Loving Leslie
Bad Boys Book Five

Christine Young

Chapter One

Winter 1826

Leslie Stewart, Duke of Southcliff, stared out the open window in his family's chateau just north of Bordeaux, France. The water that filled Gironde estuary shimmered with a silvery hue, sunshine sparkling off the ripples. Egrets and other birds took to the air in a silvery cloud of wings. Today was beautiful, the clouds having cleared early this morning. The rain cleansed the air, leveling any smoke or dust.

He was going to his home tomorrow, back to Glasgow and his new wife, Lacie MacTavish Stewart, the Duchess of Southcliff. The thought gave him reason to smile. The last words he said to her were stay put. He wanted her to remain in his townhouse in the city, but the more he thought on it, he realized doing that would be devilishly uncomfortable for her.

She'd been just seventeen when he wed her, something he felt he needed to do before he left on his final mission for the government and Drake Montgomerie. He wanted her to have the protection of his name and title. The commitment, he felt, was essential. Lacie had been in his thoughts from the moment he first kissed her when she was all of fifteen, the same age as his sister was now. At this time, he regretted his hasty departure, taking leave of his wife without consummating the marriage.

It wasn't right of him to take advantage of an underage lassie and making love to her at such a tender moment in her life would have been exactly that. Yet he needed to bind her to him before setting off on what he'd told Drake Montgomerie was his last and final mission. Drake had a hell of a time taking no for an answer, but Drake finally convinced him that he was the only one with the skills to succeed in this particular assignment. The ridiculous thing was that he believed Drake.

"You're leaving?" Jolie, his mother, waltzed into the room with her usual flamboyant style. "I hope you have every intention of begetting an heir sooner than later. It's what your father would have wanted, no expected. If I'm honest, I suppose I want that too, a grandbaby to hold and spoil."

Leslie let out a long slow exasperated breath of air, taking his gaze from the window to turn it toward his mother who had a way of annoying him even when she was being sweet. "You do know I've wed. She will just be turning eighteen when I return. I'm not going to rush things with my new and very innocent bride. That's why I've stayed away from Glasgow these last few months when I could have left earlier. I've no intention of terrifying my wife."

Jolie waved her hand in the air, grinning at him. "You are too stoic by far, Leslie, and I suppose some of the fault lies with me, certainly not your father. He would have seen you play all day and night with every skirt that wandered past your nose. You should take a page out of your brother's book and have some fun before you have children to raise and a wife to keep amused."

"I take my responsibility seriously and by the way, weren't you just talking about me begetting an heir. Playing with each and every pretty bit of muslin that comes along will not have the desired result. You don't want any bastards, neither do I." He sighed again, the air leaving his lungs slowly. This was the same conversation he had daily with his mother. "And we all understand the ways of Link. That isn't for me."

"Of course you take your obligations well in hand, it's what you've been tutored to do since you were born. We both understand the responsibilities that go with the title. Is your new wife up to those requirements? Will she make our family proud?"

"I'm sure she will do fine," Leslie said, turning his attention back to the scene outside as well as thoughts of Lacie.

"Brandy? Or perhaps an aperitif, dinner will be served soon." His

2

mother effectively changed the conversation to something less annoying. It seemed his mother knew just how far she could push him.

"You choose." His thoughts returned to Lacie then, "Actually, I've no idea how Lacie will handle the duties. She's always been a handful for her guardian, impulsive in nature, a bit like Merry. We all understand the kind of innocent trouble my sister can get herself into without even blinking."

"If it's left up to me, I'll have a brandy now and an aperitif later."

Jolie found the brandy, pouring them both a glass before she sat down. Her gaze riveted on him as if she was trying to see into his mind, ferret out his plans for his future. Sometimes, Leslie was sure she saw too much, more than he ever intended for anyone to see.

He sipped, once more turning his attention back to the view he'd been admiring earlier. From his vantage point, he could see the ship that would return him to Scotland. On board were several cases of wine. One was filled with Sauternes, a sweet wine he was sure Lacie would like. The other cases were filled with varying Bordeaux wines, red as well as white. Even from this vantage point, he could see the hustle on board his ship. He was eager to get on his way, excited to see his new bride.

"Your last night here, you could pay me a bit more attention." Jolie sighed dramatically as she waltzed across the room to stand next to him. "I won't see you for months, I'm sure. Should I join you in Glasgow when your child is born? I believe I'd enjoy a diversion."

He turned, leaning nonchalantly against the windowsill, his eyes narrowing. "You don't need me to pay attention to you, mother. There are others in this household who do that." He paused thoughtfully, "Please, don't come to Glasgow until you're invited. Your appearance would only serve to make Lacie nervous. She has sisters who will help her if she needs anything, and of course she will have me."

"Doesn't mean I don't enjoy it when you do pay attention to me. Thank God you don't want me to help out. Crying babies are not my forte." Jolie smiled prettily, lowering her lashes for a moment. "Changing the subject, my son has become very handsome and debonair. You never told me if your wife will be able to perform her wifely duties. If she is so young..."

Leslie wondered what was behind the smile as well as her attempts to pry into his life. Nothing she asked was appropriate here. "Because it's none of your business, mother, and I'm not really sure what duties you're speaking of."

"Really, Leslie, do I need to get specific. The most important duty of begetting an heir, of course, can she perform or is she a cold fish in bed?"

He choked back a laugh. "That will happen in due time. I'm sure as to the others, Lacie is a quick learner and she will please me. Have you seen my brother? He's due here. We have important subjects to talk about." Like how he is a walking scandal even though he's the most handsome and amenable devil to ever show his face in Bordeaux.

"Don't tell me you intend to lecture him on his dalliances," she said, sipping the brandy and looking over the rim at him as if she disagreed with his intentions. "You should take at least one page from his book. He's enjoying life to the fullest."

"Need I remind you that Link is the second son and has very few responsibilities in this world. He can afford to be carefree and lighthearted as well as tardy whenever it suits. His constant dalliances are different. He will bring shame on our family name if he keeps this up."

"Your words are all true. I'm sure in time he will settle down rather than finding the most beautiful widows to entertain in the evenings." Leslie sat down on his desk, swinging one leg while wondering how he could ever convince Link to change his ways. It was, he decided, most likely an impossible task.

"You know he doesn't like to be summoned. So, I'm sure he'll show up when he feels like it and not a moment before," Jolie laughed, staring at the door as if he was about to walk through it. "I do appreciate your younger brother. He is, you know, a breath of fresh air in an otherwise stagnant pool of dead air."

"You're referring to me as the stagnant pool I suppose," Leslie said dryly, a dark brow arched intuitively. "Doesn't suit you to take favorites, especially when I control the purse strings."

"Neither of you are a favorite child. I love you both as well as your charming unique ways. I'm merely pointing out the differences."

"Nonetheless, Link and I need to talk and I would prefer to do that in privacy, if you understand what I'm trying to say. Pour yourself another brandy then go visit with your daughter. I'm sure she could benefit from your years of wisdom and motherly advice." He slanted his mother a pointed look, which he was sure she would ignore. "That means when he arrives, I need to have you leave."

She waved a hand in the air, seeming to stay put, "Balderdash, you can't keep anything from me. Between the gossip of the servants and your sister's penchant for blurting the truth, I learn everything. I would quite enjoy listening to the forthcoming lecture to Link."

"Hate to admit it, but I'm sure you're right. It's just I'd like to have a few minutes alone with my brother before I leave for Scotland. I've something important to talk to him about as you well know. At the moment, I'd rather the conversation be man to man."

"Well, I can find something to do. Perhaps teach your sister a bit more about being a lady. She does have a penchant for climbing trees and running around the properties like a little hoyden in her britches, which she seems to prefer over dresses." Once again, Jolie stared at the door as if the object of her words would waltz through and plop herself unladylike on a chair just to prove her point.

Leslie held back a burst of laughter. His sister was a breath of fresh air. Merry had been named well, but her nickname was the name that stuck. Everywhere she went she left people feeling good about themselves while laughing. His mother was right, however she would need to learn how to be a lady and soon. Angelica Louise was almost fifteen, the same age as Lacie when he met her and kissed her.

He'd been unable to resist the young woman who beguiled him with her smile and tender sensibilities as well as the bit of the hoyden inside her. Even then her eyes simmered with what he was sure was passion or wickedness. He smiled then quickly cleared his throat, hoping his mother would not see the expression and comment on it.

Suddenly, Link burst into the office, windblown, smelling of leather and horse as well as the sunshine, alive as the wind, showing lots of white teeth, very nearly on time. It was only five minutes past the hour. After all, Link was nearing an ample age himself. He was almost twenty-five. He should consider settling down and starting a family.

"I've been summoned. I'm here." Link stepped through the door then quickly hugged his mother. "What is it you want to talk to me about?" He poured a brandy, his gaze focused on him. "Thought you two would have been drinking some of the Sauternes before dinner."

"Mother wanted both a brandy then an aperitif before dinner. I was willing to oblige her in this." Leslie regarded his brother who had grown into a devilishly handsome man over the years he'd been living in Scotland. Perhaps he should have come home more often. If he had then mayhap there would not be so many bastards to take care of.

The two of them should stick together in this. "It's time for you to find Merry, don't you think?" He pointedly addressed his mother, arching an eyebrow for emphasis.

"Very well, I shall leave the two of you to discuss, well... things, men things." She didn't move from the chair. It didn't appear Link had any qualms about discussing his entertainment with his mother in the room.

"Lord, but it's a beautiful day. I was riding with Suzette along the banks of the estuary. Nothing like it, I tell you," Link began with a wink directed toward his mother.

"That's nice." Leslie meant to remain patient in this, yet his brother was making it devilishly hard. He had no qualms where it concerned women and bedding them. What he always had a hard time understanding was how there could be so many bastards when he always chose widows and women of experience. The women he knew personally that Link bedded never conceived.

"I'll take a brandy," Link said, sitting down, relaxing as if someone in the room would serve him before providing his brother more of his white-toothed smile, seeming to ignore what he must know the conversation would revolve around.

"That's nice," Leslie said, dryly, disregarding his brother for the moment. "No one's waiting on you. Did you manage to stay on your horse or take a side diversion to some place private?"

Link laughed, the sound rolling pleasantly off his tongue, "Just wanted to test you." He rose then returned with his drink, smiling more widely. His eyes, upon closer inspection, appeared somewhat vague.

He had the look of a sated man, a look the duke was becoming quite familiar with the longer he remained in Bordeaux and in the company of his little brother. "We need an accounting," Leslie began. "An update on all your children."

"Well," Link said after another moment of silence, "If you insist upon these meetings every time you're in town, I must do something to make them worthwhile."

Leslie turned to Jolie, nodding as if this time she would understand what he wanted. She smiled, sipping her brandy. "Don't mind me. You two go ahead and talk. I'll just sit here and not say a word. Won't even listen."

"Mother?" The pointed question should get the desired results, but she still wasn't moving. "If you don't go, we will. There are plenty of rooms in the chateau, as well you know."

"Very well," she said in a huff, flouncing from Leslie's office as if she'd been insulted. "Dinner will be at seven. The two of you don't be late."

Leslie had been waiting for their mother to leave. When she did, he turned to Link, "Suzette? Why her?"

"The widow is quite soft and sweet smelling, brother, and she knows how to please a man. Ah, does she ever do it well. Also, she'll not get caught. She's much too smart for that, my Suzette. There will be no bastards coming from her."

"She sits a horse well," Leslie said, hard pressed not to smirk or laugh. "I'll admit that much. I suppose she won't cry foul and demand marriage if by some perverse chance she did conceive."

"Hah man and that's not all she sits well," Link laughed again, thoroughly enjoying life, his life, while putting Leslie's lecture away as something inconsequential.

Only through intense resolve did Leslie keep his grin to himself. He was the duke. He was the head of the far-flung Stewart family. Even now there might be another Stewart growing despite Suzette's intelligence. Link didn't seem to care that he was siring bastards in almost every part of Bordeaux as well as Paris.

"We don't have all night," Leslie said impatiently, but Link continued as if there was nothing he had to apologize about.

He must have seen the twitch of his lips because Link laughed outright one more time.

"Yes, we must proceed in ways that make us the happiest. There are better things waiting for us around the corner, so to speak, don't you think?" He raised the glass of brandy toward Leslie. "Here's to all women and the sweet pleasures they share with us the male species."

"Now," Leslie continued reading the top sheet of paper in front of him and trying his best to ignore Link's toast to women, "I need to confirm some things. As of this meeting you have three quite healthy sons, four quite healthy daughters. Poor little Jacque died during the spring. Julia's fall doesn't appear to have had lasting injury to her arm. Is this up to date? Or do you have more children to be accounted for?"

"I will have another baby making its way in February. The mother appears hardy and healthy. So, in a few months I will have another precious child. They are very important, you realize. They must be taken care of and given every opportunity in this life."

Leslie sighed heavily, staring at the floor for a few seconds before continuing the conversation. "Very well. Her name?" As Link replied, Leslie wrote. He raised his head. "Is this now correct?"

Link lost his smile and downed the rest of his brandy. "No, Roger died of the ague last week. He is no longer with me, poor fellow."

"You didn't tell me." Leslie thought he should be informed sooner than later, but Link had his own timetable he followed.

Link lifted his shoulders in a nonchalant shrug. "The poor baby wasn't even a year old, but so bright, Leslie. I knew you were busy, what with the trip home to your new bride, the mission as well. Didn't want to bother you with something like that even though I knew it was important."

"I'm sorry," Leslie said again. Then he frowned, concentrating, thinking he must be missing something. "If the babe is due in February, why didn't you tell me when I arrived home?"

Link said simply, "Because I didn't know until recently. Can't tell you something I don't know, now can I? The mother didn't tell me because she feared I wouldn't wish to bed her any longer." He paused looking out the same window at the estuary that fascinated Leslie earlier. "Silly woman. I wouldn't have guessed she was with child, although I suppose I should have conjectured. She's already quite big with the baby. She might well give me twins. Wouldn't that be splendid? Two blessed children instead of just one."

Link turned his gaze from the window before swigging more brandy, unable to fathom what seemed to drive his little brother.

"I forgot, Leslie. There is also Sadie."

Leslie dropped the paper. "Sadie who?"

"Sadie Arbuckle, the draper's daughter on St. Jean Street. She's with child, my child. Well, of course it is my child. She will have it in May, my best guess. She was all tears and woes until I told her she needn't worry. The Stewarts take care of their own. It's possible she might even marry a sea captain. It doesn't seem he cares if she's carrying another man's child. He loves her, you know. So, we most likely won't be accountable for the baby or the mother, although I would dearly love to see it when it is born."

"Well, that's something." Leslie picked up the paper he dropped and tallied the numbers on the sheet. "You're currently supporting six children and their mothers. You have impregnated two more women and their children are due early next year."

"I believe that's right. Don't forget the possibility of the twins or the likelihood of Sadie marrying her sea captain."

"Can't you keep your damned rod in your pants?"

"No more than you can, Leslie."

"Fair enough, but why can't you remove yourself from the woman before you fill her with your seed?"

Link flushed slightly, a rather strange occurrence for him

considering, and said, his words defensive, something else unlike Link. "I can't seem to keep my wits together when I'm inside a woman. I forget everything except the pleasure, the damn pleasure. There is no rational thought in my muddled brain except the sheer pleasure of it all."

"You need to figure this out, Link," Leslie said. "It's not up to you to singlehandedly populate the entire world."

"I know it isn't much of an excuse, but I just can't seem to withdraw once I'm there, so to speak when the lady is all warm and willing to have me there. Her sultry core quivering with desperate need." He stared hard at his brother then. "I'm not a damned cold fish like you, Leslie. Your mind never runs off its track. Doesn't it ever turn into vapor when the pleasure of it all takes over? Don't you ever want to just keep pounding and pounding in the velvet warmth and the consequences be damned?"

"No."

Link let out a long slow breath of air, thrumming his fingers on the arm of his chair. "Well, I'm not so well disciplined as you. Have you not wanted to lose control and everything else could rot?"

"No, can't say that I've ever felt that way. I've controlled myself my entire adult life. As far as I know there are no illegitimate children. Now, your lust becomes more costly by the second," he said after a moment. "Damned costly. You really must do something about this infatuation you have with sex."

"Stop your frowns and your posturing, Leslie. You're bloody wealthy, as am I. Where money is concerned, we've nothing to worry about even if I sire another ten children."

"Doesn't matter, this is not well done of you. I'd like to see a stop put to it in the future. Perhaps in the future you could sire legitimate children."

"You're always saying our bastards are our responsibility and so I agree with you. I also agree with this plan of yours, the meetings you know. It ensures we don't miss any children. I would have quite forgotten about Sadie if you weren't here to remind me. That would not be well done of us at all."

Link was chuckling when the door opened. He looked up to see their sister dart quickly into the room then stop, watching them, a hoydenish expression on her beautiful face.

"Ah, if it isn't Merry. Come in, our meeting is nearly finished. Leslie has already reprimanded me about my bad boy behavior. I'm sure he will find something to lecture you about also. What have you done wrong in the last few months, I wonder?"

Leaning against the door with her arms crossed, Merry seemed amused at all that was happening. Leslie was sure she knew everything that was said by the all-knowing smirk on her face. She was far too intelligent for her age. He would have to be wary of her from now on. She was, after all, nearing the age where she would have to be chaperoned. He groaned at the thought of Link taking over those duties.

Turning to Link, Merry asked, "So, how went the meeting? Mother told me you kicked her out and that she has every intention of getting even."

"The smirk doesn't become you, brat."

"Now, Link. I'm young, true, but I've grown up around the two of you. I'm not stupid or innocent. With the two of you as older brothers how could I be uninformed about the ways of men?"

Shocked by what Merry said, the small sip of brandy Leslie just imbibed spewed from his mouth. Leslie wiped the drops off his pants with a handkerchief, staring at his little sister, wondering if he knew her at all. *Ways of men?*

"Forget what you think you know, Merry. These things we're discussing are not for the ears of someone your tender age."

Merry grinned at Link, "How are all your beloved ones?"

"They all do very well, thank you."

"I won't say a word," she said then grinned at him, blew him a kiss before walking toward Leslie who was still sitting on his desk.

He didn't like the expression on Merry's face any better than Link's countenance. She was up to something he knew he would dislike.

Holding his breath for a moment, he eyed her critically. "What are you up to, brat? It isn't enough that I have to put up with your brother but now you have that same look in your eye."

She laughed, staring at the brandy glass as if she was about to partake before she turned her attention back to him. She clasped her hands in front of her, appearing sweet and innocent, lowering her lashes a trifle, something she could do very well when she put her mind to it. Now, Leslie was sure he wasn't going to like what she was about to say.

"I'm going to Glasgow with you. Mother already gave me permission. My bags are packed and on the ship."

"Blessed hell, you can't... Jolie can't... none of you are serious."

Chaperoning his little sister was not going to be a duty he was prepared for. Thoughts of Flynt MacTavish and his horrible attempts at guardianship of his four younger sisters spread through him too fast for him to contemplate thoroughly. Lord, he was wed to Flynt's youngest sister and the man wasn't even invited to the hasty wedding.

"I'll either go with you, Leslie, or I'll book passage on another ship. Would you like that better?" That smirking look she did so well was plastered on her beguiling little face again. She lifted her shoulders slightly, the smug expression still there, "It's your choice."

"It's a hell of a choice," he told her, like being caught between two evils. "I'm leaving first thing in the morning. If you're not on board, I won't wait for you. You should also know the weather isn't the same as here. There is no sunshine, only rain. It's dreary and won't suit your sunny disposition."

"No worries about that either, I'm going tonight. Holcum, you do know the man, the chateaux's butler. He's taking me in the carriage right after we eat, which I assume is in a few minutes." I won't be a problem, I promise. You won't know I'm even there. The weather will be a welcome change for me, something different."

"I'll hold you to that, brat," he said, understanding the whirlwind of problems he was about to face.

~ * ~

Lacie bent over the ledgers at her sister's bakery, her mind in a cloud. Making sense of Daryl's figures on a good day was difficult, but today her mind was in the clouds. She couldn't think, couldn't concentrate. There were just too many things swirling around in her head. It seemed Leslie was coming soon. He'd written that he would arrive within the month. That was two months ago, she thought letting go with a heavy breath of air.

It seemed she felt Daryl's gaze on her back. The more receipts and numbers she scratched out, the harder her sister stared. She sighed, long and deep, wishing she could escape somewhere, find a hole to climb into where she didn't have to get out.

Daryl's scribbling was always hard to decipher. The ledger was nearly unreadable, except for the ones Justine made which were neat and precise. But Daryl wanted to take on all the responsibilities here at her business, and she was doing just that.

Once again, though, nothing made sense.

Lacie put this off for as long as she dared. She didn't want to stay here, in the bakery or even the city any longer than she had to. "Justine, can you come over here for a second and look at something for me?" Lacie really needed someone to explain this last notation.

"Of course," Justine replied, wiping her hands on her apron as she left the kitchen to sit down beside her. "What do you need? Ah, I see you're trying to make heads or tails out of this ledger. Sorry for that."

Heads together, Justine pointed out different things and explained what her sister wrote down as well as the items she purchased that cost the listed dollar amount. She wanted to tell her sister not to touch the board, but she didn't have the heart to hurt her feelings.

"Thank you. I might need your help again. Don't go too far," Lacie said as she pushed flyaway hair from her eyes that seemed to be crossing when she looked at the numbers in front of her.

"Not until the shop closes and that's hours away. Hopefully, you will be done by then," Justine laughed, heading for the kitchen. "The boys are delivering leftover goods today. They tell me they don't need us."

"I would have turned the job down anyway," Lacie said, unable to swallow the painful memory ricocheting in her head.

She no longer wanted anything to do with the deliveries, always found some excuse to keep from joining.

"You could have asked me for help with this. It's my fault, after all, that everything is such a mess for you." Daryl sat down beside her, clearly annoyed at her.

"True." She didn't want to tell her sister just how absurd that idea was. Daryl would never be of any help where this was concerned.

"True? That is just not very well done of you," Daryl said, eyeing her critically then exasperated she puffed out a breath of air, "I want to learn how to do this the right way, and I did believe I was doing a better job."

"You are doing better, but it's still devilishly hard to decipher your writing and while I could have asked you, when I do, you never seem to be able to recall what isn't written down. Asking would have been a horrible waste of my time as well as yours."

"I see, you don't want me to do any of this," Daryl said, standing before starting back to the kitchen in an obvious huff. "Perhaps you are right. For the good of the bakery, I should only bake."

"I didn't say that," Lacie said to Daryl's retreating back then looked to see if Justine was watching. Perhaps it was true.

She turned then, "You didn't have to. You're my sister and I can read your mind. I'm going to stay in the kitchen for the remainder of the afternoon. At least I can bake and no one criticizes me except to sing my praises." She continued, back stiff, striding into the kitchen.

Lacie sighed heavily, understanding nothing was going her way. Well, what did she expect? She had spent time trying to teach her sister the ways of making all the numbers make sense as well as readable. As usual, those teachings eluded her sister. Numbers were foreign to Daryl and that was that. Her mind just would not wrap itself around numbers and where organization skills were required, Daryl had none. Her brain was so scattered.

Abstract, nothing in sequence.

The numbers seemed to blur in front of Lacie, and all she could conjure in her head was what happened nights ago, too many to recall exactly, the terrifying feel of the man on top of her as she lay sprawled on the hard ground. She didn't believe anything could erase that memory from her head. He smelled. Remembering his yellowed teeth made her nauseas even now. Her body shook as the memory collected in her brain.

She touched her breasts, still feeling the pain of his teeth as they closed over them. Suddenly, she ran to the back of the kitchen, reaching the door to the outside just before emptying the contents of her stomach.

"No," she moaned, "Not again." She closed her eyes, wishing all thoughts to evaporate into the day's sunshine. Facing her future seemed distant and bleak.

Breathing was nearly impossible as was walking and talking. She cleaned her mouth, drinking water then made her way into the kitchen. Justine didn't say anything, just handed her a cup of tea and a cookie.

"Thank you," she said then went back to her table and the work that was in front of her.

Still, concentration on something that was usually so easy for her, now eluded her. Her stomach rumbled again, but she didn't have to make a mad dash anywhere.

The tea must be doing its job.

This could not go on indefinitely. The nightmares as well as those images ransacking her brain during the day had to stop. She didn't know how to go about it though. No one could tell her how to make the nightmares all go away. Daryl told her with time she would no longer remember. She didn't believe a word.

Despite her best efforts in the following weeks that had passed since the incident, she could not get the horrific night as well as the images out of her head. She breathed in a deep breath, filling her lungs with new air yet nothing helped. Closing her eyes made the horrific pictures clearer. She had not slept, barely ate.

Daryl sat down beside her with a gentle smile, placing a hand over hers, "I know I've done a horrible job with the books, ignored most of what you tried to teach me, but losing your meal over my ineptness?"

Lacie wanted to laugh at her sister's attempts to make her feel better. Nothing helped her forget. She didn't even believe time would ease the pain as Hope, her brother's wife, also told her it would.

Hope knew things though, things no one else could comprehend, at least none of her friends or family. She'd had lived in a harem where women had no rights, were abused on a daily basis. The knowledge didn't help her. She doubted if it helped the other women either. Hope knew how to listen in ways her sisters did not. When the images became too real, she would visit her sister-in-law. The time spent would give her some optimism for the future.

"You know why I lost my breakfast. It wasn't your insufficiencies with numbers. I'll figure this out, but you really need to let Justine take care of the ledgers from now on. She is very good, you know. This business is yours. So, it is your right to delegate the responsibilities. It's just stubborn pride that keeps you doing something you can't."

"I don't like thinking I'm stupid," Daryl said, leaning back against the chair, looking at the ceiling as if that would give her the answers or teach her how to overcome her issues with computations and organization.

You're not stupid, Daryl. Numbers have always puzzled you. Nothing has changed. There is no reason to deny that fact. It's the same for me with cooking. I burn everything or what I make ends up like mush and tasteless. I can't read a recipe to save my soul. We all have the things we are good at as well as the things we don't do so well."

The little bell over the shop chimed as Bliss entered with her twin boys, Garret and Grant, in strollers. They were walking now and the mischief they caused always gave Lacie a reason to smile and forget her troubles. They were heaven sent in her world that was fraught with nightmares and fear. The twins looked so much like Broc. Even at this tender age, it nearly stole Lacie's breath.

Bliss bent over so she could see their cute little cherubic faces. "See, there is Aunty Lacie and Aunty Daryl sitting at the table, poring over the numbers. If you ask nicely, maybe they will give you a cookie."

"They don't say very much yet," Daryl said. "Let me hold one and Justine will bring each a cookie."

"Can't help but try. They do say da, da, a few other words as well.

Haven't gotten either one to say ma, ma and Broc holds the fact over my head on a daily basis even though I tell him if he keeps it up, I will withhold his nightly privileges. When I do that, he just smirks at me with the grin that tells me he knows ways to get around my threats."

Lacie wanted to tell her sisters they could say whatever they wanted because she was married too, but she didn't feel comfortable telling them. Yes, she married Leslie with only the minister, his wife and Kelly as witnesses then he left. She hadn't seen him since.

It wasn't well done of him. He did write though. She had to give him credit for that tiny bit of consideration.

"Really, you don't have to pretend with me. It won't be that long before I'll know everything you're speaking of. Perhaps I'll learn something I can make use of in the future. You tell me all about these nightly privileges and why withholding them would be a punishment."

"Well, Leslie should marry you as soon as he gets back from whatever it is he's doing and teach you himself. I don't understand what is taking him so long," Daryl said to her, assuming an angry edge that matched Lacie's feelings.

"Lacie is not yet eighteen. Maybe he is honoring that magical birthday and he won't return until January," Bliss pointed out. "I for one have never quite understood that number or the magic. We all know women who have wed before eighteen."

The thought made her smile. For some reason, at least for the self-proclaimed bad boys, they didn't touch a woman who was under that special age. So, perhaps that was why he was still gone. Her birthday was a couple months from now.

"He might be like Cam and refuse to even kiss you," Bliss said. "Chelsea was so angry and frustrated. She didn't know how to tell Cam she would never tell Flynt if he kissed her."

"Leslie has kissed me so I suppose the age limit doesn't apply to kissing," Lacie said with a small smile, remembering the few times yet with that memory the nightmare returned.

"We all know kisses lead to other things and it's those other things they forbid themselves," Daryl said with and all-knowing smile.

One of the little boys tugged at her skirt, looking at her with gorgeous aqua colored eyes just like his mother's. He's going to be just like his daddy," Lacie said, grinning at the little boy and ruffling his hair.

"And how is that?" Bliss laughed, seeming to know the answer before Lacie could say the words.

"He's a charmer and totally irresistible. All he needs to do is look at me and I want to give him anything he is asking for," Lacie said. "Including all the cookies he can eat."

"He probably wants his diaper changed," Bliss pointed out.

"Well, he won't get a diaper change from me. I'd most likely botch the job. Believe that's your department, big sis. Comes with having children, which I don't."

"Probably should learn some time," Bliss said. "If you're still thinking you might want to marry Leslie someday."

"Did you know anything about babies before you were married?" Daryl asked, a smug grin on her face.

Bliss laughed. "Of course not, it wasn't one of the things we were taught at home," Bliss said.

"Who would have taught us?" Lacie pointed out.

"Flynt was the only one available. I'm sure he didn't know the intricacies of diaper changing," Daryl said laughing.

"A bad boy knowing how to change a diaper...? Who would have ever thought such a thing?" Lacie asked, wondering if Leslie was just as ignorant about babies as she was. Then with a sigh, it didn't really matter anyway. After what happened to her that night, she didn't want anything to do with men or babies. She supposed he would have to seek an annulment to their hasty marriage.

"Hardly," Bliss said and the conversation lagged for a moment.

Lacie went back to the myriad of numbers in front of her with Daryl and Bliss chatting about their husbands.

She had a husband she barely knew, a nonexistent husband for that matter. A husband she wanted to remain nonexistent because she didn't know if she could bare his touch. The irony didn't escape her.

A few minutes later, the little bell chimed again.

"Grams," Lacie rose to give her grandmother a big hug. She wished she could confide everything to the woman who helped Flynt raise her, wished too she could tell everyone she was married. Grams had always been the person to listen, to wipe tears away in bad times and to laugh with in good ones.

"How are you doing? I've been worried about you. My, I still can hardly believe I'm a great-grandmother. I feel just too young." She gave the twins each a hug and a kiss on the cheek before she sat down next to her then turning to Daryl. "Could I get a cup of tea and a ginger cookie?"

Lacie grimaced, looking at her grandmother once again thinking this would be so much easier if she could tell everything. Yet Leslie had never said not to mention their marriage and had expected her to stay in his home. Maybe she was the only one who didn't want anything to be mentioned about the quick vows. "I'm taking one day at a time."

"Are you able to sleep at night yet, without the nightmares?" Grams set her hand on Lacie's, squeezing gently. "I could stay at the townhouse if that would help. I'd be happy to do that."

"I just want to get away and be alone. Nothing is going to help accept time, at least that's what Hope is telling me. But how much time?"

Lacie needed to scream and pound her fists on something hard. Needed to ride across the fields and let the wind sift through her hair, until she couldn't remember. Perhaps that was all she needed, the wind on her face as well as a little alone time.

"I think everyone is different in this," Bliss said as she watched the boys toddle their way into the kitchen.

Daryl rose to go after them.

"Stay here and relax, I'll go after them," Grams said, standing and heading toward the kitchen.

Justine brought them out, one in each arm, laughing as she set them on the floor near their mother. "Look what I found in the kitchen. I believe they want a second cookie. They are so adorable."

"Don't you dare," Bliss said. "They are incorrigible enough without the sweets. If they eat too much food like that, they will be awake all night and Broc will spend the hours frowning at me wondering why there is no peace and quiet to be had in our household."

"See, I'm learning all the time," Lacie sipped the tea while ignoring the cookie. "I would bet that with one-year old twin boys there is never alone time despite what they eat."

"Speaking of food, you need to eat more," Grams said, "You are growing too thin."

"Really, you haven't noticed her bosom lately then," Daryl said. "She is growing daily, nothing thin about that part of my sister."

Lacie felt the heat rise to her face. Her large bosom was not something she needed to be reminded of. She was painfully aware of the fact, second by second, her breasts were still getting larger. They were a source of embarrassment to her and even the good-humored jests didn't make her feel any better.

"So, when did you decide to move back to the country?" Grams patted Lacie on the hand, still appearing concerned. "It's not an impulse decision is it? You'll be all alone since everyone is in town for the winter months."

"In a week or so. I've really nothing more to do here as long as Justine keeps the ledgers. I'll pack up my things and have Ashford help me settle in. I'm sure Flynt and Hope are getting ready to welcome a baby into this world and don't need someone else in the house to get underfoot. They need their privacy. In subtle ways I'm reminded of that fact daily."

"Well, someone should help you pack and move," Daryl said, looking into the kitchen. "Donal probably won't mind lending you Ash for the day, that is if Emilia will also let him go."

Lacie picked up Grant who was once again tugging at her skirts. "Are you after my cookie, little man. Can't give it to you unless your mother gives the go ahead. What do you think? Should we ask her?"

The little boy gurgled something unintelligible as he reached a pudgy hand for the desert.

"Don't you dare," Bliss said again this time a bit more sternly. "One cookie is enough. Now where is Garret?"

"He likes the kitchen." This time Emilia brought the little boy out. "Maybe he's going to follow in his aunties footsteps and become a chef."

She set the boy in his stroller then to Lacie. "Of course Ash can help. If he doesn't, he'll be relegated to the couch for the week."

Bliss laughed. "There is nothing like keeping men in line by telling them no when they ask for their husbandly rights."

"You can do that? Tell them no?" Lacie asked, filing away that bit of information for the time, if ever Leslie comes home.

"Of course you can, at least we can," Daryl laughed. "When you finally marry Leslie, you'll have to figure it out for yourself. There will be ways. I'm sure you can let him know he's gone too far with his manly demands and righteous airs."

"It depends on the man. I couldn't tell my first husband no. If he wanted me, he took me and he never cared how I felt," Emilia told her with a heavy and long drawn out sigh. "Ash isn't anything like that. I don't think I would ever have a reason to tell him no. I like the way he makes love to me, the way he feels next to my body when we are in bed."

"As do I," Bliss said, laughing. "Broc is a wonderful lover just as he showed me time and again before we married. He doesn't let me forget. Has an ego bigger than anyone's, but again I love the fact that he is so confident."

This time when the bell chimed, Hope walked in. "Can I get a cup of tea, strong with a little milk and lemon," she asked before she sat down across from Lacie.

"Coming right up."

"How are you feeling?" Grams asked, pointedly looking at Hope's swollen stomach.

"Now that I'm no longer throwing up, I feel fine." She reached for one of the cookies on the platter in front of her.

"Ginger cookies are supposed to start labor. How close are you?" Grams asked.

"Still a month to go." She nibbled on the cookie. "Wouldn't mind having the baby early as long as he's healthy. I'm exhausted and tired of not being able to see my feet."

"He?"

"Flynt is positive it's a boy so I humor him."

"That is hard to get used to. Broc is already talking about more children. I keep telling him to bite his tongue. The twins need to be more self sufficient before I go down that path again."

"When will that be?" Hope asked.

"Another year or so, praying there are no mistakes. He has a horrible time withdrawing from me, and he says he doesn't want to use a condom, so there we are."

"What about you, Daryl? When are you going to have children?" Bliss asked. "Shouldn't be too much longer before you become pregnant if you aren't already."

"I'm late. I know," Chelsea rushed in breathless, her baby in a stroller.

"We're all here then," Bliss said grinning.

"I can't seem to get anywhere on time."

"Babies will do that to you but back to Daryl. Are you expecting yet?" Grams asked.

"No, I don't believe so. Perhaps it's too early to tell," Daryl said with a shrug.

"You've only been wed a few months. Of course it's too soon to tell for sure, but I'm guessing you have an idea," Bliss said, watching her younger sister very carefully.

Lacie didn't think they should be prying, but they'd always wanted to know each other's business. "You all should leave her alone. After all this issue is between the newlyweds, don't you think?"

Good Lord, but she'd been married longer than her older sister and she'd yet to have her husband make love to her.

"Any news on when Leslie will make an appearance?" Chelsea asked, picking up the baby from the stroller. She stood by the table, swaying while she gazed at the child.

"Haven't heard anything from the man for several months," Lacie murmured. "I'll probably know when he shows up. Doesn't seem to believe in schedules. Told me he'd be here but that was over a month ago." She paused. "But then he has no real reason to apprise me of his whereabouts. We've no commitment to each other." What a bunch of nonsense. She was his wife, or had he forgotten that fact?

~ * ~

A few months earlier

The duke was beyond anxious. He felt in his gut something was going to happen, something he wouldn't like. He didn't know just now what it was. Yet he had volunteered for this mission. So, here he was, waiting for something to blow up in his face when all he wanted to do was go home to his wife and make love to her.

He hated feelings like this. They made him feel helpless and that was something he didn't enjoy. He should have stayed home and taken his chances with Lacie and her brother. He knew he would have never been able to keep his hands off her until she turned eighteen. So, sparks would have flown.

Damned age, why was it so important? It was only a few months. So why couldn't he wait that long? For that matter, why did a month or two make so much difference?

Leslie dismounted from his stallion, slowly striding to the edge of the surf. The water unhurriedly rolled onto the sand, inching higher as the tide seemed to be coming in. Wind swept the waves turning them to frothy peaks and spewed ocean water into the air. He sucked the salt air into his lungs, felt it gritty and wet against his face. The breeze was strong and sharp, blowing his hair about his head, making his eyes water. The day was cloudy, a dull gray just like his mood.

He cursed, wishing this was not the job assigned to him, but he wanted out of the country. So, Montgomerie sent him to France, his home away from home. Because he was fluent in the language, Montgomerie told him. Because of this he could move about without anyone being the wiser. An added benefit, his mother lived there.

Two days passed. Leslie was bored and restless. As it turned out, he received his instructions from a one-legged beggar who sidled up to him and poked a thick packet into his coat pocket.

He read the letter twice, memorizing the precise instructions then carefully studied each of the enclosed papers and documents. He was in disbelief at what was expected of him. Shaking his head, he folded the papers into their packet, once again wishing he had declined the mission.

It was obvious hours had been spent formulating a plan to rescue this woman, this Caroline Dubois. Montgomerie never explained the reason for this. Leslie was beginning to think it was a ruse to give him what he wanted, an escape from Glasgow for as many months as he needed.

Now, after reading the documents, it was becoming increasingly clear the woman he was supposed to rescue was the mistress of Jean Laurent. She had been stolen a few months ago. He didn't completely believe that particular story, but the evidence was pointing in said direction. So, some of the tale must be true. Laurent was important to the working political scene in France.

Now after chasing leads, he found General Denis Caron and the location of Caroline. If all the stories were true, she was now the general's whore. He sold her to the highest bidder, pimping her out to make money. Sometimes she was the wager in card games. He didn't understand the motive in this scenario. He assumed comprehension was not imperative to rescue Caroline.

He was playing cards with Denis who possessed the key to the room where Caroline was kept prisoner. To Leslie the game seemed rigged in his favor. Perhaps the general enjoyed giving her to men. Now he was handed the key, told he could perform sexually with this woman since he won and that he was to be pleasured by her. This time it was free but if he enjoyed himself, he would have to pay the going price for further encounters.

He said the wench loved threats and a bit of pain, liked the sex rough. The bloody fool decided to shadow him. "Because," he said as they climbed the stairs to the third floor, "she isn't exactly trained fully as yet. She's a novice, if you get my drift." Leslie watched the man unlock the door and stride inside, hoping and saying a few prayers as well that the man was not intending to watch.

He followed, saying nothing. It was a spare room with only a bed and dresser and one small circular rug in the middle. There was only one occupant, a single woman standing in the middle of the room wearing what appeared to be just a robe. Was this Caroline Dubois? He assumed so.

The general grinned drunkenly at her and said with a flip of his hand. "Strip off the robe, Caro. Lord Stewart needs to see what he's going to be enjoying tonight."

The woman hesitated then complied. He'd expected someone younger, though why he should have he didn't know. *No, she wasn't really a girl,* Leslie thought, looking at her more closely, rather a woman in her mid-twenties. She was obviously scared and she was lovely, despite her pallor, the shadows beneath her eyes were very dark. She was overly thin.

The man waited silently until she'd stripped to her shift. Then he lurched toward her, grabbed her chin in his fingers and kissed her, fondling her breast with his other hand through the thin lawn. Suddenly, he grabbed the front of her shift and ripped it off.

He laughed, saying over his shoulder to Leslie, "I wanted to see if you approved of her. A bit thin for my taste, but she does have nice bubbies."

He pushed her onto the bed, leaned over her, and said low, "You see this man, my girl? You do everything he wants you to do or... you know the punishment, don't you? I would like to stay and watch, but I'm tired." He straightened and turned to Leslie. "You are quiet. Don't you think she is lovely? Not a virgin, but not overused either. She belongs to me, and now, because she isn't stupid, she obeys my every command. So, you may enjoy her but as I said, just for tonight."

The man stumbled out of the room. Leslie moved after him, listening as his footsteps receded along the corridor then down the stairs. He listened to another door open and close on the second floor. He turned back to face the woman.

She was standing now by the bed, trying to cover herself with her hands. Leslie couldn't believe his good fortune, but he wasn't about to doubt it, not for a moment.

His voice was urgent as he strode to her. "Is your name Caroline Dubois?"

She was tiny, very fair, her hair falling straight down her back nearly to her waist. She had light blue eyes, very blond brows and lashes. She was lovely.

"Are you?" he asked again.

She nodded, taking a tiny step backwards.

"Don't be afraid of me. I'm here on behalf of Jean Laurent. He wanted me to find you and bring you some place safe, somewhere out of the general's reach. He seeks revenge for your kidnapping."

She was cowering in front of the bed, speechless and Leslie was losing patience with her. He wasn't about to do anything here that would send the general after him. This was the woman he was sent to rescue. He would see her safe even if she decided she would be better off with the general.

"Do you know Jean Laurent?"

She nodded, still obviously afraid of him, not believing for a moment despite the flare of hope he'd seen flash through her eyes.

"You need to dress, quickly. I am here to take you away, to Jean. We must hurry."

"I don't have any gowns."

Leslie looked around the room searching. "A cloak, anything. Come we must hurry."

"Why should I believe you?"

So, there was some spirit left in her.

She was nearly strangling on her fear but she still kept talking. "I know that he gave me to you. He said so, and I know why he did it."

"It's because I won a wager."

"Oh, no, not that," She became even paler. Her rouged lips parted then closed. She shook her head, saying in a rush. "He wants me to find out what you will tell me about the government when you return to Paris. He's worried also that you are a spy and will deceive him. If you try to take me away from here, he will discover it and kill us both. He told me I must learn the truth or he will kill my daughter. He says he has her and she won't continue to live."

"Ah." Leslie smiled down at her and gently began to run his hands up and down her thin arms. So, the general hadn't been drunk after all. The game, the wager, his loss, it had all been the generals plan to trap him. Not bad. It was nice of Caroline to inform him.

He felt the usual surge of excitement in this adventure, wondered if he would be happy living without it. "Easy now," he said absently, trying to calm her, all the while thinking furiously. "Where is your daughter? Once we get out of here, we will get her and bring her with us. I promise she won't be hurt."

Caroline started. "She's at the farm, two miles from Saint-Émilion to the north. He says he has a man there watching her and that the man will kill her if I don't do as he orders."

"If I know Jean, he's already taken care of any guards at the farmhouse. Truly my job here is to save you. Jean will save your daughter. Now let's get you dressed in something. I am taking you and your daughter to London where you will be protected until Jean can come to you."

"London," she said slowly, her dark eyes wide with surprise. "We only speak French. I wouldn't know what to do or say?"

He waved his hand, dismissing her fears. "It doesn't matter. Many people speak French in London and you will learn. Jean lives in the city much of the time and he can teach both you and your daughter the language."

"But—"

"No, I can say no more. We can't linger here any longer. Jean wishes me to take you to London, so that is what I will do. You will be safe there until he returns to fetch you. There are chores he must attend to in France before he can leave. Will you trust me?"

She looked at him, worship and trust shining from her face and said simply, "Yes."

"Good. Now, listen to me. Here's what we will do. First, we will find something for you to wear even if I have to wrap that bed sheet around you." Leslie wondered as he stared down into that pale tense face that she held such trust for him why people in general and females in particular believed him to be some sort of Saint George. He hated it but at the same time he found it amusing. He thought of Jean Laurent and fervently hoped she would remember him in her thoughts. After all, he was a married man now.

Chapter Two

Leslie wasn't scowling. He was anxious and once more he felt deep inside something was wrong. The sensation simmered in his gut. He hated such feelings because they made him feel helpless and vulnerable. On the other hand, he knew it to be stupid to ignore the gut instincts that had kept him alive in so many harrowing situations.

As soon as he stepped inside his townhouse in Glasgow, Merry beside him, he sensed raw terror. The home was too silent, seemed empty and devoid of people.

"Lacie," he called out. "Are you here?" Dropping his valise on the floor he strode through the downstairs rooms searching for her. "Lacie you here? Where the devil are you?"

In his mind he understood she might just be at the bakery or visiting her sisters. His concern for her safety could very well be hollow and meaningless. Yet his gut never lied.

"Perhaps it would have been wiser to send a message ahead of time as to exactly when you would be home." Merry sat down on a sofa in the parlor, her hands folded primly in her lap, her grin all-knowing, smug as hell. "You can't expect people to know your wishes unless you tell them even though you are the duke. The world is not at your beck and call as you'd like to believe. Some women have minds of their own."

"Brat," Leslie said through gritted teeth needing to focus on everything but his incorrigible little sister, "Stay put while I run upstairs. I do understand what you're saying but this is different. It's an emptiness that's telling me she hasn't been here for quite some time. I told her to stay put."

"Is that what you told your wife of only a few hours? Stay put? I would have been inclined to flee the house too if you spoke to me that way. Perhaps that's what I should do now, explore the city while I've the freedom to do so, while your dukely mind is elsewhere. After all, it's not all that late. There are hours of daylight at my disposal. The sun is still shining, not a rain cloud in sight, mores the pity."

Leslie raked his hands through his hair, "Fine then leave. Go out and explore on your own. I won't be around to rescue you until I find Lacie and figure out why she isn't at home where she belongs."

His heart pounded in his chest as a fine sweat broke out over his body. He didn't ever remember being this afraid, his logical mind telling him there was no reason for the terror.

"Well, when you put it that way." She all but spit out the words.

He strode up the steps taking them two at a time, once more calling out to Lacie and poking his head into every room. Completing the process on the third floor, he knew he wasn't going to find her. Discouraged and now terrified for her, he returned to the foyer.

Westcott, his butler, met him on the first floor. "If you're looking for your wife, she left the same day you did. Since then she hasn't been back. Told me she didn't think anyone would understand what she was doing or why she was living in your home. No one knows the two of you were wed, not even her sisters whom I've been told confide everything."

His breath caught in the back of his throat on hearing Westcott's announcement. "She did what?" The only thing he'd ever really asked her to do was to live in his home. "No one knows we're wed? All this time, she has not had the benefit of my protection?"

Westcott was shaking his head, a dour look on his always-stern features. "Didn't tell me where she was going, just that this arrangement was very awkward for her and she didn't feel comfortable. Not comfortable at all. Assumed she was going home to live with her brother."

"Didn't you ask her?" he probed, thinking this was truly incompetent of his butler who was always on top of things.

"Figured it was none of my business," Westcott said with a slight shrug of his narrow shoulders along with a shake of his head. "It's up to the two of you to work it out. Besides there wasn't anything I could say that would change your wife's mind."

"It's not raining today." Merry stepped into the foyer grinning widely.

Her announcement left him shaking his head.

Then to Westcott, "Will you show me to my room?"

Westcott frowned, looking to him then back to Merry with a disapproving air. "As long as his lordship tells me what room he'd like you to stay in, I'd be glad to."

"It's not what you're thinking. Merry is my incorrigible and very wild little sister, and if you had ever agreed to go with me to Bordeaux, you would have known that for a fact."

Leslie would have laughed at Westcott's expression but he was far too concerned about Lacie and her whereabouts to find an ounce of humor in this situation.

By leaving, Lacie thwarted his plans to begin his seduction of his wife tonight. While she was not yet eighteen, the date was close and a few days shy of her birthday didn't make a wit of difference to him. Violent storms had waylaid them on the journey home. Twice they had to stop in ports along the western coast of England to wait out the tempests. He should have been home at least two weeks sooner but here they were.

Glad to be home, he had not expected to have to chase after his wife. Yet, when he stopped to think, he understood a little of her discomfort. Perhaps he expected too much of her. The marriage had been in haste to suit his needs with no consideration for Lacie or what she might want.

"Put Merry in a guest room in the opposite wing from me. I'm sure she will appreciate the privacy and make sure she has everything she needs," Leslie told him.

"Make yourself at home, brat. I'm sure there will be something in the kitchen for you to eat if you're hungry. The stables are around the side of the house. Make friends with a few of the horses. I'll let you know if your choice for a mount is acceptable. The black stallion is mine however and off limits."

"I'm guessing you won't be home tonight." She wandered around the foyer, poking her head inside different doorways, sighing before proceeding to another door. "What am I to do for fun with you gone?"

He laughed outright. "You were the one who wanted to come to Glasgow, remember? Against my wishes, I might add. Sit tight for a day or two and I'll make sure you see everything there is to see. The university is not far. I hear they have an excellent library."

"I'll find something to do. A fast ride tomorrow morning will be sure to lift my spirits."

She grabbed her bag and before Leslie could blink, she disappeared from sight. Merry would do what she wanted. At this moment he had more to do than chase after his sister to make sure she wasn't bored. What difficulty could she possibly get herself into? He would say something to Hope. Perhaps Flynt's wife would find a way to manage his sister's penchant for finding trouble.

He groaned inwardly, remembering a bored Merry was a Merry who would find herself in predicaments up to her ears despite everyone's best attempts to waylay her. Well, in any case he didn't have the time right now. He told his mother as much after she allowed Merry to come with him.

Then to Westcott, "Make sure the master chamber is ready for me. I'm off to the MacTavish townhouse to retrieve my bride."

He was sure Lacie would be there, hoped he wouldn't have to ride out to the country estate this afternoon. Thankfully the weather was cooperating for now, although it was cold, the threat of snow lingering in the air.

"You might have some explaining to do. I don't think anyone in the city including Flynt MacTavish knows you wed his youngest sibling. I would have heard the gossip. As it was the only rumors floating around were the question as to why Lacie stayed here as long as she did."

"Over night? Rumors you put a stop to I would hope."

"No, only guessed at the truth. I honored her wishes. She's a lovely lass, your duchess, but she didn't want anyone to know about the marriage. Thought it would be best if she just waited until you returned home and you could explain so that everyone believed her."

"She was embarrassed about staying here?" Leslie couldn't fathom what she was thinking.

"Don't think so, just didn't feel comfortable pretending to be something she wasn't. Heard she got herself into a bit of a scrape a while back. After that, I haven't seen her or even heard she was in town. I'm thinking you probably won't find her at the house in the city but of course you have to try there first. Would be stupid to ride all the way to the country if she was still in town."

He was puzzled by the words, confused as well. "Do you know what kind of scrape?"

Westcott was shaking his head, his snow-white brows drawn together in concentration. "Best I don't spread hearsay. Best you find out from the lass herself. Don't even know if what I heard is true."

"Very well. Try to keep track of Merry for me. She might try to go out tonight in order to explore things on her own. Don't let her. She's only fifteen and draws trouble to her before she sees it coming."

"Sir, don't know if I can do that. Maybe it would be best if you just lock her in her room." Westcott was rubbing the back of his neck as if he really disliked this new arrangement. "Don't think I'd be a very good guardian or chaperone. Don't like telling people what to do, particularly young lasses, ones with a pedigree and all."

"Novel idea, locking her in her room. Wish I could do that but she's going to need some food. We haven't eaten since breakfast on board the ship. Guess I'll just have to deal with any fallout tomorrow, if there is any." With every tick of the clock, he was growing more and more impatient. He needed to find his wife.

"You go on, Sir. I'll watch her for you and if she goes out, I'll follow her. Best I can do."

A few minutes later, Leslie was mounted on his favorite stallion, Garth, while he rode through town. He shaded his eyes as he stared into the brilliant sunshine, hoping he would find Lacie at his first destination. His thoughts returned momentarily to Merry. Even the weather wasn't helping him with his sister. He hoped her first days of rain would send her back to Bordeaux. Brilliant sunshine in December would not do the trick for him.

The ride to the MacTavish townhouse didn't take long. He pulled up in front, tying the horse to a post and hoping his search for Lacie would be finished here, but he was afraid that it might not. At least he would learn something about what happened to her, that scrape Westcott spoke of.

When he knocked, Hope, Flynt's wife, answered the door.

"Hello, Leslie."

"Hope." He nodded.

After a moment of shocked expressions, she threw her arms around him for a huge hug. "You're back. When?"

"A half hour ago, long enough to learn..." He quit, unsure of what anyone knew about his marriage to Lacie and accepting Westcott's assumption that no one knew. "You wouldn't know where Lacie is, would you? It seems we have unfinished business to discuss."

"Lacie is not here. I have instructions from Flynt not to tell you where she is," Hope said, looking over her shoulder for a moment. "But I'm sure a man as astute as yourself can figure it out. Would you like to come inside?"

"Why is that?"

This reception seemed worse than what he imagined. Not to tell him where she was? What had he done except marry her?

And leave her to her own devices.

"You've been gone for such a long time. Lacie was beside herself for too many days to count then she suddenly turned inward. Lacie's not like that. She's impulsive and wears her heart on her sleeve."

"Something happened?"

"Not that I'm at liberty to speak of, but I'm sure it did." Hope poured him a brandy after he followed Hope into the drawing room.

He accepted graciously. Sipping and thinking about Lacie, "There are not a lot of places she could be if she's not here. Flynt doesn't think I'm smart enough to figure out if she was hiding from something she'd run to the country where she feels at home."

Lifting his shoulders slightly, he just wished Lacie would have gone to his place instead of hers because he meant to bring her home with him. He would have to ride to Southcliff first before confronting Lacie if she was indeed at the MacTavish estate. He wanted the place to be dusted with the furniture uncovered when he brought her home.

"Not sure what Flynt is thinking? Never am, where it concerns his sisters." Hope smiled at him, which left him shaking his head at her in disbelief. He honestly didn't see how Flynt was able to resist her for so many years particularly when she was living in his home. She was the most beautiful woman he'd ever seen including Lacie. Not that Lacie wasn't beautiful, she was but it was her impulsive and fun loving personality that drew him to her in the first place.

"Tomorrow sometime, if it's not too much trouble for you, could you stop by my house. My sister Merry came with me. She's going to find herself bored to tears. If I know her at all, she will find a way to get herself into hot water if you know what I mean. When she's bored, she doesn't think before she goes off on some impulsive tangent."

"No problem. I'd enjoy meeting your sister. I'll bring her to the bakery. I can introduce her to Daryl too. Can she bake? If so, we could put her to work."

"Bake? Don't have a clue."

"Well, then perhaps Daryl will teach her."

"Tell everyone you see I'm home now. I won't be back in town until everything is made right with Lacie, but you will be able to find me at Southcliff Hall." He slapped his riding gloves against his leg, thinking about Lacie and how she would feel in his arms.

"What does that mean?" Hope pointed a finger at him. "Right with Lacie?"

"Never you mind." He turned on a heel and left, mounting his horse before quickly winding through the streets of Glasgow until he left the city behind. What was between Lacie and him was no one's business save his and Lacie's.

The sun was nearing the horizon when he pulled up in front of the MacTavish estate. With the sun going down, a chill permeated the air.

Dark clouds littered the sky to the west, the hint of snow on the air. He had hoped to arrive before sunset, giving him time to convince Lacie to return with him to Southcliff manor. Now it would be dark so, it seemed, he would have to stay the night here.

A storm was coming. Maybe more than one if he had to guess. Sunshine would disappear and be replaced with snow or rain. Looked like snow to him.

Pushing his hat back, he spotted a rider due east of the house. It was Lacie, racing the wind as well as the darkness. He watched her as she neared the house and veered toward the stables. She would take care of her horse first then leave for the house. In the stables where he kissed her for the first time, he would confront her. Perhaps this scrape of hers was really nothing and could easily be dealt with.

The gallop looked reckless, but he knew her expertise when it came to riding. Still he worried a hole in the ground, a small animal, anything could spook a horse and throw its rider. For the duration, he held his breath, his heart beat doubling in time as his breath held steady in the back of his throat.

Once she was safely inside the stables, he walked Garth toward the barn, handing the reins to the stable boy then proceeding to the stall where Lacie was brushing down her horse. Her dark hair had come lose from all its pins and was in glorious disarray framing her delicate features.

He crossed his arms, leaning against the stall door, much like he did the day he first kissed her. Watching her was like seeing heaven, and he'd been away for so long all he wanted was to pull her into his arms, feel her soft warmth against him, filling his soul with heat and fire. He realized he missed her. Her face was flushed from the ride. He was sure her skin would have a sheen of moisture covering it, much like he imagined when they finally made love.

Tonight he hoped if everything went as planned, she would be in his arms and sweetly beneath him. Perhaps a start on an heir, he needed to stop tongues from waging and his mother from nagging.

Her start of surprise made him grin and raise one eyebrow.

"It's you." She sounded panic struck, one hand just above her heart as she gasped for air. She closed her eyes for a second, her breasts heaving.

"Welcome home would be nice." He stepped forward only to see her back away from him, terror on her face.

He stopped midstride but had no words, unsure of how to proceed. He couldn't fathom why she was afraid of him, why her eyes were wide with terror.

She swallowed, wiping her hands on her riding habit. "I'm sorry. You did surprise me. Welcome home, Leslie." Then she turned her attention back to her horse just as if her husband wasn't standing two feet away from her. Picking up a blanket she started to cover the animal.

"A hug would have been nice, too, as well as I missed you my dear husband. Perhaps even I'm glad to see you or a kiss on the cheek. At the moment you look as if you detest me, or are terrified of me. I don't know which scenario is worse." He wanted more than a kiss on the cheek, but he knew by the sheer terror he saw in her dark blue eyes flecked with tiny particles of green even that intimate gesture wasn't going to happen any time soon.

What to do?

"You've been gone so long. I nearly forgot what you look like," she spoke softly, unable to look at him, continuing to administer all her affections on her mare. She stopped to stare at him, her eyes still wide but this time more uncertain than terrified.

This was not like Lacie. So foreign, he didn't understand. Couldn't comprehend what was happening here. For the longest time, he stood unmoving, watching the jerk of her muscles as she worked.

She turned back to her horse as if she was hiding from him. He knew he wasn't going to pull her into his arms then kiss her as he did that day so long ago. Now, it seemed, he needed to tread lightly until he could figure out what was going on with her. That scrape must have been devilishly more than a minor incident. He needed for her to tell him what it entailed.

"What do you want, Leslie."

She didn't look at him. No, she sounded as if she wanted him to go away. Her voice was cold, icy.

"You know what I want." He didn't move toward her, just settled for watching her for the time being.

"Of course I don't."

She was acting obtuse now, but he calmed his anger trying for a patience he had very little of. "My bride. I came for the woman I married and to take her home, to our home. Not tonight though, it's late and the darkness as well as the cold is prohibitive. We will sleep together tonight. It's something I've wanted since the day we married."

At the look on her face, he understood he gave her too much information. He thought for a moment she might send the brush she held in her hand straight to his head.

Suddenly, he wanted answers to the myriad of question swirling around in his poor man's brain. Enough innuendos had been spread since he returned; rumors, gossip, things he needed to put a stop to. He stepped forward taking the brush from her hands before turning her around.

"Don't touch me."

Once again, she seemed terrified of him, her body shaking as she distanced herself. Wide eyed, she backed against the wall, her hands outstretched as if she needed to defend herself against him.

What the devil was going on here? She'd never been afraid of him before. If anything, she'd been a bit forward, wanting his attention, melting into his arms as she lifted her face in anticipation of a kiss.

"Your horse is thoroughly groomed. Come, let's go to the house where it is warmer. You can explain a few things to me. I've heard you were in a scrape while I was gone. If that's true, then perhaps you can shed some light on that. Tell me what happened."

He offered his arm. Refusing him, she walked along beside him her tiny little hands fisted at her sides, her chin held high, tipping all his conceived plans out of balance.

It seemed she was determined to keep her distance.

His breath caught in his throat. His heart nearly pounded to a sudden and abrupt halt. Her flushed face turned pale while her body seemed to shake even more. His close proximity to her terrified her. In the past his closeness excited her.

"Don't touch you? Don't touch my wife? That will not be imaginable."

Of all the possibilities that had swirled in his head since this afternoon, that was not one of them.

"I'm sorry. It was just a reaction. I decided while you were gone that I didn't want to be any man's wife nor touched by any man. I got an annulment. The papers are in the house."

A hoarse laughter was his only answer. He wondered about what she just said. Her words weren't true, the annulment not valid. He'd signed no papers so, of course, she was still his wife. "What brought you to that decision?" he asked, more concerned than ever that what his butler told him was the truth.

He had work to do in this relationship, needed to mend it as soon as possible, so he sorted through the months he'd been gone.

If she wouldn't allow him to touch her, that would be devilishly hard. He would have to use words to show her he was not what she was thinking, a cad or worse someone who would hurt her.

She looked away, seemingly unwilling to talk to him. He noticed the moisture in her eyes. Perhaps she would be swayed. They walked in silence then. A full moon peeked from behind clouds. Somehow, in the time he spent in the stables with her, night had fallen. His life as well had taken an abrupt turn into darkness with no visible silver lining. Blackness filled his soul.

In his hasty wedding, he took too much for granted. His arrogance might well be hard to fight. Nothing he could think of that he might have done or said could have caused this distrust as well as the distance between them.

He found his heartbeat double-timed again and he needed a way to find his usual calmness, the impassiveness he was known for in troubling situations. The stoic man his mother spoke of was not apparent tonight. Everything he put into action before he left town crumbled at his feet.

They entered the main house through the kitchen door. She hung her coat up. "If you're hungry, I'm sure cook left something in the warming oven. She always does."

She continued inside, leaving him to wonder about her intentions.

His stomach had been turning into knots since she told him she didn't want to be his wife, since she told him not to touch her. Feeding his hunger was the farthest thought from his mind. "Not now, maybe in a little while."

He followed her into the parlor, studying her, searching for some clue to her irrational words.

"Suit yourself."

She lifted her delicate shoulders which seemed to him to be thinner than when he left, her waist more slender. The trimmer figure wasn't due to a tighter corset.

"You need to eat something," he told her, his words more brusque than he intended.

"As do you."

They were in the drawing room now. Arms crossed, he leaned against the wall for a moment. She poured a glass of brandy for both of them before kicking her shoes off and settling on the couch with her feet tucked under her, eying him as if she thought he was about to attack her.

Leslie sat down across from her, holding his brandy in both hands, warming the liquid for a moment, taking his time as he searched for the words he needed. He sucked in a deep breath of air when he noticed her clothing. She seemed to know where his gaze lingered, fastened on buttons that had somehow come undone. Quickly, she pulled an afghan from the couch and wrapped it around her shoulders.

"Why aren't you wearing the riding habit I bought you?" His question was met with the stiffening of her back and for the longest time, no answer. So, this was how the discussion looming in front of him was going to proceed. He would ask questions and she would remain mute.

Then with a heavy sigh, "I am wearing it. You picked out the fabric yourself." She pulled her covering tighter. "Don't you remember?" Her question was accusatory.

For a moment, he felt a twinge of guilt before it vanished. "I see."

He was beginning to put a few sentences in her story that needed telling, beginning with her still expanding bust line. For the life of him, he didn't see how any of that was his fault and why that fact would cause her terror of him or create a need for an annulment.

There was so much more to learn. Well, he had all night as well as the next day or longer.

He decided to continue in this vein. Clearly, a well-fitted riding habit nearly a year ago no longer fit her. Breasts that he'd wanted to fill his hands with but had waited to feel, were even larger now. He was a man well blessed if he could convince her he wasn't the enemy.

"You are quite literally popping from your bodice," he told her, beginning cautiously and with that which was obvious. "I shall take you to the dressmakers tomorrow morning. Buy you everything you will need. It's a simple thing, you know, going to the dressmakers. Most women love to buy new clothing. While I was gone, you could have purchased anything you wanted or needed. I made sure your name was on my account before I left."

"No." She looked down and once more pulled the afghan tighter. "No, we won't. It will only cause gossip. Gossip I don't want. Which in turn, will create more problems for me. No one knows we are wed. As I said earlier, there is the annulment."

Setting his glass on a side table, he walked to the sofa then sat down beside her. "Tell me what is going on here. There is so much you are not telling me. If I'm to give you what you want, I have to know all the facts." Hell would freeze over before he consented to an annulment.

She stiffened with his words that sounded more like a command rather than a request. As more moisture formed in her eyes, he felt the cad but he was desperate to know the answers.

"Nothing," she paused, wiping tears away with the backs of her hands. "Everything."

He kept the smile behind his teeth. At least now he had a start on the problem, vague as it was. "Care to explain what that means? Nothing? Everything?"

"No," she told him, her fingers nearly turning white so tight was her grip on the blanket covering her. She pulled it higher as if the tiny gesture could give her more protection from him.

"Very well." He stood, retrieving his brandy, breathing deeply and telling himself he needed to take this slowly if he was going to discover the truth. "I'm a patient man and can wait right here with you until you trust me with this knowledge. How long do you suppose that will take? Hmm...?"

"There is nothing to tell." She wrestled with the blanket a bit more refusing to meet his gaze.

"Oh, but I believe there is. Westcott, my butler, told me rumor has it that you got into a bit of a scrape while I was gone. What was that? By the way you're acting this problem affected you in more ways than one. I'm willing to bet it's why you decided an annulment was the best or only way to proceed and that you didn't want me to touch you. Am I right?"

Her tongue swept across her lips then she nodded as she lowered her lashes for a moment. Then reluctantly, told him. "It is."

"You care to elaborate?"

He felt as if he was pulling teeth in this conversation. He detested the fear in her eyes, but he also knew this would not end for her until she talked about it, released her terror.

"No."

"What does it have to do with the size of your breasts?" He put his thoughts out there, was willing to wait an eternity if necessary.

The color on her face darkened from pale pink to rouge, embarrassment seeming to take over all feelings. Once again and with obvious reluctance, "Everything but not all of it."

"You know I can't help you unless you elaborate about the cause. I also understand you were a little self-conscious about the size of your breasts months ago, but nothing like this. Here, allow me." He took her hands in his, the afghan pooling around her waist.

He felt the shaking of her hands, disliked what he was doing but he saw no other course of action.

"You know they, your breasts, are beautiful to me. At least what I've seen of them." He did smile this time but it quickly changed to a frown as he unfastened the remaining buttons of her riding habit. Her hands were batting at him, trying to stop him. He was determined to make his point. "What is this?"

Her lashes fluttered shut for a moment then after a lengthy pause. "Bindings." She ran her tongue across her lips again. Then in a defensive tone, "I bind my breasts when I go riding."

"Whatever for?" He brought out a knife he kept in his boot. "I'm going to slit the fabric. Don't worry I won't touch you. Just don't move. This can't be comfortable and the wrap has to go."

Yet he did touch her, the back of his hand felt soft skin as the knife glided through the fabric. His body shook as he finished the chore. The material fell away revealing the luscious curves of her breasts while tears slipped down her cheeks, running down her face until they slipped from her chin only to slide down her breasts.

"How dare you?" her voice, whisper thin rippled through the stilted air. "You had no right to do that."

Refusing to answer, she was after all his wife. In his mind, he had every right. He asked with more specific words, irritated beyond belief that she would do something so stupid. "Why do you bind your breasts?"

"Only when I ride." She looked at him, eyes filled with moisture. "I'm tempted to keep them that way all of the time." Her voice grew in strength as her hands tightened and her back stiffened while she tried to pull the fabric of her gown closed.

His first thoughts were that he would never allow anything so absurd. Tonight was the beginning of the return of his Lacie. Then, "Why? I'd like to understand. Can't if you won't trust me with the story."

She looked down then up again then down at her breasts, once more trying to tug the bodice back together. A moment later, she inhaled a huge breath of air. "You know how much I love to ride."

This time she stared into his eyes, hers shimmering with passion and something else he couldn't quite figure out.

"Yes, I do. You were probably riding before you could walk."

He did chuckle then, smiling at her. He held her hands away from her, studying her, while looking for any sign of the old Lacie.

"They hurt."

"Your breasts?" He was totally and completely dumfounded. "How so?"

"Yes, my breasts," she said indignantly, one small tear slipping from her eyes. "You're a man. You don't know anything, only your own pleasure. They bounce when I do anything but walk the horse. They hurt when I ride." She shrugged, staring at him, defiance in her expression. "If I could cut them off, I would."

His heart nearly stopped before it suddenly pounded out of control. Easily, he traced the visible curves of her breasts, wishing he could somehow fix her problem, despising the fact that for the first time, she flinched when he touched her. "Can I show you something?"

"As long as you don't hurt me." The rapid rise and fall of her breasts could mean just about anything, nerves, desire...

"Have I ever hurt you, Lacie?" He was trying for the strength to carry this forward, but under the circumstance it was damn hard, his body aching with his need for her.

"No."

"I promise you I won't now either." Slowly, he unfastened the buttons that were left on her bodice before pushing the fabric aside so she was bared to him. She was shaking. He didn't think it was with desire for him. "A man has the right to look at his wife, you know," he paused then, "but only if his wife gives her permission."

She swallowed hard while he watched the rapid increase of her pulse at the base of her neck. He wanted to kiss her there, but for now he had one purpose.

"Even if she doesn't want him to?"

"Are you saying no?"

For the longest time, she didn't answer but she finally shook her head, seeming to give her permission. One small step along a road he couldn't see or understand.

This whole process made him stop for a moment and think. "Yes, it does but I would never force you. I just want to show you something. May I?" he asked again, knowing how important this could be for their relationship.

"If you have to."

"Indeed, I do believe this necessary."

"Get whatever it is you want over with." Her voice squeaked in her frail response.

She was obviously not ready to give her consent yet she had. He was going to move along with this.

If he had his way, this would be the start of their lovemaking, not the end as she implied. He understood she didn't want him. At the moment was only tolerating his actions because as he told her, it was his right as her husband. Once she enjoyed his touch, once there was passion simmering deep inside, passion for him.

"If that's what you want." He cupped each breast with a hand. "All in good time, we will get this over with. You will see I treasure you, your body, all of it."

She was looking at him then, where he was touching her, her eyes seeming to cross when his thumb passed over a budding pink nipple bringing it tighter.

"Does this hurt?" He gently touched her nipples again. He heard the swiftly indrawn breath of air, the slight catch in her throat. When she didn't answer, "Lacie? I need to hear the words from you. I'm not going to assume anything."

"No, but it makes me feel very strange in a certain part of me. I remember when you kissed me. I felt that way too. Before you left me..."

"That's normal. Now, Lacie, I want you to look at your breasts." When she did, "See how they fill my hands. I've quite large hands, so a woman's breasts have to be large in order to satisfy me."

Good lord how he was making things up. He should be shot. Truly, he didn't care how large her breasts were. "Your breasts overflow my hands. I wouldn't have them any other way because they are yours. I want to suck them into my mouth, lave the velvet hard tips with my tongue. They are perfect. You are perfect, absolutely wonderful."

"It doesn't matter because I'm not going to be your wife. I can't. I..." Her breaths were short and shallow. "You cannot expect me to lie with you."

He knew how this would arouse her and perhaps it wasn't well done of him or maybe it was. He could introduce her to the pleasure of lovemaking. Perhaps she would change her mind. Whatever it was that had her terrified still needed to be uncovered so he could deal with the fear. The terror had very little if anything to with her breasts but went deeper than this.

"Where are the papers? The annulment papers? I'd like to see them for myself." Part of him hoped he was calling her bluff. When he remembered the bleak sad tone of her voice along with the terror in her eyes, this was most likely not a bluff.

"You have to take your hands off me," she whispered but there was some note in her voice that told him perhaps she didn't want him to let her go, that she was coming over to his point of view.

With a lot of patience as well as tenderness, he might be able to change her mind. He would have to change her mind because she was his wife and he never intended to be celibate, neither did he intend to grant an annulment.

He released her. She pulled her bodice together the best she could under the circumstances. He studied the stiff lines of her body as she slowly walked to the sideboard before opening a drawer. There she pulled out several pieces of paper. She looked at them for a few seconds before bringing them to him and handing them over.

"There they are. My brother's solicitor drew them up for me. They are legal and binding. No, Flynt doesn't know about the marriage or the annulment. His solicitor promised his silence to me."

He studied them, reading each line, his face draining of color as he realized this was, at least for the moment, what she wanted and believed she needed. She had gone about this meticulously, even having an advocate he knew and respected draw up the document.

His heart thundered, the life he wanted with her falling apart. He would have to find a way to convince her this was not at all what she wanted or needed. If she chose to do so, she would have to have the proper papers drawn up again because he was getting rid of these.

Slowly, he ripped the papers into quarters then walking to the fireplace tossed them into the flames. He stood back, hands clasped behind him, watching as the last piece vanished, turning into ashes. He'd expected her to cry out or to fight him, but she didn't.

Lacie was behind him, her hand lightly touching his back. A gesture at the moment he didn't know how to interpret.

"You had no right to do that," she whispered too unevenly. "Doesn't matter though, I can be your wife in name only if that's what you want. There can be nothing else between us. I won't let a man touch me again. I just thought you would like a way out of something that will never give you the heir you are looking for."

"That's the way of it then."

When hell freezes over. A man touching her? He spoke, trying for the deadly calm he was known for. It had never occurred to him that his choice for a wife could unhinge him with just a few words. "I will never force you to have sex with me but..." He meant to leave the sentence hanging, hoping she'd interpret this the way he meant it. "I will find a way to coax you into enjoying my touch, to setting you on fire once again."

"I ken it," she said, moving away from him to sit on the sofa again, her hands resting on her lap.

She'd poured another drink for herself, was now watching him, a cautious and very suspicious glint in her deep brown eyes.

"I will, however, get back to what we were speaking of earlier. I need to know about the scrape you got yourself into and what it has to do with the size of your breasts."

Her following sigh was deep and heavy with what emotion, he couldn't be sure. "You're a kin to a dog with a bone. Don't you ever let anything go?" She hesitated. "I don't like talking about what occurred that night. Talking about it embarrasses me, makes me relive something I'd rather forget. The memory is seared deep. When I think on it, I have nightmares."

"If we are going to continue on in this manner until you tell me what has you doing a complete reversal in thought, I will stay here until you can put the words together. I have to know. It seems half the city including our servants have a better idea than I do. If I have to, I'll seek out someone who is willing to continue to spread the rumors."

He was adamant in this. She would not hold herself away from him without telling him the cause.

"I'm sure to have nightmares tonight if I speak of it," she said, her voice weak, a slight quiver to her words. "It's not well done of you to make me relive something all I want to do is forget."

His heart went out to her, but he would never back away from this. "I will hold you through the terror haunting you, help chase the demons away. You don't have to endure this alone. I'm here for you and I don't plan on leaving." He watched the surprise in her eyes.

"You said you would not force me." She challenged him with his words.

"That's true.

"But..."

"Didn't say anything about us not sharing a bed. I will hold you and stroke you, hoping to change your mind, however."

He was suddenly aroused, something that strangely had not happened when he held her breasts in his hands, touched the tight pink buds. Thoughts of lying with her changed his perspective. His control now was mandatory as he fought the fire burning inside, the flames she so easily enticed into life.

She turned away from him then, returning her gaze to meet him, "If I tell you what happened, will you let me sleep in my own bed?"

He kept his chuckle behind his teeth. She was trying to bargain with him, something he wasn't inclined to do. "When I'm not at home, you can sleep in whatever room you like. If you choose your own bed tonight, I will still join you."

She grimaced, catching her lower lip between her teeth. "That's not fair. In a way it is forcing. I'll just get up when you're sleeping and leave."

"You can try."

He folded his hands in his lap knowing her words were true. What she didn't know was that he was a very light sleeper. The slightest movement nearby would always rouse him. At times, his vigilance had been a matter of life or death. She would have a hard time leaving, day or night.

"What's that supposed to mean?" She downed her brandy, setting the glass hard on the table, her eyes dark.

"It means that you can try. Lacie, I keep what is mine close. I'm not saying that to be unkind or back you into a corner. I remember a time not so long ago I supposed you were eager to be with me, to lie with me, to feel my hands in intimate places. Which brings us full circle. What was the scrape you got into and what does it have to do with the size of your breasts?"

She looked to the window then the fire. It seemed she couldn't keep her gaze on him. "I..."

He waited but she didn't seem forthcoming. "I understand. You don't want to tell me. I can and will out wait you. The sooner you get this over with, the sooner you can relax and we can both get on with the rest of our lives."

Lacie inhaled a swift breath of air. Seeming resolved, "You know that we, Daryl, Justine and Emilia deliver day old bread to the poor and needy at the end of the day."

His gut turned over. He could almost see where this might be headed. Daryl, her sister, had been hurt doing the same thing. They all agreed to bring a man with them. No wonder she didn't want to say anything. He prayed the worst scenario was not true. At least it was his understanding they were supposed to take someone with them. The sisters, however, were always impulsive. They would go anyway, damn the consequences if no one showed up to help.

"Go on."

Frown lines formed on her face while she scrunched her lips together, hesitating again. "You also know that Sandy and Ashford go with us or we promised we wouldn't go at all."

"I did know that and I'm glad to hear you accepted the help."

He was sure the next statement would be that the girls didn't wait for their escorts. Justine and Emilia were the only ones of the bunch who weren't impulsive by nature. He was also sure the MacTavish girls could easily persuade them.

"One night a couple of months ago, the men were late. Don't remember the reason, not that it makes a difference any longer. There is nothing we can do now to change what happened."

"So, the four of you set out on your own."

"Daryl wasn't there. She and Donal were celebrating something. I can't remember what it was. So, Daryl went home early leaving the three of us to close the doors. I'm not usually there, mind you. It must have been the end of the month because I'd been working on her books. The ledgers are always quite the mess, not so much now since Justine started working for her."

"You need to get to the point, Lacie. The hour is growing late. We've a lot of things to finish up tomorrow, including a trip to the dressmakers. It would also be nice to go to bed before the sun rises." He felt his impatience growing as well as the need to tamp it down. She might sleep in his arms tonight, but that was probably as far as his husbandly rights would go.

"All of us, Emilia included, wanted to go home. So," she paused, staring out the window.

"So..."

"We knew Ash and Sandy would catch up to us. They know the route we take. It's always the same." She plucked at her skirt, her fingers trembling.

He wanted to reach out and hold them, yet had the feeling such a gesture would be counter productive. "Everyone knows the streets you travel. Ever think that wasn't the wisest of ideas?" He watched her pale again at his sarcasm and regretted his hasty words even though they were true. He did want the story to come to its conclusion, so he could begin to work on the cure.

She smoothed the folds of her skirt, her bodice slipping lower as she did so. "If you want the quick story, I was attacked."

His body tightened. He had a swift deep urge to kill the man.

Gritting his teeth together, "What happened?"

Tears slid down her cheeks as gut-wrenching sobs coming from her chest seemed to envelop her. He pulled her into his arms, running his hands along her back, trying to ease the pain even with the realization the pain was still very deep and present.

"The man, it was the same man who hit Daryl that night when he was looking for Emilia. He ripped open my dress, pressing his hands on my breasts, digging his fingers into them. He hurt me, Leslie." She couldn't speak then, her sobs so terrifyingly real, Leslie was hard pressed to remain calm. "I don't know how to forget or even put the horrifying night out of my mind."

"Did he force you?" His mind went to rape, but he wasn't ready to assume anything. Whatever the case, as far as Lacie was concerned it didn't matter to him. She was still Lacie.

"Sandy pulled him off me before he could do much else except leave bite marks and bruises on my breasts. He touched me, where a man shouldn't touch a woman. He called my breasts kettle drums and said they were his now." She opened up to him, needing to tell everything now that the floodgates were open.

She sobbed again, shaking while wiping tears from her cheeks with the backs of her hands. Leslie didn't have the words as anger simmered deep inside. He should have been there for her. "I'm so sorry."

"I don't want kettle drums," she blurted. "I just want to be normal, like every other woman."

"It's only words. Did the man hurt you in any other way?" He tried to keep his mind from delving more deeply into all the possibilities. He couldn't stop the horrific thoughts.

"No, but..."

"Is that why you asked for an annulment?"

"Yes, I don't want to ever have those sensations again. I don't want a man on top of me, doing things, hurting me."

His thoughts went to so many different ways to make love with his wife. Too bad he still had to convince her he was trustworthy and would never hurt her. Yet their first time... Surely, she must know. Hope must have spoken with her.

"What if I can teach you that what you felt that night won't happen with me?"

He hoped she would give him a chance. He would find a way to convince her. He had to. This marriage had to be real, all of it.

"It's not possible." She was quick with her words. "Men are..." She gulped in air, "Men are beasts."

Some men were. He didn't appreciate the comparison. He was never hateful or cruel with a woman. He loved them. He wanted to show Lacie how wonderful it could be between them. "I understand you're afraid. For the time being, I want you to go back to those days before I left, when I kissed you. Will you do that for me? Can you remember how much you enjoyed me and what we did together?"

"It's hard to remember. The other incident is so fresh in my mind."

She reached out to him though, touched his chest. He put his hand on top of hers, hoping the gesture would keep her from withdrawing at least for a few seconds.

"We need to put new memories in your head. Can you trust me enough to at least try?"

"I don't know."

He felt the sudden constricting of his throat. The man forced her but from her account, he didn't rape her. If he were gentle with her, thoughtful as well, she would come to accept him. At least he prayed he could change her mind, reconstruct her thoughts, fill her body with fire and need. He yearned to discover the raw passion he sensed simmering deep inside Lacie.

"We could try now," he spoke softly. "If I do something you don't like or if it hurts, just tell me. Give me—us a chance."

He believed this was the first time in his adult life that he pleaded with anyone, especially a woman to let him make love to her. If it weren't' so damn serious, the situation might be funny.

She reluctantly nodded, her eyes focused now on his mouth. It was too bad she didn't know the affect that simple gesture had on him. If she did understand, she'd remove her gaze and stare somewhere else. He was

Christine Young

fully aroused in need, a vibrant tension in his body.

Lightly, he bracketed her face with his hands, gently brushing her lips with his. The mere touch sent an even greater unrestrained inferno racing through him, "Is this what you like?" he whispered as he felt her breath feather against his cheek.

He swept his tongue across her lips, wishing she would open for him as she used to do. He needed to feel the sultry heat that was hers alone. Indeed, as she'd done the first time he kissed her. Her lips were soft and moist, ready for him as he hoped other parts of her body were also. He groaned low in his throat as he trailed kisses along her jawline upward to her ear, finding the lobe and tugging gently with his teeth.

She moved against him, her hands now around his neck. "Yes, I do like your kisses. If that was all you ever expected from me, I would like that. I could be with you then, but I ken you want more. I'm afraid of what you want, that I can't give you what you need."

He lowered himself on the sofa, pulling her on top of him. "I'm giving you all the control. Do what you will with this poor man's body."

She pushed against his chest. He witnessed the first smile since he returned home and a soft giggle. He inhaled long and deep, realizing this might work as long as he moved slowly, kept his hands mainly to himself or at least as much as was humanly possible.

"What should I do?" she asked, tilting her head slightly, her eyes shimmering with what he hoped was passion, not fear.

"Anything you want." He held a strand of hair that had come lose from her tight chignon. Holding it for a second between his fingers, he slowly placed it behind her ear. He touched her earlobe, traced the shell with his fingertip, noticed the fine trembling so unlike earlier in the night.

Her slight weight was on him. He spread his legs so she could lie between them. His heavy rod pulsed against his doeskins, signaling its need for more, more of Lacie. Something he could not take just yet.

"I don't know what to do," she told him, suggestively running her finger across his lips.

He opened for her and his tongue touched her silken flesh. Her eyes widening, slowly, he drew the finger into his mouth, gently biting, lingering.

"Kiss me if you like." He had not meant to make the suggestion, the words seeming to slip uninvited from his mouth. "Do you want to feel my tongue inside your mouth?" Lord but he needed to feel the warmth, the sultry heat.

For a moment she frowned, seeming to contemplate his words. "I liked the feel of you before. But no, I don't..."

"Perhaps you would like it now also." He stopped her, didn't want to hear her say nay.

"Maybe."

"Kiss me like I taught you. Do you remember how, lass?" *Is tu mo sholas na greine.* Yes, she was definitely his sunshine, when she smiled, or looked off in the distance as if she was thinking of something to do to him. That had been the way of it before.

Lacie was staring at him as if she thought he was crazy, another first since he returned home. Now, he noticed a bit of the impulsive woman in her expression. Hesitantly, she touched her lips to his then looked at him expectantly.

"Like that?"

"No, little imp, do it right. You know how to kiss me." His hands rested at the small of her back then moved lower so he could press her closer to him.

She placed her hands on either side of his head and once more pressed her mouth to his. This time she hesitantly swept her tongue across his mouth. The lazy glide of the small pink tongue was exquisite, warm and soft. He opened for her and she slipped inside him, dancing with his tongue, tracing his teeth, exploring the dark sensitive underside of his lip.

He felt her rapid breath, tasting the brandy and the woman, smelling the sweet scent of lavender and her special woman's scent. Her hips moved against him as he heard the tiny raw passionate sounds she was creating in herself. In short, she was seducing herself. He would never tell her though. Delighted, he assumed she was wet and swollen ready for his entry into her most intimate lady parts. All that needed to be done was to convince her she wanted him again.

She pulled away. "I like kissing you but I ken that's not all you want. Perhaps we should go to bed now."

His heart leapt at her words even though he was quite sure she meant separate beds. If he had his way, and he would, that wasn't going to happen tonight or any other night.

"Ach, lass, does this mean we are ending the kissing? I thought there would be more."

"You don't want to stop?"

"I'd like to kiss you all night long," he said, grinning widely, "but you are right. Tomorrow will arrive soon enough. You will come home with me then?" He phrased the words as a question even though he didn't intend on giving her a choice in the matter.

"I'm staying here as I'm going to sleep in my bed tonight and all the nights after that. The kiss was nice but that's all I want from you. Nothing more. That's why I got the annulment."

Her words would haunt him forever if he couldn't' change her mind. Stubborn lass, he would change that notion, "Go get ready," he sighed as she got to her knees.

"You're not going to insist I sleep with you?" she asked, as she stepped onto the floor.

"I didn't say that now did I? You are my wife and we will sleep in the same bed as I told you earlier. I won't force you though," he told her once more, hoping she would begin to trust him. "I want you next to me, to hold you if you have that nightmare again and soothe your fears."

"I ken it but I've never slept with a man before. I wouldn't know what to do."

"Sleep, perhaps?" He couldn't help the soft chuckle he would have rather kept behind his teeth.

"Oh..."

"I will be up in about ten minutes. If you're not in the master chamber in the bed, I will find you and carry you there. It's a promise. I will sleep with my wife."

She stood as if frozen to the ground, her hands clasped beneath her chin, eyes wide with alarm. "You..."

"The rights are mine, Lacie. Don't ever forget you married me willingly. I'm not going to let you forget that fact. Ten minutes." He didn't like the harsh edge to his voice, didn't want to lose the tiny bit of control he had or the fact that he'd weakened her resolve, but she did test him.

She turned and fled. He was pretty sure she would not be curled up on the bed in the master chamber when the time came. Meaning to go gently with her, she would discover tonight he would not let her have her way in this and they would move forward accordingly.

He poured himself another brandy, sitting back and watching the clock as the seconds ticked by coming ever closer to the ten minutes he thought it might take her to get ready for him as well as bed. Thoughtfully, he sipped the amber liquid, swirling it around in his glass, determined she would see the reality.

Noting to himself to discover the name of the man who attacked her, his deed would not go unpunished. He was a scourge in the city of Glasgow and seemed to have a way of going underground whenever someone was after him. He didn't doubt for a minute after he hit Daryl, a search was forthcoming. Yet no one found him, no punishment impending.

The minutes seemed to take hours to pass. Finally, he rose from the chair where he'd been sitting watching the clock as the minutes ticked by. He wondered just how to go about this, thinking he should check her room first. He didn't even know which one was hers. Deciding on trust, he strode up the stairs to what he believed to be the master chamber and pushed the door open.

This time he couldn't keep the smile behind his teeth. Lacie sat on the large bed made specifically to fit Flynt, wearing a white nightdress that fastened around her neck and reached to her toes. Her look of innocence nearly brought him to his knees as he reminded himself Lacie was truly the innocent she appeared.

A line of pillows separated two sides of the bed. A precious attempt to keep him on his side, he believed. Perhaps after those kisses, she needed the pillows to keep her away from him. He laughed at the thought, unable to hold the feeling inside. Perhaps he'd made a tiny bit of progress.

"Thank you," he said, unfastening his shirt before shrugging out of it, his hands resting on the fastening of his pants. "I truly did not want to have to come after you."

She gasped, her urgent loss of air seeming to catch with her words. "You aren't going to undress right in front of me, are you?" she paused, running her sweet pink tongue across her lips.

"I'm not going to bed in my clothes."

"You're going to wear something though."

Clearly amused, he sat on the bed, pulling his boots off then stood again, facing her. "I don't sleep in anything. I'm not going to change now just because I've a wife. A wife, I might, add who seems to be a bit hesitant to fulfill her wifely duties." He smiled fondly, reaching out to caress her cheek before thinking better of it and pulling his hand back.

When he lowered his pants, he thought she would look away. Instead, she stared at him, her eyes wide. For a moment he felt a bit self-conscious then realized her expression showed only appreciation of his body. He couldn't remember a woman ever staring at him this way.

"Do you like what you see?" He smiled, strolling slowly to the bed, letting her look as long as possible.

He quickly tossed all the pillows separating the two halves of the bed onto the floor then pulled the covers back, slipping beneath them.

"I..."

"Come to bed, Lacie. You need your sleep as do I. I don't intend on ravishing you tonight unless of course you want me to. You will have to ask sweetly though. A gentle please might be in order. A man has to be sure that his wife wants him." He patted the bed. Then, "You didn't say if you liked what you saw of me."

"My mouth is dry." She drank from the glass of water beside her bed.

"What does that mean?"

"You've more muscles than I thought. Well, that your clothing covered them up. You're intimidating and very large."

"I am large, but I assure you I will fit when the time comes."

She was staring at his face this time, her eyes crossing with his words. "You don't mean... I couldn't possibly... Well... We are not going to find out. You do understand I intend to be a wife in name only."

"We shall see."

~ * ~

Merry strode around the Stewart townhouse, picking up objects then setting them back, never in the original spot. What the devil was she supposed to do with her time? She was bored to tears then she reminded herself this was what she wanted. Not to be bored, of course, but to be in Glasgow. She had choices and this was at the top of her list.

She had her reasons, valid reasons. None of which she could tell Leslie.

She visited the stables last night and picked out a beautiful brown stallion with a white star on his nose. a matching one on his hindquarters as well. The horse seemed to like her at first glance, letting her rub his nose and feed him the bites of apple she brought with her for bribery. The horse wanted to run, go right now if he had his druthers. She was sure she heard the stallion talking to her, telling her how much he wanted to race with the wind just as she did.

Merry laughed when he nodded to her suggestions as if he understood every word. "You are precious," then leaning against him and stroking his nose. "What's your name big fella?"

"He's called Regan." Westcott stood behind her, hands clasped behind his back, rocking a bit on his heels as if he knew things she didn't. Well he probably did know more about Glasgow as well as her older brother.

"Nice name," she said to him.

"Don't think master Leslie will like you taking that big stallion. He's much too spirited for a little girl. This mare," he pointed in the opposite direction, "might be a better choice for you. She's docile and will do exactly what you ask of her. I won't have to worry about picking

58

up the pieces when be bucks you off."

"So, will Regan. He will do exactly what I ask of him. You'll see."

Merry bristled at the words, feeling an immediate rise of anger when the man assumed, she couldn't ride this magnificent animal because she was female. She was an excellent horsewoman. This man had no idea along with no business telling her what she could or couldn't do.

"I would not wish to gainsay you. Just making a suggestion that I thought was appropriate under the circumstance," Westcott said calmly. "I'm sure you ken what you're about. I'll leave..."

"My brother told me I could pick out any horse except the black stallion, which was his."

She turned away from the man, stroking Regan's nose, trying to tamp down the anger that was already threatening to rise and let itself out despite her attempts to vanquish it.

"This one is not a good choice," Westcott persisted, seeming to change his mind. "That little mare will take you anywhere you want to go. This one," he pointed to the stallion, "will set you on your arse before you can blink. He only lets Leslie ride him."

"He will let me."

"We shall see," Westcott said with a loud hrmph.

Merry ignored him even while she realized he was just carrying out Leslie's orders. "You and I are meant for each other, aren't we, big fella? You won't buck me off, will you?"

The hose nickered his answer.

"Of course, you would be allowed to make a choice, but he also told me to look out for you. That's what I'm doing. Don't want you to get hurt on my watch. I'd have to answer to the duke. Are you going out this afternoon?"

She let out a long slow breath of air then, "No, well yes, tell me where I can find Hope and Flynt MacTavish. Leslie told me she would keep me company if I was lonely or had an urge to explore the city. Suppose I could ride to her home if it's not very far. Can you give me the directions?"

"Is that all you mean to do?" Westcott asked, clearly disapproving yet the frown lines vanished from his brow. He seemed pleased after he thought on it for a second.

"What did my brother tell you about me?" Merry demanded.

"He said you might want to explore the city. It's much too late for a young lady to be by herself in the city. Not safe out there, no, not safe at all."

So now she was a young lady. That pleased her immensely. Much better than a little girl. "For now, I could of course change my mind."

She kept the laughter inside her lips, not wanting to offend this man who had been charged with chaperoning her. He seemed quite nice and caring. Once again she reminded herself he was merely following orders.

"I'd appreciate it if you didn't," he paused, "change your mind. Master Leslie warned me that it might be difficult to keep you from doing something foolish. You won't do that, will you?" Westcott asked. "Something foolish? I'm too old for watching over you. Told the duke that too, but he didn't seem to pay me much attention. Suppose his mind was on his wife."

"No, I never act foolish. He's been away for so long he really doesn't know me very well. I will promise you that I will go to Hope's if you give me the directions and come right home after I've spoken with her. You needn't fear for my safety unless the streets of Glasgow are unsafe for a woman during the day."

"Not during the day they aren't, but you will be home before dark, won't you?" he asked, running his hands through his thinning grey hair. "You are after all very important to your brother. He would be here if he didn't need to find his wife." He cleared his throat as if he thought he shouldn't have said that.

"How does a man lose his wife?"

Merry laughed, enjoying her brother's discomfort as well as Westcott's. She'd known from the start Leslie would do this to her. Her mother always asked what she was doing but never sent anyone to follow her. Only her brother would do something this absurd to make sure she had a chaperone, an elderly man at that. If she wanted, she could lose him in a blink but in just these few moments she was becoming fond of him as well as his fatherly ways.

"I'm sure it wasn't easy." A tentative smile creased Westcott's stern expression. "Master Leslie will find the duchess and bring her home. Then everything will be right dandy."

"Good then, I'm off to see Hope as soon as you give me the directions. Should be home in an hour or so."

She felt a moment of exhilaration at the thought of riding this spirited horse even though the ride would be sedate since she would be on city streets.

With the directions firmly planted in her head, she turned Regan toward the MacTavish townhouse in hopes of the day revolving in a different direction and becoming a little less tiresome. The thought brought her to the point of whistling a bawdy tune Link taught her last year.

Regan suddenly reared, pawing the air. When Merry finally grounded the horse, she gasped, surprised by the man staring at her from his seat on a beautiful black and grey horse.

Someday I'm going to marry that man.

Chapter Three

When Lacie woke, there was no sunlight filtering through the windows. Only the dreary gray sky, which shed a few drops of light into the room. Unlike yesterday, it was a day the clouds would make their appearance and stay until rain drenched the ground or perhaps snow.

Leslie was gone from the bedroom. The crazy thing was she missed him. She had not expected that. He held her through the night. When she woke the first time with the nightmare, she sobbed against his naked chest, actually seeking the comfort he gave. He didn't do anything except hold her and talk to her softly trying to ease the night terror.

She wanted to feel differently about the marriage. She was so unsure of herself now that Leslie returned, remembering against her will all the pleasant time they spent together. So handsome and debonair, every time she saw him her breath caught in her throat. He was tall, lean and so very powerful. His chest was broad, well-muscled and bronzed from time in the sun. Truth be told she was hard pressed not to want him in her arms as her husband. Yet the ugly truth reared its head, terrifying her away from the man of her dreams.

Men hurt women.

Before this she had been positive an annulment was what she wanted. Before he held her in his arms, absorbing her horrific nightmares into him, she knew it would not be difficult for her to absolve the marriage. If they could just be married and not have sex, she would make a go of this without further hesitation or complaint. She could be his duchess in almost every way, if he would never pin her beneath him so expertly that she could not escape his hold.

He tried though, attempted to soothe her and somehow she understood he was different and she should give him a chance. At those thoughts, the fear entered into her and she began to shake. He would pin her down, hurt her and she understood the fear was irrational. She couldn't absolve herself of the nightmares that encompassed Leslie also.

For a few seconds, she closed her eyes as well as her mind and put the past behind her concentrating on the man who suddenly and unexpectedly returned to her life.

Rising from the bed she shook her nightdress so the gown fell to her ankles. She walked to her room to discover steaming water waiting for her to bathe. Quickly, walking back to the door she peered down the hallway. No one was there. Only Leslie could have ordered her a bath.

How did he know when she would get up?

Happily, Lacie slid into the steaming water, noticing an extra pail of hot water for rinsing. Her favorite lavender soap sat on a dish close by as well as a sponge. She looked to the door, hoping Leslie would not take it upon himself to walk into the room. There were no sounds from the hallway, not one boot step indicating her privacy might be invaded.

For a few seconds at least, she could relax, would not have to guard her feelings. Leslie was far too receptive and he wanted, no needed, to learn everything about her.

Deciding it was necessary to know what was going on down stairs and where exactly Leslie was, she hurried with the bath. An hour later, with her hair dry and coiffed along with a tiny amount of makeup on her face she picked out a gown. At least she could still fasten the bodice of this one, although it was quite tight.

You shouldn't even care what you look like, she said to herself as she preened in front of her mirror. *You expect to convince him that an annulment is the best way to proceed for both of them.*

But you do.

I know. She let out a long slow breath of air, realizing Leslie was slowly drawing her back into his web. She didn't think she cared about the annulment any longer, not if he continued as they had begun last night. Only her stubborn nature would resume that plan.

That was the trouble though. After what happened to her, she didn't trust men. Her sisters trusted their husbands though. Not once had any of them spoken of any wrongdoing. They confided in each other. If anything had happened, all would know the truth.

With her hand on the doorknob, she hesitated before turning back to the mirror for one more quick glance. For some reason, she wanted him to like the way she looked. She decided it was due to old habits, ones she needed to break.

"Don't be a ninny." Before she could convince herself to stay in her room and wait for Leslie to confront her here in her secure and very private domain, she rushed out the door. Hand on the railing at the top of the steps she paused in confusion.

A young and very pretty woman stood at the bottom of the steps staring at her. Her jet-black hair tumbled around her shoulders and she was showing lots of beautiful white teeth. Her dark blue eyes, eyes reminding her of someone, sparkled with pleasure Somehow, Lacie felt as if she knew the woman, girl.

She stepped forward, hand outstretched to her as she walked down the steps. "Hi, I'm Merry, Leslie's sister. You're very pretty."

Lacie wanted to punch herself for thinking this girl might be one of Leslie's mistresses. She was much too young, even younger than she was. She thought she'd been about Merry's age when she fell in love, no lust, with Leslie.

"I'm Lacie."

"I know. Leslie had a fit when I showed up here this morning. He told me I was supposed to stay put in his townhouse until he could attend to my needs. Figured since he wasn't home last night with you, I should find out where he was. So, I did." Then, with a small shrug and a pause for emphasis, "I've never stayed put in my life. Don't intend to do that now. I'll be sixteen in a couple of months, and that's old enough to make most of my decisions. I even saw the man I intend to marry. Will have to find out what his name is though. Dear me, I pray he isn't already wed."

"Really," Lacie said with a smile, remembering how she'd thought the same about Leslie the first time she saw him. "That's how I felt too, when I was sixteen yet everyone was still telling me what to do. That's when I knew I wanted your brother."

"We're much alike you know."

Lacie regarded her closely. "I was bored in his townhouse too. No one knew we were married. I couldn't stay there, living a lie. It was a lie, you know. I told him I wanted an annulment."

"You want what?" One of her dark eyebrows arched skyward, a hint of amusement quickly disappearing. "He didn't like that."

"No, he threw the papers in the fire."

"That does not surprise me. Now, as to why I am here, there was nothing to do except watch Westcott who seemed too quiet for my taste. He wouldn't even talk to me. Had the audacity to gainsay Leslie's orders that I could pick out the beautiful stallion to ride and suggest I choose a docile mare."

Lacie couldn't help herself, she laughed. "So, going backward, you decided to join your brother in Glasgow? May I ask why?"

"I needed a change of scenery. Bordeaux held no excitement for me," Merry laughed, "and mother gave me permission before Leslie could say no. He would have too."

"Translation?" Lacie asked with a smile. "I've three older sisters as well as a sister in law. So, I ken there's more to this story than what you are telling me. If you want to share, I'm more than willing to listen. No judgments."

"Lucky you, I have two older brothers. Neither of them understands me. They never will. I've already fallen in love with the man on that horse. Saw him once before when I was in Paris. Believe I might have been ten."

"You've got plenty of time for that." Lacie paused in thought. "I fell in love with your brother when I was just fifteen. It was a long wait and now I don't want to be wed."

"You could do worse." Merry lifted one eyebrow in a gesture that reminded Lacie of something Leslie would do. "Do you still fancy yourself in love with him?"

"Why did you want to get out of Bordeaux? You just said it wasn't exciting but... elaborate please," Lacie asked as the heavenly aroma of cooked bacon rose in the air.

She needed to divert the conversation from her to Merry.

Merry seemed to notice the scent also. "I'm hungry."

"Back to the question. Must have something to do with a boy. You can talk to me you know," she repeated. "I wouldn't want to say anything to Leslie. He's bound to overreact. Of course, you are too far away from the lad, I suppose your young man is a lad, to do anything..."

Merry's features drooped. "Perhaps we can talk over breakfast, but only if you promise silence where Leslie is concerned. He does have a tendency to overreact just like you said when it comes to me."

"Deal," Lacie said. "Where is the man anyway?"

"Your husband?"

She had to laugh as Merry diverted the conversation back to her. "That fact remains to be seen, although more than once last night he told me that he would never let me go and that he always gets his way."

"That's the way of it then? If so, I'm glad. He's much nicer now," Merry said. "He was smiling when I rode up to the house. He didn't even lecture me. He's never like that. You make him better."

"He does have that way about him. He's tried not to lecture me, and I've noticed him biting his tongue in the process," Lacie looked to the door to the kitchen, sure Leslie was the person cooking the bacon.

"Yes, it's true. He always gets his way. You do understand you won't ever beat him. He's patient and can outwait everyone." They walked into the kitchen where her cook had an amazing breakfast set out for them.

"Leslie ordered it before he left," the cook told them.

She was disappointed and didn't want to admit the fact even to herself. "Thank you." Then, "Where did he go?" Lacie sat down, dishing up a huge plate of food that she knew she wouldn't be able to eat.

"Don't know. Leslie never says anything about his business."

"Why are you here?"

"The duke ordered me to show up here and make you a meal you would enjoy."

"Since we don't want to spend the morning second guessing him, why don't you tell me about this person you left Bordeaux to get away from," Lacie suggested as she stared at the meal in front of her, her stomach rumbling with enthusiasm.

"Not a lot to tell. He made my skin crawl and he showed up to the house way too often. Mother did her best to dissuade the visits, but she doesn't have the same persuasive qualities in her voice as does Leslie. I didn't want to tell my brother."

"So you thought a change of scenery might do the trick. Would you like to go for a ride after breakfast?" Lacie waved her fork in the air a moment, grinning with pleasure. "How did you find him here?"

"It wasn't hard. I asked Westcott a few questions. Found myself at your brother's townhouse and Hope told me Leslie was most likely here because that was where you were." She inhaled a long slow breath of air. "Yes, I would very much like to go for a ride, if Leslie will allow you to leave."

Lacie sucked in too much air and coughed. "Let me leave? Leslie doesn't have a voice in what I do."

Merry shrugged, "He is your husband and he's explained to me numerous times that when I married, which is of course a long ways away, I will finally have to obey someone. It's something I should have learned as a toddler but mother was far too lax in the discipline department."

"Oh." Lacie was mulling those words over in her head and silently chuckling. "So, you didn't stay put as he ordered, and you are still here eating breakfast with me when you should be obeying his order to stay in Glasgow and not venture too far from the townhouse. We shall go for a ride. Leslie is not even here to have an opinion."

"I think he has something planned. He left this morning after I arrived, calling me incorrigible, mumbling something about the perfect dresses for you," Merry tilted her head to the side. "What does that mean?"

Lacie looked down at her ill-fitting gown then back to Merry. "My constant problem. I have nothing to wear because I have kettle drums for bubbies." There, she'd said the words. It didn't seem so bad when she called them kettle drums herself. It was when others said the same words.

"I wish I had your problem or at least half of it." Merry looked at herself. "I'm as flat as one of these plates on the table." She held an empty plate up next to her as if she meant to compare.

"Well, obviously not flat enough to dissuade the man who makes your skin crawl."

Merry grimaced. "He was just after my trust fund, not my body, I'm sure. Has nothing to do with my nonexistent bosom. If he had his way, he would spend it all then move on to another conquest."

"Don't sell yourself short. You are a beautiful young lady. I was that flat when I was your age. How old did you say you were?"

"Fifteen," Merry said.

"Yes, I was definitely that tiny when I was fifteen. That was the first time Leslie kissed me though. It was not well done of him. I wanted him to kiss me and there was no way I would have told him no."

"Tell me more?"

"My sisters and I snuck into one of the bad boys' card games. When they saw us, they gave chase. I thought I lost him when I darted into the stables, but he found me and kissed me." Lacie did remember that time fondly as well as all the expectations for her future as well.

"Bad boys?" Merry laughed. "Not Leslie, now my other brother Link, he's a bad boy, a very bad boy indeed. He has children you know, illegitimate children, lots of them. Leslie and Link have accountability meetings every time Leslie comes home to figure out the finances of my brother's infidelities and what it will cost to feed and clothe his children."

"How many?" Lacie was curious now, smiling at the thought of Leslie not really being a bad boy but a rather steadfast and conservative man. "I don't believe Leslie has any children, but he has a mistress." At Merry's startled look, "Had, I think."

"No, I'm sure he doesn't have a mistress now that he is wed to you. He tells Link to have more control over his manly parts but it's not possible. He must lose his seed outside the woman's body and he won't have to worry about children. Link has six or seven children. I've lost count."

She inhaled a desperate gasp for air. "What did you say?"

"That Link should..." Merry waved a hand in the air. "Sorry. I listen at doors. Not well done of me, but I learn things."

"I'll accept that. In any case my brother, Flynt, and four of his friends decided they would dub themselves the bad boys. I think now it was to dissuade mothers from considering them good catches for their daughters. They didn't like the debutant scene or recitals and balls. This way they could stay away and not have to be expected to court women they weren't interested in."

"My oldest brother is the farthest from a bad boy anyone can get," Merry laughed, finishing her breakfast. She leaned forward as if she wanted to make her point stick. "He's known for his conservative stoicism. Better words to describe him might be stick-in-the-mud."

"Since Leslie is not here to put a damper on our ride, let's go now. I don't have a riding habit I can wear. He cut what I use to bind my breasts so there is nothing to delay us."

"Bind your breasts? Whatever for?" Merry asked, eyeing her critically.

"To keep them from bouncing so hard it causes pain."

Lacie grimaced at the thought. Without her bindings she could not gallop, race the little mare across the field.

"Well, then I'm ready also. This is what I wore to ride out here. Leslie let me have my pick of horses in his stable in town. I daresay he won't like my choice, but he only told me I couldn't have the black stallion. It wasn't there any way." Merry laughed. "He's such an autocrat. Has to have his way in everything."

Once mounted and on their way, Lacy headed toward the small creek that meandered through theirs and the Wallace property. Crisp air as well as the threat of colder weather hovered over them. Winter might well come in with a vengeance tonight.

Lacie understood she'd have to make this a short ride. She was sure Leslie would return soon and would most likely meet them in the stable with a few chosen and pointed words about their escapades. After all, he'd not given her permission even though she'd been living on her own ever since he left in the middle of their wedding night.

"Tell me about your sisters?" Merry said as they rode. "I would have loved a sister or two. Much more fun than two brothers."

"Or three? The best fun was ganging up on Flynt. Most of the time though, he didn't care what we were doing. He was preoccupied with his business interests as well as his mistress."

"Until someone would tell him what was going on?" Merry asked before continuing. "That's the way Leslie is. If he finds out something, he reacts. The rest of the time," she lifted her shoulders a bit, "he's never there."

"I'm sorry for that but now you will still most likely be on your own. Leslie isn't in Glasgow often either. Rumor is he's a spy and works for a man in London named Drake Montgomerie. I don't know if any of that is true, but it does make sense."

Lacie was staring straight ahead, studying the dark clouds on the horizon that seemed to be growing in size.

Merry seemed to think about that for a few seconds. "Back to your sisters. I'd much rather learn about them. What is it you all talk about when you visit?"

"First, we mostly talk about our bad boys."

"Alright then, tell me who your sisters are."

"Very well, then in order. The oldest is Bliss. She's an artist. She has twin boys. Before they were married, Broc left her because she didn't tell him she was Flynt's sister. He was angry since he seduced his best friend's little sister."

"Is Broc one of the bad boys too?"

"He is, that's why Bliss knew he would never look twice at her if she told him who she was. Finally, he returned wanting to marry her the day she gave birth to the boys. It wasn't well done of him."

"No, it certainly wasn't. I can imagine Leslie's reaction if something like that happened to me. If he liked the man though, I hope he would insist on marriage," she paused, "that is, if that's what I wanted."

Lacie laughed, her chuckle catching Merry's attention. She could also imagine what Leslie would do. "Chelsea is the next oldest and Cam, her husband tried to learn from Broc's mistakes. For the longest time he attempted to, what he called, court her properly. Chelsea didn't like that at all. She was always trying to seduce him. She wanted his kisses. He wasn't obliging her even though he was having the devil's own time refraining."

"I wonder how a woman would go about seducing a man," Merry said, a sparkle of humor in her eye. "I know it probably wouldn't be that difficult to seduce Link. So, who is next and what is her story?"

"Daryl, she's married to Donal, but she vowed she wouldn't wed just enjoy his company and sex. She figured if a man didn't have to get married to have sex, why should she? Only problem, Donal wouldn't let her get away with that notion. Told her he'd only make love to her when they were married."

"That must have been a real conundrum." Merry grinned widely.

"It was for Daryl. She was beside herself. Well, there is the river and the pond we swim in during the warmer weather. We used to skinny dip there." Lacie recalled the memories, ones she was fond of.

"Something else Leslie would have a fit over if he knew," Merry said. "He would not like to think of his wife swimming naked where anyone could come along and see her.

"We were children. What would it matter?"

"Darned if I know but I'm sure it would to him. Are there any more bad boys in Glasgow? Younger ones?" Merry laughed. "I think I'd like to meet a bad boy. When I'm older of course."

"I'm sure Leslie could lead you that way if he wanted, which he wouldn't. But I certainly don't have any idea. The only reason I met Leslie was because he was a friend of Flynt's."

"Do any of them have younger brothers?" Merry asked, curiosity evident in her tone.

"Well, Cam has a sister but she's married to Flynt and Donal has a brother, still too old for you. He's in the highlands overseeing his inheritance there. Don't have any idea when exactly he will be back in town."

Still looking to the east, Lacie had growing concerns about the weather. A brisk wind picked up a few minutes ago. Leslie would not be pleased if they got caught in a nasty storm. Neither would she.

"We should get back to the house." Lacie turned her horse around. "This time of year, the storms can be unpredictable. They can roll down from the hills and take you without warning."

Merry followed suit and they rode in relative silence as they cantered their horses toward the MacTavish estate. Lacie placed one arm beneath her breasts, trying to hold them still, uncomfortable, reminded once more of the nagging weight she bore day in and day out.

Leslie just didn't ken what she went through and she could not think of the words that would explain it to him.

Merry watched her closely, "I'm beginning to understand your problem. Don't think I'll ever wish for what you have even though I know men like large bubbies on a woman."

"Leslie says he wants them to fill his hands. Mine overflow," Lacie said, disgusted and wishing once more she could get rid of them somehow. "A magical genie would be nice. One of my wishes for him would be to shrink my breasts to at least half their size."

When they reached the house, there were carts and people unloading fabric from them. Leslie stood nearby supervising, gesturing with his hands. While Lacie could hear his voice, she didn't understand what he was saying.

"I think he's home," Merry whispered with a light feminine giggle.

"Well, he hasn't seen us yet. Do you want to turn the horses around and ride somewhere safe? I'm thinking I won't like what he has planned for the rest of the day." Even though she was in dire need of a new wardrobe, she didn't feel up to the fittings or the comments today. No, today she wanted to brood and sulk about the directions Leslie was spinning her life.

"He would come after you," Merry told her. "If he's brought the store to you, he won't have his plans ruined. My brother is just that way."

"There is nowhere to hide from him. I thought I would be safe in my home, but he found me and insisted we sleep together even though I asked for an annulment," Lacie murmured her unhappiness.

"You didn't. Did you mention that earlier? I don't recall. An annulment, really? You don't want to be married to my brother?"

"To any man," Lacie said with a long dramatic sigh.

"That's difficult to believe when I can see you love my brother."

"I do, but after everything that has happened since he showed up in the stables when I returned from my ride yesterday, I really don't know what to think. However, I do know what he wants."

"Then I showed up to put further confusion into the mix. I should go home, let the two of you work out your differences."

"Yes, but you're a breath of fresh air. I've enjoyed your company. In just a few hours I feel as if I have another sister."

"He's seen us," Merry said, pointing in the direction of the house. "His expression is exactly what I would have expected."

Leslie, hand shading his eyes from a nonexistent sun, stared in their direction. Now, with his feet firmly apart, he set both hands on his hips. Lacie recognized the posture.

He wasn't pleased. No, he wasn't pleased at all. There was no reason for him to think they should remain at home unless he told them they could enjoy a ride. She would be hard-pressed to get used to this dictatorship of his.

"What will he do?" Merry asked, "He doesn't appear happy. He doesn't punish you in any way, does he? At least with me, he's usually all bark and no bite. When he calls me brat, I know he's finished with his sermonizing."

"Probably lecture me. Suppose I should have left a note, but I've never been married before. Don't quite know how to go about being a spouse." She found she was holding her breath, waiting for some unknown explosion from her new husband.

"He couldn't have been too worried about us. He didn't come looking for you," Merry said, with seeming knowledge of her big brother. "Maybe we're just imagining something that's nonexistent."

"Perhaps you're right and whatever he has planned, we're obviously not late for it. Don't understand what he's doing though."

Lacie pushed her horse forward despite the pain. She really wanted to get home and find out what Leslie planned. Waiting and speculating wasn't easy.

"Isn't it obvious? Like I said a minute ago, he's brought the dressmaker to you. If you drove into town, he would lose that part of the day with his new bride then you would either stay at his townhouse or you would insist on returning here." She grinned. "More riding. More lost time. He's always efficient with his time, plans ahead."

"Really? I would have never thought of anything so ludicrous or expensive."

Lacie smiled and waved at him. Reminding herself there was absolutely nothing wrong with going for a ride on a dreary day. She did it after all, to lift her spirits and Merry's as well. After a thought, "He would really bring the dress shop here? He has that much money?"

"Wealthy as Midas, all of us are. I'm an heiress and even though the younger brother doesn't have a title, he has holdings and so much money he couldn't spend it in a lifetime."

"I had no idea."

"Perhaps that is one of your charms for him. Can I trust you with a little secret?" Merry tilted her head slightly, a sheepish expression adorning her face.

"About Leslie? I'd love to have something to hold over his head, something to barter with."

"No, about Link."

"You would tell me a secret about Link. Why?"

"Perhaps not, it would be too hard for you to keep it from Leslie, especially if he ever discovered you knew something you weren't sharing."

"I can keep a secret." Lacie said adamantly, a bit offended at the idea she couldn't.

"Even in bed when he has seduced you until your mindless?" Merry asked, once again showing a wealth of beautiful white teeth and knowledge a fifteen-year-old should never be privy to. "If he thought you knew something he didn't, he would pull out every trick he knew to get you to spill the secret."

"I don't know. He's never really seduced me and I've never been mindless. Can that happen?"

Lacie didn't like to think about something like that. After all she had no idea what really happened in the bedroom, except what little her sisters had been willing to share, which was practically nothing. It seemed to her, Merry must knew more than she did.

"Of course, men like Leslie and Link know just know how to do it," Merry said with seeming knowledge of it all. "They are experts at giving a woman her pleasure."

"Good lord, you are fifteen. How do you know all of this?" Lacie asked, suddenly confused then blurted out her thoughts. "You're much more worldly than any fifteen-year-old should be."

"Listening at doors or just being so unobtrusive they forget I'm sitting in the same room with them. It's what two older brothers do for you, give you an education in the way of men. In any case, when I was younger and playing with dolls, they didn't ever think I was listening. So, do you want to know a secret?"

"I believe I do." Lacie couldn't help the grin emerging and growing wider.

"Those children I told you about, the ones Leslie pays for every month are not Link's. He also pays for two of the mothers so they don't have to prostitute themselves in order to put food on the table. As far as I know, Link doesn't have any illegitimate children. He's just as careful about that kind of thing as Leslie is, but he will never admit to the fact. He enjoys the role he has cast for himself."

"Then what? Who are they? The children?" Lacie was baffled, pure and simply bewildered.

"They are children who Link has found abandoned, usually in the streets of Bordeaux or Paris when he visits. He rescues them. He has a home in the country where he keeps them and a woman who treats them as hers. She's a very special woman in so many ways, but she's not one of Links paramours. Their relationship is platonic which is strange. Link doesn't ever do platonic."

"Why doesn't your brother tell Leslie? He wouldn't care. He would probably be proud of him."

"Because Link has a wild sense of humor. He wants Leslie to think of him as a second son who doesn't care about anything except his pleasures. He's really not that way though. He's almost as serious as Leslie. Thing is, he really does love women, all women and he's never hidden that fact. He seems to know them too, exactly what they are thinking, what they want and what they will do next. Don't understand how though. He can always second guess me, knows how I'm going to react to everything."

"How did you find out?"

"Listening. It really pays to listen."

"You are devious. Remind me not to share anything with Leslie I don't want you to know."

"He doesn't like secrets and at first he thought I would divulge the truth. But their banter is too much fun to listen to even though some of the things they say I don't understand. Some of the words aren't even in the dictionary, which I make excessive use of."

~ * ~

When they reached the stable, Leslie moved quickly to help Lacie from her mount, calling for the stable boy to get the horses. Merry didn't wait for aid. She swung her legs over Regan, landing easily on the ground, a grin on her face.

"We went for a ride," Merry began albeit a bit breathless, "and it was all my idea. Lacie was loath to leave the house. Against her wishes, I did manage to talk her into it. The task was really quite difficult. She said you wouldn't like the notion of us leaving without your approval."

"You don't have to lie for Lacie, brat." He laughed showing lots of pearly white teeth in the process. "Lacie fends for herself quite nicely. I'm sure she had as much to do with the decision to go out riding on a cold winter day as you did. I would have liked to have known where you were as well as the direction you took."

His gaze raked his wife from top to bottom then lazily settled on her bosom with seduction in mind. All through the night, he thought of little else, save kissing her lushes body, kissing and teasing every beautiful inch. He craved to learn the sweet taste of her.

"True," Lacie responded pleasantly, "been fending for myself for a long time now, but thank you for the effort. I'll return the favor someday."

She turned her attention on her husband. "What are you doing here? Merry says you brought the dressmaker to me. Is that true? If so, don't you think I should have had some say in the matter?"

"Knew you didn't want to ride into the city and have disapproving stares. Wanted you to be comfortable. You should be pleased. We should get on with this, clothing of my wife," he said, watching his wife closely, seeing the slight dark circles beneath her eyes, the shuttered trembling when she looked at him.

"The way you put it, this clothing me thing doesn't sound like much fun," Lacie said with a grimace. "You're right about me though, never liked to go to the dressmaker. Did it only when I was desperate."

"You're desperate now." His voice was a bit harsh. He wished he could take the tone back and change it even though the truth was out.

"I ken it."

Leslie wrapped an arm around her as they walked up the steps. "I'm going to enjoy this, clothing my wife even if you are not. May I present the seamstress, Madame," he paused in thought, "Now, what is her name?"

"Madam Robina," Merry interjected. Before he could ask, she pointed, "Says so on that box."

"Ah, brat, you're always so astute it boggles the mind. Now, Lacie and I will be engaged all afternoon from the looks of it. I want you to mount Regan and ride back to the city. I notified Westcott you would be home before five o'clock. See that you are."

"I don't want to go." She placed her slender hands on her hips, defying him, all the while grinning as if she would get her way. "I find your wife pleasant to talk to and she is close to my age."

"You will this time. Lacie and I need private time together in light of the events that transpired while I was gone."

Merry wasn't going to challenge him with this. Lacie's and his few moments together were precious as well as necessary. He understood it would take some time before he could convince Lacie to truly become his wife in every way.

"If you put it that way, I understand completely. Want you to know you dashed my hopes," Merry said, clearly disappointed but accepting his dictates. "Do I have time to eat something and let my horse rest before I have to hightail it out of here?"

"You do." He ruffled her hair, which gained him a look of disapproval. "Have the time but not a second longer. Get yourself home so you'll be there before dark."

"Very well." She hugged Lacie before she left them for the kitchen and a bite to eat. "I'll let you know when I'm leaving."

Leslie nodded while his attention was focused on Lacie and Madam Robina. "Should we get started now?"

"I don't think..."

"You don't have to think at all. I believe your seamstress needs to take your measurements." He sat back in one of the more comfortable chairs in the parlor, arms crossed in front of him with his gaze riveted on Lacie. He didn't say anything for the longest time, just watched her, plotted to find a way to make love to her.

"Here?" Her mouth dropped open as she was clearly shocked by his proposal.

"Is there a better place?" His grin stretched from ear-to-ear, as he was quite pleased with his idea.

While he didn't want Lacie to be too uncomfortable, he needed her to get used to him seeing her wearing little to no clothing. This would be the perfect time to begin introducing her to some of the very proper as well as the more pleasant things that would occur between a husband and wife.

"My bedroom?" Lacie asked. "Would be better."

"I see you don't want me, your husband, to look at you. Rest assured if you choose the bedroom, I will be there also. There is more space here. As you see, Madam Robina has brought nearly half her store, so we have fabrics and fashions to choose from. Would you want her helpers to carry all these boxes up the stairs when they don't have to?"

"Of course not, but why do you have to be part of this?"

"I've a need to oversee what I am paying for. As we both know, you are quite splendidly endowed. I want to make sure I'm the only male person to see your breasts."

He did that quite well, pleased with the tenor of his words. She would get used to him. Even now her blush was fading from her cheeks.

The seamstress cleared her throat. "I would like to get started. You must remove your outer clothing so I can take your measurements. Have to do that since they've changed over the last few months."

Lacie looked to him, a panicked look on her face. "I..."

"Go ahead." He gestured with one hand then feeling as if he should give her a moment of respite, "I will take a look at the fashion plates on the table while you undress."

He poured himself a brandy then turned his back on the two while he shuffled through the dress patterns, setting a few aside for future consideration. The sound of her dress slipping to the floor gave him reason to smile. He heard a few more garments touch the floor. His heart pounded and despite his best efforts he grew hard.

Before turning his attention back to the women, he picked out additional designs. Turning, "Stunning," he said, smiling at his wife. "I believe you are very beautiful."

Her breasts were rounded globes pushing above the corset. The aureoles could just barely be seen, tantalizing every male part of him. Her blush enchanted him even more thoroughly, spreading now from her cheeks to the tops of her breasts. He wanted to take her breasts into his mouth. Sitting down, a glass of brandy in hand, he watched the process as the Madam measured every part of Lacie writing all the numbers down or her note pad.

When she noticed him looking at her, she turned her back. The act didn't bother him at all. She pleased him. Her shyness satisfied him. Lacie would learn he meant her no harm. Besides her back was just as intriguing and beautiful as her front. He made a note to give as much attention to her rounded derrière when he finally taught her sex was about pleasure not pain.

"If you would sit here," Robina pointed to a chair, "I'll find out what pleases your husband. We'll proceed from there."

She sat down, her hands folded in her lap, very nearly naked. "Do I get a say in what I'm to wear? Shouldn't the gown and underthings please me also?"

She played into his hands nicely. His smile widening at this new plan, "Come here." He patted the arm of the chair where he was sitting. "You can look with me and approve of my fabric choices if you want as well as the fashions."

The glare she shot him was amusing. She stayed where she was for several seconds then standing, she walked to him. It seemed she was more interested in the fabrics or perhaps him than he previously thought. He believed she would have remained on her chair at least ten more minutes before giving in to his command.

The fashion plates rested in his lap before he set them on the table for her perusal. "Do you like any of these?" he asked, spreading them out after he wrapped his arms around her.

Every chance he got he touched her, ran a finger across her arm, her hand, up the middle of her back, enjoying the tiny shivers of passion she couldn't conceal from him.

She reached for them, "Let me see."

He wouldn't allow that, instead he held them close enough for her to see. She would have to bend closer. Her breasts so close that if they were alone, he'd find a way to taste them.

"Leslie?" she squeaked, her voice thin, transparent.

A swift indrawn breath of air was all that kept him from touching her breast with his lips. "What do you like?"

"For you to give me some room," she said on a strained whisper, almost as if she felt his breath across her skin.

"I want you to be close. I like the lavender fragrance that still clings to your skin from your bath and the way your hair feels like silken fire when it falls against my skin."

She licked her lips then, nervously pushing at the chemise she still wore. He would love to see her in less. For now, he would have to satisfy himself with this delightful picture. His hand now rested on her thigh, tracing patterns ever higher. He felt the shifting of her body, the slight tremors sifting through her. She was not immune to him. That fact pleased him immensely.

Between them a few patterns as well as the fabrics were decided upon. Madam Robina as well as the other seamstresses she brought with her cut the fabric for two of the dresses and tacked them together.

"Are you cold? I'll stoke up the fire if you are." Leslie watched as she rubbed her arms. While he was thoroughly enjoying watching his wife, he didn't want her to take a chill.

"I'd like to put something else on, perhaps a robe?" she asked. "Would that be so horrible?"

"I'll retrieve one from your room." He gave in to her discomfort thinking there was more to be gained by keeping her happy or at least happier than she was at this moment.

He strode to her room, rummaging through her clothing until he found the garment he sought. There was little guilt for him in this. After all, it was their future together he was vying for, but he suddenly felt she needed more room some space to make a few decisions if not about the gowns but about their future.

Downstairs, he handed her the robe then wandered into the kitchen in search of something for them to eat. She must be hungry. Finding a tray of ginger cookies, he brought them to the parlor as well as a hot pot of tea.

When he arrived, she was standing, one of the gowns draped over her shoulders as the seamstress pinned and stitched the fabric together all the while commenting on the size of her breasts.

He cleared his throat, distraught for Lacie, having seen the tightening of her lips, the tiny shudder of her slim shoulders. "You are not to speak of her body parts, their size or lack thereof if you want to continue with me as a customer. I can assume you will respect my wishes."

Madam Robina stared at him, her jaw dropping a fraction. "Of course, sir. Anything else? It was not well done and I will see to the lady's punishment."

"No need for that, just refrain from discussing my wife's shape and size." He handed Lacie a cookie then thought better of it before setting the cookie on a nearby table. "Oh, well... I suppose you will have to wait. I won't pour you tea until you can drink it."

He sat back down, eating and watching then suddenly realizing now that the initial undressing had passed, he had no interest in this scenario as it played out. At Flynt's home he had nothing to do. He needed to busy himself or he would go crazy.

"I'm going outside," he told her. "Perhaps take a quick ride. I'll be back by the time Madam Robina is finished here."

He left with a quick kiss to her cheek. In the stables he found his sister, just mounting Regan.

"You haven't left yet?"

"No, I figured you would get bored soon enough. When that happened, you might enjoy accompanying me at least part of the way back to the city." She smiled prettily, cocking her head to one side while she waited for his answer. "Nothing bores a man more than fashion plates and fabric choices. I think Lacie has excellent taste. You don't need to pick anything out for her."

"You thought right. I'll be saddled in a minute."

Merry skipped happily toward her ride.

For the first few minutes, Leslie rode behind his sister, marveling on how grown up she had become over the years he'd been away. He'd never asked her the real reason she wanted to go with him to Glasgow, supposing she would tell him when she wanted to.

This was a time for a few questions, not that he didn't try for answers when they were on board the ship. He did but he didn't receive any. He brought his horse next to hers.

"Tell me the real reason you wanted to come here, where you

don't know a soul." He made sure his look was stern, rigid enough for Merry to know it was about time she gave him an answer.

"I know Lacie now, and I'm sure Hope will be quite nice. Hope told me she'd show me around the city if I'd like. She doesn't even know you married Lacie and neither does Flynt. Don't you think you should tell them, her brother and sisters?"

"I'll tell them when Lacie is ready to accept the role as my wife, the new Duchess of Southcliff. It all happened so fast. I had to leave right after the ceremony. My horse trainer was supposed to tell them. Don't know what happened."

Somehow, he let her sidetrack him. From experience, she was accomplished at it.

"So, who was there? At your wedding?" Her pointed question left him a bit put off.

"Are you questioning the validity of my marriage? Westcott, of course, and the minister's wife were witness as was Kelly who is now tending my race horses. That's all we needed."

"Obviously Westcott wouldn't tell a living soul. In his prim voice and manner, he would keep everything to himself."

He laughed hard at his sister's portrayal of his butler. "That's really good. I didn't vow anyone to silence. Now tell me the real reason."

She let out a long slow breath of air. "I suppose it's safe now. Didn't want you to kill anyone."

"That sounds ominous. You were afraid I'd turn the ship around if I knew the truth?" he questioned, wondering now more thoroughly than before about the reasons. "Did mother know?"

"Yes. That's why she gave me permission to go before you were told. We were both concerned about things and the way they might transpire if I wasn't careful."

"Continue." He was more than eager to hear this rendition as to the reasons for her hasty flight from Bordeaux.

"You remember Nevil Boucher?"

He sucked in air. "The cad, yes. What's that got to do with you? He's about my age."

"All true, but mother and I were not sure. He started coming around, asking me to ride with him. I declined of course. The man makes my skin crawl," she paused, watching him closely, "as you say he's an old man." She smiled at him.

"Brat."

"I didn't say anything sooner because I didn't want you to kill him. He didn't do anything. It was just what was implied." She shot him a glance then pushed her horse a bit, picking up speed as if she was finished with the conversation.

He wasn't finished, not by a long shot. Once again, he drew alongside. "I can always send a message to Link. If the man, the old man, has been bothering you, I'm sure Link would love to make sure he doesn't even think your name again."

"I'm sure he would but that was the point of our silence, mother's and mine. Don't want to hear about you or Link ending up in the Bastille. Besides, I handled it by leaving."

"Suppose you made a prudent decision. Can't say I'm all that surprised though. There are, however, ways to silence a man without being caught." Leslie smiled. When it came to men, Merry had always been wise beyond her years. "I'll bow to your wishes. We're close to the city now. Can you find your way home?"

"Think I'll visit Hope first. She said to come to dinner if you didn't let me stay the night, which she was sure you wouldn't. Flynt will make sure I get home safely."

"Promise me you'll let Westcott know your plans," he told her. "He's been charged with keeping track of you in my absence."

She shot him a meaningful glare. "Whatever for?"

"So he doesn't worry about you."

"No, because you told him to follow me. He's probably been keeping his distance all this time. I'll wager he will know exactly where I am."

He continued to stare at her until she sighed softly.

"Alright, I'll send him a message as soon as I get where I'm going. But I still think he's just far enough behind us so he won't need the message."

"You should have Flynt invite him to dinner as well. He did tell me he would make sure he shadowed you. Since he understood you wouldn't stay in the house."

"You're conceding that I'm right."

"No. Westcott is loyal. If he told me he would do something then he would."

Leslie made a note to himself that he needed to give his friend and butler of more years than he cared to count a raise in wages. Chaperoning his sister, he deserved the raise and more. The deed would most likely age him more quickly.

"Well, brat, don't get into too much trouble. Hope will introduce you to the sisters. Perhaps they know of someone your age you can play with. I will see you in a few days if the weather holds and if Lacie becomes less prickly when it concerns our marriage."

"Good luck I like her and would be very disappointed if you two cannot kiss and makeup."

"This will take more than a kiss to draw her to my side. She's been wronged by a man and now holds all men accountable. Something that would never have happened if I'd stayed home."

He waved as he turned his horse around, wondering if he would see Westcott trudging after his sister.

Pushing Garth to a gallop, he was in a hurry to see Lacie again. As he was no longer bored, he had plans as well as a few more ideas to set into motion. He just hoped they would work to his advantage.

A few minutes later, just as Merry predicted, he topped a hill and there was Westcott. He was trailing after her.

When he pulled up beside him, "You're doing a fine job. Didn't really expect you to chase her all the way out here. What would you have done if she stayed the night?"

The older man looked to the road, "Should probably keep going. Don't want her to get to far ahead of me. And sir," he paused then, "I would have asked for one of the empty rooms in that great big old house. Not partial too sleeping on the ground or in haylofts."

"Good, glad to hear that. Always knew you had a lot of common sense. Now, she says she's headed to the MacTavish townhouse. Don't have any reason to think she's not telling the truth. She doesn't know anyone in the city but them. Hope invited her to dinner. I told her she should ask Flynt if you could join them."

"You didn't have to do that."

"Wouldn't have it any other way."

~ * ~

When Leslie strode into the parlor, Lacie was curled up on the sofa, a glass of wine in her hand. "They are gone. Finally."

"Good. I have you all to myself for a minute or two."

Her look of confusion didn't surprise him. She would be expecting him to stay the night again, but he had enough time to ride to his country home before the night arrived. If he tried to convince her to come with him, it would take too long. Besides, he meant to leave her to think. He just hoped she didn't intend to think too long.

"Where were you?"

"Ah, wifely concern, I like that. I rode part way home with Merry. She is stopping at your brother's for dinner tonight. Thought I'd like to have some time with you before I too traveled home."

Her eyes widened. "I can't possibly go with you tonight."

She was planning on defying an order he wasn't going to give. "Don't expect you to come with me. I would like to share a glass of wine and a few kisses then I'll take my leave."

He prayed he wasn't making a grave mistake, prayed too that after a day or two she would miss him and come to him. He meant to give her every opportunity to make the decision herself.

If it took longer than his patience could withstand, what to do then? He would go after her because she was his wife. He would make damn sure she always would keep that title. Living a celibate life was not in his plans.

Pouring a glass for himself and refilling hers he sat down next to her. He remained silent, studying her. His eyes focused on her breasts. "How were the rest of the fittings?"

She grimaced, looking over the crystal glass. "Do you want to know about all the pins that were stuck into me or something else?"

He laughed, "You would bring out that point. Madam Robina is known for her precision. If she stuck her wealthy clients too often, they would go elsewhere. Really, did you get stuck a lot?"

"No, only once or twice."

"Why are you so surly? You should be kissing me, thanking me for my grand generosity. Purchasing all that finery, the gowns as well as the lacy frothy underclothes takes a lot of groats."

Gently, he placed a stray piece of hair behind her ear, realizing it would be him to remove them, him to touch the soft white flesh beneath when he eventually convinced her to give herself to him. Perhaps a bit more courting would be necessary.

"I'm your wife, you don't want me popping out of my dresses any more than I want that. You are clothing me to suit your purposes, so why should I thank you?"

She turned stiff and pompous on him. He truly didn't understand unless she guessed his thoughts.

"You have a valid point I must say. I'll thank you for being my wife and behaving so nicely when I know the fittings were the last things you wished to endure today."

His lazy grin seemed to be getting a rise from her, a bit of anger might solicit a bit of passion.

"That's blackmail. You want me to kiss you."

"Yes, I believe I do."

"Then you will leave?" she asked, a bit too eagerly for his taste.

"I will finish my wine first. If your kiss doesn't satisfy the first time, I'll take the lead in that endeavor and make sure I am content," he smirked. Couldn't help himself. He would have the kiss he desired before he left here tonight even if he had to ride home in the dark. It wouldn't be the first time.

She sipped, watching him over the rim of the crystal, her eyes wide studying him. "I don't know when you want me to do it. Can I just get it over with?"

"That's not the proper way to treat kissing. Proper kissing takes time and should be treasured." He set his glass on the table, wanting both hands free. "One does not get it over with, one savors and enjoys all the subtle nuances and some not so subtle."

She moistened her lips. He followed suit gazing at her and running his tongue along his mouth. Her eyes seemed to cross.

"What are you doing?"

"Getting ready for your kiss. One's mouth must be soft and moist, prepared for the other person's. No one wants dry lips when they kiss." He was beginning to think he was a besotted fool as words he'd never said before tumbled unwittingly from his mouth.

"I really don't ken what to do." She set her hand on his chest just above his heart.

He would have liked to reciprocate that movement but at this point in time, the gesture on his part wouldn't be prudent. He would have to appease himself with the feeling of her small hand on his chest as he thought to close his hand over hers.

"Scoot closer to me then you can put your hands on either side of my face." He brought her hands upward to hold him. "Now place your lips on mine."

"You make everything sound so simple." She sighed a soft evocative sound, a soothing sound. The whisper of her warm sultry breath flowed across him.

He felt the breath of air against his lips, smelled the tiniest sent of her wine. As she leaned closer her breasts pushed against his chest. He groaned low in the back of his throat, understanding what he would not be enjoying tonight yet reminding himself patience would win out.

"That's right."

Her lips met his just as his hands held her close. He pressed his tongue against her mouth, tracing the line between her upper and lower lip she was keeping closed to him, teasing her to give him what he was silently asking of her, the need to taste her nearly overpowering his control.

Hesitantly, her tongue met his, the velvet glide across his bottom lip, her mouth opening just a little. Inside he smiled. She was a fast learner. She would come around to his way of thinking, forget about the man who hurt her. He pressed his tongue inside her then removed it waiting for her to explore in return. She did.

A tiny sound of pleasure escaped her. This was more as he remembered. Before he left, before her attack, she enjoyed kissing. She would again. He nibbled gently at the corners of her mouth, across her jaw, up to her ear, taking the lobe between his teeth, tugging.

He pulled away. "I should finish my wine and go." He downed it then, wishing he hadn't made such a damned awful decision.

"So soon..." her voice trailed off, her eyes wide with what appeared to be disappointment. "You are satisfied?"

"Very."

~ * ~

"I really didn't believe, not for one minute he would stay away this long," Lacie murmured to herself, distraught, her body aching for another kiss. Admittedly she missed him, his gentle teasing and coaxing. She was sure she'd done something terribly wrong. It had been two nights since he left saying he was satisfied with the kiss. She was feeling ignored again and she didn't like that train of thought.

What to do?

She should just show up at Southcliff and see what he would do then. Ride to the country estate and barge inside. What if he didn't want her any longer? Perhaps that was why he stayed away. While she enjoyed the kiss, he must have thought she'd done a horrible job. After all he wanted a wife, someone to make love to and to sire an heir. She told him that woman would not be her. Why was she having second as well as third thoughts now?

Because she remembered the way he touched her breasts that one night, how the sensations inflamed her, set her on fire. She wanted that now, realized he wanted it too but she was still terrified.

What then? What if he sent her home? She was assailed with doubts. Better to find out sooner than later.

Determination to discover the game Leslie was playing with her she strode up the steps to her bedroom. A riding habit arrived yesterday evening but none of the other gowns came with it. She now had a riding habit and that was what she would do. She would go riding.

She was told the purchases were sent to the duke's home. Madam Robina, at Leslie's direction, constructed a tight fitting garment to circle her breasts and hopefully keep them from hurting her when she rode. The gesture was greatly appreciated as well as endearing. She would soon find out if it worked and she considered the action to be very thoughtful. Mayhap he did listen to her.

When she finished dressing, everything fit nicely. She was pleased. Nothing was too tight or too big. She looked at herself in the mirror from every angle satisfied with what she saw, praying he would be at home this afternoon and not with some woman.

She told him she wanted an annulment. So why would he waste his time with her? Perhaps that was why he left so abruptly. He didn't want to spend more time with her than necessary. She shuddered, afraid she'd been stupid, more than stupid by pushing him away.

It didn't take her long to reach the stables or mount her mare, yet second thoughts assailed her. The weather was changing. Snow fell but the ground was still bare. She was dressed in her warm cape and ridding gloves. She wouldn't freeze to death, not in the short time it would take for her to reach his home.

In fact, a lightness of heart enveloped her at the thought of seeing Leslie again. The snow was exquisite, beautiful. Soft flakes floated around her as she exited the stable. This was so amazing. Christmas was almost here as was her birthday a few days into January. She would finally be eighteen, yet she didn't think Leslie cared about that. Perhaps that was why he stayed away so long. He was waiting for that magical age.

With desperation she didn't understand, Lacie needed to see him. She touched her lips remembering the kiss they shared a few days ago.

He was satisfied, he'd told her but she wanted so much more than just satisfaction.

Her fear was still very real, nightmares waking her the last two nights. The difference was that Leslie was not there to soothe her and whisper to her everything would be fine as he did that evening he stayed with her. The closeness she felt that night was right and very good.

Now that he was home, she missed him. Missed him far more than she cared to admit.

Truly, she didn't know how to proceed with him, her husband, or without him if it came to that. Annulling the marriage now would be difficult even though her fears were still very real. He would protest. As a man he would win. Now, though, after the kiss she didn't know if getting out of her vows was really what she wanted. If that was what she wanted, why was she riding through a blanket of snow to see him?

Bloody eyes, no one in her immediate family knew she had wed Leslie Stewart, kenned that she was a duchess. So, what did it matter? What would they do if they learned? She closed her eyes for a second, slowing her horse to a steady walk. Racing to see Leslie would be counter-productive to her plan of ending the marriage.

Second-guessing her husband was not something she excelled at. It seemed to her he was always one step ahead of her. She barely knew him, she realized. The thought did not sit well with her. How did one continue on in a marriage when the wife didn't truly know their husband?"

"What do I know about you, Leslie Stewart? I don't even know your favorite color or food. Nor do I know any of your secrets. I don't know what you like to do when you want to relax." She was talking to herself as she rode toward Southcliff. "I'd like to know why you chose me, what you saw in me, besides the size of my breasts. What were you seeing in me that you thought would last a lifetime?" All legitimate questions she decided, and she meant to ask them of her husband.

A frigid blast of cold air wrapped around her, enveloping her. She shivered, realizing that because of her daydreaming, she needed to pick up her pace. Another fifteen minutes and she should see his home. When she looked to the sky it was gray and white with a hint of midnight blue in the clouds. At least they weren't black, but the snow was falling harder and beginning to stick to the ground.

She grinned thinking about snow angels and snowball fights. Leslie would never participate in such things. Even though he was reputed to be a bad boy at heart, he was too stoic and conservative by far just as Merry told her. She couldn't see him playing. As a little boy he must have played with his brother and sister. He was most likely never was a little boy. She laughed at herself and her musings. She would find a way to change that.

Now the snow fell so hard the view was obscured. She panicked a moment, her mount sidestepping nervously. Getting lost in a snowstorm had not been part of her plan when she left the house today. If she did get lost, he would certainly be angry with her. Coldness penetrated through the layers of clothing she wore, her body suddenly shaking uncontrollably.

She wondered if they would arrive more quickly if she let the horse lead himself. The animal would instinctively know where the closest food and shelter was. Unable to see where she was going in the whiteout, she would fail miserably. Moisture filled her eyes as she pushed it away refusing to wallow in self-pity.

Inhaling a deep breath of the frozen air, Lacie bent close, talking to her favorite mare. "Go on, take me to Leslie's home. Take me to Southcliff. We've been there before. Remember? Do you know the way?"

Silently she looked upward saying a silent prayer to help her. As if she conjured a miracle, the snow slowly stopped falling. When she looked into the distance, she saw Southcliff, standing bold and beautiful on the horizon.

"Thank god," she murmured.

Spurring her horse forward, she smiled, relieved she was not going to freeze to death. Images of Leslie finding her frozen in the snow, popped into her head. When she drew close to the home, Leslie stood on the porch, watching, feet firmly set apart his arms crossed in front of him. It seemed he expected her but that was impossible.

He couldn't conceivably know she planned to ride to Southcliff. No one would have been able to tell him. Shaking her head at her crazy thoughts, she wondered at that and why he was outside in the cold, watching the road.

She was near the porch now. She heard him call out for the stable boy as long strides brought him closer to her. When she slid off her mount, it was into his arms. She had no protest. His warmth and strength encircled her. She felt as if she finally found her home.

"You shouldn't have come in the storm, but I'm very pleased to see you, to hold you close," he murmured, lightly kissing her forehead and running his hands up and down her back. "Are you cold, lass? Would you like to warm yourself by the fireplace?"

"It wasn't snowing when I started out." She spoke in her defense then she looked into his eyes, seeing desire simmering in their depths. Perhaps she didn't need words in her defense

"Why did you come?" He twirled her around, seeming to enjoy the moment. "I'm glad you did."

"I missed you," she told him as he set her feet on the ground. He turned to walk into the house expecting her to follow. "I love the snow."

"You didn't come to me because you love the snow. I missed you too, and I'm—"

He appeared shocked when she hit him with a well-formed snowball in the back. She laughed and danced away from him, bending over to make another missile, which she sent toward him before he could figure out how to proceed with her. A frown formed on his handsome face for a moment.

"You don't know who you're dealing with." He stepped toward her, his eyes gleaming. "I'm verra dangerous with a snowball."

She gave a little cry and skipped from him, enjoying this new side of her soon to be annulled husband. She zig-zagged between a few trees, taking a moment to make another snowball before sending it his way. She had a good arm. The missile hit him squarely in the chest.

Her laughter occupied the snow filled air, because the snow had begun to fall again. She twirled in a circle, enjoying this moment and wishing it could last forever. She knew he wouldn't play fairly but she didn't care. He was a man and would be determined to win the game. She could allow him his way.

"You little devil."

She saw his grin, knew she would pay, but somehow it was like the night she and her sisters invaded the bad boy's space. They chased them. She needed this moment of carefree play. So much had passed between them this was a breath of fresh air in their ever-changing relationship. His laughter was low and filled with happiness as the wind carried the sound to her.

She wanted him to catch her and that revelation gave her pause. The slight hesitance brought him closer. Racing to the right then the left she tried to put a tree between them but was unsuccessful.

"You've met your match," she told him, standing still for one second before she darted in the opposite direction then he lunged.

Standing straight and tall, he strode in her direction. "What makes you think that? Perhaps I gave you that win."

His question was not one she could answer. If she didn't have her wet skirts dragging her down, she might have prolonged this a bit longer even though she knew unequivocally he would catch her then he would kiss her.

Did she want that kiss?

At the thought a moment of panic swept through her. Perhaps her impulsiveness was getting her into more trouble than she wanted to deal with. He dove at her and she whirled away. The second attack was successful.

She was in his arms on her way to the ground. He rolled so his big body absorbed the impact when they hit the earth. He held her close, his body hard and warm against her. His arms wrapped around her lent her a sense of security.

She lay on top of him, laughing. He took a moment to put snow down her back. "Leslie!"

He grinned at her, their gazes seeming to lock. She squirmed trying to get away from him. His cold hands were on her waist tickling her. She laughed attempting to reclaim a handful of snow to put down his shirt.

He rolled over, her back now on the snow then she was on top of him again. His hands were on either side of her face as he lifted his head to brush his lips against her mouth. Once, twice then one more time.

"It's too cold out here. Your dress is soaked through. Let's get you into the house where it's warm where we can pursue this to its logical conclusion," Leslie murmured, his lips barely touching hers. He kissed her again.

When she started to say something, his tongue probed inside then he drew away, watching her. She wondered if he saw the longing in her eyes.

Rising, he pulled her from the ground then into his arms. Quickly, he strode to the house, holding her close. She placed her head on his shoulder, soaking up his warmth, realizing her skirts were soaked through just as he said and she was shivering.

"Have you ever played in the snow, Leslie? Ever made a snow angel?" she asked, reaching out to touch the side of his face. "You have a very nice face. I do believe I like the way your eyes crinkle at the corners when you laugh."

With a groan, he set her down close to the fire where he placed another log. Turning to her, "You've got to get out of your wet clothing."

"Have you ever played?" she asked him again, determined to have an answer before she complied with his wishes. His fingers were on her cloak, unfastening it before setting it near the fire to dry.

"I suppose so, but it was so long ago I don't actually remember. What I do remember is that father was very ill for a long time and mother expected me to assume the role as head of the family. I wasn't very old. There were a lot of responsibilities."

"We shouldn't change our clothes yet." She said the words but her arms were wrapped around her and she couldn't stop the shaking of her body.

"What should we do?" he asked, a tender, expectant smile on his face. "Mine aren't wet. They are only slightly damp."

"While we are still wet, we should go outside again and make snow angels," she told him, realizing of course he would find an excuse to avoid the small moment of play she so wanted with him.

"Do you hear the wind howling?" he asked as one perfectly shaped brow arched in question. "Staying inside where it is nice and warm would be prudent, perhaps a hot cup of something to warm the insides."

She poked him in the chest, hearing the wind as the storm increased its intensity. "You're deflecting. Tomorrow, if there is still snow on the ground, we will make snow angels. I will hold you to it?"

"You're not taking your wet clothing off." He stood back crossing his arms in front of him watching her as if he expected her to disrobe then and there.

"No, what would I put on? If I take them off, I must have something dry."

A twinge of fear swept inside. It wasn't the debilitating terror she felt before at the thought of being with him. The feelings were generated by something else.

"If you don't, I'll do it for you." He paused seeming to reflect, "I'll fetch a robe from upstairs and make sure the upstairs maid knows to stoke the fire so our room will be warm. You must be hungry. I will take care of that too."

He turned, leaving her to watch his retreating back with too many questions filling her head.

Until now, she was having fun. He was fun to be with even though he didn't have a clue as how to play. She supposed when they had children, they would have to teach him a few things. The thought of children didn't scare her just the process of conceiving them.

Fiddling with the fastenings on her riding habit, she waited for him, unsure of the next few minutes.

He returned with what appeared to be a dressing gown and robe but they were very shear. She guessed he had motives other than keeping her warm and dry.

"After the other day, I didn't think you would still be shy."

His shirt was unfastened and it hung loosely from his shoulders baring his broad chest. She yearned to touch his rippling muscles, discover more of his sleek, taunt belly. Unable to help herself, she ran her tongue across her lips.

He saw and watched. The very fact he was staring at her started a flame inside that no snowstorm could quench.

From the other night, she recalled exactly how he appeared unclothed, tall and well-muscled, lean hips and strong thighs and... She swallowed, her throat suddenly very dry.

"I..." she began, "I hoped you would give me privacy."

He pointed to the other room, handing her the sheer gown. "Be my guest, while I'd much rather watch my wife, I'm trying to understand your feelings and be compassionate. I'm not going to lose you before we've even given ourselves a chance."

Wishing she could give him what he wanted, she hesitated for a moment before leaving for the room he indicated. Quickly, she undressed, unsure if he would change his mind and appear in the doorway. Holding the gown and robe in front of her, she wondered if it would cover her. Well, of course it would cover her, but what would he see?

Lacie inhaled a quick breath, hoping for a bout of courage she didn't think possible while dressed. Looking in the mirror, she saw the stark, facts in front of her. She might as well be naked. For some reason, she felt a small measure of protection. She inhaled a long deep breath, hoping for courage as she watched the sheer fabric floating and billowing around her.

When she returned, wine was poured and someone brought a platter of food, not a meal but enough to ease whatever hunger she had. She'd toyed with the idea of coming to Southcliff or not coming all morning. She'd forgotten to eat.

"You're beautiful," he told her, "I picked the lavender negligee out when I was in Paris because I thought you might like that color. "Come sit by me." He patted a spot beside him on the velvet sofa.

"You have ulterior motives," she said yet she accepted the glass of wine as well as the place on the divan next to him as she curled her legs around her.

"You saw through me. I want to kiss you and talk. I want to hold you in my arms through the night, convince you we are right for each other. We will only do what you want."

"Talk about what?" She wanted to tell him they should talk first and kiss later because she was pretty sure if they kissed, they would never get to talking.

"Anything you like." He watched her as she sipped her wine, her eyes then lower to her bosom.

She felt her nipples harden as if they needed something from him. While he watched her, her blood pounded harder, the air around her growing sultry and hot. For a moment she looked away in an attempt to regain the equilibrium she'd lost.

"Why did you decide to come here this afternoon?" One of his calloused fingertips traced a path down her neck before silently gliding across her collarbone. "You do know because you came on your own accord, I will assume certain things."

"Like what?"

She was suddenly extremely nervous, didn't know why she asked the stupid question. She understood what he would believe while she ignored the little voice inside her head telling her the answers.

"You tell me. You're an intelligent woman. I've never lied to you. What do I expect?"

"You think I came to visit because I want to sleep with you again." The words rushed out in a sudden panic.

"That's part of it but not all. Tell me the rest."

He pulled the small ties holing the robe together until they came undone. His exploring finger followed a path between her breasts. Maybe this was too much too soon, maybe it wasn't but she was suddenly overwhelmed.

She swallowed hard, sipping more wine to ease her parched throat to help make it easier for her to talk. Somehow the wine didn't have that affect. "Lesl..."

When he reached for the stem of her glass the back of his hand lightly brushed one hardened tip. He set the crystal on the table beside him, his eyes darkening.

"Talk in a minute." His questing finger settled beneath her chin, slowly lifting until he brushed her lips with his. "Open for me, *is tu mo sholas na greine.*"

She heard the words, knew what they meant and was surprised. *His sunshine.* For a moment she couldn't suck in even the tiniest bit of air. She opened for him, tasting him as her tongue met his as more fire danced in her body, heating her from the outside in. She was burning. Steadying herself, emotions rapidly tumbling through her, she set her hand on his chest, felt his nipple beneath her palm, heard the low masculine groan rumble in his chest beneath her hand.

It seemed he wanted more of her, kissing her, pulling away then returning and deepening the contact. Urgent with desire for him, she ran her hands down his torso, stopping at his waistband then up again to rest over his nipple. One hand still held her while the other found its way into her hair, dislodging all the pins, hearing the clattering sound as they landed on the hardwood floor. She arched, feeling her breasts rub against his chest. A tiny ripple of sound caught in her throat.

An inferno swept through her as the kiss went on and on and he filled his hands with her hair. Slowly, he pulled away, staring at her lips. She wished he would kiss her again.

"That was nice," she told him. "I like your kisses, the way you taste. Your scent, a bit of lavender and woman."

He handed her the wine then sat back appearing relaxed, pleased with himself. He looked as if the kiss between them had no effect on him while she inflamed with fire, her body restless in a way she didn't understand. "What else do I want besides you in my bed?"

"To see me with no clothing on?" she asked, nervously sweeping her tongue across her lips, remembering what Hope told her about staring at his lips and what that simple action would do to him. Then, plucking at the sheer fabric of the nightdress, before her gaze returned to his, "Seems you've got that."

"True, I can see every part of you, but it's still not the same as holding your warm, soft body next to mine nor is it what I was referring to."

His hands settled at her waist, slowly moving upward, stopping just beneath her breasts, turning his large hands so he gently cupped her breasts, his thumbs gliding easily over the hardened tips.

She gasped in a crucial breath of air. "You've touched my breasts before. I know you wanted them to fill your hands. That still isn't what you are talking about?"

"Yes, you remember. Did you like it when I held your breasts, stroked them, kissed them? It's something you need to appreciate if we are to move farther into our marriage."

"I like the way this feels, yes, but that isn't what you wanted me to tell you, is it? Leslie, I can barely inhale a breath of air let alone think." She watched as he slowly untied one of the straps holding up the sheer gown. Her body seemed to quiver in anticipation.

"No."

"You want me to tell you I no longer want the annulment?" His fingers were now toying with the ties on the other strap. She felt frozen unable to do anything but watch him slowly and with a strange reverence undressing her.

"Yes, I want that, but it's not the words I was looking for. Try again."

"Then what? My mind is muddled. Cobwebs are filling it."

Slowly, what there was of the sheer negligée pooled around her waist. She closed her eyes waiting for him to touch her, but there was no caress forthcoming. Her lashes opened suddenly.

"I'm waiting for you to say the right words." He lifted her. What tiny amount of fabric covering her slowly drifted to the floor. He smiled, seemingly pleased. "You are just as God made you and you are mine now."

Pleased, with her or with himself, she couldn't be sure of anything.

"You want to put yourself inside me," she blurted out.

"I've had my tongue inside you, and yours in me. So you should be more specific," he coaxed her. His words were slow and hypnotic, winding her under an enchantment she could not understand.

As if she wasn't sitting in front of him naked, he handed her the wine. "Truly, I've no idea what you want me to say." She moistened her lips. "You should take your clothes off too. It's hardly fair."

The front door banged open then closed. "Leslie, where the devil are you?" Booted footsteps followed.

"Bloody hell." He stood, tossing her a quilt. "Wrap this around you. Go upstairs."

~ * ~

Pacing Leslie's townhouse in Glasgow, Link read the letter several times before folding the paper and placing it back inside the envelope. He'd made up his mind to go in Leslie's place, but he still had to inform his brother, the duke, what was happening. He needed the duke's permission to deal with the trouble as he saw fit, especially since Graham Campbell left the states.

Link hoped Leslie would be here, in Glasgow, and not at Southcliff. Of course his wishes were not part of his brother's plans and a few minutes ago it started snowing. Snowing? Be damned. He didn't want to do anything in the snow let alone ride to Southcliff."

A man didn't need to be cold when he had news. Merry was feasting with her new in-laws and he decided he wouldn't bother her. Westcott told him she settled in nicely, despite Leslie's abandonment of his sister in deference for his wife. As of this moment, Merry had not caused trouble. According to Leslie though, he shouldn't hold his breath.

His being at Southcliff Hall would have to do with his brother's need to consummate the marriage, which took place months ago. He'd spoken with Merry for a few minutes. She informed him Lacie wanted an annulment. That made him smile. Leslie was used to getting his way in things. This young woman must be an unexpected challenge for his big brother. She married him then changed her mind. That gave him reason for thought.

So, Lacie was putting his big brother to the test. That was good. She would need to stay on her toes also. The duke was formidable and unpredictable as well. There might be a few battles, but he didn't doubt for a moment Leslie would not come out on top.

Westcott was behind him, helping him into one of his brother's winter coats. One that would keep him warm on the ride to Southcliff. He wasn't looking forward to this. He'd grown accustomed to the warmth of Bordeaux where they rarely if ever saw a snowstorm.

"You should stay the night, Sir. Start out in the morning. That would be prudent and wise."

"Leaving right now, I should still arrive not too much after dark." Westcott wouldn't have trouble talking him out of leaving, but Link kept his purpose in mind and headed out the door.

"Don't get lost, Sir. It's nasty out there and you're likely to freeze to death if you wander off the road."

"I've been to Southcliff before, Westcott. The road would be damn hard to wander from." Link peered outside, studying the snowfall as well as the clouds before jovially saying, "See, Westcott, the snow has stopped."

Once on the road, Link thought of a dozen reasons why he should have stayed in town where it was warm. Though it was too late now to do anything about his decision, he still thought about it. He hated the cold and the snow. Warm weather and sunshine were so much sweeter on his body as well as his disposition.

On his way to Southcliff, he did manage to veer off the snow-covered road twice. Again, he swore at himself and his damn decision. This news could certainly have waited one more day to be delivered. Late morning would have been just fine.

If he'd stayed in town, he might have a woman on his arm and a brandy in his hand. This was not well done of me, he mumbled, just as he made his way into the Southcliff stables and handed the reins of his horse to the stable boy who didn't seem pleased to be up this late and having to take care of another horse.

Link was certain he might interrupt a tryst. Now he was afraid he might interrupt his brother and his efforts with his very reluctant new wife. Should have stayed in town until the morning.

Well, the deed was done. There was no going back now that he was here. Whistling, he strode up the steps, trying to make as much noise as humanly possible. He was sure he was loud enough to wake the dead. Walking in on his brother and his wife playing husbandly games was not his intention.

"Leslie, where the devil are you?" he asked as he poked his head into a room.

"Bloody hell," echoed in his ears as he stepped into the parlor in time to see Lacie, a blanket wrapped around her, frozen to the spot where she stood, eyes wide as saucers and a sheer negligee with a matching robe lying on the floor at her feet.

"Go on upstairs, come down when you're ready," Leslie told his wife, his voice tender. "Some of your new clothes are in the armoire in your room."

Link had never heard his brother speak so gently or with such sincerity. He also didn't miss the blush he assumed went from her cheeks to her darling little toes. "Sorry about that." He pushed the hood of the coat off his head. "Didn't mean to interrupt anything."

"This better be important." Nodding toward the brandy before glancing up the steps to where his new wife disappeared. "Help yourself."

"Again, my apologies."

"It's done. Why are you here?"

"Where did you get this?" Link picked the delicate lingerie off the floor. "It's quite the thing you know. Believe I'd like to have one made up in every color of the rainbow. One doesn't really have to remove it."

"Paris. I see you're going to perversely take your own sweet time giving me the reason for your sudden appearance at Southcliff Hall," Leslie muttered, pouring himself a drink before helping himself to some of the food on the tray.

"No, I'm not. Plan on telling you what I came here to say, find something to eat and maybe bring a bottle of brandy to my room. I'll leave the two of you alone to carry on with whatever you were doing."

"Afraid the mood has most likely passed. Perhaps if Lacie feels comfortable enough to join us we can eat dinner together and I'll try again later. I certainly won't be able to get her into that skimpy confection again, well at least not any time soon." Leslie said, drumming his fingers on the table before shifting his attention to the second floor.

"Seems to me you'd rather have her out of it," Link laughed hard, gaining enjoyment from the situation, simply because that would be his intentions. He understood his brother didn't stray far from that mark.

Leslie sat down, drinking from the glass he just poured then, "Get on with it. Why are you here?"

"Just after you left Bordeaux, you received a letter from our plantation manager in Maryland. In your absence, I took the liberty of reading it and deciding if I should deliver the news personally."

"Personal delivery, I see. What did it say?"

"Just that there is trouble brewing at a neighboring plantation that seems to be affecting everyone nearby. Things aren't right at all, superstitions, strange occurrences, and more." Link didn't want to tell his brother about the young lady who had become the village whore. Before they were finished, though, he was sure Sophia's name would come into the conversation.

"What sort of trouble?"

"Grayson wrote of strange doings, of black magic, voodoo and visions from hell itself, murders and the like, of slave uprisings. You undoubtedly get the idea." Link sat back, stretching his legs in front of him, wondering what conclusions his brother would come to.

"Grayson excels in exaggerations," Leslie said. "If a fly flew past his head, he would call it a gigantic wasp and claim it was bedeviling him. This talk of perversions sounds interesting, but knowing Grayson, it involves nothing more than two noisy cats."

"Ah, but he is a good man and an excellent manager for the plantation," Link said, thinking about his children and frowned.

When Leslie was home in Bordeaux, the two of them dealt with all that needed to be done in his absence, but still, he would miss the little hellions.

"So, what's to be done?" Leslie methodically tapped the glass on the table.

Link suddenly spoke aloud realizing he'd been silent overlong. "I've need of an adventure. I'll leave for Baltimore as soon as I find a ship sailing in that direction. So, in that case, if Lacie returns fully clothed, I presume it will be my one and only chance to ingratiate myself with my new sister-in-law. Would an introduction be forthcoming? By the way she looked at you before she fled the room, I do believe you've got your work cut out for you."

"If you haven't scared her off for the duration. Think I'll go upstairs and check in on her." Leslie rose but stopped when he saw Lacie regally descending the steps as if she hadn't just been sitting naked in the parlor and very nearly seen by a strange man.

Chapter Four

Leslie couldn't believe his efforts at coaxing his wife into his arms as well as his bed had come to such a sudden and abrupt halt. Of all the people to show up on a snowy night the last one he would have expected was his brother, Link. His body was still on fire simply because an innocent kiss set flames spiraling through him.

What the devil was Link doing in Glasgow?

Lacie surprised him too. He'd expected her to stay in the room, hide away, not want to see the man who might have caught a glimpse of her when she wore nothing. He didn't think Link saw her naked, at least he hoped not as he didn't like the thought of sharing any part of Lacie with his brother or anyone else for that matter.

Leslie smiled at the thought of Lacie naked and giving in his arms. He needed to touch her, explore every silken inch, prowl every soft, silken part. He prayed, for Lacie's sake, Link had not seen her, that she had wrapped the blanket around her before Link entered the room.

It seemed she endured the embarrassment without hesitation. That pleased him. He hoped she would survive the night without a flinch also. He meant to...

What did he mean to do? He'd thought on this numerous times. He knew he wanted her to come to him, to beg him for his manly favors. Today she took the first step by riding to Southcliff in a snowstorm. She missed him, she told him. Good God, but he played in the snow with her.

He would continue in that vein, gentle and undemanding. She had to come to him, wanting him, before he could be sure she was ready to be his wife in every way.

Riding to Southcliff in a storm, he paused in thought, perhaps was not well done of her. As she told him, though, the weather had been fine when she started the journey. She was hardly in the position to know a storm would threaten her or what would happen from second to second.

A few minutes ago, Lacie excused herself and walked upstairs. Now when he watched her from the bottom of the steps, he found he was pleased. She was quite fetching in her new gown that hugged her breasts just right. While they revealed very little, they did give a small hint as to what might lie beneath.

Madam Robina did well. Indeed, he might request a few more items from the seamstress.

Lacie walked into the room, sitting down near her husband, her hands folded quite primly in her lap. "You must be Link. I heard Leslie greet you as I left the room."

"She is really quite precious," Link clapped his brother on the back, his gaze roaming from Lacie back to his brother. "Go on upstairs and be with your wife. I can keep myself company. This bottle of brandy will keep me warm this evening."

"I won't see you for a while so we should chat." Leslie wondered at his decision, wishing he would be able to convince her to be more amenable to him.

While he didn't completely understand her fear, he knew it was real and potent, possessing her emotions as well as her thoughts. She was doing the best she could under the circumstances. Patience was needed, he reminded himself once more.

"You want to chat with your brother instead of bedding your new wife? Your control amazes me, or is it steely purpose that has you choosing me over Lacie. Do you have other motives when it comes to the woman of your dreams?"

He heard the tiny gasp rippling from Lacie's lips. "Perhaps you should wait for me upstairs. I need to speak with my brother about our holdings in the states. I will join you as soon as we are finished here." Leslie sighed, not sure how much he should tell his brother about his wife. Mayhap nothing.

She nodded, rising from the couch, her face unreadable. He was afraid this would not be good. Starting all over might be the way of things. With a heavy heart he watched her walk upstairs, inflamed by the easy grace that was so much his wife.

When he could no longer see her, "Lacie was attacked while I was gone. She still fears a man's touch. I have to teach her I won't hurt her."

"Attacked, you say." Link poured them both full glasses of brandy. "Sounds like a long story."

"Not so long. Before I left, she was quite willing in every way. As I've told you, we were wed but I did not get the chance to teach her the pleasures found in a marriage bed."

He regretted that. A few more hours with his wife would have sufficed to make her more willing now. Two or three hours with his wife would not have changed the outcome of his mission. That evening was not well done of him, and he would take it back if he could.

"There is no justice in this world. Am I right in assuming I interrupted what might have been the first time?" Link had the gall to laugh, seeming to enjoy the discomfort he was feeling.

"True enough," Leslie drummed his fingers on the nearby table, looking upstairs again as if she would somehow materialize. "I'm thinking it was for the best."

"Why? What are you waiting for? Go on, go upstairs, bed your wife before she begins to think you don't want her. She has feelings. I'm sure with your skills you left her very aroused, maybe even on fire for you. She will remember that." Link laughed again, his smile broad.

"No chance of that. At least I don't think she could possibly..."

After this afternoon she couldn't conceivably wonder if he wanted her.

Link laughed again, lifting his shoulders before lifting his glass of brandy to his lips. "Women's minds do not work like ours. Go see to her."

"No, and yet..." He looked upstairs, his gaze lingering on the top steps then searching the hallway to the master chamber. "She has to want me and come to me."

"Second thoughts?" Link asked. "Never took you for a coward. I won't have a problem if you choose Lacie over me. Indeed, in my mind that's exactly what you should do. It's what I would do if I were in your shoes."

"I want her to need me, come to me with a smile on her face not fear in her eyes."

Leslie picked up his glass, standing then and walking to a window. These few days were crucial and he didn't want to fail. Time would help her heal and the sweet touches he would give her, enticing her, enticing her to come to him would work in his favor.

"For her to plead for sex? For your manly prowess?" Link appeared clearly amused with his brother. "By the look in her eyes when I interrupted the two of you, she was more than willing. I saw no fear in her eyes. If you're expecting her to plead, embarrassment might stop her. She is a virgin, right?"

"I don't look at it that way."

Leslie lowered his lashes for a moment, listening to the steady beat of his heart and easy breaths. A little while ago it had not been that way. She touched his soul, aroused him like no other, inflamed him. With only a kiss, he couldn't think straight. Now, he burned.

The snow was still falling. She wanted to play in the snow tomorrow. He couldn't remember if he'd ever done that. "Have you ever made snow angels?"

"With my children. You should have a child soon, an heir. God willing in nine months, give or take. The little devils change your perspective on life." Link stood beside him then seeming fascinated by the falling white stuff. "Yes, snow angels are quite the thing, you know."

Without looking, Leslie knew Link was grinning, showing all his perfectly white teeth. It wasn't as if he didn't want a child, an heir. He did. "She has to want me before that can happen."

"She looked pretty willing this afternoon."

"Only because her body was responding. I wasn't giving her mind a chance to catch up. I don't know what to do. If it's only her body saying yes, I won't force her."

"Do you need more than that? Hell, charming her to come to you is quite all right. She is a virgin. Lovemaking is new to her."

"I'd like more from her, all of her. We both know I can sweet-talk her to respond to me. Persuading, seducing, whatever you want to call it is easy." He paused in thought. "I should wait until she seduces me."

"That is a plan." Link rocked back on his heels. "Not a good one though. How long are you willing to wait for her to seduce you? You need to take the first step, perhaps see what follows. You are experienced. Your wife is not."

He turned to look at Link, probe his mind for answers to his questions, "Am I forcing her? If so, I won't be any better than the man who hurt her."

"You're right of course. Taking this slow is perfect. So, my showing up this afternoon might have been a good thing, a blessing in disguise. You can wait until late tonight or possibly tomorrow morning to consummate this marriage. That will give her time to worry and brood about what is going to happen. It's a splendid idea, big brother." With that said he downed the remaining brandy in his glass.

"I wouldn't go so far as to say that but maybe." Leslie looked to the steps again, drawing in a long slow breath of air. "I'll wager she is sleeping in the adjoining room."

"She wouldn't go to your bed on her own volition?" Link asked.

"Doubt it."

"Then you go to hers and hold her close." Link followed the direction of his brother's gaze. "Either that or take her to your bed. Two simple choices for you. Shouldn't be hard to figure out what you want."

"Soothe her when the nightmares come to her," Leslie added, thinking about the one night he was able to do just that.

Holding her and not making love had been difficult, but it was better than sleeping alone.

"You will be pleased when your patience pays off and she jumps into your arms and pleads with you to make love to her. Play with her in the snow tomorrow. It's not hard to make a snow angel. The happiness you see on her face as well as in her eyes will pay ten times for your embarrassment."

"I'm going to give her space and I'll try to play tomorrow." Leslie grimaced but the memory of the snow fight while rolling in the snow with her, feeling her on top of him felt right, very good. Possibly his brother had a good idea.

One thing might lead to another.

"I'm going to leave bright and early in the morning. You don't need to get up and see me off. I'm a big boy. Can find my own way home. There is a ship, I believe it's leaving for Maryland in the afternoon. Can't wait to see what the states will offer. Never been there before." Link was grinning, his gaze in the distance. "New adventures. The little whore, who is supposed to be a lady I heard about might prove amusing."

"Keep your rod behind your pants. Whatever you do don't sire any more children. It's not well done of you."

"Control you say. Damn hard for me, you know. When I'm inside a woman, I can't think. I lose myself in her perfection, the magic of the moment. Women are all so unique."

"Think about what you're doing, Link." Leslie hoped this warning would be heeded by his brother but had few hopes.

"You've never been that way? So mindless with your pleasure, you have cobwebs for brains? Have a hard time believing that, big brother. You can't possibly enjoy the sex as much if you don't fall completely under a woman's spell and in the process lose all control, so much so you can't think, can barely breathe."

"No."

It was true. He prided himself in his ability to withdraw before he left his seed inside a woman. To his knowledge, thus far in his life he'd sired no children. God willing a child with Lacie would be his first.

"When you are over a woman who is your wife and you don't have to think about leaving her willing warmth, perhaps then you will experience that mind-numbing state I know so well."

Leslie couldn't keep the grin hidden before he laughed out right. His brother had a way about him that was so easy and carefree. He spoke of women, the spell they cast over him, but Leslie was sure that with Link it was the other way around. That lack of control was nothing he'd ever experienced, at least not that he could remember. He hoped Link was right that when he finally made love to his wife, he would feel that wonderful moment Link was describing, mindless soul shattering loss of power. Somehow, he didn't believe it would happen, although just watching her set him on fire.

"I most certainly hope what you've just described comes true for me. I've often wondered how it was you lost conscious thought when you found your pleasure with a woman."

"Perhaps that's the reason you've never felt that way. You have sex. I make love. If a woman is worth having, she is also worth the time and effort to make love to her."

"I see," Leslie said but he was pretty sure he didn't. For a few seconds he drummed his fingers on the table. Lost in thoughts of Lacie and what his brother described, he groaned.

Watching him Link chuckled. "Changing the subject since you need to get your mind off your wife, what's the weather like in Maryland this time of year?"

"I suppose it's much like northern France. They do have snow and cold weather but you won't arrive until early spring. There are hurricanes in the fall and tropical storms as well if you stay that long. I hope though you can figure out the problem and solve it before autumn comes. It would be nice to know everything has been taken care of quickly and with no difficulties. From everything we've heard, I rather doubt this is something simple."

"So, warmer perhaps by then. If the coat I wore here is a spare, could I take it? You wouldn't want your brother to freeze to death before he can find out what all this magic is about."

"Of course, take it."

"My thanks. Will need the money if I do sire another child. I'll write and let you know." Link laughed, slapping his brother on his back. "We both know that is likely to happen."

"There is a young woman who seems to be willing to bed just about anyone," Leslie said, focused on his brother and the crease in his forehead. "I presume you intend to discover who she really is and if the rumors about her are true as well."

"That's part of the adventure. I will certainly enjoy finding out the truth about Sophia and how she uses her female charms to lure men into her web as well as why." Link lifted his empty glass to his brother. With an eyebrow arched and a speculative look in his eye, "Sometimes rumors are far from true."

"There was something that didn't quite ring true in Grayson's letter. It seemed the man didn't believe what was being reported about the lady, Sophia. I believe that's her name. Said she was a good honest and innocent young lady. Something about her uncle was mentioned."

"Nice name," Leslie said, musing.

"There is always something a woman hides from a man. The fun comes in finding out what the secret is. I can't wait to test her mettle."

"You will treat her right," Leslie said, a strong warning in his voice.

"I always treat women right, but I don't bed whores for the obvious reasons," Link said. "I should be able to size her up in less than an hour. If there is something not quite right about her, I'm sure I'll figure it out."

"You seem eager."

"This escapade is something new. Don't believe in magic or voodoo. Perhaps I just need a change of scenery. Been bored lately with the mundane life I've been leading." Link moved back to the sofa, twirling his glass between his hands then pouring another.

"Your widow pursuing you more closely than you'd like?" Leslie asked with a laugh, watching his brother closely for a reaction to the question.

Link ran a finger around his collar then broke out with a chuckle. "Not the widow. She doesn't want marriage again, enjoys her independence too much. I will miss her though. She sits a horse very well, among other things."

"You never make mistakes with her." Leslie reminded his brother with a smirk. He felt better now that the subject changed to Link.

"Never. For some reason, she never makes me mindless, holds

herself apart from me just a little bit, just enough so I do possess conscious thought when I'm deep inside her. Guess it's enough so I can think. Perhaps she knows me to well and does it on purpose. Maybe she doesn't want to give up that part of her to me that would make her vulnerable."

"Did you know this Sophia has a little sister? Believe the little one is about nine years old," Leslie said. "The little girl might change the way you handle this one."

"I didn't. How did you discover it?

"I've corresponded over the years. Been privy to some of the goings on in the vicinity. Graham, Donal's brother, just came back from the states. He had a few tales to tell, but Donal needed him at their holding in the highlands and Graham wanted to go. The manor house is Graham's inheritance. So, he won't be there to help you out."

"A younger sister." Link seemed to be mulling this newfound information in his head. "Do you think Sophia might be forced to be a whore to protect the younger sibling? That does put a whole new spin on this."

"Anything is possible," Leslie said, grimacing "But you should make sure you keep this all up front in your head. Be careful with the woman. Remember that Graham doesn't believe the rumors about Sophia either. Says she was always a sweet girl."

"That makes two men who don't believe the gossip about Sophia. Does anyone believe there is really magic going on and ghosts? Ah, the possibilities and intrigue as well expand as we speak. I promise you I will go with an open mind." Then he shrugged. "Women are women, I recognize their strengths and well as weaknesses. I ken how to handle them."

"You might brush up on the paranormal elements we've been speaking about while you are on the ship; magic and voodoo, anything supernatural. Wouldn't want you to feel the pins as someone pushes them into one of those dolls that's supposed to look just like you." Leslie was turning his attention once more to the second floor, distracted. "Any ghosts involved in this?"

"You need to go to your wife," Link said following the direction of Leslie's gaze. "You don't have to entertain me. I'll be out of your hair in the morning. I promise I'll be careful."

"Another hour, I think. She should be asleep by then. I'll find her and hold her. Need to show her just how much she needs me, would miss me if I'm not there for her." Leslie had hopes for the evening, prospects that could be dashed just as easily as fulfilled.

He was eager to go to her, his control slipping with thoughts of Lacie in his arm as well as his bed. It could be true that once he made love to his wife, he would be mindless and out of control. The thought gave him reason to smile, something new for him.

"She should be asleep by now," Leslie murmured, once again his attention focused on the floor above. "I'll have to wake her if I'm to proceed with my plans."

"Mind telling me those plans?"

"I do mind. You would tell me how they won't work and it's not your damn business in any case."

"Didn't think you would. Thought I might learn something," Link said, grinning still. "Older brothers should pass their expertise down to the younger sibling."

"Not a chance."

Link couldn't hold back the laughter. "Go, go to your wife. I don't expect to see you in the morning." They clapped each other on the back for a quick hug.

"Stay safe."

Quickly, Leslie strode up the steps to his bedroom. He was surprised to see Lacie on the big four-poster bed. He expected her to hide from him. Instead, it appeared she waited for him. Westcott must have brought a tray of food and wine for them, or possibly her. She held a glass in her hand, sipping before she looked at him, holding her glass in the air as a toast.

The sight brought a smile to his lips. Her long dark hair that held so many different colors when any light reflected off the strands was spread out around her. She wore her prim nightdress, buttoned to her neck. He let her keep it on the other night but not this evening. He would take one more step forward in making her his own.

He sat down beside her, tracing the line of her jaw. Smiling when she seemed to move into the caress. He kissed her on the lips, a soft brushing of mouths. His body ached with need. Just looking at her, touching her with a fingertip, the tiny kiss made him wild with need.

"Your eyes are nearly closed, wake up Lacie." He wrapped an arm around her. "I want you to know tonight is going to be different in so many ways. I'm pleased you waited up for me."

"What are you doing and why do I have to wake up? I'm just sleepy not asleep." She stared at him through sleepy lidded eyes.

It must be the wine he thought as he wondered how much of it she had to drink.

"I waited for you. I couldn't stay away. Is everything all right with your brother? You didn't seem too happy when he came into the parlor."

He wasn't happy because his wife was very clearly naked when his brother burst through the front door. Link should have known better than to show up without sending a message.

Her drowsy voice aroused him. He was eager to get on with the night. "Lift your arms." He'd unbuttoned the nightdress even while she tried to bat his hands away. He stared down into her quite lovely face, those remarkable dark blue eyes of hers bright with humor, mischief, and intelligence at least when she was fully awake. His understanding swamped him. She was not interchangeable with any other woman. For a moment, the thought scared him straight down to his toes. He raised his hand to smooth back a thick tendril of rich chestnut hair that had come loose from its braid.

"Why?"

Her eyes suddenly opened. She was clearly wide-awake now. He didn't see a spark of fear in her eyes. He liked that. It was well done of her. In time they would do very well together.

"Too many questions. Just do it for me. Everything will be fine, you'll see," he told her.

When she did raise her arms, he pulled the gown over her head.

His breath caught in the back of his throat at the sight of her stark white breasts, perfectly rounded to fit in his hands, soft pink circles surrounding the tight buds. He couldn't help himself. He stared at her, hoping he wasn't drooling at the sight of the flair of her hips, the soft white belly. When his gaze traveled lower, he stopped at her woman's mound, the dark nest of soft hair he wanted to caress as well as the petal softness beneath. He hoped the sight of his wife would always have that effect on him. This would be damn hard if she responded in any way.

"It's cold," she murmured, wrapping her arms around her beneath her beautiful breasts, the nipples puckered and hard.

He wetted his lips, leaning forward to suck one into his mouth, caught himself.

She had no idea what that tiny gesture did to him. His body hardened further, aching with the need to bury himself deep inside her. Unable to further resist, he touched one nipple, amazed at how rapidly they both hardened. Given time, she would suit well.

"Go ahead, go back to sleep now. We'll talk in the morning."

He settled her into bed before pulling the covers over her, leaning down to kiss her lightly on her slightly parted lips. She looked surprised as she stared at him, tilting her head to the side, questioning. For a moment he caressed her cheek, her ears, her throat.

Lacie stared at him blankly. She touched her fingertips to her mouth, looking thoughtful. "You don't want me?" she asked but she was very nearly asleep.

He was sure she had no idea what she was saying.

Link's words registered in his head now more than ever. "More than anything." He walked to the other side of the bed, stripping his clothes from his body before dropping them on the floor as he walked.

Crawling into the bed, he pulled her close. Her head settled against his chest, the hard tips of her breasts pushed against him, tantalizing and burning every part of him. Was this heaven or had he found hell?

He wasn't sure what to do. Sleep, he supposed. But he was new to this situation, understood sleep would elude him.

"Leslie," she murmured as her hand settled on his belly. She seemed fascinated with his torso, running her hands upward then down to his stomach. He groaned, understanding fully now just how hard his plan would be to carry through with. If she moved her fingers lower, he would not be accountable.

"What is it?" He placed his hand on top of hers, relocating it higher while he sucked in a deep breath.

"Are you going to make love to me now?"

She pushed away from him, staring at him as she lowered her exotic dark lashes. Her voice was dreamy, whisper thin, intriguing him. The idea of making love to his wife haunted him for months on end, setting his blood on fire at the most inconvenient times. Now she asked if he was going to do what he'd wanted to do since that first time he kissed her too many years ago to count.

If she wasn't half asleep, he might think she wanted him. He couldn't tell now, so he let out a long breath of air, running his hand along her back, enjoying the feel of her naked flesh.

"Not tonight."

His voice was gruff, hoarse with the emotions he felt as he cursed himself for his damn decision. He supposed he would swear all night since he would find no relief. *Maybe in the morning.* "Soon."

"All right then, can I put my nightdress on now?" she asked, pressing herself against him, every part of her touching him, arousing and enticing him ten times over. No woman had ever brought him to this instant state of need so quickly and so often. He was tempted beyond anything he'd needed to endure before.

He tried to keep his laughter behind his teeth but he did chuckle. "No, tonight and every night after this we will sleep like this. I want to feel you against me. I also want you to know the warmth from me."

"Oh, why, if you aren't going to...?"

"Make love to my wife?"

"Because I like the way your naked body feels next to mine. I want to fondle you and stroke your breasts when I wake up in the middle of the night."

"Hmm... I like the way you feel too, so hard everywhere, everywhere that is except your mouth."

His rod pulsed so ready to find fulfillment. Truly, he didn't think he would survive the night. She set him on fire with her subtlest movements.

Suddenly, she was asleep in his arms. He took a second to close his eyes, dreaming. Then, almost as suddenly, she was crying out, sobbing, pushing him away. He understood she was not afraid of him. He felt an instant rage at the man who created this incessant fear in her.

A fear that kept them apart.

"Hush, everything is fine. It's just me. I'm not going to hurt you or take anything from you you don't want to give."

His words were soothing and calming, at least he hoped they were. He ran his hands along her back all the way to her buttocks then back, massaging her neck muscles before repeating the promise.

"No!" She was hitting him with her fists, trying to push away from him.

"I'll keep you safe. I'm never going to let anything happen to you." He had no idea what to say or how to make the night terror vanish. "Wake up, sweetheart."

She was crying. He felt her tears settle on his chest before running to the sheets below in rivulets. He wanted to make everything right for her. He decided then when they returned to Glasgow, he would make it his mission to find the man who did this to her. Who, for the foreseeable future, changed her life as well as his, irrevocably.

"It's not. Don't think it ever will be fine or safe. I can't live with the nightmares every night." Her nails dug into his shoulder, her fear very real and disabling.

She would have to live with them until enough time passed and he was able to find a way to vanquish them. "I'm going to make this better for you. I promise you. Time will chase the bad memories away. I'm sure of it."

"That's what Hope told me." She was on her elbows now, looking at him. Her eyes were huge blue-green pools, the tips of her beautiful breasts touching his chest. "I like your kisses. Will you kiss me again?"

He did and the brush of his lips against hers left him panting with need, sweating. "Now, go to sleep."

His hands rested on her rear, pulling her close. She turned over then, her body curled sweetly against his. He cupped her breast in his hand, playing with her taut nipple. She flinched slightly at the touch but he didn't withdraw. He moved his hand lower until his fingers caressed her intimately. She was wet, ready for him.

Truth be told, he was shocked by the knowledge. Massaging the small velvet nubbin until her hips moved against his arousal, he hoped this was comforting. The devil but he wasn't all that sure. She didn't push him away, nor did she tell him no.

On the other hand, his plan might well be taking shape. He would leave her in the morning, praying she would come looking for him. For nearly an hour, he smoothed his hands along her silken flesh, explored her body, leaving her aroused and needy. She didn't know though what she was missing, what he could do to make her feel wild, bringing her raw passion to a sweet bliss.

The sun was beginning to peek in through the windows. The sky was still mostly overcast but the snowfall had ceased. Link would leave soon. He meant to wait until he heard the hoof beats of his brother's horse before he continued his strategies with his wife.

Time would tell in this too.

Pushing the hair from her neck he placed kisses along the column, nibbling his way to her ear, tugging a bit as he worried the lobe with his teeth. He heard a soft sigh of pleasure. With his hand holding her breast he felt the thrumming of her heart, the easy breathing of sleep. He didn't want to wake her up. She needed to rest.

Leslie rose, picking up his britches from the floor as well as his other clothing. He slipped them on along with his shirt and strode downstairs. Link was just stepping from the bedroom door.

"Thought you were going to stay in bed all day." Link laughed. "How was your evening? Did it go as planned?"

"Getting better by the minute."

"Then you shouldn't be standing here with me. Go to your wife."

"That's where you're wrong. Like I said, I want Lacie to come to me. I think she might do that today as she did yesterday when she rode through a snowstorm to be with me. She told me she missed me, you know."

"If you make a snow angel with her, she will fall into your hands or is it your bed where you want her?"

Link headed out the door with a smirk on his face and a chuckle behind his teeth.

He wanted both. Hell, he wanted everything. "Write and let me know what is going on," Leslie said, relieved there was one less person in the house.

Leslie stood at the window until Link disappeared from view, thinking about bringing breakfast to the master chamber. Thought better of it. He didn't know how to wait, to do nothing.

She appeared then, at the top of the stairs, dressed in the sheer negligée of the night before. It would have been nice if she wore nothing at all. Yet this sight stunned him, called to all his senses. She surprised him, truly she did.

His member pushed against his britches, the fire burning at just the silent promise of something to come. "Good morning," he smiled at her, reaching out his hand to her as she approached the bottom steps.

"I don't think I like waking up to an empty bed," she said, her voice soft, her eyes filled with desire. "I understand I've only slept with you two nights, but it's so much nicer when I reach out and you are beside me."

"I suppose I should have stayed with you. Thought you might like some privacy. I wanted to say goodbye to Link as well."

Beneath the gown he could see her curves, see everything and he wondered if she was still aroused and ready for him. He hoped he would discover the truth soon.

"That would have been nice." She set her hand in his and he walked with her to the couch.

"Link has left."

"I heard his horse, the hoof beats," she murmured. "I would not have come down dressed like this if I thought he would be here."

"I guessed as much. When I saw you at the top of the steps the sight stole my breath, robbed me of a heartbeat for a couple of seconds." He picked up her hand, placing the palm on his chest above his heart. "Can you feel the rapid beating of my pulse? You do that to me make my blood race. Looking at you sets me on fire."

"Leslie, why didn't you make love to me last night? I was sure you wanted to, and I think I was ready to put as many fears as I could behind me."

"I wasn't going to seduce you, didn't want your body to be asking for sex, just want your mind to be there too." He schooled his voice to an unusual softness, yet the sound was still husky with desire and the wanting of a young woman who would take more than seduction to come around.

"I'm not sure I know what you're saying."

"Do you want me to make love to you?"

She hesitated, looking to the ceiling then to him. Placing her hand on his chest, she moistened her lips before catching the bottom one between her teeth. "I think I do."

"I'm a sorry man then. I need you to want me deep inside you more than anything. With desperation I've never felt before I want you to be on fire with need for me. You have to be sure." He found himself holding his breath as he watched her, keeping his hands folded together.

"How do I know?"

"Can't answer that for you. It's something you're going to have to decide for yourself. Lacie, do you want me inside you? Do you want to have so much pleasure it will leave you mindless?" He grinned shamelessly at her, playing with a tendril of hair, wrapping it around his finger, tugging on the strand to bring her closer.

"Nothing like that exists," she said, her eyes seeming to search him for answers she would have to learn for herself.

"It does. All you have to do now is tell me you want me." His voice was gruff but his words were soft.

"Make love to me," she whispered, her voice thin.

"Are you sure?"

Seconds seemed to tick by then, "Yes. Yes, I'm sure."

~ * ~

Her body thrummed with sensations she didn't understand. She wasn't sure she was deciding with her mind as he said he wanted. In any case and despite her fear she wanted Leslie to make love to her. His fingers, last night, tantalized and enticed every part of her that he touched.

"You will be open with me? Tell me everything you think and feel?" he questioned. "If you say no, I'll stop."

"I don't understand." She didn't know what that had to do with making love or consummating a marriage. "I won't ask for an annulment if that's what you're referring to."

"When I make love to you, you need to tell me everything you like as well as what you don't like," he paused, his eyes twinkling with something unknown to Lacie. "A husband has to know these things."

She let out a long slow breath of air. "You're talking about where you touch me?" So far, she liked everything he did. At the moment, his eyes had darkened, his hair was disheveled from running his hands through it. She wanted to touch his mouth with a finger. "All right. I believe I can do that."

"You don't sound too sure of yourself." He smiled, walking to her, reaching out to touch her face with the back of his hand.

"I'm not. As you well know, this is all new to me." She felt as if she was drowning in new sensations and ideas. He was asking things of her that were alarming, that left her embarrassed yet longing for more. Last night brought no conscious memories of the attack to her, and for that she was thankful.

"I think we should go to the master chamber now," he told her, scooping her into his arms before carrying her up the steps and into the room. "Would you like that, lass?"

Breathless and nervous, she leaned into him, relishing the feel of his strong arms around her. Next to him, she felt so small yet protected. He sheltered her in so many ways. She settled her hand against his chest, thinking it would be nice if she could touch him without his shirt on. Hesitant, she placed her lips on his neck, kissed him there. He groaned. Surprised, she looked up, questioning.

She told herself he wouldn't hurt her but Hope had said the first time would be painful, just for a second then the pleasure would offset any pain. It would only be once.

She began to say I think so then changed her mind. Sweeping her tongue across her lips unable to keep herself from looking at his mouth. She was sure they were soft and warm, remembering the other kisses they shared. "Yes, but can..."

"Would you like a cup of tea? We could talk if you'd like that." He stopped part way up the steps to look at her.

She caught her lower lip beneath her teeth.

It didn't seem he was in any hurry. "Yes, to tea and we can talk later. While I'm sure I want you to make love to me, I'm still nervous more than a bit terrified of what I don't know. I do want you to kiss me."

"No reason to be frightened." He kissed her on the forehead then lightly brushed her lips with his. She leaned into him, her hand on his shoulder. "I will make sure you gain your pleasure. You like my kisses so we'll start there. Just kisses."

She touched the side of his face with a hand. "I do like your lips on mine, I like your tongue inside my mouth, the way you taste."

She heard the low masculine chuckle, watched his grin widen.

"What else do you like?" He pushed open the door with a foot and set her down by the fire. He stirred the logs making sparks jump before setting another log on the flames. Standing back, he brushed his hands.

She was afraid to say the words, wasn't sure what she could and couldn't say to a man. He's not just any man, she reminded herself, he's your husband. Heat flushed her face while the palms of her hands were damp. Nerves stretched thin, she began, "Like..."

He was still standing, watching her, seeming to wait for something. She wasn't really sure what it was he wanted from her. Then, "Remember, honesty. You can tell me everything, ask me anything. It's the only way I'll learn how you feel, the things you like as well as the things you don't."

"What about you? Shouldn't I know the same about you?" She really did want him to share if that's what he expected of her. "Where do you like me to touch you? I would only give you pleasure."

He laughed again. "Of course, but there isn't a thing you could do I wouldn't enjoy. You can touch me anywhere. Now, what is it you like?"

He poured the tea and handed her a cup, his teeth a bright white behind his lips. When he sat beside her, his leg brushed against hers.

She felt his warmth. "The way you touch my breasts, stroke my nipples. When, when, you do that I find there are tiny butterflies fluttering around inside my body." Pausing, "And kiss them." She sipped needing liquid in her parched throat. She could barely swallow and her insides seemed to be swirling, her mind in a jumbled mess.

"Anything else?" He watched her now with a heavy-lidded gaze. His fingers traced a path along her arm before exploring higher to her neck then her jaw.

More butterflies, larger ones seemed to dance in her stomach. Her tongue glided across her lips while she played with the fabric of the gown. More seconds passed. When she lifted her gaze from her hands, she knew she had to tell him everything despite the embarrassment.

"Last night," she hesitated, her breaths shallow, "Last night you touched me places you never did before. Places I never thought anyone would touch me and... let alone a man."

"Your husband?" he reminded her, a half smile on his soft lips. She wanted to reach out, stroke him there run her finger along the full bottom one.

"Yes, I liked the way you made me feel." She remembered the heat, the tempest of longing sweeping through her, the ache as well as the pleasure. "Will you let me see you?"

"How was that? The way you felt?" His grin stretched across his face. "How did my touch make you feel?"

He ran his hand down her other arm, picked up her hand. When he turned it over, he kissed her palm then each fingertip lightly biting each one until a tiny sound echoed from the back of her throat.

In a shuddery voice, "Hot and wet and there was a strange ache and so much pleasure I couldn't breathe. I wanted you to never stop then you did. I guess I fell asleep. I'm not sure how."

"You were very tired I suppose. We will do that again tonight before we pleasure each other if you ask me. But tonight is a long ways away. What do you want to do now?" He set his cup on the hearth then hers. He slipped from his shirt, his muscles rippling with the movement. "Ach, but you did tell me that you wanted to touch me. Where would you like to start? My body is yours to play with."

She nodded, a shudder ripping through her; reaching out to touch his chest, feel the hardness beneath her fingers. "I like to look at you too. I want to see you without your clothes on again. Can I ask that?"

"Then you shall."

He kicked off the rest of his clothing. Now he stood naked in front of her, appearing as if this was something he did all of the time. There wasn't an ounce of embarrassment showing in his face, only a smile that seemed to glow with concern.

She plucked at the robe covering her, staring at him, wondering what exactly he would expect from her now. "Do you want me to take this off?"

"If you want to." His husky voice reached into her, calling her.

Again, she needed to say I don't know but she'd thought he would do that, take her clothes off without asking for her approval. He'd never been so solicitous before. She wasn't sure what to make of it. She looked at him expectantly. "If I want to?" Her heart thundered. Did she?

"Today, tonight, tomorrow those days are about you, what you want, not me. Do you want to be naked with me?" He lifted an eyebrow then shrugged his broad shoulders. "Tonight the choice is yours."

"I kind of thought you would do it." She spoke so softly he leaned forward, in an attempt to hear every word.

"I didn't hear you."

"I thought you would take them off, my clothes, like you've done before."

She didn't know if she could as her fingers toyed with the tiny strings. A tug and the gown would fall to her waist. If she closed her eyes and didn't think, the deed would be done.

He crossed his arms over his chest, waiting and watching. She inhaled a ragged breath while he picked up their cups and walked to the bed. He settled there, his legs stretched out in front of him, sipping the tea before he placed it on a table.

"Not tonight. I want to watch you but..." he paused as if thinking. "I've an idea. I told you today is about you, what you are willing to give and it is. That part hasn't changed. What if I meet you half way?"

"I don't understand." She walked to him, sat down beside him on the huge bed, her hand resting on his chest. This was where he would do it. She wanted him to do it.

He toyed with the string on her robe holding it together. She felt the fabric slide from her shoulders. "I've done half now you finish." He touched her breast, "First though," He bent close to her, sucking her nipple into his mouth. Sucked and pulled with his teeth. Moving away from her, he watched again. "I've done my part. Now it is up to you to finish."

She cried out softly, "Kisses first?"

He bent close to her, brushed his lips across hers. "I am kissing you. My lips are surrounding you, stroking you, tasting you. That's a kiss by my definition."

"I thought..."

"Don't think, just feel and do whatever you want. Are you hot and wet? Has the ache returned? Do you want me to find out?" He tugged on her nipple again, his hand cupping the other breast, rolling her nipple between his fingers. He laved the nipple with his tongue. Sitting back now, he seemed to wait for her.

"My turn. You want me to finish undressing me?"

Truly, she didn't know if she could do it, carry through with her part. Undress for him while he watched and she could tell herself a thousand times that he'd seen her nude body before, still it didn't help to think of herself as being so brazen.

"If you want. I would like that. To watch you slowly reveal

yourself to me, knowing this is your choice." He relaxed, lying on the bed, one arm draped on a knee.

She could barely swallow her throat was so dry. Downing her tea, she played with the remaining shoulder tie for a few seconds trying for the needed courage. He'd seen her naked before, slept with her the entire night while she wore nothing. This should not be so difficult.

If she didn't do this, he might walk from the room, look for a woman more willing to do these things with him, for him. He had a mistress and could return to her. Did she undress for him?

She tugged. The bow holding the garment in place was gone. The fabric slipped to her waist. He wasn't smiling though, his eyes were simmering in the light of the day. He looked hungry, ravenous.

"Perhaps this would have been easier in the dark," she murmured, wishing she dared cover herself with her hands.

He seemed to understand her predicament, clasping her hands in his, smiling, "This man is pleased. You please me."

"I don't know." The words slipped out. She knew she should have told him yes.

"If the room was dark, this would not be as enjoyable for me. I don't want you to hide away or run from me."

It seemed he couldn't resist as he reached out to cup her breast then he groaned, tenderly pulling her to him. She was on top of him then. The heat of his lips was molded against hers while his hands rested on her derrière, pulling her closer. She felt his arousal against her belly. Honey as well as searing heat seemed to flow throughout as sensations rippled within.

She met his tongue with small forays of her own, caressing and exploring, dancing with his, seeking the hot velvet depth of his mouth. His hands roamed and touched, excited and aroused. He placed swift tiny kisses along her jaw then down her neck. He sipped and nipped across her collarbone then lower, leaving nothing untouched. His hand splayed across her belly then down her leg stopping to stroke her intimately.

The feelings delicious, creating that ach deep within her. She ran her fingers through his hair then down his neck. He pulled her closer.

His rod pulsed, tempting her with the promises of pleasure while he continued with the explorations that sent an inferno of desire rolling through her. A primal enchantment coursed through her. He rolled her so she lay on her side. His kisses traveled down the length of her to her belly then lower still while he parted her legs by pushing one of his between them.

An odd shivery feeling undulated through her from her breasts to her knees but changed to a burning ache when his fingers found her intimately and caressed. She couldn't hold back the tiny sounds rippling in her throat.

"I wanted you to open your lips for me. Now if you like you can part your legs for me? Let me feel your sultry rain caress my fingers as well as the welcoming heat of your soft swollen petals."

He watched her now, holding himself back from her while she spread her legs. Then he was between them, his lips on her belly slowly moving lower until he was kissing her so very intimately, stroking her with his tongue. Her hips moved while her body ached with need. "I'm on fire."

A startled cry of pleasure seethed through her as he continued, her hips moving of their own accord. She was helpless, beyond need for him, running her fingers through his dark hair, pulling on it when she could do nothing else.

"Do you like this?" He lifted his head to look at her. "You taste sweet, just like a woman should."

The heated glide of his tongue searching her body scattered her thoughts. She forgot that she was supposed to tell him what she liked and how she felt. At this moment she found speech impossible, her brain and thoughts a muddled mess.

All her attention centered on her feminine parts, which were now vividly alive, hot where his tongue touched and cool when he pulled away to watch her.

Her fingers tightened in his hair as he set her on her back.

"You haven't answered me," he spoke softly, his gaze now riveted on her eyes.

"Yes," she managed to say. Her breathing was ragged, her heart pounding frantically. She was able to say. "I... I like everything." She was desperate in her need.

Her breath came in brokenly as she opened her mouth trying frantically for air that seemed to elude her. He changed his focus now, gliding up her body, his weight pressed against her even though it seemed he held himself away. His tongue dipped beneath her upper lip, gliding, probing, circling. His teeth caught her lower lip tugging gently. He kissed her and kissed her again. Some kisses hot and hard, others long and sweet as she found she reveled in all he did, her body arching, seeking more of him.

She heard the ragged sound she made as all the sensation increased in intensity and she opened wider. Lord but his tongue was plundering inside her now and the taste of his kiss was sweet and tantalizing beyond bearing.

Understanding he needed to know what she felt, she couldn't tell him how sweet the kiss was because she didn't want to end the moment. So, she gave him back the kiss, sliding her tongue over his, probing the sultry corners of his mouth then catching his tongue gently between her teeth.

His breath whooshed from him in a hoarse sound. She heard his deep throaty response that was more growl than rumble.

Instantly, she pulled back.

"I'm sorry," she spoke fast. "I don't know anything about kissing. "You didn't like what I did?"

He rose on his forearms, sweeping hair away from her face, laughing softly as he stared at her. Inhaling deeply, "This time I'm at a loss for words. I loved your kiss and virginal exploration. All I want now is to cherish every moment with you, make this last as long as possible."

His voice was husky and his eyes were a smoldering deep brown, very nearly obsidian between his nearly closed dark lashes.

"You groaned," she said, "what does that mean?"

"So did you. Well it wasn't exactly a groan but you made tiny noises. Those whispers of sound told me how much you enjoyed what I was doing with your body."

"I don't recall."

"I'll tell you next time, and there will a next time, when you make that throaty little noise again." Then he merged his mouth with hers once more. He kissed her hard. She gave back to him, feeling a desperate urgent need rising inside her.

Lacie met him breath for breath, touch for touch, hunger for hunger. When he pulled away, hesitating, he stared down at her again.

"What are you going to do now?"

She was watching his mouth now and wondering what came next. There had to be something else. She touched his lips then his chin. It seemed to her he touched her everywhere. The primal ache within her increased with every movement he made.

Sensations swept through her, at an unstoppable pace. Embarrassed, fascinated, enthralled, held in a delicious net of pleasure, she watched as his finger moved down her body, lower, until once again they caressed her most feminine parts while his lips nibbled gently on her breast, sipping at the tip, laving with his tongue.

Her back arched instinctively as his mouth and hands seemed to find every sensitive place she possessed. He responded by continuing, coaxing and persuading her body to his will, seducing until she whimpered and clung to him. He was her lifeline.

"I don't think I've ever made love to a woman, only had sex," Leslie said, "At least that's what Link implied since I've never lost control, but I'm on the verge of just that right now. You've set me on fire. I burn to finish this, to show what pleasures there can be."

At first she didn't really hear the words. She was too caught up in the pleasure that rippled and shimmered in a blinding array of colors through her to understand anything else.

"Never made love?" she managed to say in a tiny voice, clearly not understanding his meaning.

"Not like this. Not ever like this."

"I thought..."

"I want to take the pain away. Only leave the sweetness in its place. I'm so afraid of hurting you and yet in order to make love with you that is what I will have to do. Before this moment, there was just the notion, not the sweetness, not the burning that can be found no other way."

His voice died as he kissed the inner soft flesh of her thigh then raked his teeth down one leg and up the other. She jerked in response, her fingers clenching suddenly in his hair.

"Blessed hell," he said huskily. "I can't even remember how it was before you. I just know it wasn't like this. Never like this."

Propped up on his elbows, he was watching her. He came over her again, lowering his head and delicately consumed one breast then the other, lingering over the hard, pink tips.

"Do you think you are ready for me, for this first time. I need to make it right for you. If not, there's more of you I want to pet and pleasure. Will you let me inside?"

Her only answer was a dazed sound with her fingers silently urging his head back to her breasts.

"You'll let me inside now, not just your mouth but your tight sheath?"

"I know it will hurt for just a little while. Yes," she breathed softly, looking at him with an absolute trust she'd never felt for anyone before. "I need, you know. I ache with a hot burning pleasure. You've given me that, taken away the fear of you, at least."

"Are you sure?" he asked, seeming to need the reassurances that only she could give him.

"Yes," she said unevenly, her voice raw with the passion shimmering deep inside.

"I'd give my soul to take back what that savage man did to you," he whispered.

Tears came suddenly to her eyes. She touched his mouth tenderly with her fingertips, ran it along his lip.

"Don't speak of that man. You taught me not to dwell on the past. I can't go backward, only enjoy what you can give me in the present," she whispered.

With a hoarse sound, he put his forehead against her heart. She clung to him, realizing in some way she changed him, perhaps changed his heart.

Gently, he continued. She forgot that she was vulnerable to his much greater strength. She forgot everything except the pleasure he created within her as well as the puling ache he created deep inside her.

"Leslie."

He made a hungry, questioning, oddly soothing sound.

"You're inside me," she said in wonder.

"God, yes. Your silken fire is *tu mo sholas na greine.*"

He moved his hand again, slowly, touching, caressing her silken moist knot.

Heat flowed through her once more. Her hips arched to pull him more deeply inside.

"Silk and fire enough to melt the snow," he whispered before he kissed her mouth then lower to her breast. "I want to melt the winter with you then touch the spring."

She tried to speak. She couldn't form words. A wave of intense pleasure was bursting through her while she arched her back to match the rhythm he set.

He continued, slowly and steadily moving within her. She no longer wondered about his hand so intimately between her legs as she gave herself to his caresses with complete trust.

A ragged throaty sound came from her.

"Are you alright?" he asked.

She tried to tell him how good what he was doing felt, but her words became a husky cry of pleasure as his hand moved again. When he was deep inside her once more his thumb rubbed over her creating more undeniably pleasant, soul shattering sensations.

As he continued, powerful, shocking pleasure exploded inside her, drenching her with heat.

"Tell me if I hurt you," he said huskily.

She barely heard the words. She knew only a sense of heat between her legs and a stretching that went on and on, delicious, frightening, endless, sensuous beyond anything she'd known before.

Leslie made a throttled sound as it seemed he felt the resistance of her body both pushing against him and at the same time inviting him to penetrate more deeply.

"Lacie?" he asked hoarsely, "am I hurting you?"

"No but I feel so... strange." She shivered rhythmically.

"A good strange?" he asked.

"Yes," she sighed.

"I'm coming all the way inside you now. I'm touching your maidenhead. When I burst through, it's going to hurt."

His warning gave her pause then she felt him stretching her, all of her. He was deep inside. With her cry, he stopped, holding himself so very still, his body taut.

"I'm so sorry." He froze still inside her. "There was no other way."

Seconds seemed to grow into minutes. "I'm alright," she finally told him. "What now?"

Only pleasure as she felt him move inside her again, then again. Slowly at first, his hands beneath her, lifting her hips to meet each movement with one of her own.

He made a hoarse sound. His fingers finding that place that seemed to give her the greatest passion, circling, retreating circling, spreading the liquid heat of her response between them.

Eyes closed, shivering, whimpering with each breath, Lacie tried to get closer to his maddening, wildly arousing fingertips. He moved within her. He was a hard, full presence that wasn't hurting her at all, not any longer, just touching her soul.

She felt incredibly good.

Something both wild and beautiful spread up from their hot, joined bodies. Lacie's eyes widened. She shuddered and moved hungrily against him, needing more of Leslie, needing to feel every bit of him as deep into her as he could get.

Pleasure erupted through her beginning with tiny spasms that grew to puling tremors. She couldn't move her hips in response, but she discovered she could respond in other ways while he pulsed deeply inside her, giving her so very much.

The shivering sweetness doubled. She clenched her body around him again and again and gasped at the shattering pleasure. Talons of fire flowed into her, pulsing, releasing, pulsing again and again as a frantic need encompassed her.

Tiny throaty sounds sprung from her as she moved against him, trying to get closer, desperate for something she couldn't name.

Leslie put his hands on her hips, jerked forward and drove into her again, harder and deeper than ever before.

A wild heat pulsed through Lacie then she too was free, unstoppable tremors ripping through her over and over again, her cries fading into his mouth as he covered her lips.

With each broken breath she inhaled there was a cry of ecstasy that was also his name.

~ * ~

Flynt rode as fast as he could toward Southcliff knowing the rest of family followed accompanied by a preacher. His anger intensified with each beat of his horse. True, Kelly told him about the hasty marriage between his sister and the duke months ago. He didn't believe Leslie would marry his sister without family present. Lacie would have wanted Daryl to stand beside her. In his mind, there was no marriage. He meant to rectify that situation right now.

Merry was visiting Hope this morning, telling her Lacie spent the night at Leslie's home. Her brother Link had been there too, with news for Leslie so she knew it for a fact.

At first, Hope was reluctant to say anything, but her good sense finally got the better of her need to respect Lacie as well as her feelings for Leslie. She didn't want the man to take advantage of Flynt's littlest sister.

Flynt agreed with Hope. Another wedding, a real wedding, was in his sister's future. One he knew would be valid. He was not going to allow her to sleep with Leslie while she was not married to the man, duke or not, dangerous spy or not. Hope went for the minister, sent messages to all the sisters including Merry to meet at the MacTavish townhouse as soon as possible. "It's urgent," were the last words on the messages.

"Blessed hell," he murmured,

Chaperoning his sisters had not been a choice. Grams had been way too lenient. It was always left up to him to set things right. He drew in a deep savage breath of air, realizing he couldn't drive his horse this hard.

He slowed his stallion to an easy trot, understanding it wouldn't be good of him to exhaust the poor animal even though he felt an urgent need to arrive as soon as possible, even while his gut told him his arrival would be after the fact.

Finally, he pulled up in front of the house. The stable boy must have heard him, because he was outside offering to take his horse before he dismounted.

Thank goodness. Racing he strode up the steps two at a time, he didn't take time to knock, just bolted through the door.

"Stop right there," Westcott demanded, his hands outstretched as if that simple gesture would stop him. "What are you doing here?"

"As if you can't guess," Flynt said, looking up the stairs, meaning to bypass the stodgy man who would protect Leslie with his life if necessary. His heart beat too rapidly in his chest. He tried to inhale deep breaths, calming himself before the altercation.

"I can't." His voice was calm and that fact further infuriated Flynt. "Now, what can I do for you?"

"Tell Leslie I need to talk with him now, not a moment later." Flynt was beside himself with unleashed energy.

"He's busy but I'll tell him you're here. Don't know if he will see you." Westcott turned to make his way up the steps.

Flynt followed, standing behind him at the door.

"Leslie, someone's here to see you."

"Tell them I'll be down in about an hour," Leslie's voice thundered through the door. "I'm busy."

That's what Flynt was afraid of. "I'm giving you five seconds before I'm coming in."

Flynt counted to five then passed the older man who was trying to block his way before throwing open the door.

He wasn't at all sure what he thought he would see. "Get off my sister," rumbled from his chest.

"Get out of here." Leslie was pulling on his pants and fastening them as he strode toward him, his face contorted with anger. "You're embarrassing my wife. I won't have it."

"Not without my sister." Flynt stood his ground.

"My wife," Leslie grit out, his fists clenching and unclenching as if he meant to hit Flynt.

"I've a minister on the way as well as the rest of the family." Flynt looked around Leslie to see Lacie covered with a blanket burrowed deep inside the bed, her cheeks flaming with color.

"Send him home, send them all home and get out."

"I'll leave for now," he said, suddenly feeling the intensity of the intrusion and trying to respect his sister.

Obviously, his arrival here had been too late. The rest of family should be downstairs within the hour. They would have time to prepare.

"When they get here, send them all home." Leslie said, glancing back to the bed.

"You can't keep Lacie in your bed if you don't do the right thing," Flynt persisted.

"I've already done the right thing by her. She agreed to the marriage months ago, as you well know. We were married then. If Lacie wants another wedding, the choice is up to her. Not you and not in the next hour or so. If she wants a big wedding or a little one, I'll give her whatever she desires."

Chapter Five

Link was right, when he made love to his wife, he reached that mindless and out of control place his brother spoke of. There was no way in hell he could have withdrawn from her. He smiled as he dipped a soft washcloth in water.

"Let me help you." Tenderly he bathed his seed and her blood from between her legs. This was a moment he didn't believe he would ever forget, at least not until he stuck his spoon in the wall.

"You don't have to do that," she told him, her voice whisper thin, thready. Her cheeks were stained a beautiful shade of pink. Her small fingers pushed at his hands, even while she turned away in an attempt to hide her embarrassment from him. Her actions were charming and he'd remember this moment forever.

"Don't be embarrassed. There won't be blood again, only my seed, and perhaps it took root this first time. Would you like that, a child in your womb?"

"I'd like some wine." She breathed in long and deep. keeping her gaze averted from what he was doing as she tried to pull a sheet around her. He stopped her.

He kept the laughter behind his teeth. "As would I but you ignored my question. Do you want a child?" He finished washing her before he poured them wine this time instead of tea. God, he hoped she did. This would be so hard if she drew away from him now after he experienced the most amazing gut-wrenching climax of his entire life. Hell, but he'd never felt anything like it before.

"Leslie..." Her voice broke off, seemed to catch in her throat.

"Leslie..." she began again clearing her throat.

He wondered what exactly she meant to tell him. "What?"

She seemed to gain the courage although her lashes were still lowered slightly. "I liked the last part of what we did. Where you..."

"I liked it too." No, he loved the sensations, the mindlessness of it all. "Do you want to make love again?"

"Right now?" She gulped the wine, her eyes wide with burgeoning passion. "Can you do that?"

"If you like." He reached out and touched the hard, pink tip of her breast then smiled as it seemed to pucker and harden even more with the light caress. "All you need do is ask."

"I would but I can barely breathe yet and don't know if I can move." He watched as she closed her eyes slowly then opened them. The pulse at the base of her neck beat furiously fast, and he wanted to stroke it caress all of her.

He liked the way she watched him, her gaze following him around the room as he set the cloth in the basin of water. Sitting down beside her, "Perhaps we should eat something first, gain your strength back. As for me, I'd like to make love to you all night long until neither one of us can breathe. Hold you in my arms, feel your softness pressed against me until the sun rises, perhaps until spring is here and the daffodils find their way above ground."

She nodded, her eyes wide with the growing passion she was just learning from him. Sweeping her tongue along her lips, unconsciously moistening them for his kiss. "That would be nice."

He laughed. It would be more than nice. He was definitely pleased she still wore nothing, had made no move to cover herself with sheets or even the sheer nightdress she slipped out of earlier in the morning. She seemed comfortable with him looking at her sooner than he had expected.

Leslie held out his hand, stopping her from moving. "No, don't get up. Stay right where you are. I'll bring this platter of food to you, to our bed." He set it on top of the covers, picking up a pastry before holding it to her mouth to share.

"You're feeding me?" she laughed, her smile infectious. "I

probably can do this myself. I'm not that weak or boneless anymore."

"Good, but this is more fun," he murmured as her lips brushed against his fingers, his body instantly hardening even more than he'd been a few minutes ago. He didn't believe he could have been more aroused or that arousal would come so quickly.

"I'm not sure this is a good thing, if you really want to eat."

Her breath seemed to catch in her throat. She waved a hand in front of her face to stop him.

"Probably not." His voice filled with hunger as he watched her eat then held the confection to her lips again, delighted by the tiny mew of pleasure he heard. "You like the way I taste or the pastry?"

"You. Yet you persist in feeding me," she whispered, touching him, his chest and running her finger down his torso to end so close to that part of him that needed her right now more than anything. "I like the way you taste, a little bit salty and all male, I think."

He drew in a shaky breath at her words, realizing she told him exactly what he needed to hear. He looked at his wife. Her eyes were open, her mouth parted. He saw the tip of her tongue glide suggestively across her bottom lip. She looked utterly uninhibited, a wildness about her, her hair curling sweetly around her shoulder as well at the velvet hard tips of her large breasts, tangled around her head. He touched a finger to her soft flesh. She quivered. "I can't help myself. Seems I've lost all control and would have you again, right now and again as soon as we recover then possibly another time if you've the strength."

She laughed, moving away from him, watching him, staring at his mouth as if she wanted him to use it to possess her. Her focus traveled the length of him, stopping at his sex then back to meet his gaze, her eyes wide with recognition of his need.

He rolled onto his back, pulling her to him so she straddled him. Her hot wet core touched him, caressed and enticed him. The passion he felt was primal and all-consuming.

"Really?" Her hands rested on his chest, nails scraping his skin as her breasts were so close to his lips he needed to taste another time, suck her into his mouth, savor her essence.

"Take me inside, hold me in your heat and silken sheathe until I find myself mindless again, with no control whatsoever." He understood his brother now but wondered how it was that way with every woman. For him, this was the only woman who had ever brought him to that state, a place where every coherent thought vanished except one.

Seeming to understand what he asked, she lowered herself on him. "Is this what you're asking?"

"Yes." He was impaled on her, deep inside the heat of her body. She held him within herself, quivering around him, small tremors encapsulating him. He thought he'd gone mad with lust; savage passion while he tried to control his unruly body. "Look down, look at us, together."

They were as one, united. He delighted in her swift indrawn breath of air. "We..." She moistened her lips before looking at him. They were parted slightly, kiss swollen, "I never thought... I don't know what to say."

"Don't say anything."

"Leslie..." she breathed his name and the word seemed to float on the air as she arched her back, taking him farther inside. Her breasts rose and fell, the rosebud tips hard, alluring, beguiling. He cupped them with his hands as they overflowed his fingers.

"Come closer," he told her.

She leaned toward him, the softness of her breasts brushing against his chest. He groaned. Desperate in his need, his body wanted to explode within her again. Yet he held himself in check needing to give her, her pleasure first, see her eyes while he heard the soft cries as she climaxed.

Slowly, erotically, as if she was experienced, she slid up then down his shaft bringing him ever closer to that mindless place where he couldn't think let alone breathe. She did it again and again. A sultry rain poured from her. His husky groan of delight surprised him. The magic surrounding her enchanted him, creating a mercurial heat deep within that could never be denied. She was part of him. He hoped this very night they created a new life together.

His hand moved. Fingertips searched through her slick dark thatch until he found the swollen knot of passion. He circled the nubbin with his thumb, worked it until she tossed her head back, her eyes closed, as he created the tiny cries echoing around him, more warm honey surrounded him as she moved.

Trembling, moaning with each breath, Lacie's body responded sweetly to his caresses. Her hips rocked against his aroused male flesh between her legs. He was a hard, full presence inside her, giving her as much pleasure as she was giving to him.

He was a man well pleased.

Watching her, Leslie teased Lacie until her pleasure drenched both of them, until he felt the first tremors of her release, until her body clenched tightly around him pulling him deeper into her sultry core. Her primal nearly savage response to him was his undoing.

Her hips moved sharply, sinking so far into her that his hand was pinned between their bodies. Only then did he finish what they began a few minutes before, teasing and teaching her with every driving motion of his hips just how good love could be between them.

Something both primitive and stunning spread up from their hot, joined bodies. Lacie's eyes widened with the deepest pleasure and passion. There was no color in them, only dark centers dilated with pleasure. She shuddered and rocked hungrily, seeming to want more of him. It was raw and savage and something he wanted to hang on to as long as he could only then he would create the unrestrained passion, the violent joining of their bodies and the raw primal climax.

Suddenly, her body tensed and the ripples of bliss began. It seemed they washed through her into him. She cried out then again and again. In response his body corded and tensed. With repeated, throttled shouts he spent himself inside her sleek heat.

She responded in kind, crying out his name as she tried to breathe then relaxing against him, her body slick with moisture.

Behind them, behind the closed door, he heard Westcott's voice. Thought he made it clear he was to go away. He didn't want to talk to anyone, didn't want the beauty of their first time together disturbed. Looking to Lacie he smiled. The look on her face was poignant, beautiful and once again when he made love to his wife, he was out of control, mindless with desire that could not be stopped even if he wanted to. He realized he could never let her go.

Behind him the door suddenly burst open. His instincts cut in as he flipped Lacie over as gently as possible. His back was to the open door, "Get under the covers." He blocked her from anyone's view until she was hidden, turning to confront whoever invaded their privacy. He saw Flynt, realized the anger on the man's face was very real and deep.

"Get off my sister." Flynt's voice thundered in the master chamber, even while the man strode toward him, his fists clenched tightly at his sides.

He was quickly moving toward Flynt, yanking on his pants and fastening them, rage simmering, threatening to boil over. The violent conversation between the two men continued. Leslie wasn't all too sure how he convinced him to leave but Flynt finally backed from the room.

What was happening here? First his brother interrupts them yesterday and now today her brother. At least Link did not surprise them with the purpose of ending what he so carefully began. "What was the talk about a minister and the rest of the family on the way?"

What to do now?

"It's clear. Your brother left the room." He sat on the bed, reaching out to touch Lacie's back. Unable to help himself he traced a line down her spine. An act of reassurance he hoped would help her adjust. This was not supposed to happen. He could only pray this did not set them back. "Flynt left, so you can come out from below those covers."

She poked her head from beneath her hiding place, her eyes wide, shocked. "Why on earth did Flynt bring a minister to Southcliff? Kelly did tell him we were married, didn't he?" he asked, beginning to think he might know the truth and why would he barge into his private sanctuary demanding he get off his sister.

"I never told anyone we were wed, not even Daryl, who I'm closest with. Only Flynt knew. He agreed to keep the news a secret. I guess I was embarrassed at the quickness of the ceremony, that you left then later I saw no reason to say anything after I decided we needed an annulment." She sounded a bit contrite and apologetic.

Why Flynt showed up like this is a mystery.

"The picture is becoming clearer as we speak. We both need to dress then explain ourselves to the family. Flynt also needs to enlighten us as to his bazar behavior given what he knew. I suppose all of your sisters along with their husbands will be in the parlor." He rose then and called for hot water enough for two baths. He decided he was going to have a tub made large enough for both of them to fit into.

"No one's going to barge in here?" her voice quavered on the question. "I don't want..."

"I promise. While you bathe, I'm going to take a few minutes to talk to Flynt and see if I can explain what has happened. I wish to find out as well why he doesn't remember we are wed. If they wish to stay here at Southcliff, that's fine. We'll celebrate our marriage with family. I would bet Merry had something to do with this fiasco. It's just the kind of thing she would revel in."

Once the water arrived, Flynt headed downstairs trying to decide the best way to approach this matter. He was disappointed Lacie chose not to tell anyone except Flynt. In any case he would have to deal with the past now, as well as the future while trying to convince them they were indeed wed. In his parlor he saw Flynt had not joked about the entire family coming to marry them.

"Brandy?" he offered, striding to the cabinet and pouring one for himself before turning to see if anyone else wanted a drink.

"Helped ourselves to your expensive French brandy already before I decided to confront you head on, but don't mind if I take a second glass," Flynt informed him, the anger still very apparent in his voice as well as the bearing of his shoulders.

"We should speak of the misunderstandings between us then. I'm really quite innocent of all wrong doings here." He surveyed the room, seeing the smirk on Merry's face, realizing while she could have told Flynt he and Lacie were wed, she chose not to do so.

"What are those misunderstandings?" Flynt asked.

"You had no right to invade mine and Lacie's privacy, no right to see her naked and in my arms. It was not well done of you, Flynt, and I hope you apologize to your sister. And," he paused, "Lacie told me you knew about the marriage. Perhaps you should take this golden opportunity to explain why you're feigning ignorance."

"You had my sister beneath you..."

Well, he mused fondly, she was actually on top of him. With no luck he couldn't keep the smile from spreading. "My wife," he said with complete calm, watching different expressions flit across the faces of those assembled in front of him. "And should you be saying these things in front of all of these people. It's not anyone's business but Lacie's and mine."

It seemed Flynt ignored his statement as well as the earlier question. "The minister is here, ready, eager to marry the two of you. It's best we get this accomplished as soon as possible. When that is done, we'll celebrate. Justine is in your kitchen baking a wedding cake for the two of you."

"After I bathe, I'll see if Lacie wants to stand through a second ceremony. I'll do anything she likes. Her wishes here are what is important not yours, Flynt, or anyone else's."

Leslie started for the stairs, his shoulders squared while he seethed inwardly. The calm façade was just that a pretense.

"You're not going back to the bedroom." Flynt blocked the way by stepping in front of his long-time friend.

Truly, Leslie didn't feel an argument would do any good, but he needed to bathe and check on Lacie as well. Her feelings were of the utmost importance here. These two days had been an ordeal, pleasant as well as troubling. Now, the extent of his patience was coming to a quick and final ending.

He stepped around Flynt, not bothering to look at him. "Don't stop me, Flynt. You'll come to regret it if you do. When we are both ready, Lacie and I will talk to all of you and not a moment before."

Wisely, Flynt moved away. Leslie walked to the second floor without looking back. Stepping inside his room, Lacie was still in the bath. Kneeling beside the tub, he touched her cheek with the back of his hand, "Would you like me to rinse your hair. You can dress and dry it while I bathe."

"That would be nice," she murmured, her eyes drowsily half closed.

He realized how tired she was and how he kept her awake most of the night.

He rinsed the soap away then handed her a large bath sheet as she stepped from the tub. "Next time let's do this together."

"What? Do what together?"

She appeared baffled by his comment, yet she was smiling, reaching out her hand to caress him.

"Bathe," he whispered close to her ear before he pulled her to him and brushed his lips across her. Then, "I don't think there will be any snow angels in our future today but if the white stuff is still on the ground tomorrow, I'll make one with you. Seems right now we have to deal with one furious brother and several amused sisters."

"You're deflecting," she said. "Thank you, I'd like to do that, snow angels with you and if the snow vanishes, I'll have your promise for the next time the white stuff sticks to the ground even if we have to wait a year."

His heart felt lighter now. His future with Lacie seemed more secure than yesterday at this time. Her family needed to be dealt with, but they would cross that bridge together. Unfortunately, he couldn't prove their marriage took place or when. The signed documents were in a safe in his townhouse. So, it was up to her family to accept hers and his word on this.

With the towel wrapped around, her she sat by the fire, combing her hair, the strands picking up light from the flames and shimmering softly around her face. He washed quickly then sat beside her.

"We need to tell them together. Flynt isn't taking my word." He chuckled, remembering the look on his face when he stepped around him to come back to the room. "I suppose if I found my sister in such a compromising position I would act first and ask questions later." He finished then dressed, knowing that thought for the honest truth.

"Is Merry here too?" she asked, her comb stopping as she paused. "I like your sister a lot."

"She is and that's my question too. Why didn't Merry tell everyone we were wed months ago before I left on the last mission at Montgomerie's request and stop this fiasco before it started?"

"And Link would have told Merry that I was at Southcliff with you," Leslie spoke, trying to piece together all the previous events in order to make sense of this invasion. "I know some of this was my fault. I should have stayed at your home. If I had done that perhaps none of this would be happening now."

"No, Flynt would most likely have hauled you from my home even though he knew we were married. Kelly was witness to the fact. He was also supposed to inform Flynt."

"Didn't Link realize what would happen when he told everyone where I was?" Lacie asked.

"Without a doubt, but I put this squarely on Merry's shoulders."

Leslie knew though, Merry enjoyed the drama and was most likely punishing him for sending her back to town a few days ago. She would have been bored to tears if she stayed here. While he understood her motive for coming to Glasgow, he, after all, had a life of his own, one that did not include babysitting his little sister. Sighing heavily, he realized then that MacTavish had four such little sisters and Lacie was the youngest.

She stood, looking around the room, "Suppose I should pick out one of my new gowns. What do you think would be appropriate? Something that would serve as a wedding gown or a normal day dress?"

"It all depends on what you want. Whether there is a wedding or simply a celebration is up to you."

He walked into an adjoining room. A few minutes later he returned with a dark blue day dress that was trimmed with Belgian lace and cinched beneath her bosom, pleased with himself. "This will be perfect. Do you like it?"

"Yes, it's beautiful but I will need all of the underthings. Do you want to pick those out too? A corset? A shift? Does this mean you don't want another wedding?"

"Here, of course you have everything you will need. We can purchase more anytime you like. If you decide on a wedding, we can return and dress you accordingly." He felt a bit of embarrassment but she did that to him, left him mindless and unable to think when she was in front of him in all her stunning glory. He left and returned again, helping her with the laces and into the garment as well.

When finished, he held out his arm to her. "Are you ready to confront those who are in disbelief of our marriage?"

She was shaking her head, her face turning pale. "I don't want to have another ceremony. We don't have to but Flynt should take our word for it. Especially since I know Kelly told him about the wedding at your house."

"Yes, I'd like to know that reason too." His voice was gentle, but he also knew she heard the demand in the tone.

She sighed softly and he understood this was not something she wanted to discuss with him at the moment. If Flynt and the entourage would leave of their own accord, he would allow Lacie to hide away in the master chamber until she felt more comfortable with all the decisions she had made in the last twenty-four hours.

They wouldn't though and even if they did, there would come a time for explanations. No one in her immediate family, even Catherine, her grandmother, would stand for them living together if there wasn't proof of a marriage.

Hand on his arm, they walked down the staircase together. He heard her inhale a long breath before they turned into the drawing room to confront the family.

"Be brave," he whispered, taking her to an empty chair then he stood behind her, studying the landscape.

A clamoring of voices echoed in the room, everyone suddenly asking questions they had no right to hear the answers. His sudden need to protect Lacie from her family and further embarrassment washed over him.

Then Lacie cleared her throat. "I'm sorry all of you came all the way out to Southcliff. I didn't, don't need protection of any type from my husband." She held up one hand as the others began to talk all at the same time again. "I am married. We are married. Flynt was supposed to know. For the life of me, I don't understand why he is acting this way. You don't need to be concerned about Leslie's and my relationship."

"Why didn't you tell any of us?" Grams asked her, clearly appearing disturbed about the announcement and ignoring the fact she told Flynt. "I knew for all these months you were keeping something from me, but I never thought for a moment it was something like this, a secret marriage."

"Why?" Daryl asked. "We share everything and you knew I would want to know. You also know I would never say anything to anyone."

"You might have told Donal, your husband and I didn't want to risk that."

Thankfully, the remaining sisters stayed quiet, seemingly content to wait for the answers.

She stood up straighter, clearing her throat and seeming to think. Then she began, "I was embarrassed at first and confused. So much happened in so little time. I was totally overwhelmed. Leslie was gone and couldn't reassure me."

"Why?" Flynt asked his sister. "This..." he waved his hand around the room, "seems to me to be more embarrassing than telling us Leslie married you. If I'd known, I would have never barged into the master chamber."

"You did know," she insisted, more convinced than ever Flynt was lying. "I would be shocked if Kelly didn't tell you."

Flynt was running his hands through his hair, pacing, "I don't recall."

"You weren't eighteen so it was not well done of him," Broc said seeming to take the words straight from Flynt's mouth. "He should have waited for you to grow up."

"Which is part of why I didn't consummate the marriage when we were wed." Leslie felt a sudden need to defend himself in this even though at the time he had every intention of making love to his wife. "I wanted her to have the protection of my name while I was gone as well as my money."

"She's still not eighteen," Flynt reminded him.

"What difference does a couple of days make?" Daryl spoke up in her sister's defense. "I've never really understood the magic of that age. Do girls suddenly become women when they turn eighteen and the day before they are not? Emilia was wed and had a child by the time she was thirteen years old. I realize of course that isn't the same but truly, Lacie and Leslie can make up their minds."

Leslie chuckled softly, amused by the words yet also realizing how true they were. Daryl was a fighter just as her younger sister. He wondered what would finally be decided. A celebration would certainly be nice. Lacie deserved that. His mouth watering, he could already smell the cake baking in his kitchen. Of course they could eat the cake without getting married again.

Leslie waited a few more seconds, enjoying the quiet of the moment. Then, "So, we're not going to discuss Lacie or our marriage. Suffice it to say we are legally wed or I would have never taken her to my bed. If all of you would like to you can stay and have a midafternoon luncheon with us then allow us to cut the cake that is even now being prepared for our consumption. You're welcome but that is the extent of what Lacie and I are willing to do for you even though you are family. She has told me unequivocally, I might add, that she doesn't want another wedding ceremony. So sorry to disappoint."

"We've the minister here, we can make sure—" Flynt stopped short when Lacie spoke up.

"You doubt my word? How dare you? What about the rest of you?" She turned her attention to her grandmother then her sisters. "Do you all really believe I would let Leslie bed me without benefit of marriage?" Then it seemed she realized what she'd just said. Two of her sisters did just that

Grams spoke up first, "I've no reason to doubt your word, but you said at first you were embarrassed. Why?"

Lacie was quick to speak. "Because my new husband left two

seconds after the wedding. What was I supposed to think? I certainly didn't know having had no experience in these things."

"It wasn't well done of me," Leslie said then shrugging. "When Montgomery summons, you obey. I had no choice but to leave. If all of you are wondering, if I'd had more time, yes, I would have bedded my wife, eighteen or not. I'm no saint but I'm content that everything happened in this order."

"After the ceremony, I was attacked. I decided I didn't want any man touching me." She spoke softly, her dark lashes lowered. "Leslie had to encourage me not to be afraid of him."

"Any man except me," Leslie smiled, his hands now on her shoulders, caressing gently and attempting to reassure. "I was successful in convincing her I was not like that man."

"If I'm not needed here, could someone take me home?" the minister asked, seemingly eager to be away.

"Well, that would mean someone, one of us, would have to leave. No one here wants to do that."

Grams walked to the minister, "You should stay and eat with us. Nial and I will take you home when we are finished."

"I don't believe anything that's been said here," Flynt spoke, anger still in the tenor of his voice. "I for one want to see these two wed. Then and only then will I believe the marriage vows complete and true. The truth lies in what one sees, not in what someone tells you."

~ * ~

Lacie was furious as well as disappointed with her brother who would not take her word. He actually thought she lied to him. Her heart pounded and she felt a deep need to hit something. Instead her fingers tightened on Leslie's arm, her nails gouging his skin. He placed a hand over hers. She smiled then, understanding he was as angry as she was.

"This will all turn out. Don't take this personally."

His whisper was close to her ear, which seemed to have further impact on her brother as his brows drew together in a deep furrow, his lips thinning.

"How can I not?"

She tried for several deep breaths but all the air caught in her throat. She was shaking so hard, she knew Leslie felt the tremors. This was not acceptable to her now that she decided she could trust Leslie.

What to do now?

"I would like a moment with my wife. Come."

He didn't wait for permission or to answer any of the clamor that was going on behind them. He led her from the parlor then into his office, closing and locking the door behind him. For a few seconds he held her before pulling away. Smiling down at her, "You must relax, my sunshine. By the end of the evening, we will all be laughing and your family will be well on their way home."

She watched as he moistened his lips, knew he was about to kiss her. She needed this closeness and reassurance as well. Quickly, he brushed his lips across hers, nibbling on the corners as she parted for him. His tongue entered briefly before he pulled away, once more staring into her eyes. The day had turned traumatic in an instant. What had begun as a tranquil and peaceful morning was now in chaos. It was almost as if he read her mind, understood what would make her feel better, give her the confidence she yearned for.

Lightly his lips brushed hers, softly and slowly he touched her lips with his tongue. She answered in kind. She brushed her tongue across his mouth and he opened for her, caressing and exploring, setting a slow lazy heat to simmer within her. Closing her eyes, she let all the delicious sensations wash over her, encompass her, replacing the emotions her brother and family single handedly been at the forefront.

He pulled back, a gentle expression on his face, concern for her seeming to simmer in the depth of his eyes. "I would make love to you here with the benefit of a locked door all the while knowing your brother would be pacing and swearing just outside. We've something to discuss. You'll understand the importance and hopefully realize the impact this decision will have on the rest of our lives."

"I would rather make love with my husband than talk about

anything right now, particularly if it concerns Flynt and what he set in motion a few minutes ago," she told him, still feeling the brunt of her family's betrayal. "They didn't believe me, us, didn't take my word as truth or yours. That was not well done of them. I would have expected it of Flynt, maybe even my older sisters, but Daryl... She didn't believe me either. I could read it in her eyes."

"That also bothers me but the fact of the matter is, I would have consummated the marriage on the day we said our vows if the opportunity and the time presented itself. That's why I married you that night before I lost what little control I have when it comes to you. It's also true, your sisters' husbands bedded their wives before the vows were said. So, why should they believe us?" he asked, his hands around her waist, drawing her close to him.

She was shaking her head furiously, distraught and wondering how she could put up with this. "All that is true but even Grams didn't believe us. Just like Daryl, I could see it in her eyes and the judgment. At this moment I don't want to see or talk to any one of them and if we don't come out of here soon, they will all be pounding on the door, believing that you are taking advantage of me."

He chuckled, laughing for a moment and his hands ran up then down her sides as if he did want to make love to her. "I saw that too, but just as the husbands did, I would have told the truth. If we were not married and they managed to find me in bed with you, I would have never lied about the marriage. I'm a man of my word and Flynt knows that for a fact. He's been a good friend for many years and we've shared a lot."

"What should we do? You have a suggestion and I'm not sure I'm going to like it."

She was beside herself, emotions pummeling through her from every direction.

He didn't answer right away. Instead, he poured them both a drink before leading her to the sofa in his office. Her hand in his was warmed by his gentleness and gave her a moment of peace. She breathed in deeply waiting for him to explain his thoughts.

"Sit down. Have a sip then we'll talk."

He did what he advised then placed both the crystal glasses on a nearby table, taking her hands in his once again. His expression so serious, she nearly looked away, felt a need to run.

"What if I don't want to talk?"

She felt petulant and unforgiving at the moment. When she looked to the door, she understood she would eventually have to confront her family but not this moment. Confront them with what exactly she didn't know.

"You don't have to talk. We'll go out there and make sure they understand they cannot bully us into doing something that is so very unnecessary, a second ceremony."

"Alright..." She touched his face with her hand. "What then?" she asked not liking the way he was approaching this, knew though they would succumb to the wishes of her family.

"Would it be so bad to give your family and Flynt what they want?" he asked, putting his finger beneath her chin. "It would only take a few minutes of our time and everyone would be pleased. Families need to ban together even when it means one party does something the other doesn't like."

She understood what he was doing as he lifted her head so he could see her eyes. "I don't know what that is," she said, her voice bitter and strained. "What do they want?"

"You're the only sister who did not have a proper wedding of some sort," he paused in thought, "I suppose one could say that Broc and Bliss did not have a proper wedding either, but they did have a ceremony in front of some of the family. Theirs was rushed and with good reason."

"Neither did Cam and Chelsea. They married in a church by themselves on the way to the beach. No one made them marry twice."

"Yes, that is true but..."

"So, what are you trying to say right now, or am I supposed to read your mind?"

Her fingers were winding in her gown, twisting the fabric. She still couldn't breathe right, her heart pounding fiercely beneath her ribs. It seemed she was asking questions she already knew the answers to.

"Well, I am reading your mind, but I'm going to disagree with you. Sometimes it is best to compromise for the greater good." He showed her a row of even white teeth just as if he was pleased with either his thoughts or what he was sure she would decide.

She was sure she knew what was behind that smile and so much more. After all, she already told him she didn't want another wedding yet he was implying another one would appease everyone. One wedding was enough for her. She wasn't going to change her mind no matter how sweet the words, no matter how much sense he made.

"I don't want another wedding," she told him petulantly, yet her voice wavered slightly.

She saw the look in his eyes, the moment he knew he could convince her this notion of a second ceremony was for the best. "You can't change my mind about this. Please, Leslie, try to see things my way."

"Your family will be placated. You will make them happy if you decide to go through with a second wedding. It makes no difference to me. In my mind we are married and need no further validation."

"At the moment I don't really care if I make anyone except you happy."

She stared into his dark brown eyes that seemed to see into her soul, knowing then how true those words were.

"I'm pleased you want to make me a happy man. You already have, you know by accepting me and allowing me the honor of making love to you. You had me terrified for several days. This matter is still your choice, but I thought you should look at this situation from your family's perspective. We have time to think. Sip the brandy, let it warm you from the inside out."

She did as he said, felt her conviction wavering. Everything he said was indeed true. A little bit of compromise would go a long way. After all they weren't expecting a huge church wedding in a few weeks or months, just a ceremony they could be part of.

How would that be so bad?

"What you're asking is difficult, since they don't want to consider my feelings. They don't even believe me." She didn't want him to convince her, bowing to Flynt's wishes was the best for everyone, but he was well on his way to doing that very thing. The fact of the matter was that he already convinced her but she wasn't going to give in quite so easily.

"I understand all you are saying as well as what you are not saying," he paused, seeming to think. "Again, this decision is still all yours but what will it hurt to give in to your brothers wishes?"

He pulled her into his arms, cradling her gently, his hands soothing the tense muscles of her back.

"It wouldn't hurt if he believed me. If he could tell me he knew, we, I wouldn't lie about saying our vows, I would do anything he asked." She paused, "Well almost anything."

"That's the crux of the matter isn't it?" He lightly kissed her forehead. "Think about what you're telling me and just how stubborn you are being. Perhaps the moment is not about us. We're already pleased with our relationship." He pulled away slightly, looking at her. "You are pleased. Am I right?"

"Yes." She didn't like what he was getting at. It would mean surrendering to her brother's dictates, yet when she thought about it, she had rarely ever yielded to his wishes. What would it hurt now?

"So," he paused, handing her the glass of brandy then wrapping his arm around her as they sat back on the sofa, he encouraged her once more, "Take a few minutes to think about what would be the best for everyone."

"You really want to have another ceremony?" She was reconsidering as she closed her eyes, going over all the good as well as the bad points of doing this a second time.

"No," he was grinning and shaking his head, "but I do believe that by having a wedding with our families present and a part of the ceremony is best in the long run. What do you think?"

Sighing heavily before smiling at him. "I want the same for us, but this doesn't come easily. Shall we tell them?"

"We should but you've a more appropriate gown upstairs. You go on up. I will tell your sisters all about it and you can get ready." He kissed her gently then smoothing her lips with his thumb, "You will be an absolutely stunning bride."

"This is happening way too fast." Her heart suddenly sped at the thought. "I don't know which dress."

"The cream-colored ball gown. Go on with you."

He kissed her lightly again, this time on the forehead and watched her leave before he stepped into the parlor.

Lacie raced up the steps, emotions overwhelming her. She didn't understand why she agreed to something so preposterous. All the while Leslie made her believe it was her decision. He was a man. He, of course, would be determined to have his way. In this case, however, he made sure she made the final decision.

How astute of him. It seemed he easily wrapped her around his little finger. She supposed that would be the way of it for the rest of their lives together.

She didn't know how he did it. She would have to think on it for a while, figure out how to combat that skill of his.

When she stood in the master chamber, the bed had been made and everything was in order. One of the maids had pulled out a tub and strangely it was filled with steaming water as if Leslie had ordered it for her.

"Milady," she curtsied. "I was told to have a bath brought upstairs. We keep the water hot in the mornings for just this purpose. Cook said, since it was a special night for the lord and the lady, to keep it hot all day."

"I see," she said but she really didn't understand anything at all. Leslie could not have ordered the bath, simply because there had not been the time.

"My darling granddaughter." Grams stepped from the adjoining room. "I ordered it. When the two of you disappeared into Leslie's office, I was pretty sure I knew why he wanted to speak privately with you so I took the chance."

"I just had a bath and washed my hair. I'm not taking another one," Lacie said, eyeing the steamy water distastefully.

"Suit yourself," Grams laughed. "Didn't know if you had time before you encountered the family.

"Lacie!" The sisters burst into the room, chattering nonstop.

It seemed to Lacie a whirlwind swept into the chamber. Holding her hands beneath her chin, she watched and wondered once more if this had truly been wise. They set a tornado into action that couldn't be stopped.

"You're getting married," Bliss said, laughing. "It's about time the two of you did this the right way."

"As if you and Broc did anything the right way." Lacie couldn't stop the words yet she didn't regret them.

"Well, a younger sister is supposed to learn from the mistakes made by their elders not couple them with new blunders," Bliss said, still laughing and seeming to enjoy herself immensely.

Suddenly, all Lacie's reservations rose to the forefront of her mind. "Only if the lot of you believe I've told the truth. That's the only way I'm going forward with this." She meant to stand her ground. Hands on her hips she stared at then, her chin higher by a couple of notches.

"Well, of course we believe you," Daryl stepped forward. "I know you would never lie about something like that. I also knew you were keeping something from me all of these months. I'm pleased to finally know what you were hiding and I don't blame you. Under those circumstances I would have done the same."

"I believed you as well," Chelsea said, shrugging her shoulders and smiling. "You never lie so why would you start now over something as important as marriage vows? Can't say I know Leslie well enough to say the same, He does strike me to be much like Flynt. He might bed you but he wouldn't lie about a marriage that never took place."

"I've found the dress and underthings Leslie told us about," Bliss said as she emerged from the adjoining chamber. "This gown is stunning and the color should suit you quite well. Now, Lacie, it is time for a bath. Flynt is being autocratic. He gave us an hour to get you ready, but we will let them wait an extra fifteen minutes. It will do them good and Leslie will learn a valuable lesson."

"And what would that be?" Lacie asked, looking at the bath again and thinking she was going to turn into a prune if she couldn't convince everyone she didn't need a bath.

"Beauty cannot be rushed," Bliss told them smirking.

Lacie wondered what could be beyond that smile.

"A man should be willing to wait at least a few minutes for his wife, don't you think?" Chelsea laughed with the others as they continued to agree with Bliss. "Now is the time to begin training your man. The rest of your life will go so much better."

"I see you aren't wearing a ring. Maybe Leslie will have one for you this time," Grams stepped through the door again with a platter of food. Daryl followed with glasses and a couple of bottles of wine.

"I have a ring but I chose not to wear it since I didn't tell anyone that we were married. It's at home. So, no, he won't have one to give me."

She wore the ring one day and one night. That was all. After that twenty-four-hour period, she placed it in a box in her room.

"Well, that doesn't matter," Daryl said softly. "The vows are what matter now. Both of you will have a chance to speak them in front of witnesses that make a difference to you."

"I suppose."

Lacie still felt the reluctance deep in her bones, wished Leslie was here with her. He was probably drinking with the bad boys in the parlor, waiting and laughing.

"You having second thoughts?" Bliss asked, stepping up beside her and placing a reassuring hand on her shoulder. "We can walk down those stairs right now and send the minister home if that's what you want. You have to be sure."

"No, I'm just nervous I suppose. Everything seems to be happening backward and for all the wrong reasons. Let's do this before I do decide I can't go through with it."

She was in then out of the lavender scented bath in what seemed like flurry of soap and rinse water.

Now, she stood in the middle of the room while the girls helped her with all the new clothing. Even though this wasn't a wedding gown, it was beautiful a very light shimmering cream satin studded with pearls, fitting her to perfection and dipping just low enough to see the swell of her breasts but little else.

"You are a very beautiful bride," Bliss said.

"I am? I've never thought of myself as beautiful."

The reflection looking back at her seemed foreign to her. Never in her life had she worn anything this elegant. She turned to the others, her heart in her throat.

"You are so beautiful." Grams stepped forward, hugging her gently, seeming to agree with Bliss. "Leslie will be pleased to see you. I'm sure his mouth will fall open at his first sight of you." She handed her a silver comb for her hair. "Your grandfather gave this to me the day we were married. I'm going to lend this to you today. When I'm gone or too old to appreciate the jewelry, it will be yours."

"I think Leslie saw something in Lacie none of the rest of us did. She was always the youngest and into trouble, her hair disheveled, her clothes torn. But now..." Bliss held onto her hands then stepping back to admire her more. "These are for you."

"Garters with tiny blue flowers embroidered on them. Thank you." Lacie was very nearly to tears.

"Now don't cry," Grams said. "I know they are tears of happiness, but they will smear your makeup."

"They are your something blue, good luck you know," Chelsea said reverently. "Bliss gave them to me when she thought I would marry Cam and I to Daryl so the three of us are handing them down to you."

Lacie's heart swelled with love for her sisters. "Thank you, all of you. This is more than I ever expected. All of you must have been pretty sure of yourselves. When did you decide...?"

"Last night, so we did have a little time to plan. When Merry told us at dinner, we were left with no choice."

"Where is Merry?" Lacie had not expected any of this and was so used to her sisters she didn't miss Leslie's sister until this moment. "Shouldn't she be here?"

"She stayed with her brother but implied she would be up later with something for the bride."

"A toast," Hope said pouring the champagne Daryl had brought earlier, "and something to eat. While I'm sure Justine has prepared more than just a cake for later, the bride should have something in her stomach before the vows are said. Don't want her to faint. By the way we found you earlier, I'm assuming neither of you has eaten."

"I'm not hungry," Lacie murmured, realizing the truth. Her stomach was in knots. She couldn't possibly keep anything down.

"You will be once this is all done and you are even more legally Leslie's duchess than right now," Bliss said. "Because of his title, this is truly important. You don't want anyone questioning the legality of the marriage."

"I never thought of that," Lacie murmured.

"Drink and eat. Don't want the bride fainting." Grams laughed but there was a serious note to what she said.

"Can I sit in this?" Lacie asked, rubbing her arms, a chill seeming to sweep through her. "My legs are suddenly very wobbly."

"Lady Lacie." Westcott knocked on the door. "Merry is here and she has something from Leslie. He wanted to give this to you before the ceremony. Can she come in?"

"Of course," Grams was at the door, opening it for Leslie's sister.

"Here, oh my you're so very beautiful." Merry handed her the box. "He wanted me to tell you that this is a family heirloom. Been handed down several generations. This is for Lacie now. While it is not exactly new, it is not borrowed or blue." She sat down, watching.

"What is it?" Daryl asked as Grams handed the box to Lacie. They all gathered around.

Slowly, she undid the blue ribbon tying the box shut before she opened it. She gasped at the sight, the jewels glistening and sparkling in the light of the room. "It's stunning."

"It's something you will have to get used to," Daryl said, a bit of awe in her voice. Then, "Who would have known our baby sister would marry a duke? A rich duke."

"You are truly marrying a duke and a man of wealth," Chelsea said after her sister. "You will do well, I'm sure."

Lacie found herself backing away, shaking her head, wishing Leslie were a commoner and not a titled lord with seemingly more money than he knew how to spend. "I don't know how to be a duchess. I'm not sure..."

"Of course you know how. There is nothing to it." Grams waved her hand in the air for emphasis. "Of course you will have responsibilities, but you will learn as you go. Leslie will not expect something of you that you cannot do."

"Your soon to be husband is not a typical duke either," Bliss reminded her. "He was a spy for the British government. At the beck and call of someone named Drake Montgomery. I truly hope he is no longer a spy and will not be called away on dangerous mission now that he is wed."

"All you're saying is true, but why me?" Lacie asked, turning the necklace over in her hands. "Why would a man with so much power and wealth want me?"

"Perhaps he appreciates how wild and free you've always been," Daryl said. "There is no drama with you. What you see is what you get."

"And your honesty. I'm sure it was clear to him from the very start that you didn't care about the money or the title that came with his name," Bliss said. "You just wanted him. That one fact had to be refreshing for a man who would have been bombarded constantly by women who wanted what you didn't seem to care about, his title and money not him."

Grams took her by the shoulders, leading her back to the mirror. "Look at yourself, sweetheart. A few minutes ago, the woman looking back at you surprised you. You are beautiful from the inside out and should never doubt your abilities. It's obvious by the way Leslie stares at you that you please him immensely."

"I was? He does?" She was having difficulty inhaling air.

"The physical beauty isn't all. You are beautiful everywhere it counts, always have been," Grams said. "When you smile you have this sparkle about you that draws people to you that is brighter than that necklace you are holding. I believe your duke has chosen the perfect duchess."

Lacie didn't know what to say in response. When she first saw her husband, she never thought about him in any way except to her he was the most handsome man she'd ever seen.

"Now, should we put this necklace on, sip a bit more champagne then go downstairs for your wedding?" Chelsea asked as she handed Lacie a glass filled with the bubbly stuff.

"Here's to you and your new life," Daryl spoke up.

"Amen to that," Grams joined in.

Once the necklace was around her neck, she touched the stones, running her fingers along them. This was beautiful but she didn't care about jewelry, never had. He told her she would have to go to a ball or two. What else would be expected of her?

"How much time do we have?" Lacie asked, fiddling with her dress.

"Not thinking of changing your mind, I hope," Daryl said. "We would be forced to change it back if that is what you are doing."

"No, just thinking I want to get this over with so life can get back to normal." Lacie downed the rest of her champagne, thinking of Leslie and the delicious things she experienced this morning. He would make love to her again tonight, and she would let him do anything he wanted.

"We have five minutes left. Do you want to go now?" Grams asked just as the knock sounded on the door. "You understand letting your man know you have control is important."

"Time for the wedding," Flynt's impatient sounding voice boomed through the door. "Not going to put this off a moment longer."

"We have five minutes," Grams said, winking at Lacie before handing her a piece of meat and cheese. "Eat this, it will help calm your stomach as well as the pre-wedding jitters I know you're feeling."

Lacie didn't think she could possibly swallow the food. Setting it on a small plate, she smoothed her skirt. "I'm suddenly terrified." She held her hands up. "I can't stop the shaking."

"No, you're all ten minutes late," Flynt said, sounding more than just a little bit peeved, his annoyance showing.

"It's up to you." Grams looked at her before asking. "Five more minutes or right now?"

"Let's go now. Truly, I would like to put this behind me as soon as possible. My throat is so parched, I doubt if I can say any words. I'm so terrified I'm chilled bone deep."

"You 'll find a way to say whatever is necessary," Daryl said encouragingly. "But the chills don't seem right. Are you sure you feel well?"

"I'm feeling a bit dizzy and cold but I think I'm fine," Lacie said, once more rubbing her arms, trying to feel warmth where there was none.

"Too much champagne on an empty stomach. Did you eat anything?" Grams asked, clearly seemingly more concerned now than she was before.

"I don't know. I don't remember. In any case whether I ate or not makes no difference now. We have to leave."

"Hold on to Flynt's arm on the way down the stairs then make sure Leslie knows you're a bit wobbly and you'll be fine. They will take care of you," Chelsea said, holding her hand to her forehead. "She is a bit warm."

"Just nerves," Bliss said. "I'm sure she will be back to normal as soon as we finish the ceremony and there is no more stress."

"Are we ready then?" Grams stepped to the door and opened it. "I will go first. I assume that your sisters will be your bridesmaids and Daryl your matron of honor. They will follow and line up on the bride's side while the husbands will escort them and line up on the opposite side of the minister."

"I never thought about any of that. Yes."

Perhaps this was for the best. Everyone was taking care of her, making the decision she couldn't. A huge wedding would have been even more stressful. All was good.

This time the knock was more insistent. "Lacie, I want to see you open this door now."

Grams smiled at her then slowly opened the door, facing Flynt.

Her brother stood in the doorway a scowl on his face that changed to perhaps a look of awe before he spoke. "My God, Lacie. I never knew."

~ * ~

Flynt didn't think he'd ever really looked at his littlest sister, at least not closely. No wonder Leslie couldn't wait to hop into bed with her. He couldn't condemn his friend for lusting after such a beautiful woman. Until this moment he'd never thought of Lacie as anything but a little hoyden and his baby sister.

"What are you staring at?" Lacie asked, seeming confused and irritated as well. "We aren't that late."

Flynt swiped his hand across his forehead, still wondering at the site in front of him. "You. I'm staring at you, wondering when you grew up to be such a beautiful young lady. A woman a duke would want to have in his life."

"Me? You've never stared at me before. Indeed, you rarely looked at me," she told him.

"If I had paid any attention to you, I would have kept you tied up in the house until I found a suitable husband for you, because I never would have picked Leslie although he obviously adores you. Lucky for you, your older sisters wore me out. Now, shall we go?" He held out an arm. "Your groom is waiting for you. I for one want to witness the expression on his face when he sees you."

"No, we have to wait for the others to go in front of me or are your own wedding memories so far away you can't recall the sequence of events?" she asked, her voice soft but she was smiling. So, perhaps his insistence was not such a bad thing.

He stepped aside as his wife passed by, kissing him on the cheek. After that, his sisters followed. Laughing and feeling a huge weight lifting off his shoulders, he said. "No, I don't remember much about those moments, just the ones after everyone said their good byes."

"I'm not doing this for you," Lacie told him with a tight voice. "You know that don't you?"

He had to lean in to hear her. "Doesn't matter who you are doing this for or why, but I'm curious. Just who are you doing this for if not me and the rest of the family?"

"For Leslie of course. He's a duke. As both he and Grams explained to me, he needed a real wedding, including proof of such, so his heirs are all legitimate. Someone might contest the marriage. Of course, his sister, Merry, will be here as witness," she told him.

"So, it was Leslie who convinced you. I thought as much but didn't want to say anything to you," Flynt wondered at that. His friend had seemed just as adamant that the first wedding was legal and binding. There was absolutely no need for a second one.

"Yes and no. He told me it was all up to me, but he had a way of making the point for another wedding that he had me convinced."

Lacie plucked at her gown before running her fingers along the necklace.

"You decided in favor. Somehow I'm having a hard time believing..."

Lacie cut him off quickly, motioning with her hand. "It doesn't matter. I just want to get this over with so I can send everyone home, no explanations required," she told him. "I don't want to spend the rest of the evening with anyone except my husband."

They started down the steps. Flynt was shocked at the trembling of his sister's body close to his as well as an unnatural warmth emanating from her. She clung to him while he tried to steady her.

"You are nervous? Is that all this is?" he asked, concerned, as they reached the bottom of the steps. Then, "It will pass."

"I'm a bit tipsy too," she acknowledged.

He laughed, "False courage I see. Don't worry, I won't let you fall but the rest is up to your soon to be husband. You must somehow let him know how you're feeling before the ceremony begins."

"Husband," she said, "He is my husband. I don't need this wedding to have that validated. All we need is to go back to Glasgow and present you with the signed papers."

"You're not thinking of bolting?" he asked, suddenly wary.

"The thought did cross my mind, but no, I committed to this, the second wedding. I will follow through even though technically, I don't need to do that. Don't want to disappoint my husband. I think he's counting on this."

"Soon to be husband," Flynt said as they stopped at the open door.

Chapter Six

Leslie's first sight of Lacie stole his breath and stopped his heart for a brief moment. He was used to seeing her in day dresses or riding habits, her hair in disarray around her face. Hell, half the time she was falling out of her gowns. When he first saw her, the dresses were usually worn thin and barely covering her ankles.

He remembered their first kiss in the MacTavish stables when she was only fifteen. She was beautiful then. He knew he wanted her at that very moment in time, understanding he would have the devil's own trouble, waiting what would seem a lifetime. From the start, her beautiful features haunted him.

Here they were now. She was waiting for Flynt to walk her down the aisle to him. The fact amazed him. She wanted to become his wife but didn't care about his title or the wealth. Lacie wanted him just because, just because... maybe she loved him.

Her hair was swept up, artfully arranged with tendrils of hair delicately framing her face. Even from the distance her eyes sparkled with desire. He remembered how she looked at him when he was deep inside her as well as the soft sounds she made.

He needed to concentrate on something else.

The sisters stood on one side of the minister now, the husbands on the other. As she walked toward him, he held his breath, smiling, with his heart pounding double time. When she saw him, she smiled, too, but he had to admit it looked somewhat forced.

When she and her brother finally reached him, it had seemed a damn long time for the short walk, Flynt handed her over to him. She was shaking now, her face pale. He had not expected her to be this nervous.

He grasped her hands in his, feeling the delicate trembling and the fine sheen of moisture on her ice-cold hands. Trying to give her encouragement, he smiled at her again, realizing she wasn't entirely well.

Fear for her pooled in his gut.

Watching intently as she squeezed her eyes together, he was even more concerned, was about to call this off.

She seemed to read his mind, "No," she whispered, shaking her head. "Just too much champagne. That's all. Hold on to me."

"Is everything fine here?" the minister asked, searching the duke's face, "No second thoughts."

"None," Lacie whispered, staring into his eyes. "I want to marry you again, right now, today."

"None for me either," Leslie said, gently squeezing her hands, concerned for her. She didn't look right. Her face was slightly flushed. "Can you give us the shortest version possible? I think my wife needs to rest. This has all been extremely taxing for her, unexpected as well."

Words were said as well as the vows of obedience and love. Leslie wondered at those promises even while Lacie answered with no reluctance. *Obey*, he mused thoughtfully. Only when she wanted to but he didn't care. He would delight in every challenge she presented him with.

He'd given her a ring the first time they said their vows, now he would give her another one. This one he purchased in Paris at a small store on the Champs Elysees, mulling over all the possibilities and finally settling on this one with a diamond and sapphires surrounding the large stone, not too large because he didn't want it over power her hand.

"Would you like to say something?" the minister asked him. "Any words to your wife?"

Well, he did and he didn't. Prolonging the ceremony might not be wise still, "Yes," he brought her hands to his lips, kissing them slowly while he looked into her eyes.

"Lacie," he began slowly. "I wanted to marry you the first time I kissed you in the MacTavish stables, maybe even before that." He wasn't sure how much he should say here. So much was private between them yet he needed for her to realize how he felt about her. "You were too young. I knew I would have to wait for you to become a woman."

He inhaled a long deep breath, staring at her. "Didn't know how I could do that when every time I saw you, I wanted you more. So, I went to Drake Montgomerie in London, requesting an assignment that would take me away from Scotland. No matter how hard I tried, I couldn't stay away though. I kept coming back to make sure you weren't falling in love with someone else." He inhaled a long deep breath of air. "Not sure what I would have done if that happened."

"You left on purpose?" she asked, sounding surprised.

"I did. Drake sent me to Paris then Bordeaux following a lead."

Without thought, he picked up a tendril of hair, holding it between his fingers. Everything about her enchanted and mesmerized him. She was magic to his soul and changed the hard jaded man he'd once been to someone who looked at the world in a different light. She melted the ice surrounding his jaded heart. "Seemed I waited forever for you. The requests I made however, sent me once again from Glasgow only months before you would turn eighteen. I had no choice but to bind you to me. The only way I could think of was through marriage. I apologize for that. It wasn't well done of me, but now all I want is to make this right for you, your family as well."

"I guessed as much but I was confused as I'm sure you comprehend. I didn't tell anyone about what happened. That we said vows to each other, that evening months ago then you left me."

He laughed then feeling lighter. He couldn't resist the question, "Are you going to obey me?"

"I promise, whenever you are right."

"Do you have anything you want to say?" the minister asked Lacie.

"No, just that I'm very happy you wed me the first time and that you always wanted to do the right things where I was concerned, even the second marriage which somehow you talked me into. Now, I would really like to finish this, because my knees are still shaking so hard I think might fall. I don't feel all that well."

"I will always hold you up," he murmured, kissing the backs of her hands again. "Support you in every way possible." *I love you, Lacie Stewart, with all my heart, is tu mo sholas na greine.*

The minister cleared his throat with what sounded to Leslie as a disapproving gesture. What did he care?

"Perhaps you would like to give your bride a real kiss and proceed to the refreshments which I'm sure your new bride is in dire need of," the minister said.

Leslie looked to the man, chuckling at his words. "Of course. That would certainly be the best way to proceed."

Then, "I pronounce you husband and wife. You may kiss your bride." He leaned back slightly, his bible clasped in front of him, smiling as if he enjoyed this part of the ceremony.

"May I kiss you, wife?" he asked, yet didn't wait for an answer as his lips brushed lightly across hers before shaping pleasantly over the softness he found, his tongue briefly sweeping across her mouth only to draw back. "More will come tonight. Can you wait? Or should I sweep you into my arms and scandalize everyone by carrying you upstairs and into our room."

Breathing heavily when he pulled away, "Yes, to both even though I don't think you can scandalize anyone in this room. My sisters and their husbands have had more scandal in their lives than I would have ever thought possible," she said even while he felt her weight lean against him.

"You're right, so let's give your family a few more minutes of our time before we seek our privacy for the rest of the evening."

"And yours, Merry is also here. Although I will have something to say to her about the events of today and her part in them."

"Indeed, now all you need do is to walk to that sofa and sit down. After that I'll make sure you eat your fill of whatever Justine and my cook have prepared today."

"I'd like that."

"Good." Yet he was suddenly very worried about her again. When he touched his hand to her forehead, she was hot. Now her skin was dry to the touch, parched.

To the applause of their families he led her to the sofa, kissed her again then made sure she was comfortable. "You stay here. I'll return with two plates of food and something to drink as well."

He knew she needed sustenance and hoped this was the only reason she was hot to the touch. Experience was saying otherwise. She would not be sick, he decided, not on their wedding night although they had a very wonderful wedding morning. Under the circumstances and if he'd know what the day would bring, he might have acted differently.

No, he'd waited too many months, nay years to feel his wife beneath him. He would have done nothing differently.

Now, what to do?

He would watch her and wait he decided as he made his way to the dining room table that was now adorned with all kinds of delightful food. Dishing up two plates, trying to put something of everything on each, he made his way back to the parlor where Lacie waited for him.

With new color on her face, he was pleased that perhaps all the worry was just over wedding day jitters. When she looked at him though and he saw her eyes, he changed his mind abruptly.

"How are you doing?" he asked, handing the plate and fork to her.

"Suppose I could say that I'm a bit dizzy for you." She ate a small bite of baked salmon but still seemed disinterested in the food.

"Dizzy for me? If it's the truth and you're not dizzy because of the champagne, I'm pleased."

He continued to watch her while he ate then realized the sun was nearing the horizon and of course everyone was still here.

"Dizzy for you." She closed her eyes swaying slightly. "Is everyone staying the night? Do you have enough rooms for all of my family and Merry as well?"

"I'm sure we'll find a private room for every couple. You need not worry. With any luck, we fill this home with children." He kissed her forehead hoping to discover a cooler temperature, but to no avail.

"You want that many?" she gasped. "I don't know anything about children. I'm the youngest." It seemed she was reminding him. "I've stayed away from Chelsea's and Bliss' children. Didn't want to have to change any diapers."

He laughed softly, moving damp strands of hair from her face to place them tenderly behind her ears. "We will figure it all out. You have Grams and your sisters to give you advice," then he leaned closer, whispering in her ear. "After this morning, my child might even now be growing in your womb. Would you like that?"

He watched her touch her belly then looked at him, her eyes wide. "You might be right, I suppose. I don't know much about those things."

"Not something to think about now though," he told her, realizing he would be well pleased if that was true but he would also take delight in working on making a baby.

"What should we think about?" she asked him.

"Eating."

"I'm not hungry. That bite of salmon seems to be sitting like a lump of lead in my stomach." She played with the food and sipped a small amount of wine. "It's sweet."

"A sauterne from my family's winery in the Bordeaux valley. Promise me that for every sip you eat two bites of food."

She nodded at him, "How long do we have to stay here. I'm really quite tired," she paused, "And I'm chilled, shivers seem to envelope me every few seconds. I don't feel well, Leslie." Her voice was weak and the few words she uttered were strained.

"I will have Justine take food and drink upstairs. If we cut the cake, we will have done all the obligatory things."

He left to organize the next few minutes, realizing the best for Lacie was to get her upstairs and into bed.

Daryl sat down in his place. "How do you feel now? The things he said they were so nice. He loves you, you realize. Do you love him?"

"I never knew he felt the way he did. What he said was very nice," she smiled, "and as to how I feel, not well."

"You should excuse yourself and go upstairs to rest. I'm sure it's just exhaustion and nerves that you're responding to. You will be much better in the morning."

"Leslie says we have to cut the cake before we can leave, but I'm not sure I can stand up for that long," she sighed heavily, closing her eyes. "Perhaps if he holds me around the waist."

"You're that tired?" Daryl asked, looking to the dining room and meeting Leslie's hard gaze.

He was in front of them in seconds. "What is going on here?"

"Lacie is more tired than she should be. You need to make sure you get her upstairs soon. She needs to rest," Daryl said.

"I noticed the same thing. Justine is bringing in the cake as we speak." Leslie said focusing on the other room.

Flynt was suddenly beside him, slapping him on the back, "Welcome to the family. It's about time you're finally married. You are the last of the bad boys to tie the knot."

"Thank you and welcome to mine. I'm glad we're friends but friends trust each other's words." He was still put off by Flynt and his overzealous need to orchestrate this wedding.

"Of course I believed you. You're a man of your word and you would have never made up a story such as that one."

"Then why..."

"For the very reasons I'm assuming you told my little sister. You're a duke and no one should question the validity of your marriage to Lacie. We both know you have enemies. Your years of work as a spy have assured that. My sister needed to be protected from anyone who intended to question this marriage. If I hadn't interfered, I'm sure you would have come to your sense as soon as a she carried your child."

Leslie understood the truth of Flynt's words all too well. He ran his hands through his thick dark hair. "Lacie is sick. We are going to cut the cake then retire for the night, at least Lacie is going to retire. As soon as I'm sure she is sleeping peacefully and no longer at risk, I'll return. If I don't, I trust all of your entourage can find sleeping quarters in the west wing."

"Lacie is sick? I thought it was just the champagne or the nerves," Flynt said.

"No, it's more than that. I hoped to come to the same conclusion that it was just exhaustion from the last day and a half, but I believe she is truly ill," Leslie looked to his wife.

"Why would she be sick?"

"We spent some time yesterday playing in the snow." As soon as he said the words and watched Flynt raise an eyebrow, he knew how ludicrous his words would sound to anyone who knew him.

"You, Leslie Stewart, Duke of Southcliff played in the snow? I suppose you made snow angels too." Flynt let out a roar of laughter. "That is something I would have loved to see."

"Well, you won't ever. Snow angels as well as playing, is between Lacie and me." He cleared his throat searching for Lacie, relieved she remained on the sofa, remembering also the snow he put down her back and front as well in retaliation to the wet white missals she flung at him.

"No, I suppose I won't see it. You would never let down your guard when anyone else is present. However, it delights me to understand how much you love my sister. You are not as stuffy as you let on."

Yes, I do love her and should tell her sometime soon.

"Needless to say, she was soaked through to the skin." Instead of getting her warm and seeing to here needs I seduced her, tried to convince her to make love to me. A wave of guilt washed over him. It was not well done of him. He made a mental note to never do anything like it again. He certainly didn't want to risk her health.

"I think I understand a little too well. Go, do what you need to do with Lacie and we'll all see ourselves to our rooms for the night. I'm sure Justine and Emilia will help our wives with the accommodations."

Without further comment, Leslie strode quickly to Lacie. "The cake is ready then I'm going to get you into bed... by yourself." He had not envisioned Lacie sleeping alone this night.

She nodded her agreement. He helped her to stand, surprised by her unexpected weakness. Keeping a hand around her waist he led her to the dining room table. Fear rushed through him.

"Our happy bride and groom are about to cut the cake. Then they will retire." Flynt motioned for everyone to gather around. "Make sure everyone has a glass of Champagne."

The glasses were poured and Leslie held the cake knife in one hand while Lacie placed hers over his. He smiled at her. A wave of terror tumbled through him when he looked into her vacant, glazed over eyes.

As if she read his mind, "I can do this."

"Are you sure?"

"Now, yes."

Quickly they cut a piece and set in on a plate. He fed her a bite, taking care to get only a small amount of icing on her lips. Then she did the same.

Brushing his lips against hers, he tasted the sweet confection. He heard her moan, felt the weight of her slide through his arms.

"Lacie!" He swept her into his arms, heading for the master chamber.

~ * ~

She recalled Leslie scooping her into his arms before he set her on the bed in their room. Remembering also, that he undressed her before putting her in her nightgown.

A vague recollection of eating cake came to her then it vanished. She sighed, rolling over on the bed, reaching for him, finding nothing, only air and another pillow. Everything seemed foggy a mist in her mind.

More time seemed to pass as she heard Leslie sit down beside the bed, place her hand in his. Lacie tried to open her eyes. She somehow understood he was worried about her. She needed to reassure him but when she attempted to speak her lips were dry, didn't want to move. She tried to moisten them but there was no moisture.

"It's time you woke up, Lacie. I need to see the sparkle of your eyes, hear you tell me how I should learn to play and relax. There is more snow today. When you get better, we can make snow angels together. You must throw off this silly sickness that has you wallowing around in the bed. You must wake up. I'll remain stodgy for the rest of my life if you don't obey me now."

She did try to do as he commanded, after all, she told him she would when he was right, now he was right. Opening her eyes would be the prudent and acceptable thing to do. Yet she didn't want to leave her dream world right now. She knew she would hurt if she did.

"Open your eyes, my sunshine, is *tu mo sholas na greine*," he murmured so close to her she thought she might have felt his breath tickle her cheek.

If she only could do what he asked.

Finally, and with great uncertainty, Lacie opened an eye, stared with blurry vision at the large man sitting in a chair beside the bed. The swallow she tried for didn't happen. She needed water, tried to tell him so with her eyes. While she spoke the words in her mind no sound came from her.

"You've slept the night away," he told her a, hesitant smile on his handsome face. "Our wedding night. You know you will have to find a way to make it up to me. I would that you could watch the snowflakes fall with me."

She needed to remind him he had a wedding morning and that should be sufficient for the time being but groaned instead. Just as she anticipated, the pain seemed to come at her full force now that she opened her eyes.

"Are the others gone?" Her voice came out a croak, hoarse and raw. Lacie blinked to clear her vision. The gesture didn't work. A shaft of pain over her eyes nearly knocked her senseless.

"Not everyone." He stroked the back of her hand with his thumb.

"Oh, my," she moaned and moved restlessly against her pillow. "I'm ill," she told Leslie, wishing he could do something for her. "You shouldn't come any closer. Don't want you to get sick also."

Leslie wasn't paying any attention to her, his large hand rested gently against her cheek. "You're very hot, Lacie. It was not well done of you to drench yourself making snow angels as well as that snowball fight you tried to draw me into. No, it is you who will have to make it up to me."

A fever. How had that come to pass? That was all she needed to go with the pain in her head. She had to get up and start learning how to be a duchess. Lying in bed was not the way to begin her new life as the duke's wife.

She tried to push herself from the mattress, she really did but she couldn't make it. She was just too weak and exhausted from doing nothing. Every muscle, every fiber and every bone and sinew ached horribly.

Worry in Leslie's voice caught her attention. "You must rest. Flynt has gone for the doctor. The snow held him up but he will be here soon. You must lie still. Grams will also come up here to see what she can do for you. I have to leave for a few minutes just to make sure everything is going as planned. I've some correspondence then I promise you, I won't leave your side."

Grams did come to see her some ten minutes later, worry lines on her forehead. "You're not feeling any better? You should be recovering by now. You're a MacTavish and strong, a fighter."

Lacie managed to open her eyes a second time. "No, don't seem to be able to do much except breathe and ache in every imaginable place then wish I could go to sleep so I can wake up feeling like a normal person."

"You sound horrible. Drink this, it's honey and milk. It will coat your throat, make you feel better. I'll tell Leslie you're doing better. He's beside himself with worry, blames himself he does. Thinks he made you sick."

"He shouldn't blame himself. May I have some water, please?" Good lord, but she sounded just like a frog.

"The carafe is by the bedside. I'll make sure there is a full glass when I leave," Lacie watched as Grams poured her a glass then held it to her lips so she could drink."

"I'll fetch Leslie, He'll want to talk to you now that you're awake again," Grams smiled. "I'll wager though by the time he gets here you'll be fast asleep. I put some laudanum in the water. The medicine will ease the pain in your head as well as help you to sleep."

Most likely, Lacie thought. She never got sick, didn't understand how any of this could happen to her. Even with the water, her throat was so sore it hurt to breathe. Finally, she fell into an uneasy sleep, dreams bombarding her from every direction.

When she awoke, Daryl was standing beside her bed. She'd hoped Leslie would be there, but no, he told her he had work.

"Leslie sent me to keep you company, also to make sure you are going to get well," Daryl said.

"Water, please." She wondered what her sister was doing here and where was the doctor? She was told would come soon. Daryl should be home with her husband, not ensconced with a sick person.

"Of course," Daryl turned and poured her a glass, sitting on the chair beside the bed where Leslie usually sat.

"Drink slowly, now," she said, her voice soft, concerned. "You really don't look well at all. It's passing strange because of all of us, you are the one who never gets sick. Don't think you've been ill a single day in your life. Goodness, but your face is too pale. Leslie is beside himself with worry. You need to get better for him, you know."

"Is he sleeping?" she asked, needing to know if he was taking care of himself through all of this. "He needs rest too."

"No," Daryl said. "Last night he sat by your bed the entire night. Don't suppose he slept much if at all. Now he's working. That's why he sent me to stay by your side."

"You have to tell him he needs to sleep." The world seemed to move in slow motion while she had the distinct impression she was repeating herself and Daryl was being very patient with her.

"Need to change your nightgown, it's all sweaty. No, you don't look well. Just don't understand any of this. It came on you so quickly." Daryl left the bedside and Lacie heard her rummaging around in the adjoining room. "Here we go. Now I'll help you sit up."

Somehow, Daryl managed to change the nightdress, not from any help from her though.

Lacie didn't care what she looked like. While the dry nightdress actually felt good, all she wanted was the water Daryl gave her. She drank and drank. When she didn't want any more, she lay back, panting with the effort it had cost her.

"I can't even sit up without help, Daryl."

"It's because of the sickness. You'll get better soon and be back to your normal self."

Lacie didn't know about any of that. She wasn't getting stronger. She felt as if Daryl kept saying the same things over and over. "Has Flynt come back with the physician?"

"He probably got held up by the snowstorm, but it hasn't been snowing for a while. I'm sure he managed to leave a few hours ago. Hopefully Flynt will have the doctor in tow before nightfall. All depends on the weather."

"Alright then, where is Grams?" she asked, wishing for the best but feeling alone even with Daryl sitting by her bed. "Won't she know what to do?"

"I'll fetch her and Leslie as well. They will want to know that you are awake. I will get you some more water." With that said, she left.

Leslie came in first, at least that is what she thought. She'd fallen asleep again, so exhausted she'd been unable to keep her eyes open even though she tried. His head was resting on his forearms, which were beside her on the bed. She was hot and sweaty again, thinking she'd never felt so miserable.

When she moved, she must have woken him. He looked at her through sleep-deprived eyes. Then he touched her forehead, jerking his hand back. "You're burning with fever." He rang the bell cord then returned to her bedside. "Got to get you cooled down."

He dipped a cloth in the basin of water near the bed, setting it on her forehead. "That feels good," she murmured. "Thirsty. Always parched. Need water."

Leslie held her head in the crook of his elbow, putting the edge of the glass to her lips. She was so weak her head lolled against his arm.

"You're going to come out of this just fine. Wait and see, in a few days we will be outside playing in the snow. Would you like to go for a ride on your horse?" Yet even when Leslie spoke of playing and riding, Lacie heard the hint of fear in his voice.

She didn't want him to be afraid for her. "I hope so, Leslie, and I'm glad you are here. The cloth truly felt wonderful, but I think it is as hot as my head now. Don't believe it's going to help any longer."

He chuckled slightly, dipping the cloth in the water, once more placing it on her head. He found another cloth and when it was wet and cool, he pulled her nightgown around her shoulders so he could bathe her body. She shivered at the first touch of the cloth against her heated skin.

"No need to protest, I've seen all of you and will again. Just going to cool the rest of you off. Catherine told me what to do when you are hot as well as when you are freezing. I will climb in beside you to keep you warm, give you all the blankets there are."

"I feel much better now that you're here. The cloth is divine. No, I won't complain about you seeing me, Leslie. You're my husband. It's your right." Inside she smiled, thinking Leslie wouldn't see the tiny gesture because she didn't have the strength to move her lips.

Still though, she was incredibly tired, so very weary that she just wanted to sleep and sleep, perhaps forever. She moaned softly, the sound of her voice odd to her, far away actually, as if that rumbling noise came from someone else.

She didn't understand.

Tired so very tired. How could that be? She heard a man's voice, echoing in her head as if it came from a great distance and wondered if it was her voice she was hearing and if it was why she was speaking. Had she fallen asleep again? The voice didn't sound like Leslie's because it was muted somehow, but she thought it should be her husband. She didn't want anyone else but Leslie looking at her, touching her.

Yes, it had to be Leslie. His voice was strong, deep, impatient, and commanding, surely Leslie's voice. Her husband wasn't pleased about something and she wanted to please him. She'd heard that tone of voice enough times in her life from her brother to hear the anger.

It wasn't Flynt. It couldn't be. He'd left to fetch the doctor. Held up by the snow. So, it had to be Leslie even though it sounded like him but certainly, just so far away.

Now the man, her husband she was sure but wasn't, was speaking more closely to her, next to her ear, but she couldn't understand his words. They weren't important, surely not. She heard another man speaking as well, but his voice was old, softer, blurring at the edges of her mind, not intruding, bumping gently against her consciousness.

The hard man's voice was retreating at last. The need to understand everything vanished with it. Soon she would be free of all the voices as well as the blinding confusion and the need to please. All the voices were gone now. Her head lolled to the side, her mind eased. She felt her breath slow and slow some more. She was floating in a mindless fog. She could see her body, stretched out on the bed, Leslie beside her, his expression strained.

"Blessed hell, wake up! I'm not going to tell you again, Lacie, wake up! You're not going to give up. I'm not going to lose you. I won't let you stop trying to live. Granted, you got worse over the last few hours. Now, that nonsense is over with. You're going to get better. This has gone on long enough, too long, truth be told. You promised to obey me."

The shouting brought her back with a lurch of pain. Flynt shouted like that but she knew it wasn't her brother. No, he was at home or still trying to bring the doctor here. She felt as if she was teetering on a cliff and could not gain her footing. Drawn to something seductive, but also wary of it. No, it was Leslie. She just saw him sitting by the bed.

Leslie's voice echoed close to her again. It was a loud, horribly grating sound that made her head pound and ache with ferocity. She hated the sound. She wanted to scream at him to be quiet, give her a moment's peace, needed to go back to sleep.

She stepped back from the edge, so angry at the interference that she even opened her eyes, wanting to protest, to yell at him for intruding on her. She opened her mouth but didn't make a sound. She was looking up at the most beautiful man she'd ever seen in her life and she knew him. It was her husband but then she thought he had left her again so it couldn't be him. He was off on some mission.

Her mind absorbed his image, his black hair and incredible dark brown eyes, that cleft in his chin. She managed to say in a raw whisper, "You are so beautiful." She closed her eyes again because she knew he must be an angel and she was here in heaven. She wasn't alone anymore, and for that she was grateful

"Damn you, open your eyes again. I'm not beautiful. Blessed hell, I haven't even shaved."

"An angel doesn't swear," she said clearly then once again forced her eyes open just so she could look at him.

"I'm not an angel. I'm your husband. Wake up, Lacie. Do it now! I won't have another moment of you scaring everyone to death. Come back to me. Do it this second or I might never forgive you."

"Husband?" she repeated slowly. "Yes, you're right. I'll obey this time. I must come back. You are right in this. You need an heir. I haven't given you one yet."

"Do it now. I've waited too long. I'm not going to let you give up. Do you understand?" His voice was still a harsh command.

She wanted to tell him if he would speak to her nicely, she would do as he asked. "Yes, I do agree. You are right this time so I will obey." She felt as if she was repeating herself, but the man staring down at her didn't seem to care because he was grinning foolishly.

"Good. Now I'm going to pick you up, hold you upright. I want you to drink the water."

"All right?" She thought she could do that with his help.

She managed a nod. She felt a strong arm beneath her back. Felt the cold glass touch her lips. She drank and drank and the water was ambrosia to her parched throat. It ran down her chin, soaking into her nightgown. She was so very thirsty nothing mattered but the sweet water trickling down her throat.

"There, enough for now. Listen to me. I'm going to bathe you, get that fever down. The washcloth was not enough, didn't do the job. Think I need to douse you in a tub. Do you understand me? Your fever's too high. I've got to get it where it belongs or things won't go as I've planned. You won't sleep again. Do you understand me? Tell me you understand."

She did then his words vanished. Her brain tripped off into another direction unable to focus for very long. The words he wanted to hear vanished from all her thoughts.

Lacie moaned again because she wasn't sure she could do everything he was asking. She just wanted to go back to sleep, float around in that surreal world he pulled her from. Taking a bath wasn't something she wanted to do. She surely didn't understand how she could accomplish such a thing because she couldn't even sit up. She'd most likely drown if she tried to sit in a tub.

"The doctor came, told me the cloths were not enough. Your fever is too high. He's gone now and your fever is worse, just like he said. I'm not going to leave your side or sleep until you are ready to go outside and play in the snow with me. You do want to make snow angels with me, don't you? That can't happen unless you get well."

He pulled her to a sitting position, stripping her of her nightdress. His arms encircled her. She was floating in his arms.

She felt the cool air touch her skin. She vaguely realized he took off the sweaty nightgown she wore. She was thankful for it, for quite suddenly she felt the itchiness of her skin.

"I'm going to put you in the water, but I'm going to stay with you. Don't trust you not to fall asleep and slip beneath the water. Don't know if you have the strength to sit in this by yourself."

She realized then that he wore no clothing. She felt his solid chest against her. The sensation was delicious, intoxicating. She knew then she would not go to sleep, not if he was naked beside her. Since she appreciated him this way, she knew she must be improving.

She felt the tepid water wash over her, his chest against her back, holding her still, but the coolness didn't go deep enough. She was still so very hot, deeper inside. The wonderful touch of the water didn't reach far enough. She tried to arch her back to bring the amazing feelings into her.

She felt Leslie's hands around her, holding on to her. He was saying quietly now, that beautiful man, "Hush, I know you burn. I've had a very bad fever before. I understand what you are going through. I felt as if I was in flames on the inside, where nothing could reach, and I was burning from the inside out. Be patient. It will be over soon."

"Yes," she said, understanding the truth he spoke.

"We will stay in here until the burning vanishes. I promise I won't abandon you."

"Leslie," she said, as she opened her eyes, turning her head so she could see him and smiled. "You're not an angel. You're my husband. I'm so glad you're here."

"Yes," he said, "I won't leave you again."

It seemed then she must make him understand. She tried to lift her hand to touch his face, to gain his attention. Her voice was hurtling from her throat, the words trembling. "You can't stay here. You have to leave. Don't want you to get sick too."

"I won't get sick."

She closed her eyes again while the water continued to encompass her, soothing her body. He continued holding her. She felt more water as it was added to the tub. It was cooler than the bucket of water that was taken out. She supposed her body heated it. She didn't know though. All she was doing was guessing about things.

Then she heard his voice and he was praying.

"Please, God, please let her be all right," he said aloud in the silent bedchamber.

He covered the tub with a bath sheet when he heard the chamber door open.

"My lord?"

She didn't recognize the voice. It wasn't Flynt or one of the husbands she supposed. Who else would come here? The doctor maybe, she couldn't remember anything.

"Her fever is down. I did what you said. Thank you for not leaving."

"It will rise again doubtless, but you will handle it, I'm sure as you do everything else."

"Catherine went home as did all the rest of the family," Leslie said, "It was for the best. There was nothing they could do here. I will put my wife in a nightgown then stay with her the rest of the night. Thank you for everything. Will you remain here at Southcliff?"

"Yes, my lord. If she will survive, we'll know by tomorrow morning."

"She will survive. She's tough. You will see, besides she has a powerful incentive she's said she's has to get well so she can teach me how to play."

He laughed.

~ * ~

General Denis Caron paced the small room he rented in Glasgow. Trying to be inconspicuous he leased a place in a seamier side of town. The braided rug he strode around took up most of the room and was probably its best feature even though it was worn and ragged around the edges.

He gazed out the window on the dreary January day. Snow fell but the worst of the storm seemed to have passed. A hazy sun tried to poke its head through the dense clouds.

He had a score to settle with Leslie Stewart, Duke of Southcliff and spy. When he discovered both Caroline and the little girl were missing, all the evidence pointed to Lord Stewart. Denis had expected some sort of subterfuge, but not that. He'd offered Caro to him on a silver platter and what did he do? Lord Stewart ran off with her, sent her to Montgomerie, putting her in protective custody where he couldn't reach her. Caroline was not accessible for him, but perhaps he could find another woman to take her place.

Well, he would find a way to grab his revenge. Stewart would pay. While the duke was distracted, he planned on stealing his wife. Stopping at the kitchen table he slugged down a half pint of Guinness, but he needed food and a woman.

Damn the snow, the frigid weather was getting in his way. The cold tore through him all the way to his bones. He slipped on his warmest coat before heading for the door. He needed something to warm his belly and satisfy his other manly needs. Heading out the door then down Queen Street he looked for a pub.

Damn the foul weather. He needed sunshine and warmth. Southern France was much more amenable this time of year than this ungodly place.

"Want some company?" A young woman stepped up to him, latching on to his arm. "I'm more than willing."

"Wouldn't mind some," Denis said his smile wide. "Company." He could do worse and he meant to come to the point. "Anything else you want to give besides companionship?"

"I'd give just about anything you asked for if you'd buy me dinner," she held herself slightly aloof.

"Anything?" He stroked her cheek and chuckled when she jerked away.

"I'm willing, are you?" She looked at him with wide blue-gray eyes. Eyes that might shimmer with desire if he coaxed the passion from her and he meant to do just that.

"Not a practiced whore, are you?"

Denis was delighted with this new prospect for the evening. Perhaps a longer relationship would be in order. This girl seemed to be a delicious morsel that appeared just for him. Well, if he had to bide his time in this god forsaken city, he might as well spend it in bed with this delightful lady and see what she could give him in payment of meals.

He knew what he could teach her and he would reap all the benefits.

She inhaled a huge breath of air. He watched the tempting curve of her partially concealed breasts rise then fall. "Need to eat. The lady with the leftover bread hasn't been around for several days. I'm hungry and this is all I know."

"Leftover bread, that's intriguing. Tell me about her," Denis encouraged as they headed into a small pub. After dinner he would take her home with him, perhaps keep her through the night or longer if she satisfied him.

"No, the bakery has been closed for several days now so no deliveries. The ladies come around and give out bread and muffins and whatever else they didn't sell."

"I see," he said but he'd never heard of anything so bazar. "A bakery? Who owns it?"

"Yes, her name is Daryl that's all I know."

They sat down. He ordered bangers and mash for both then a pint of Guinness.

He sat back, hands folded in his lap, watching her. She'd taken off her coat. The gown she wore had seen better days. It was cut low but he guessed that wasn't the intention. He wondered if she carried the pox and if after all this, he dared bed her.

She was very young, seemingly new to this game she was trying to play, naïve also so perhaps she was clean.

"How old are you?" Not that age made any difference to him. The younger she was the more malleable she would be. More thoughts on how he could use this chance meeting to his advantage. If she suited him and she didn't have the pox, he would take her with him when he went back to Sant-Emilion. There were men there who would pay him nicely for her use.

Her mouth stuffed with mashed potatoes, she stared at him her eyes wide. For a moment she looked away, her voice quivering despite her apparent determination to carry out her promise. "Does it matter? I keep my word."

"Just curious." Casually he sipped the ale, studying her. Her manners needed a bit of refining if he was going to use her for other purposes. The men he planned to give her to would not want someone who stuffed food into her mouth. Ah, but she was hungry.

"I can do anything you want," she told him, repeating herself through mouthfuls of food. "All you have to do is tell me."

"How many men have you had?" He asked her wondering if she would lie. Of course he didn't know the truth but after tonight he would know if she was a virgin.

Eyes wide, she stared at him. "I don't know." Then shrugging, "A lot I suppose. Does it matter?"

"You don't know how many or you don't know what I want to hear." He smiled wide, more sure than ever he would bed a virgin tonight. Ah, but he remembered his first virgin. He did like untried ladies the best.

She swallowed the food, wiping her lips with the napkin then she was shaking her head. "I don't know how many." She seemed angry now and stood. "If it matters, I'll just take my leave now."

Reaching out a hand to her, he tugged on her arm until she sat down. "No, you don't. We made a bargain."

She inhaled a shaky breath, "Just don't appreciate the questions. None of your business you know."

"If I'm going to bed you, I need to know. Makes a difference to me, you see."

"No, don't see at all."

He leaned forward, resting his elbows on the table. "Ten? Fifteen? A hundred? Maybe more."

"More than ten." Her voice shook with the lie she told. "Yes, more than ten but I don't keep a tally."

He could see the truth in her eyes. When he sat down next to her and ran his hand up her leg, she jumped. He inched it higher then leaning closer, "You said you'd do anything I want. Right now, I want you to open up your pretty little legs for me so I can touch your beautiful lady parts."

"Are you sure that's proper?"

As he moved his hand higher, he was able to push his hand closer.

"Everything and anything is proper here. No one is watching so we can do whatever we want. That's why we sat down in a dark corner. I wanted privacy before I took you home with me. Do you like this?" He touched her, felt her heat and the softness of her folds. She was not moist not ready for him. He would have to make sure she felt only her virgin's pain this first time. After that, he would make sure she was ready for any man. He would teach her everything she would need to know.

"Not really." Her voice wobbled but he knew in time she would understand the right answer.

"When a man is seducing you, it doesn't please him unless you tell him how much you like what he is doing."

She ran her pink tongue across her slightly parted lips but didn't answer, only drew in a very long deep breath.

"Do you like this?" he asked again.

"Yes."

He heard no sincerity in her answer only fear. Her eyes were wide with the terror she was feeling.

"You will have to learn to do better. Do you like this?" he stroked her again.

She swallowed, her eyes seeming to cross, "I said, yes. That's the best I can do."

"Suppose that will have to do until you learn more. Good, finish up then I'll take you somewhere we can be a bit more intimate. You can please me further. Do you have a name?"

"What's yours?" she asked.

He laughed then and smiled. He was going to enjoy her very much. "Denis Caron."

"Oh, I'm Torra."

Chapter Seven

"Rise and shine, my sweet sunshine, it's time for your bath then I'll take you downstairs for some new scenery. I'm sure you're tired of the bedroom." Leslie was in an amazing mood now that his wife was on the mend.

For days he'd been terrified, even though the physician told him if she was alive the next morning, and she was, she would survive. It had taken two more days before she didn't need help getting out of the bed to relieve herself.

She sat up smiling, her eyes once more sparkling with life. "I'd like that. Do you think I'll be able to walk all the way to the first floor?"

"Most likely not but I will enjoy carrying you."

He would do anything for Lacie. She was his heart and soul, his sunshine.

He adored her. Decided the first opportunity to present itself he would tell her how much he loved her. The illness she just endured terrified him, frightened him into the knowledge he couldn't live without her. She was indeed his duchess.

He chose well.

Yesterday, he sent instructions to the dressmaker for three new gowns. There was a ball the earl of March was giving. A coming out party for his oldest daughter. He'd been invited when he was single. At the time, he did not plan on attending, having no taste for such things. Yesterday, he also sent an acceptance to the earl for both he and his wife, knowing full well the earl would not be pleased to hear of his marriage.

He wanted to show his new duchess off.

The man's oldest daughter was a silly twit. They wouldn't suit, although she was very beautiful. The daughter was enamored of his title and wealth, not him. Well she would have to find another eligible bachelor to ensnare, someone who could deal with a woman who thought only of herself.

"Can we sit in the sunshine? I have a burning need to feel its warmth on my cheeks." She swung her legs over the bed, groaning at the effort it took to move even that tiny bit. "I still need to dress. I'm tired just trying to leave the bed. When will this ever end?"

"Soon, I assure you."

"I'll hold you to that promise."

"There is a place inside, a window seat that gets the afternoon sun. I think you will enjoy it there. Now wrap your arm around my waist and I'll help you to the bath."

"I suppose you plan on helping me out of my nightgown too." She looked into his eyes. He hoped she saw the desire emanating from them even though it would be a few more days before he dared to make love to his wife.

"With great pleasure, I'll attend to your every need, wash your back as well as your front. I'd like to fondle your beautiful bubbies, but I'll save that for another time." He laughed at the expression on her face. "You know how much I adore your large white breasts as well as your splendid pink nipples."

She touched his face. "I've missed you and it was only one morning. That seems a lifetime ago."

They stopped in front of the tub filled with steaming water. She obligingly lifted her arms as he swept the gown over her head. He stepped back to admire her. She had lost weight and he made a mental note to make sure she ate well.

"Your health comes first. Now take my arm. I will make sure you get into that water without taking a tumble or slipping."

She did and with his aid she soon felt the hot warmth surrounding her. "The water feels delicious. Was it a dream?"

"What?"

"When I was burning up with fever, did you get in the tub with me, hold me in your arms? It seems real yet a dream also." She picked up the sponge along with the lavender soap.

"No dream." He walked into the adjoining room to retrieve clothing for her. "I had to get in with you because I didn't think you had the strength to sit up. The wash cloth didn't bring your temperature down, and I was frantic with worry."

"I thought you were an angel," she murmured, smiling at him as she watched him reappear.

"You told me that I had to go away because you needed to protect me," he laughed then set the clothing on the bed before walking to her. "Your words were amusing at the time but now... I don't know what or who you would have to protect me from."

"I know you have enemies."

"Most are in France. I sincerely doubt if anyone would venture this far north." Yet he thought about the General who was known to seek revenge when bested. He would have to make sure one of his men was always nearby.

He watched her shrug, observed the tiny ripples of the bath water and remembered the fear from those days. He didn't frighten easily, had spent most of his adult life challenging danger. Her illness brought him to his knees, teaching him just how fragile life could be.

"I needed to protect you from something?" she asked, seeming clearly puzzled by his statement. "I had a lot of dreams. Do you think it was a premonition of some sort?"

He sat down on a chair close to the tub, still watching her, nevertheless afraid for her even though she was well, her coloring back to normal. "You ready to get out?" he asked then, "I don't take much stock in premonitions or dreams. They aren't real. They're not based on fact. If one is to believe every dream, we might all wallow in imaginary terror."

"You're a skeptic then. Why am I not surprised?" She paused for a fraction of time. "I don't' suppose I believe in them either. I do remember I kept seeing the man who attacked me. He was sneering at me. I was afraid then, but not for me, for you. After that, I saw you fall from your horse." She shuddered, rubbing her hands along her arms. "It's time to get out. A chill seems to be invading me. I want to feel the sunshine on my body, the warmth of the sun even though there is not much of it today."

He assisted her and when he was finished helping her dress, he cradled her gently and carried her down the steps to the window seat. "Cook has made a pot of tea. Your grams sent over ginger cookies. You should have a snack now before dinner."

"There's still snow on the ground," she said with amazement in her voice before she turned to him. "You, we..."

"Don't go there, not right now. I understand my promise but you cannot get cold and wet. I won't allow you to sicken again."

At that look in her eyes his heart was beating out of control. His words were not enough to dissuade her from her thoughts, but he took solace in the fact she wouldn't be able to walk that far by herself. He wasn't about to put her in harm's way.

She smiled. It was the smile he knew he couldn't resist. He was doomed for the rest of his life.

"It might not be prudent for me to go outside, but you can go out on the lawn and make a snow angel for me. Right there," she guided him to a spot she could see from her sunny perch. "I want to watch you play for me. I want to see you grin wide and forget all your dukely duties."

His breath caught in the back of his throat. He had not expected this today. Yet what harm would it do? This could be the last snowfall for the season. Making a snow angel was the last thing he wanted for himself, but for Lacie he was pretty sure he would do just about anything.

"Alright, as long as I have your promise to stay right here in this seat until I come back inside. Not sure if I'll ever make another one even if you give me that smile I'm finding devilishly hard to refuse." He couldn't resist and kissed her lightly on the forehead.

She looked confused for a second before she grinned again, "You say you can't refuse my smile? I'll have to remember that. I might be able to use it to my advantage some time."

He roared with laughter. It was the first time in so many days he could remember laughing. "Oh, here are the tea and cookies. Don't look away because this might very well be the one and only time I make an angel in the snow." He kissed her on the forehead again unable to resist her before stepping outside.

He found the spot she'd pointed to and waved then directing her attention to the ground, he looked up for confirmation. This was the spot. He knew he wore a silly grin on his face, but he was delighted with his wife. She nodded, beaming still. He was sure he could see her laughing.

She mouthed some words which he was sure were, *I'm waiting.*

Pointing to her then the ground again, he waited for another nod and a smile. When she did as he was silently asking, he dropped to the ground and waved his arms and legs across the snow. Then he was up striding inside, ready to give her a quick hug.

He dried and warmed his hands before coming to her. "Was that what you wanted to see? My humiliation?" he asked, sitting down beside her before placing her hand inside his. She was soft and warm, fragile. He would make sure no harm ever came to her. "Don't believe I've ever done such a ridiculous thing."

She was in his arms. Despite his best intentions, he needed to kiss her, needed it for days on end now. His finger beneath her chin, he slowly lifted it so she looked into his eyes. Hers were so dark and brilliantly blue, hungry now with passion for him.

She blinked as he lowered his mouth to her lips, her luscious breasts pushing against his chest. Her mouth was softer than he remembered as he touched her lips lightly with his finger then ran his tongue across them, exploring as he delved deeper, once more learning the promise of her passion and desire.

He put the tiniest distance between them, "You taste damn good, *is tu mo sholas na greine.*"

He so needed to take this kiss further but he didn't dare, not right now, perhaps tonight. She was growing stronger with each passing second. Pulling back further, he touched her nose with his fingertip. "How are you feeling?"

"Like you just put a stop to something I didn't want to end. My heart is pounding so hard it seems I can't slow it down."

She leaned into him, closing her eyes as he stroked her before sliding his fingers down her back, wishing ending the kiss had not been the prudent and wise thing to do for the moment.

He held her, loving the way she felt nestled against him. Feeling the coward, he didn't want to bring up the ball. Perhaps he could put it off until tomorrow when the dressmaker brought the new dresses to the house.

"Hello, anyone home?" Merry waltzed into the room as if her presence was expected. "Thought I would pay you all a visit and see how Lacie was doing. Looks as if she is recovering nicely," she paused, her eyes seeming to cross, "Did I interrupt something?"

Leslie groaned. He supposed his short time alone with his healing wife was now at an end. Privacy was always just around the next moment but rarely theirs.

"What do want, brat?" he asked, refusing to let go of Lacie even for decorum's sake.

Merry was invading his and his wife's space, their privacy. She better have a damn good reason. Something better than she wanted to see how Lacie was doing.

"She has a good reason. It was me who encouraged her to come here," Westcott said as he set a valise on the floor.

"Wanted to visit and see if Lacie was up for a ride. I know she would like to try out the new mare, the one you bought her for her birthday," Merry set her hat and coat on the hanger by the door before finding a chair in the parlor and sitting down.

Westcott rocked on his heels in the doorway, his hands behind his back, waiting for further instruction.

"Brat, of course she isn't ready for a ride. It's her first time out of bed. I had to carry her downstairs," he paused angry with Merry for telling Lacie about the gift. He'd not had the chance. "I bought you a new horse. Was going to show her to you as soon as you were ready."

"A horse?"

"Yes and no you can't see the mare today. I'll take you first thing in the morning."

"Thank you, as to when I am ready to ride, I can speak for myself," Lacie said, clearly displeased with him. "No, I might fall off if I tried to ride so let's put this off for at least another day. Why are you really here, Merry?"

He liked it, Lacie was gaining her footing, more herself he decided, pleased with her spunkiness.

Merry placed her hands on her lap, clearing her throat before she spoke. "Well if a ride isn't in your future," she looked to Lacie, "then I need to speak with my brother."

Her voice was so thready and thin. Leslie was concerned for her and what Merry hadn't voiced yet. This tone wasn't normal for his sister who usually looked on life a bit like Lacie, carefree and void of problems. "Of course, can we talk in front of Lacie though? I'm loathe to send her back to the bedroom when she just now has the strength to come out of it."

Merry looked to Lacie then back to him, "I have no secrets here. This is just a fact I need to tell you. I didn't want to intrude with this but," she turned to look at Westcott, "he talked me into confiding in you."

His arm around Lacie tightened as he kept her close before glancing Westcott's direction. "What is it?"

"He's here. I saw him on the sidewalk in front of the townhouse. I think my heart stopped for a second when he looked up and saw me. Don't understand why he would follow me here. It's such a long way from Bordeaux," Merry spoke so rapidly she was very nearly breathless.

"Who?" Leslie was racking his brain for the answer to his question, but he had no idea who Merry was speaking of. "Who did you see?"

"Him," Merry said, clearly frustrated and impatient. "Nevil. What do you think he wants, really wants from me? I don't like this. It makes my skin crawl thinking about him."

"He's pursuing you," Lacie said thoughtfully. "That's the only reason as far as I can see for a man to travel such a distance. You need to take every possible caution. Westcott was right in convincing you to come here."

Merry visibly cringed at Lacie's words. "I've never given him any reason to believe I might be interested in him. In fact, I've told him to leave me alone numerous times."

"Sometimes a man doesn't need a reason that's clear and evident. Let me look into his finances. You are an heiress. That fact might be reason enough for him to think you can save him."

"If he finds a way to compromise you, he might think your family would ensure you marry him," Lacie said, looking outside. "You cannot go anywhere alone and unguarded."

"The ploy has worked with others but rest assured I would never demand you wed someone who makes your skin crawl. That just won't happen," Leslie said, smiling and attempting to reassure his sister.

"Can I stay here?" Merry asked, her voice fraught with tension. "I know you too want to be alone, but..."

"Only for another few days," Leslie said turning to Lacie, realizing it was time to tell her about the ball. "I haven't told you but we'll be returning to the city as soon as you are strong enough for the trip." He saw the curiosity in her eyes.

"I don't want to stay here by myself. For all I know Nevil might have followed me to Southcliff."

Uncharacteristically Merry was plucking at her skirts, frown lines marring her beautiful features. From time to time she looked outside.

"You don't need to be nervous. Of course you will come with us when we go back to Glasgow, and I'll make sure Westcott keeps a close eye on you," he said trying to think of all the possible scenarios. "Don't go out riding by yourself as is your penchant, at least not until we understand why Nevil is here and if he means you harm."

He needed to address Lacie, explain things to her but he wanted to do that in private and was even now afraid she would ask questions he couldn't put off answering.

When he glanced Lacie's way, she seemed calm, not over concerned about his sudden announcement to return to the city.

"Can I take the same room I had last time I was here?" Merry asked rising and starting for the front door. "If so, I'll leave you two alone to do whatever newly married folks do."

"Yes, of course. Why are you going outside?" Leslie asked, thinking Merry should be walking up the steps to the opposite wing of the house.

"Don't be obtuse, to get my bags. Left them in the carriage just in case you wouldn't let me stay. Kicked me out on my arse, so to speak." She smiled as she started for the door.

"Brat, you knew I wouldn't kick you out. I'll get your bags. Sit and chat with Lacie. Westcott will help."

Outside the air was crisper than he remembered from just a short time ago when he spread legged in the snow acting like a jackass. He laughed. The expression on Lacie's face was worth the mortification.

So, Nevil was after his little sister. It had to be for the inheritance, not that Merry wasn't lovely in her own right but she was young, too young for the likes of Nevil Boucher.

Peeking his head inside the carriage, he grabbed her second valise and enlisted the driver and Westcott to help with the trunk.

Brushing his hands together and walking down the stairs from the second floor after depositing the bags in Merry's room, he stepped into the parlor.

"Everything is where it belongs. Don't get too comfortable. As I said we will return in a few days. Do you want to freshen up?" He looked pointedly at his little sister then Lacie, her gaze meeting his.

"I see the two of you have something to talk about. I'll be down around dinnertime if that's all right. I am exhausted. A nap would be nice." She yawned and Leslie was sure it was pretense.

"Thank you." He watched his sister depart before he sat down next to Lacie, picking up her hand. "I was going to wait until tomorrow to bring up our departure, but Merry's arrival complicates the matter."

"I understand and hoped you would explain sooner than later. I knew we would have to return to the city eventually. You have duties and I suppose I do too, although I don't know what they are." She breathed deeply, a tiny frown of concentration marring her face.

"If you are not well enough in two more days we won't go."

He was still putting off the explanation. Maybe it was because he knew she didn't want to attend balls or perhaps it was because he didn't want to share her yet.

He decided then they would have a honeymoon as soon as the weather improved. Perhaps this spring they could visit his home in France and his family's wineries.

"You can tell me. I won't run away. My first duties... You did say we would have to attend a ball or two, the one thing I can honestly tell you I'm not eager to be part of. However," she paused, smiling at him, reaching a hand up to touch his face. "I've never attended one before so maybe if I give it a chance, I'll enjoy it. I do like to dance."

His face fell. He was sure that one act told her what she guessed was true. "You're right. It is a ball and we've no real obligation to attend except that I want to make sure the young debutant who this is given for realizes I am a married man."

Lacie smiled then laughed softly. "So you see, you do need my protection. Why is this important to you?"

"She had her sights set on a title and wealth. Mine. I wasn't interested, was never interested. Now she will move on and I'll be happier for it."

"So you married me just to get away from this lady?" Her lips turned upward then she swept her tongue across them. "Perhaps Nevil would like an introduction to this young lady and Merry's fears will be put to rest."

"Perhaps," he said as he watched the slow glide of her tongue across her mouth, wishing he dared to taste her.

He was enchanted, mesmerized by the simple gesture, understood she was purposely flirting with him. Then she was shamelessly staring at his mouth. He liked what she did. His body hardened with vivid pictures of her naked in his arms, her soft curves pressed against his aroused flesh.

"Should we take this upstairs?" It was too soon to make love to her. Blessed hell, she was so weak a few hours ago he'd needed to carry her down the steps, but it seemed with each passing second she was growing stronger, more like herself.

Perhaps if he was careful.

"Not yet," she spoke softly, her eyes still on his lips as she slowly lowered her lashes for a second. "I would like a kiss then one of those ginger cookies Grams is tempting me with. You did want me to eat something."

"It's not nice to tease your husband," he murmured as he bent close to give her exactly what she was asking for.

He stood and held out his hand. She placed hers in his. It looked so tiny resting on his palm. Bringing her fingers to his lips, he kissed each one, gently sucking them one at a time into his mouth. Tiny sounds vibrated from her chest. He delighted in the gentle trembling of her body resting so close to him there was no space between them. He hoped she was strong enough for more sensual play. He wanted all of her, every part of her willing and healthy. The scent of lavender melding with her special woman's scent intoxicated him.

"Now it seems you're teasing me," she murmured. "I don't want to wait another second or days as I think you've planned."

He needed to take his time with this moment. Rising, he brought her a cookie as she'd asked and one for himself. He poured her a cup of tea, taking brandy in his cup instead of the tea.

"I don't want to tease you, need to make love to my wife but only when she is strong enough. The problem I'm having is keeping to that promise I made to myself. Your cheeks have a rosy blush to them and your eyes are shimmering with what I believe is desire."

"You see right," she murmured setting the half-eaten cookie on the saucer before setting both on the table.

"Where should we start then? I wonder, perhaps here or here?" he asked, his voice raw with desire, but he brushed her hair to the side as he trailed kisses across her neck and collarbone.

"That seems a good enough place to me," she said, her breath a puffy little sigh of contentment.

"Me too." His hands rested on the tiny sleeves he wanted to push down her arms. He looked upstairs. It seemed quiet but so far both their brothers had interrupted them. Didn't want Merry to intrude and learn more than a fifteen-year-old should know about what transpired between a man and a woman.

Her head fell back, giving him more opportunities for pleasuring her. He pushed the sleeves just far enough so he could see most of her lush breasts. Lord, but he needed to finish what they were beginning here.

"How do you feel? Do you still want to wait to go upstairs or not?" he asked praying for the right answer.

"You're making me so hot. You always have that way about what you do to me. I can't think."

"I want to make you hotter, need to make your body weep for me, need to feel your honey fill my hands. Will you let me do that? Is it too soon?" Of course it was too soon. He was a damn besotted fool.

"As long as you can carry me up those steps, I think I'll be just fine. You'll have to do everything, of course."

"That's not a problem.

~ * ~

She was swept away with the beauty and the sensations Leslie so easily brought to the surface. He touched her soul but more than that he created a magical enchantment she didn't want to live without. She would do anything for him, give him whatever he wanted.

The fire simmered deep inside, burning bright as his hands and lips explored all of her, touching her in places that could not be ignored. Primal in its nature, the inferno creeping within until the flames broke free in a mysterious way created tremors in her body until she cried out his name in pure ecstasy. He burned her with his innate fire.

His body was sweat-sheened as she curled next to him exhausted and replete in the aftermath, enjoying the warmth and comfort. She tried to calm her breathing yet even the simple gesture of running his fingers along her arm seemed to create more havoc within.

"How are you, Lacie?" He pulled away and when he looked into her eyes she smiled.

"How are you?" Her lips twitched with laughter.

He had been so cautious but in the end, it seemed he needed to give her pleasure and he did.

"Throw my question back in my face, will you? I'm good, more than good. You please me, Lacie. Now, how are you? Don't deflect this time because I need to know."

She turned so her head lay on his chest and she could play with the hair and tease his nipples, delighting in the masculine groan of desire, she heard. She wanted to explore lower, but she held back.

"I won't lie to you. I'm tired but otherwise very good and content. Would love to rest then do this again and again. You please me." She closed her eyes, recalling all he did and all she wanted him to do.

"It's nearly dinner. Should we dress and see what cook has made?" he asked, looking to the door. "Forgot to lock it. Hope Merry doesn't have some ungodly urge to talk to me."

"Don't think Merry will come looking for us, do you?"

She suddenly felt panic rip through her, remembering Link and Flynt. They had not thought to knock, barging into the room with no hesitancy. Link had been amused but Flynt was furious with not just Leslie but her too.

"Only if it was necessary," he said.

"If she is as impetuous as you've talked about, how can you believe she won't act in the same manner as our brothers?" While her pulse raced at the thought of this, she closed her eyes, trying to calm the speeding of her heart.

She felt his deep breath on her cheek, wondered what exactly he was thinking even while she heard the pounding of steps then the hush as they stopped in front of their door.

"It would seem Merry has some idea of decorum. She is stopping to think about the consequences," Leslie said, watching the door as if it would fly open on a second's notice, at the same time pulling the blanket up to cover her.

"Merry seeing me naked is not nearly the same as your brother and mine," she murmured still trailing her fingers along his chest stopping at strategic places then following the path with her lips.

"Thought you said you're tired. It seems as if you've recovered and want to do this again," he told her with a chuckle as he proceeded to explore her body as she did his.

"Just biding my time until we figure out if Merry is going to barge in here or not," she said, realizing just how true his words were. She wanted him all to herself, and she was tired of sharing.

"As soon as we hear her walk away, we can get up, or I could make love to you," Lacie laughed. "Right now, I'll bet she is thinking of the pros and cons. If the reasons for barging in outweigh those for waiting, we should be seeing her soon."

"So, while we wait, what do you want to do?" he asked as he toyed with a strand of hair, chuckling softly. "Everything I can think of would only serve to embarrass both of you if she walked in on us."

"Hmm... I should thank you properly for my birthday gift. Maybe trying to say the right things to make you understand I'm not a fragile flower. I don't need to be coddled. Truly I'm never sick. So, you don't have to be afraid this is a common occurrence."

"Lacie..."

"No," she put her finger to his lips. "I understand I was sick, but you tend to believe I need to be protected all of the time. Remember, in my dreams you are the one who needs protection."

The knock at the door failed to surprise either of them. "She is coming in. Are you ready?"

"Don't think I'll ever get used to people barging in on our privacy while I'm naked, but at least this time it's not to intimidate us and it's not a man."

The door squeaked open, as did Merry's voice. "May I come in? Didn't want to interrupt anything."

Her face was all Lacie could see then slowly the rest of her appeared. "It's alright, Merry," Lacie said. "Come in, this must be very important."

"Whatever has brought you to my bedchamber better be good, brat." Leslie sat up, letting the sheets fall around his waist, seemingly unconcerned.

"Maybe I should come back at a better time." Face beet red, Merry turned to leave. "This was not well done of me. I'm sorry."

"Stop right there," Leslie said. "Tell me what has you barging into my private life. Then we'll proceed from there. It must be important or you wouldn't be here."

Lacie almost laughed when Merry walked straight to the bed and sat down next to her big brother.

"I do have a good reason and don't call me brat," she said, her voice hard. "I don't like it."

"Tell us what's got you so terrified your hands are trembling," Lacie said, trying for encouragement rather than fear.

"I saw him again. Just now, out my window." Her voice was shaking while she looked to the window as if she would see the man she ran from France to avoid.

"Blessed hell, you best go back to your bedroom, Merry. I'm going to get dressed and see what I can find outside. No, on second thought go wait in the parlor for us. Don't want to leave Lacie alone up here."

She blushed an even deeper shade of red as she ran from the room. Before she closed the door, "Sorry, Lacie, didn't mean to intrude."

Stark naked Leslie strode to shut the door and lock it before picking up his pants and pulling them on as well as everything that had been dropped to the floor before their lovemaking.

"Nevil? Is that who she is talking about?" Lacie asked, standing then sitting abruptly back down.

"You're still weak and I haven't helped. We should not have..." He was by her side. "I'll help you dress then I'll make sure you get downstairs without incident and no, I'm not coddling you. Earlier in the day I had to carry you, remember? I'm just letting you see what you can do on your own before I interfere. Is that alright with you?"

Lacie couldn't help herself. She didn't want to acknowledge her weaknesses even if Leslie was right "I'm stronger by the second. At least you are giving me the chance to try. I appreciate that."

"Fair enough." He slipped a shirt over his head. "I'll let you try to navigate the stairs, but only if you are holding on to my arm. Don't want you to take a tumble. Agreed?"

"You don't want me to fall down the steps. Neither do I so I will hold on to you as well as the bannister, but I do want to try on my own. Need to test my limits."

She smiled as she sat up letting the remaining covers slip to her waist and was delighted to hear his indrawn breath, pleased that he still liked what he saw and that she almost felt comfortable displaying herself to him.

This time when she swung her legs from the bed, she was able to stand. Inhaling deeply, she bent to retrieve her underclothing that was spread around the floor. "I can't," she mumbled shrugging her shoulder. "Just a bit dizzy." She sat on the bed again.

"If this wasn't so damned important, we would not be leaving here for another hour or more." He helped her into her clothing then finished dressing himself. Gallantly, he held out his arm.

Without further comment she accepted the proffered help, stepping slowly and feeling the exhaustion bone-deep but refusing to admit it to herself or to him. She was determined though to make it down the steps.

"Tell me if you need more help than this." He stared pointedly at her. "You will do that, right?"

She nodded and smiled at him as they walked slowly through the door. She wondered if that was the smile he said earlier that he couldn't refuse, "I promise but I am determined."

This time she managed to negotiate half the stairway. He seemed to notice her exhaustion as well as the trembling of her body. "Time for me to carry you? Settled?"

"If you'd like. Otherwise I'm going to have to sit down right here and wait until I can walk farther or slide. I could just slide down the steps on my bottom. Perhaps we could make a game of it and you could slide as well." She was laughing now, couldn't help herself, and the look of horror on Leslie's face made her laugh even harder. "Really, you should see yourself. Would it be so bad, sliding down the steps, or I could take the steps and you could slide down the bannister."

After a long pause, he laughed then, and she understood his laughter to be a full out belly laugh for the first time since the wedding when she nearly fell to the floor, would have fallen if he'd not been holding her. "I'd like to see you sliding down the steps."

"Is that a challenge?" she asked, wondering what he would say. "Only if you slide down the bannister."

"Never to both." He scooped her into his arms, carrying her into the parlor where Merry waited.

"It's getting dark. You shouldn't go out there," Merry said, waving a hand in the air. "He could be dangerous, could be waiting to surprise you. I don't want any trouble or for you to get hurt."

"Did you or did you not see Nevil?" Leslie asked, as he slipped on his coat before he picked up his pistol. He turned to her, his expression harsh. "Well? I'm waiting."

"I saw him. I wouldn't lie about that. Still, I, could this wait until the morning?" she asked.

"I understand you're afraid so you must accept the fact I have to find out why he is stalking you. Perhaps it's just a coincidence, but I don't believe in them. Might have if he stayed put in Glasgow but out here there is absolutely no reason for him to be found on my property."

"He followed you," Lacie said, thinking about her earlier encounter with the man who attacked her. He'd followed her too, waited for her in the shadows. "You've got to be careful."

"Lock the front door behind me. I doubt if he stuck around, particularly if he saw you too. He would know you would tell me. You know I've got to check. I'm sure there is no reason for either of you to worry."

Leslie headed out the door. Merry locked it, turning and leaning against the door. "I'm so sorry I interrupted the two of you. It was not well done of me, and I sincerely apologize." The words she spoke were whisper thin, shaky.

"You didn't really. I was too exhausted and..." Well, she had already said too much but something told her that with both Leslie and Link as older brothers she wasn't entirely innocent.

Her shaking hands were now on her rapidly reddening cheeks. "I... What's it like? Making love?"

"Your brother might not ever forgive me if I talked to you about it." She wasn't sure where she was going with this. "Didn't your mother say anything?"

"Not really, she just talked around it seeming embarrassed by the topic, and my brothers just talked about the fact that Link couldn't keep his pants on." She lifted her shoulders a bit. "Link laughs about all his children and of course Leslie lectures him."

"I suppose if your mother won't talk to you about sex..." she paused, wondering what was proper to tell a fifteen-year-old girl and what was not. "Leslie is very caring. When you are older, I would be happy to explain a few things to you, but not now."

Merry sighed as she looked out the window. "Why would that man be following me? This just doesn't make any sense. He terrifies me. At home in France I just thought he was a nuisance I could avoid, but now...

"Now everything about this is surprising. It might not be anything at all," Lacie told her, but she didn't believe it. "You said you had a dowry."

"I do, but I would never say yes to him. I made it perfectly clear to Nevil that I didn't like him." Merry stared at the fire, twisting her skirt in knots while silence stretched every nerve to its snapping point.

"He must be desperate. There is no other explanation for his actions. Your dowry is large?"

"I suppose so, don't really know. Link and Leslie call me an heiress. I've money from my grandmother. She made sure we were all taken care of. Leslie says I've more money than I could spend in a lifetime, but I don't ever spend more than my allowance so I still don't have any idea how much is waiting for me to turn of age."

"But a womanizer and or gambler could go through any inheritance," Lacie mused thoughtfully. "We need to make sure Nevil never gets a chance to force you into marriage. We can't send you back to France. He would just follow you again and you would be without protection."

"I could visit Link in Maryland, but then I might never see the man I'm going to marry again. I doubt if a man like Nevil would pursue me that far."

"That seems a bit drastic," Lacie said, thinking it over, "but it is an idea. Who is it you plan on marrying?"

Merry shrugged, looking a bit sheepish. "I don't know his name but I've seen him twice, once a few years ago in Paris and a couple of days ago in the city."

Lacie was shaking her head at Merry's statement who went on to say, "Perhaps Leslie can make him understand he needs to find some other heiress and I'm not available." Merry walked around the room, staring out the windows before finally sitting down again.

"Maybe Leslie could play matchmaker for Nevil," Lacie laughed, thinking again that would be far out of character for her husband.

"He would never do that," Merry said, seeming to find a little bit of humor in Lacie's suggestion."

"Why don't you pour us both a brandy?" Lacie asked, wishing she could do or say something that would make this all go away. Then paused, "Are you allowed?" she asked with a second thought. "Flynt wouldn't let me and my sisters drink until we were eighteen, but we did anyway."

"You're not eighteen yet and you're a married woman too. You must have fallen for my brother hard."

She laughed, then with a soft sigh. "I did fall for him. I think it was love at first sight, if that's possible. He's so handsome and confident. I used to see him when he came to the house for the weekly card games. One night my sisters and I snuck up to the third floor where they played cards. They, the bad boys, saw us and he chased after me, found me in the stables hiding yet wanting to get caught. He kissed me. I knew at that moment there was no one else for me. I was afraid he wouldn't think the same way. He was older and he had a mistress, I think. So," she lifted her shoulders slightly.

"Some call it arrogance," Merry said laughing. Then, "I drink when I want to just as you and your sisters did. There is always brandy in the house. Mother doesn't care and my brothers just indulge me. You will have your work cut out for you when you have children."

"I doubt it," Lacie said, "You weren't his to discipline. I suppose he acted in a manner that would keep you safe and secure but as to things like drinking, he probably enjoyed seeing you act independent. You're not a lush. I'm sure he would have put a stop to any drinking you did if that was the case."

Merry brought her a glass. "I see you had cookies and tea earlier. Before he took you upstairs to have his wicked way with you."

"We did and yes he did, but I'm not going to say anything more. He tells me he loses control so now he's just like his brother in that matter but only with me. Tells me he's never lost control before and anytime he sees me he wants to make love to me."

"Doubt if Leslie could ever lose control, but he is different around you. He's not at all himself. You've managed to change him just a little. I think for the better. He smiles more."

"I want him to be himself," she said on a whispered sigh. "I don't think I like the idea that I've changed him. I like the man I married."

"Not love?" Merry asked. "I see the way you look at him, how he stares at you, very nearly drooling. If you ask me that's love."

"Probably just lust," Lacie said, thinking it would be nice if he loved her too.

"It's all for the good. When I got here, I saw the snow angel on the ground and because of the size of it, I'm willing to bet you didn't make it," Merry leaned forward and placed her hand on top of hers. It seemed she couldn't stop the laughter from bubbling forth. "I heard you talking about sliding down the steps and the bannister. Almost agreeing to something like that is not my oldest brother. I almost went to the foyer to see if he would do that for you."

"I see you found the brandy, brat." Leslie stepped into the parlor. "Do what for Lacie?"

"Did you see anything?" Merry sipped the remaining liquid in her glass, choosing not to answer Leslie's question.

"Yes, I saw footprints and a place where it seems Nevil must have hunkered down to watch the house."

He strode into the foyer to hang up his coat then back to the drawing room. "As to Nevil, no I didn't see him."

He poured a glass of brandy for himself before refilling hers and to Lacie's amazement he refilled Merry's too.

Westcott stood in the doorway. "I'll go see about dinner. It should be ready soon. Is there anything else?"

"No, not right now. Do relax for a little bit, Westcott. I understand running after my sister all day can be taxing."

"So you believe me," Merry sounded relieved.

"Always did, I took you for your word. I've known the man and after I thought about him, I understand more fully why he wants you. You're too young and I came to the conclusion it is simply monetary."

"Why is that? Is he a gambler and a wastrel?" Merry asked. "It's what Lacie said might be a reason he's stalking me."

"It is, at least most of it but once a while back I heard him speaking of you. I didn't find it complimentary so I called him out but he told me he was just thinking about what might be if you were older. I don't think he's the type of person who likes little girls that way because he's never pursued others your age. His mistress is older than he is."

"Blessed hell, Leslie, how old was I when he first noticed me?" She rubbed her arms, breathing in a shuddering breath of air.

"It was last year just before you turned fifteen. I set him straight but I heard later about his loses at the racetrack. He bets heavily. He usually wins as much as he loses, but he had a run of bad luck."

"So he wants my money." She sounded horrified as she rubbed her arms. "You won't let that happen, will you?"

"He wants you, too, but his fortune has reversed itself. Now, it seems he's not prepared to wait a few years. I'm guessing his finances have become even worse over the last few months." Leslie drummed his fingers on the chair, thinking as if he was trying to understand the workings of Nevil's mind.

"I can't keep running from him." Merry threw her arms in the air dramatically. "I don't like this, Leslie. Don't' like it at all." She stood, striding around the room, stopping occasionally to stare out the window.

"He's not there. I'm sure he's someplace warm and dry. So, at least for tonight, you've nothing to worry about."

"Can't help worrying," Merry mumbled. "Westcott spends all his time following me and that's just not right. The man shouldn't have to trail after me. Has better things to do, I'm sure. Don't you have some other men who can guard me?"

"You're right. Westcott can't possibly be your bodyguard. I'll find someone else, someone who is younger and can protect you if something were to happen."

~ * ~

Denis knew all he had to do was keep Torra fed and she would do anything he wanted. She proved that to him time and again. While she wasn't eager, she didn't say no to anyone. Pleased she was virgin, he spent the weeks training her and kept her locked in the small room he rented.

For her protection he told her. She would shrug her shoulders and accept whatever he asked as long as she had plenty of food.

The fee he charged for her use was exorbitant. He was making easy money, which he didn't intend to give up. The fact Torra was experienced now made her more marketable. Yet there was still an innocence about her that seemed to please his customers.

He learned his lesson with Caroline Dubois. He wasn't going to make the same mistake again. Most of the time Torra wore only a robe and a shift. When he brought clients to see her, he put her in a beautiful gown, making sure her makeup and hair was fashioned in the most modern styles, and he kept track of her. He was not about to allow someone to spirit her away from him.

Unlike with the circumstances surrounding Caroline and Leslie Stewart, he now trusted no one.

Yes, he was pleased with Torra, well pleased. She was a fine addition to his businesses and what would become his stable of girls. He meant to keep them young as well as innocently naive. Once they couldn't or wouldn't fulfill their role, he would let them go.

Now, he intended to follow Leslie Stewart. The duke owed him. He aimed to collect on that debt. In the process of trailing Leslie and his wife, he'd run across Nevil Boucher. What better revenge than to kidnap Stewart's sister and bring her to her knees. By the time Leslie could rescue her, she would be well-used.

Boucher agreed that Merry Stewart would make him a fine wife and a whore as well. Not only would Boucher gain control of the woman's inheritance, but he would make money when he sold her to those agreeable men for their pleasure.

Denis knew firsthand the duke had enemies who would be more than willing to bed his sister as well as bask in the irony. He was realistic also. Leslie Stewart was a formidable opponent and thwarting him would not be easy. No mistakes could be made.

"What has you grinning so shamelessly?" Nevil walked into the room looking at Denis before eyeing Torra. "You look as if you just won something. What is it?"

"Just thinking about the money we'll make when we have Merry Stewart at our disposal. Perhaps we can find a couple more girls, young beautiful women who will most assuredly bring a profit," Denis said. "It shouldn't be too difficult. There are many on the streets same as Torra who are forced into prostitution. We might as well reap the bounty."

"As long as they aren't off limits to me, to us, it's a perfect idea. For now though, how are we going to get to Merry?" Nevil asked. "The task won't be easy but the hardest part will be keeping her whereabouts a secret. We both know the power the duke has. When challenged he is a ruthless man."

"The old man who is trying so hard to keep up with her can be easily danced around. You should be able to get close enough to snatch her without mishap," Denis said thoughtfully. "Try not to kill the old man. Don't want murder charges to hound us."

"Westcott? No, he won't be a problem. If possible, we should kidnap the duke's wife too. That would be even better revenge for you."

Nevil strode to Torra, stroking her cheek then pushing her robe from her shoulders. "Right now, I'm in need of a woman."

"I'll leave if you want to play with Torra," Denis said smirking. "Or perhaps both of us can play. That might be fun. What do you think?"

"We should do it soon. I find I'm growing impatient." He ripped the shift from Torra then stepped back, seeming to eye her critically.

She didn't say anything, just jerked in surprise, a tiny squeak escaping through her lips.

"You should stop ripping her clothing. It's cutting into the profits," Denis laughed again. "Can't you just have her take the shift off? I've never heard her say no to a request."

"You should go. Don't want to share tonight," Nevil said as he pushed Torra onto the bed then climbed on top of her as he unfastened his pants.

"I'll see what I can do about finding another girl and you should figure out just how you're going to separate Merry from her bodyguard."

Chapter Eight

"The Duke and Duchess of Southcliff," the man announced from the top of the stairs leading to the Prescott ballroom.

Lights sparkled. The sound of the pipes gave Leslie a reason to smile. His wife was beside him in her first official duty as the Duchess of Southcliff. She dressed in silvery blue gown that seemed to change colors as she moved. He gave her the sapphire necklace for this evening with matching earrings.

He was pleased.

"You've got this," Leslie whispered close to Lacie's ear, wishing he dared kiss her. "You are the most beautiful woman here. Just take a deep breath and imagine everyone without a stitch of clothing on."

Her laugh was short and sharp. Shaking her head at his outlandish comment, she turned her attention to him. A broad grin painting her delicate features, "My hands are sweating and my knees are wobbling. So, I'm not sure how you can say I've got this but seeing all these people dancing around naked does make me want to laugh. Serves to calm my nerves a bit, at least until I think of you naked and dancing in my arms."

"You'd have to be naked too, or I wouldn't dance with you."

He chuckled, enjoying her determination to get through the ball and the introduction to the young lady who pursued him the last two years. He directed her attention to a portly and very short man dancing with a woman who was a couple inches taller with a bosom that put Lacie's to shame. "Imagine that pair without a stitch of clothing on. That should put an even broader smile on your face."

She did laugh. It was impossible not to. "I don't think I want to imagine that man naked, only you." Her sigh was soft. If the image of them dancing naked had aroused him, now he was deucedly uncomfortable.

"You don't have to imagine me. When we get home, you can take all my clothes off and do whatever it is you would like to my man's body." He was beginning to enjoy the ball, taking his advice to heart and letting the naked images of all the attendees float through his brain. "No one here compares to you but if we could find an empty room..." He gently nipped her ear then looked around to see if anyone noticed. "We could take care of my little problem."

"What is it that you want?" Lacie leaned into him, asking but knowing full well what he wanted from her and what he meant to collect as soon as they were home. She would be pleased to give him the world if that was possible.

"I think you know so don't pretend. Now, I'm having a devilishly hard time. We will leave as soon as it is polite to say our goodbyes. There is no reason to remain here longer than necessary."

As they made their way into the throngs of lords and ladies, he watched for the daughter who had set her eyes on him. She was older than Lacie and not nearly as beautiful in his eyes, but some thought there was no one more beautiful than Cora Prescott in Glasgow and perhaps all of Scotland.

To Leslie she was shallow and a twit. All she cared about was herself and what someone else could give her. He never wanted to have to deal with a wife who needed so much attention.

"There you are," Cora was suddenly beside him. She placed her hand on his free arm. "Can we have this dance? I so want to speak with you." She flirted, batting her darkened eyelashes at him while she coyly tilted her head to the side.

Her breasts were pushing from her corsage. If he wasn't married and in love with his wife, he might have been tempted to find an abandoned room and begin a discreet dalliance with her, marriage not part of that involvement. "No, my first dance will be with my wife." He shook off her grip on his arm, bringing Lacie to the forefront.

"Cora," he paused, lightly kissing Lacie on the forehead to help make his point, "this is my wife, Lacie Stewart, the Duchess of Southcliff."

He knew the mention of Cora's lost title would infuriate her. He didn't care, just hoped Cora would get the not so subtle message he was sending and move on to another man, someone she could manage.

"Nice to meet you," Lacie said sweetly and Leslie was sure the few words were spoken through gritted teeth.

He wanted to laugh and pat her on the shoulder telling her she was doing an absolutely splendid job, suitable to any duchess, but he held back deciding he would give her praise tonight in the bedroom instead.

"Of course, everyone enjoys meeting me." With that said, she turned further attention to Leslie, lowering her lashes for just the perfect amount of time before staring at him with her ice blue eyes. "After the first dance with your wife, you must come find me for the second dance. I'll be by the punchbowl."

She was cold and aloof despite her flirtatious manner. Leslie shivered as a wave of chills swept up his spine. "I've reserved all my dances for my wife." With that he shook her hand off and turned his wife toward the refreshment table. "Would you like something to eat, my love?" he queried, his voice soft and he hoped would put her in the proper frame of mind for seduction later this evening. "Something to drink. I've a burning need to wash that encounter out of my mind and what better way than a glass of champagne."

"Well..." Cora turned, walking off in a snit, her skirts swinging rapidly around her feet.

Lacie laughed softly then, "Thank you. I appreciate your efforts on my behalf. Yes, I'm suddenly very hungry. Should we see what there is on the buffet table?"

Bending close and whispering, his tongue barely touching the shell of her ear, delighted by the tiny sound of pleasure he created in her, "After we heap our plates, we can find a spot in a secluded and hopefully dark corner where I can pretend I'm still a bad boy and perhaps try my hand at embarrassing you just enough to make you ready for me the instant we walk in the door of the townhouse. "Let me see." He grinned shamelessly at her. "Have we made love on the dining room table? Perhaps that should be our first stop."

"Westcott will be there."

"I'll make sure he knows his presence is not appreciated."

"You'll embarrass the poor man."

"No more than usual when he knows what I intend to do with you."

For a moment, Lacie looked away, seeming to ignore the conversation between them as well as the question about the dining room table, but Leslie knew she was mulling it over in the back of her mind.

"Merry was surprised that you were ever considered a bad boy. Did you know that? She laughed at the notion. She told me you were stoic and conservative. You would never be bad where a woman was concerned. I suppose conservative might be the right word. You would never do anything bad and that you were always the model of decorum."

"Yes, I suppose compared to Link I'm a very good boy, but I've been bad with you, now haven't I?"

He was remembering their first kiss along with the time in the stable when he tried to show her that her breasts were beautiful. He touched her then, very nearly carried her over his shoulder to the loft above. The control he always touted was clearly in jeopardy that day. Now, whenever he saw her or watched her doing the simplest things, he wanted her.

"I'm glad you were, bad." She stroked his jawline with a fingertip obviously forgetting where they were but the gesture pleased him. "When you're around me you can be bad anytime you want."

He was pleased also that she was willing to show affection for him in front of other people, even strangers as most of these people were. Lacie was all he ever wanted in a wife and more.

He was content. He did wicked things where Lacie was concerned, but they were all for the right reasons. "Shall we gorge ourselves on these delicacies?" He dished up two plates avoiding questions from friends as they gingerly made their way around the outside of the dance floor to the tables.

"I see an empty place in the corner." Lacie directed him with a nod toward a farthest away place. "Do you need to talk to people? You can, you know. I will find something to take up my time. I do like watching the dancers and listening to the pipes."

"No, I see most of these people on a weekly basis for business. Tonight is for us and to forget there is danger surrounding Merry."

Possibly you too, he thought but didn't want to say anything to Lacie. He had enemies and Nevil Boucher knew that for a fact. Enemies who could be enlisted to help him with any scheme he might conjure.

"I like that you want to spend time with me, but I'm at a loss for words, feel so out of place I want to run from the room. I've never been to anything like this. I know Flynt has and Cam and Chelsea always get invited to events such as this one because of his connections with the university. I suppose also because he is a viscount. Chelsea loves the attention and dressing up. It's second nature to her."

"Does Chelsea like going to balls?" Placing a kiss on the back of her hand, he waited for her to answer.

"Don't know. She never talks about them. I suppose so," Lacie boosted her shoulders in a tiny shrug. "Chelsea was always the most social. She is perfect for Cam."

They sat down for a moment. He watched her play with her food. He wished he could think of the right words to put her at ease. At this moment, it was all he could do to take his gaze away from her bosom, which once again seemed to have grown. It could only mean one thing.

He was pleased with his intuition. Yet he didn't intend on bringing the possibility of a pregnancy up here but perhaps after they made love tonight, or in the carriage on the way home. They had spent several wonderful weeks after her sickness making love every day and night, some days more than that. He'd made it his mission to make love in every room of their house. Merry's and Westcott's presence made it difficult though. He longed for privacy.

They still had quite a few rooms to go. After that they could move to the stable.

"What are you thinking? Your grin is so wide I can nearly see all your straight white teeth. Tell me what's in your head." She was smiling and he was sure laughter was not far behind.

"Eat your food then I'll tell you anything you want including what has me grinning like a mad man," he told her then watched her try a few bites.

When she looked at him as if expecting answers, he shook his head. "More food first. That just won't do. What you ate wouldn't keep a hummingbird alive. You have to keep your strength up for tonight and all the wonderful things I've planned."

"I'm not really hungry anymore. You gave me way too much food," she murmured, pushing more food from one side to the other. "Where you're concerned, I've more than enough strength to keep up with your plans for this evening."

"One more bite." He waited until she grudgingly obliged him. Leaning forward and whispering, "I was trying to recall all the rooms in the townhouse we've yet to make love in."

"And what else, Leslie Stewart, Duke of Southcliff? I know that's not all you were thinking about although you were wearing that silly grin that seems to take over your face when you're making plans about fondling my breasts."

He roared with laughter, thoroughly appreciating her comment. "Take a bite of that tiny cube of cheese and I'll take you dancing. We can always come back and finish the meal."

She ate the cheese but remained in her chair seeming to wait for him, impatiently tapping her fingers on the table. "What were you thinking? I need to know and you have to tell me. I held up my end of the bargain."

"If I don't comply to my wife's wishes?" One eyebrow rose, his grin steadfast. "What then? Will you punish me some way? Believe I like that idea. Let me think. How indeed would you mete out punishment?"

"Yes, punishment would be in order. If you don't comply, there will be no favors when we get home."

Her voice sounded different to Leslie. He wasn't sure what was going on in her head. In any case, this really wasn't the place to bring up such private things but even wracking his head for a convenient lie he could not come up with anything.

So, he tried to deflect, his gaze searching the room as if the decorations might give him an idea. "What if...?"

She tilted her head slightly, a frown marring her forehead. "What if...?"

"I promise to discuss this with you in the privacy of our home. What had me smiling is far too important to risk sharing with any unwelcome eavesdropper. Starting gossip here would not be a good idea." He hoped that would serve to placate her.

She stiffened. He had the immediate impression he was going to regret what would come next. "Very well, Leslie Stewart, Duke of Southcliff, I will hold you to that. Shall we dance?" She stood a bit too quickly it seemed, reaching for the table.

He was beside her, holding her. "What is it?"

"I'm fine really. Suppose I got up too quickly." She looked up at him, her eyes a deep dark blue, compelling and magically filled with passion.

"You don't look well." Concern for her swamped everything else. "You're not having a relapse..." He thought of the possibility she was with child again and the relief he felt nearly brought him to his knees. He would have to ask someone about all the various symptoms of pregnancy.

"I don't think I'm sick," she said, her voice weak and a bit hesitant. "Never really felt better. Just more tired than usual."

"We should get you home, now. Let's find the hostess," he said, searching the room for the earl and his wife so he could say his goodbyes and a quick thank you.

"We're not leaving until I dance with you at least once. Now, they are playing my favorite Scottish reel." She held out her arms for him. "A dance first then we will go home. Didn't get all dressed up to leave without a dance."

"Are you positive?" He was sure this was not a good idea, but he would give in to her wishes and in the process keep her close.

She straightened, "Positive."

"Against my better judgment."

He walked with her to the dance floor, one arm around her then drew her into his arms. They danced across the floor. Bending close to her ear, he slowed. "You are a very good dancer." They joined the other couples as the lively music filled the room.

When the playing stopped, she leaned against him, seemingly winded. "That was nice. Shall we have one more dance before we leave?"

"Whatever you want."

"I want to dance," she told him. "I can wait for that discussion I was so eager a few minutes ago to have with you. Something tells me I won't like what you've got to say. So, now that I've thought a bit, I'm more than eager to put it off."

She smiled at him then. It was the look he had a hard time refusing. After her wink, he understood her ploy. He had unwittingly given her ammunition she needed if she wanted to control him.

"Ah, perhaps it's for the best but make sure you know if you are asking me with your smile to allow anything that would put you in danger, I will still say no."

"I wouldn't want it any other way. Now, one more dance and I will be more than pleased to allow you to take me home where you can become a bad boy where I'm the only one who will know."

Once again, they danced to a Scottish song. She hummed along with the tune. The pipers wore their kilts and sporrans. Once more, she was winded when they finished. Sweat beaded on her forehead. She leaned against him while she inhaled deep breaths.

"Are you ready to go home now, lass?" he asked, watching her carefully still concerned.

"Yes, we should try this again in another year or two. A ball might be fun. We can stay an hour or so, eat and dance then leave. We wouldn't want to indulge ourselves with such a fantastic thing as a ball very often."

"Just the right amount of time," he laughed, tenderly brushing a stray lock of hair from her forehead.

"Enough, and no more. Where do you think your friend, Cora is?"

she looked around the room.

She is off to a secluded corner with an earl. George, I believe is his name. Nice fellow but he will find himself wrapped around her tiny little finger by the end of the night."

"Should you warn him?" she asked, watching him, tilting her head a bit sideways as if she was truly concerned for the man. "He seems to be in control and enjoying himself. Perhaps we should say nothing and see what transpires."

"The man knows what he's getting into. Perhaps he's enamored of Cora. She is a beautiful and..."

"Maybe they have the same end game. He could do worse for a marriage. As you say, she is very beautiful and I'm assuming will bring some wealth. Do you suppose he will enjoy her in bed?"

"True," he mused thoughtfully, wondering if she was trying to find out if he ever bedded Cora. "There is Lord Prescott and he doesn't seem concerned. Shall we say goodbye?"

"If you want to leave early, I won't complain." She squeezed his arm, lowering her lashes for a moment then gazing into his eyes.

"Little minx. You got that from Cora, didn't you?"

"Mimic Cora? Never." She smiled at him and he wanted to kiss her right there in front of everyone.

She was his after all.

He had every right.

Outside the air was crisp and cold. A few clouds floated across the full moon. He pulled her close, "Are you cold?"

"Not with your arms around me. You have this way of making me hot no matter the temperature."

He kissed her then, a long deep kiss with the promise of more. When he drew away, "The carriage is here. Let's continue this where it's warmer and no one will see the wicked things I've planned along with the places I intend to roam with my cold hands in order to warm them up."

"Then I will have to do the same."

He laughed remembering the snow as well as the fight on his front lawn with the fluffy white stuff then the strategic placement of his hands.

He had to be careful that day not to explore too intimately, but this evening he didn't have that problem.

Inside the carriage, he kept his arm around her, wishing there was enough time to make love to her before they arrived home. If that were the case, he could cross off one more place. Perhaps...

"We have privacy now," she told him, her hand on his cheek. "We can talk now if you want."

He turned into her hand, kissing the palm, drawing his tongue along one finger to its tip, felt the tiny shudder of passion sweep through her, repeated the process. "Talk later." His hands found their way beneath her gown, sliding up the length of her leg.

"No." She drew his hand back her voice firm. "Tell me what you were thinking about when we were eating, please. I've been very patient and I let you decide when, until now."

He expected to see that smile he was growing used to instead her brows were drawn tightly together. "I don't want to worry you."

"You worry me more by not talking to me and telling me what you are thinking. Now, remove that freezing hand from my leg. What is it that has you grinning but telling me it's a private matter and we have to wait before we discuss this problem? There is no one here now except the two of us. Who knows who will be at the townhouse when we arrive? If Merry is there, it will give you one more excuse to put it, whatever it is, off."

"I'm sorry. Broaching the subject eludes me. It's a delicate matter. I don't want to embarrass you, don't know if I will though." In a perfect world, she would understand all about pregnancy, but she was innocent and he wouldn't have had it any other way.

"Just try. This won't be the first time I've been embarrassed by you, and I'm pretty sure it won't be the last. You have this uncanny way of doing just that all the time."

"Your breasts are larger. I noticed it last night." This time his brows furrowed, realizing she would not like the knowledge even though he enjoyed them immensely.

"You're wrong. They cannot possibly get any bigger. Is that the private matter you wanted to talk with me about? You've worried me all evening and for no reason. They are not bigger. You will not be taking me to the dressmaker any time soon." She sounded adamant and indignant as well.

But he knew how they felt. They were larger. "The size of your breasts is what alerted me to another situation that a husband understands and waits for his wife to tell him about."

Well, that was subtle and neither was the tone of his voice. Impatient now with this conversation, he wanted nothing more than to get it over with.

"Now you're talking in riddles." It seemed she was annoyed and a bit angry with him. "Just tell me what it is you want me to know, what this other situation is that I'm unable to figure out on my own."

So be it. He was doing his best, but he'd never experienced anything like this before, had no idea how to proceed. He'd always thought the woman would know first, but Lacie wasn't very old and her mother died when she was a little girl. He was positive Flynt never played the role of a mother, telling her about sex. That thought made him choke, good thing Flynt didn't. Who knew what Flynt would have said? So, what about Catherine? She did have sisters though. Two of them had babies. She understood their lovemaking would most likely provide him with an heir.

"I don't mean to make this confusing for you. It's just that it's new to me also." He sighed heavily, sitting back and closing his eyes to think. What to say to her now? Perhaps he should approach this from a different direction.

"Just tell me. Does it really make any difference in the scheme of things if I'm embarrassed?" she asked, leaning into him and making herself comfortable he assumed.

"To me it does. It makes a hell of a lot of difference. I'm sure Link would just blurt out what he is thinking. Your feelings be damned. And no, he probably wouldn't allow this conversation to get this far."

"You're not your brother but perhaps in this case his style of dealing with things is preferable to silence and a few innuendos. Speaking in riddles has not gotten you very far."

"We are home," *at last,* he said, seeing the porch light of his townhouse. From the look of things Merry was still up, possibly waiting for them along with her new bodyguard. What was his name? Douglas, yes that was it.

"I'm not getting out of this carriage until you tell me what you were thinking." Impatiently, she tapped her foot on the floor then jabbed his chest with a finger. "I mean it Leslie. You will not make me wait a moment longer."

A groan rumbled from the back of his throat, but he understood she was right, he was right. It just wasn't something he wanted to do. Then he began, "Because we've been intimate every night and some days for the last few weeks, over a month now," he started, speaking slowly trying to choose his words carefully. "Because we've made love in almost every room in the east wing."

"And..." Once again, she was irritably tapping her foot. "More riddles. Am I supposed to guess what you're talking about because if I am, I don't have one single idea.

"I've noticed something that you should have noticed. Also, we were intimate before you were sick. I think perhaps more than a month has passed maybe a week more than that since the first time I was deep inside you, spilling my seed."

"And..."

The blank look in Lacie's eyes told him he was going to have to be more specific. Bloody hell, how was he supposed to do that? At the moment he tried to think of what Link would say. After all, he had how many children, all with different women. He must have had this same discussion more than once or had he been so lucky that the women he had children with understood such things.

"When was your last woman's time?" He watched her, saw her pale then it seemed her beautiful dark blue eyes crossed. If she wasn't so damn puzzled, he would laugh at the expression.

"I don't know." She was breathing hard, her breasts rising and falling, tantalizing, beckoning to him.

He wondered if she understood the significance of his question or... "Are you embarrassed?"

"Yes, and I'm not sure I know why you asked..." Then her voice trailed off and her face turned a shade of pink she'd never worn before.

"You understand now?" Blessed hell, but he prayed she knew. He didn't know much more of this conversation he could take.

"Am I with child?" She smoothed her skirts before scrunching the fragile satin between her fingers. "I don't think I've gained weight."

"Your breasts are larger but no, as of yet you don't have a baby bump." He grinned now that this was over. "I believe a month is too soon for that."

He was a man well pleased.

"My bosom is not bigger. Nothing is tight or doesn't fit right. I don't remember when my last time was, but I know it was a while ago. So, does this make you happy?"

"Amazingly so." He drew her into his arms, kissing her slowly, intensely, his hand resting on her belly, wishing he could feel his child kick. In time, in time he would enjoy her new figure and the movement of the child. For now, he would be patient.

~ * ~

At first, she was shocked, stupefied, although she knew this would happen sooner or later. She just didn't expect to be pregnant within a month or a bit longer after sleeping with Leslie for the first time. He asked if she was happy, but that wasn't the emotion she was feeling at the moment.

Fifteen more days had passed and she still had not had her monthly flow. So, she must be carrying his heir because she was sure the baby in her womb was a boy. She had not been sick yet. Both Chelsea and Bliss had morning sickness, but they said not until well into the second month. Hope had been terribly sick. Well, she might be that far along. It was impossible to tell. She was riding her new mare, her birthday present from Leslie. The little mare was exactly what she wanted, perfect for her. He bought the mare at a stud farm, Weston's Corner. The duke of Weston owned it.

"You're so quiet," Merry said. "You thinking about my brother."

"No, not this time." She sighed deeply, knowing Merry would ask her more questions, would want to know what it was that had her off in some distant place. Merry was far too curious. It seemed she wanted to know everything.

She should have lied and said yes to Merry's inquiry. Leslie didn't want to tell anyone for another month. He said it was bad luck to do so. She wasn't sure if she agreed with her husband, but she would rather lie to Merry than Leslie.

"What is it?" Merry asked, grinning as if she'd already guessed. "I'm a sister to you now and I've told you everything about me and my life. Not that there is that much to tell."

"I'm not too sure I believe that but never the less, there is nothing important and my thoughts are private." Lacie urged her horse to a faster pace, hoping to put a bit of distance between them.

The ploy didn't work. Merry was beside her in a matter of seconds. Leslie warned her before she and Merry left not to ride too fast. She didn't think riding a horse would harm the child, but she would rather err on the side of caution than risk anything.

"A penny for your thoughts," Merry asked as she rode up beside her. "You have me more curious than I've ever been."

"Leslie doesn't want me to say anything so I'm going to put a stop to this conversation. Isn't the weather just perfect for the end of January? It feels like spring, it's so warm. Why on earth did you name your new mare, Sir Alistair?" She sounded ridiculous even to herself and she just knew that wouldn't stop Merry from pursuing anything

"You're pregnant," Merry laughed, seeming delighted. "I'm going to legitimately be an aunt. None of Link's children count as legitimate."

"I'm not. Why do you think that?"

Leslie would be angry with her for telling and she didn't. She didn't want to lie, but now she didn't see any way out of this predicament

Merry created by her questions.

"Because pregnancies happen. Why doesn't my big brother want you to tell anyone?" She was still grinning at her, riding next to her.

"Because I'm not pregnant." Lacie tried to be convincing, but she was a horrible liar, at least that's what Leslie told her the one time she tried to hide the truth from him.

"Of course. I'm very pleased. I won't let on that I know even if someone tries to torture the words out of me," Merry laughed again slowing the horse. "You really shouldn't be riding so fast. You could hurt the baby, all that bouncing."

"Don't be so melodramatic. Horse riding won't cause any harm to the baby. If for some reason the truth comes out before three months is up, you better make sure Leslie knows I didn't tell you." She slowed her horse thinking Merry was just like her brother and wondering if she was going to start hovering over her too. The thought made her groan.

"Ladies have to stick together. My lips are sealed. It wasn't really anything you said, it was what you didn't say. It's also the way Leslie has been acting around you."

"How is that?" Lacie asked but she knew.

No matter how many times she told him she didn't have to eat so much, he put more food on her plate. He tried to do everything for her when he was home and the way he was treating her was going to drive her nuts before she finally had this child.

"He does everything for you, more so than before. He's treating you as if you are a two-year-old. I think he'd even try to cut your food and feed you if you'd allow it." Merry grinned wide, seeming pleased with the new found knowledge. "This is the best news I've had in a very long time."

"It's that obvious?"

Lacie grimaced and decided she needed to have stronger words with her husband even though she knew it wouldn't do any good. Leslie would do what he wanted when he wanted.

"Even Bliss and Chelsea were laughing about him as well as the fact their husbands were the same way when they were pregnant. Do you suppose they also suspect your condition? It's really a little endearing, don't you think?" Merry asked.

"No, there is nothing endearing about it," Lacie said, grimacing, even though the first couple of days had been nice, now that several weeks had passed she wanted to scream when Leslie insisted on doing something for her she was perfectly capable of doing herself. Pretty soon he'd be carrying her up and down the steps.

"You wouldn't have him any other way." Merry looked at her and grinned again.

"Perhaps not, but he does need to learn I can't deal with his hovering non-stop for the rest of my time. There is relief only when he is at work or away from the house for some reason, which isn't very often these days. He has people come to the house so he doesn't have to leave."

"You shouldn't complain about a man who cares so much for you," Merry told her with seeming conviction. "When I find someone to love, I hope he's like Leslie and maybe even Link in some ways."

"You're right. He does care for me, but I do wish he would tell me he loves me so I don't feel as if he just married me for the size of my bosom as well as the heir I might give him." If that thought didn't hurt so much, she might laugh.

'You've no idea, do you?" Merry asked her, one eyebrow up just like Leslie. "Anyone with eyes can see how much he loves you. When you're in a room with him, he never takes his gaze from you and not your bosom. He's watching you, all of you."

"You read my mind. He does look there quite a lot though," Lacie said. "If he does love me, does he expect me to just know it, to read his mind?"

"Have you said the words to him?" Merry challenged. "I'm sure he would tell you how he feels if you broached the subject first."

"Only if I knew he loves me," Lacie said, adamant in this one thing.

"He does." Merry pointed toward the road. "Who is that? Not many people come out this way? I think we should turn the horses around and head for home. I've an uneasy feeling about this."

Lacie's breath caught in her throat at the site of two men riding toward them. She turned her horse, urging the mare to a gallop as Merry rode beside her. "Perhaps we should ride hard and forget that I'm pregnant."

Merry spoke to her bodyguard. "Stay behind us. Don't know if there is trouble, but the one man looks like Nevil Boucher and if it is, he's the one you were hired to guard me from."

Wind rushed past Lacie's face, her hair falling from its pins. Her stomach rolled with the sudden fear cascading inside. This was not what she'd expected from this day. For a second, she closed her eyes, thinking of a more direct path home and wondering if the mare would prove faster than the horses pursuing them.

The gunshot rang out loud and clear. Lacie tried to stay close to her horse, but the shot surprised the horse. She bucked, the little mare's forelegs rearing high into the air, terrified of the noise.

Lacie screamed, clinging to the reins, trying to hold on to anything she could find as she slid off the horse. Frozen, she couldn't move. The world circled around her in a strange fashion. Every part of her ached from the fall. She closed her eyes. trying to absorb the pain into herself.

Now she moaned and tried to see what had happened to Merry and who shot at her, but she couldn't lift her head from the ground. She couldn't move, could barely breathe. "No... no... no... no..." tears threatened to fall but she forced them back.

Seconds ticked by turning to minutes. The pain caused a hazy fog when she opened her eyes. She thought about the baby but everything seemed fine. She wasn't cramping, at least not yet. She prayed silently the growing babe was fine and unharmed despite the fall.

She saw the perfectly shined hessians before she heard the voice. A voice she didn't recognize. *What do you want?*

"Well, you're quite the pretty little thing, aren't you? You must be the duke's wife. I guess it's my lucky day. I get two and wasn't even planning on that." He hunkered down, leaning close to her as he spoke while he held a lock of her hair between his fingers.

She swallowed, trying to speak but the pain was too intense. If she could, she'd run.

"Very soft but I doubt if it's your hair that attracted Stewart to you. Now was it?" The man leered at her breasts, reminding her of the time she was attacked.

He touched her, placed his hand on her breast. She still couldn't move, couldn't swat away the unasked for invasion. Closing her eyes did nothing to vanquish the revulsion she felt.

Finally, "Who are you?"

He laughed. The sound was hollow and frightening. "General Denis Caron. Your husband took someone from me, and now I'm going to take you from him. It's quite nice of you to be out here with Merry. The two of you will do well together."

He picked her up, carrying her in his arms to a waiting carriage then setting her on a seat. Truly, she didn't know where the vehicle came from. It wasn't in sight when she turned to run from the strangers. She wanted to ask about Merry, but her question was answered in the next second.

She heard Merry's screams. She was fighting and cursing the man who held her. The man tossed her into the carriage. Merry tried to scramble out the other side, but the door was latched tight.

"No!" Merry cried out, shoving at the man's chest, pounding on him while he wrapped a beefy arm around her. She kicked him and heard the man's grunt of pain.

Merry kicked at him again before bending low to bite him on the wrist. She spat out blood.

"Hellion," he cried, shaking her for a moment before he punched her hard in the face, her head jerking backward with the power of the blow. "Give me some rope," he yelled at Caron.

"Feisty little thing. You think you can tame her?" Caron laughed. "It will be fun to watch."

"Any woman can be tamed," Nevil gritted out. "For now, all I want is for her to learn she cannot win against a man, against me. I want her to understand her life will be much easier if she gives me what I want."

Once she was tied, Nevil left and the two women were alone.

Lacie couldn't hold herself upright, understood the bouncing of the carriage wherever he was taking her would cause more pain. Lacie closed her eyes, wishing Merry had been able to outrun Nevil.

While Lacie still hurt, there were things she needed to know. "Your bodyguard?" she asked, trying to ignore the jouncing of the carriage and the piercing ache in her body all the while fearing for her unborn child.

"He was shot," Merry said, her voice whisper thin.

"Dead?"

"Appeared so," Merry said, her body shaking as she spoke. "Nevil caught me easily. My mare, fast as she was, was no match for his stallion. I will never give that man what he wants."

"Leslie will come for us," Lacie said with conviction she didn't feel. "He will find us and bring us home."

"He won't know where to look," Merry said, shaking her head with such disillusionment in her eyes. "I'm sure Nevil has someplace, but who would know where that is? Caron must have a room in Glasgow. It will take days, even weeks before they find us."

"Then we will have to get ourselves out of this mess. I for one have no intention of remaining in that man's custody. Don't know what he has planned, don't want to know either." She tried to think of Caron naked and she almost laughed, but pain stretching across her chest in a tight band stopped her.

"What is it?" Merry asked, "Are you alright? You fell. The baby?"

"I've been better," she spoke softly. "It's my ribs but what you saw just now was a game Leslie and I played at the ball."

"You almost laughed?" Merry asked. "Suppose I need to see some humor in this situation we find ourselves in."

"Leslie told me to imagine the men and women naked. When I thought of Caron that way, his fat belly hanging over the waistband of his pants and the rest of him, I almost choked at the image." She inhaled wishing she could fill her lungs without the pain. "One way or another we will get out of this."

"Well, I could imagine Nevil that way. I think it would help. Hope

I never have to actually see that man naked. I'm sure he looks nothing like either of my brothers."

"You've seen them naked?" Lacie wasn't sure if she liked the idea of Leslie parading around the house without a stitch of clothing on and other people seeing him. "That's just not right."

"Not since I was about seven. I did see him from the waist up the other day when I barged in on the two of you but other than that, no."

"Thank goodness, you're far too young to see a naked man, any naked man, especially Nevil Boucher." She leaned back then, needing air but unable to inhale a deep breath.

"We both know that Leslie thinks Nevil is intending to force a marriage. Rumor has it he's in deep financial trouble. It seems he needs money so he will try anything, and I won't allow that to happen. I won't give in to him, ever," Merry said.

"Leslie will find us before any of that can happen or you will get away. Don't think I'll be of much help right now. You have to promise me that if the opportunity arrives, you will flee." She hoped Merry wouldn't play the martyr and if the chance presented itself, she would escape and bring someone to make their fat captor pay for this crime against her.

"I won't leave you behind." Merry sounded adamant and Lacie couldn't let that happen.

"Of course you will. If there is a chance of one of us getting away, you must take it. Don't you see, as far as we know your bodyguard is dead and as you said, it might take days for Leslie to find us? Even if he calls in all his favors and uses every man available, he might not find us soon enough. You have to make use of whatever happens. It's the only way. Promise. I know you can do it."

As the carriage continued, they fell silent. Lacie tried to think of her husband and how he'd react when he discovered what happened to her. Even now the horses might have returned to the stables. Leslie would never panic, but he'd ride out to see what happened. All would take valuable time.

She wanted to believe the bodyguard was not dead and had

informed Leslie. What would he do? Douglas seemed to be a man of resources. He was strong and resilient. Lacie smiled thinking of the bodyguard who refused to call Merry by her nickname, insisting on calling her Angelica.

"We're in the city," Merry said, somberly. "I can see the townhouses and carriages on the streets. "We just passed the cathedral and there is George Square."

"Good, you should know where you are when you get away." Lacie wanted to smile but even that hurt.

Slowly she tried to sit. Instead she groaned, the pain piercing through her. She closed her eyes for a moment, wishing the agony to vanish but only time would help, time to heal.

Merry continued staring at the window, reciting landmarks as they passed them while Lacie kept her eyes closed. When they pulled to a stop, Lacie managed to push herself upright, hoping to walk.

"Should you do that? Merry asked. "Sit up? Does it hurt?"

"I want to be able to walk by myself. Don't want that man to touch me." Lacie looked to the door, waiting, her body shaking with pain as well as well as revulsion.

"Don't want Nevil to touch me either but unless he unties me..." Merry let the sentence hang for a few seconds. "He won't because he knows I'll fight him. I'll fight him with all my strength."

"He'll have to untie you sometime," Lacie said. "Take care you don't make him too angry. We need to be compliant, lure them to trust us at least enough to untie you so you can escape."

"For now, I'd rather they kept me tied," Merry muttered. "I don't like the way this feels. It's not good, not good at all."

"Remember, if you get the chance, run. Don't look back. Don't wait for me. Go to my sister's or brother's home, whoever lives closest to here. Promise me again." Lacie understood, Merry was their only chance. Every time she moved, breathed, pain from her ribs swept through her.

"Well," Denis said a grin on his face, his jowls sagging, hands on his ample hips. "I see you ladies survived the short trip. Good, this is all good. I can feel all my plans for the two of you coming to fruition."

"Leslie didn't do anything to Caroline, just rescue her from you. She didn't want you to keep raping her and giving her to other men," Lacie said, bitterly wishing she could think of something to sway him. "She is safe in London. Well out of your reach. I suppose you already know that."

"The woman was mine and just as Torra doesn't mind working for her food and clothing, neither did Caroline. Perhaps if I let the two of you go hungry for a day or two, neither will you."

Without giving Lacie a chance to walk, he pulled her from the carriage and carried her through the doors of the building and up to the second floor. Pushing the door open with his shoulder, he walked inside.

The room was small, a braided rug decorated the middle. There were two chairs and a couch along with two end tables. A door led to another room, which Lacie assumed was a bedroom. She shuddered, her shoulders quaking. This did not bode well for either her or Merry. The pain she felt was deep and dark, the strange silence in the cold room, echoing through her, sending shivers of revulsion through her to settle in the pit of her stomach.

"Welcome to your new home. I'm sure you will enjoy your life here. Not as many privileges as before, but nonetheless you won't want for anything." He set her on a sofa. Stepping back, he laughed, seeming well pleased with himself. "Make yourself at home. Too bad you're hurt and I have to wait a day or two in order to see what the duke finds so attractive about you besides your sizable kettle drums."

"Except my freedom and my husband. How can you even believe you might get away with this?"

"There is that but you will become used to it."

"Don't have to wait with this one," Nevil entered with Merry slung over his shoulder, laughing. "She's willing and eager to see how a real man treats a woman, one who is amenable that is."

"You can't just treat Merry as if she's your whore. She's a virgin."

Lacie couldn't believe what she was hearing. Shivers wracked her body, an ache sliding deep into her core.

"Perhaps you're right," Nevil said. "I never did like virgins, they just don't know how to please a man. Maybe I'll wait until she's seen a few clients before I have her."

"Yes, but if you're over eager, you might want to stay the process until she's a bit more willing, unless you like to force your women." Denis eyed the couple. "Might be a while though. Perhaps if you make her go withhold food and water for a few days," he said again.

Merry was squirming and yelling obscenities almost falling from his shoulder "Put me down!"

"Don't mind if I do, hellion." He dropped her to the floor, standing over her now, his feet on either side of her.

Merry let out an humph when she hit the floor, but as soon as she caught her breath, she scooted away from him, pushing herself as close to where Lacie was sitting as she could. "Untie me."

Nevil laughed, bending down next to her, tracing the line of her jaw with his finger then lower to travel along the top of her bodice, eyeing her. "Put my life at risk? Not a chance in hell, sweetheart."

He walked into the bedroom then came out carrying a sheer gown and a robe. Hunkering down next to her, he ripped her riding habit. The fabric hung from her shoulders. In a few seconds all her clothing was destroyed. She was sitting in front of them naked, her chin defiantly held high. Tied, she couldn't cover herself, her shoulders shaking as Nevil reached out to touch the curve of her breasts letting his gaze roam lower.

"No! Don't. Please, don't." A scream burst from her when he suddenly backhanded her and she was knocked to the floor. Unable to sit, she lay on the floor cowering.

Nevil grinned, "Like what I see. Soon sweetheart, soon. You can wear this gown now. I want you to remember how nice I'm being at the moment and understand that can change. No complaints. Wouldn't want you to get cold. No, if you're nice to me, I'll be real accommodating to you, give you most everything you want."

Merry didn't say anything as tears rolled down her cheeks. Lacie wanted to wrap her in her arms and tell her not to worry. Indeed, she wanted to tell herself not to worry.

"You will have to stick your rod in her sometime, that is, if you want to marry her," Denis said with a shrug that emphasized his point. "But that's up to you. If you get her with child, it will be so much easier to convince her brother that you are the best and only possibility for a husband. Who else would consider a soiled dove?"

"Leslie will find us," Lacie said with a calmness she didn't feel, her heart thundering as she tried to slow her breathing. "None of that will make any difference to a man who loves her," Lacie said but she wasn't all that sure about her words. She didn't think Leslie even believed in love.

"We shall see. If we have to, I'll keep moving the two of you," Denis said, stroking his chin in thought. "We will. For now, however, it should take several days for them to begin to canvas the area. Perhaps we'll just up and move back to France. What do you think about that, Nevil?"

"I prefer the south of France. Quite a good idea though."

"That won't make a difference. Leslie has friends and people who will help him. The two of you should just leave now and cut your losses," Lacie said. "If you don't, you'll hang or have a fun trip on a prison ship."

Denis slapped her and she let out a startled gasp, her head spinning. Her hand on her face, she glared at him, barely able to inhale a breath. She should not have provoked him. She would do better next time, telling herself to keep her mouth shut. There was nothing she could do or say that would intimidate either man enough to convince them to part ways with her and Merry.

"Don't test me, Lacie. You'll never get the best of me. When you are not in so much pain..."

"What are you planning?" Merry asked, still bound hand and foot. She seemed to have come to terms with her nudity. Although Nevil draped the robe and gown over her, one could still see her intimately. "We won't be a party to it."

"Not giving either of you a choice. Eventually you'll concede to our wishes and come along of your own freewill," Nevil said as he untied Merry's feet, eyeing her critically before grinning.

"I believe you've most likely guessed part of what we want.

Lacie's appearance here is a surprise but a nice addition to the fold. We've another girl. Torra is her name. She works for us, entertains clients in the room next to this one. Indeed, she is with a gentleman as we speak or I would introduce her to the two of you."

"I won't," Lacie said, a strange yet very deep calm entering her soul. "Not willingly. I'll fight you every step of the way."

"That, of course will be your choice. When you are hungry, truly hungry, you will change your mind. I will look forward to that moment. You should know this is very personal, but I mean to make a bit of coin with you too."

"We will see you in the morning. Have a good evening. Your work begins tomorrow." Denis backed from the room followed by Nevil.

"My god, they're finally gone. Can you untie my hands now?" Merry asked her, breath coming out in a quick rush. "I've never felt such vileness and revulsion."

The feat took Lacie longer than it should have but when the ropes were finally on the ground, Merry was rubbing her wrists and arms.

"Thank you. I think they are numb. Can barely move any part of me."

"Put that gown and robe on then you need to see if you can find a way out of here," Lacie told her, hoping not to waste any more time. She was more than willing to hobble out of this place given what Denis just told them. "Try the door even though I'm sure they have locked it."

Lacie watched as Merry dressed then explored the tiny room before she disappeared into the bedroom.

When she stepped back into the living room, "We're in luck. The window is unlocked. I can open it. Now all I have to do is get the courage to drop two floors to the alley below."

~ * ~

Stunned, Douglas lay on the ground, blood oozing from his head. What the devil just happened? As the world seemed to sway and turn around him, he sat up then whistled for his horse. The silence clinging to him was very dark and foreboding.

The ladies were gone, He'd failed Angelica but, in the distance, he watched a carriage rumble down the dirt road. He was angry and terrified for the girls. This was not good, not good at all. He had to find a way to make this up to them and the duke as well. He couldn't waste time seeking out the Duke of Southcliff. He needed to follow the carriage now. The only question was whether or not he could get on his horse.

"You didn't protect her, didn't protect either lady." He berated himself now, not wanting to waste time on recriminations. "Get your arse up and go after them. Find out where Nevil is taking Merry and Lacie." Struggling to stand, it seemed to take forever and just as long to finally mount his horse.

Seconds seemed to turn into hours while he tried to get on his horse. He prayed he could catch up to the carriage before it vanished into Glasgow. His head pounded as he headed toward town.

This was not what he bargained for when he traveled to Glasgow from his home in the Highlands. He needed to marry an heiress and figured guarding Merry for a few weeks would give him the groats to purchase suitable clothing to attend the necessary balls for his purpose.

The problem he encountered was that Merry stole his heart the first time he saw her and was introduced. She was a breath of fresh air, and she was also an heiress. He had to wait though because he wasn't sure how old she was. Waiting had never been a strong suit of his. He wasn't sure how much time his estate in the highlands could withstand before it tumbled down around him and his tenants.

He smiled. More than once he'd thought about finding a private spot to steal a kiss. Before he invested too much time courting, he wanted to find out if she tasted as sweet as she looked. He didn't tell the Duke of Southcliff that he was also titled. Wanted to keep the information to himself until he discovered whether or not Merry cared for him.

He chastised himself again. He understood she wasn't yet eighteen but... Perhaps she was close enough her big brother would overlook the fact. He understood the duke wed and consummated the marriage to the duchess before she came of age.

They were kindred spirits he decided. Not that he liked little girls. Merry was hardly a little girl. No, she had all the beautiful curves of a woman grown, curves he'd like to negotiate and explore.

In the distance he noticed the carriage and inhaled a breath of relief. Blood trickled from where the bullet grazed his head. He wiped it away with his sleeve. He brushed his wayward thoughts of Merry from his head, hoping to get close enough to the carriage without drawing attention to himself. With all the hustle and bustle of the city, the deed would be easier when they reached town.

The sun was beginning to set when the carriage finally pulled to a stop in one of the seedier neighborhoods of Glasgow. He watched as first one then the other lady was hauled out of the carriage and was tempted to rush the two men when he saw Merry bound hand and foot then slung over Nevil's shoulder.

His fingers tightened on the reins, weighing the pros and cons, but he didn't want to put the women in any more jeopardy than they already were. He stayed in the shadows for several minutes before retracing his path out of the city and toward Stewart land. Hoping he would meet the duke before he had to ride all the way to his home, he kept his gaze set on the horizon.

Rewarded by the sight of two men in the distance, he assumed Westcott and the duke. He pushed his stallion into a gallop until they met each other.

"What happened?" The duke's voice thundered in the encroaching silence. "Two horses came back without riders."

"Ambushed, but I was able to track the carriage to the building where they took the ladies. We should be able to get them away tonight."

"How do...?" Westcott began, rubbing his chin and looking from one man to the other.

Blessed hell, but even Douglas had not been able to protect Merry and his wife. He was obviously shot, blood beginning to crust on the side of his head. "We'll get the constables and you said they?" Leslie asked, having expected only one man.

"Boucher was one of the men and the other was older, fat belly, sagging jowls," Douglas said cautiously. "French accent. Do you know the man?"

"Caron," Leslie all but whispered.

Chapter Nine

Leslie Stewart, Duke of Southcliff had known fear before but nothing so debilitating as this. His wife and unborn child were at risk. Douglas told him Lacie had fallen off the horse. She might have already lost the baby. Now, while he rode along the same path he assumed his wife had taken, his heart raced with an incapacitating agony. Until now, faced with an emergency, he always remained calm.

He was furious and scared. He'd watched the riderless horses as they entered the stable, his heart caught in his throat. He was tracking the path of the returning horse all the while wondering about the whereabouts of Douglas.

He prayed it wouldn't rain, but the clouds building overhead did not bode well for his wishes. The ladies had been heading toward Glasgow with no particular purpose or reason. Lacie told him they just wanted a little exercise and some time to chat about girl things.

Darkness would descend soon. He didn't hold out a lot of hope for finding them tonight. Terror pooled in his gut, his blood running cold. He'd not taken enough precautions, had thought Nevil was a harmless irritant and perhaps he was but one should never take even a harmless irritant for granted.

Blessed hell, would they go to France? Rain began to fall. Leslie cursed, but it didn't help. At the moment it didn't matter, there was really nowhere else to go but into the city.

He had this feeling though, this man had never met the likes of his wife and sister. He wasn't going to have an easy time of it. Neither lady would swoon; they'd try their best to get away from him and that terrified him more than gave any encouragement. Men just weren't used to having women go against them. He knew Caron to be unpredictable and ruthless sometimes viscous. Leslie pushed harder toward Glasgow, hoping Westcott could keep up with him.

When he reached the city, he would scour it but he knew he would need all of his brothers-in-law and gathering them would take time. He decided that Flynt's home would be the most central location. They would fan out from there and hopefully Lacie's sisters would not join in the search.

He recalled another time when they could have very easily all been killed but had insisted on finding the man who shot Flynt. He shuddered at the thought.

"I don't believe this," he said to no one in particular even though Westcott rode at his side.

"The two of them are smart, scrappy lasses they are. You'll see, they'll be just fine," Westcott seemed to try for encouragement. "Probably sitting in your townhouse as we speak, sipping your fine French brandy, just waiting for us to catch up with them."

Leslie couldn't stop the long drawn out sigh he emitted. "I hope you're right, but we both comprehend all too well that scenario would have resulted in a miracle of gigantic proportions. More than likely they will hurt themselves trying to escape."

Westcott didn't respond right away. Then, "I'm going to keep my thoughts positive. Nothing untoward is going to happen to your wife and sister. They are both just too precious."

"Untoward has already happened. A crime was committed against them and if I can't get justice from the law, I'm going to take matters into my own hands. If I ask Arie, both will be on a ship bound for Turkey before they can blink. The general didn't understand I will track him down until I can hand him over to the law or kill him myself. Even if we get the ladies back unscathed, I will find both men. Killing might just be too good for them, slavery would be better." He'd never before felt such a deep simmering need for vengeance.

"Yes, Sir, I suppose you will. Just don't say those words to anyone besides me. Wouldn't want anything to happen to you."

"They could be anywhere in the city. How the blessed hell are we going to find them?" Leslie ran a hand through his hair, angry with himself and growing more frantic with each passing second.

This was not well done.

He should have foreseen this.

"Now you just stop berating yourself. There is nothing you could have done except keep those two little ladies locked behind closed doors. You'd never keep them prisoner that way." Westcott chuckled softly. "Separate they are incorrigible, but together I'd say they are a force to be reckoned with."

"When I find them, I might just do that, keep them prisoner for their own good. At least until the baby is born and Merry turns eighteen and I can wed her to someone, anyone."

"A baby?" Westcott asked surprised. "Didn't know you were expecting. Should have told me."

"Yes, and keep that fact to yourself. We weren't planning on telling anyone for at least another month or two. Bad luck and all, you know." This was one more thing to berate himself about.

"Well then I know Lacie will take every precaution not to get the general angry with her. She wouldn't want to hurt the baby. You can rest at ease now, Sir. She won't be reckless."

Leslie didn't know if he agreed with Westcott's rendition. Knowing she carried the child might make her more careless. "If he touches her, I'll kill him. Nevil too, if he thinks he can get Merry pregnant and force a marriage, he's wrong. I know Merry won't climb into bed with him. She detests the man. Rape is punishable by death. I won't even have to do the deed. What the bloody hell did the man want with Lacie?"

"Man on the horizon," Westcott muttered, reaching for his gun. "Hope it's not someone else we'll have to deal with tonight."

"I see," Leslie held his breath for a moment, watching as the lone figure drew closer. Then he called out, "Douglas? Is that you? What happened?"

"Ambushed, but I was able to track the carriage to the building where they took the girls. We should be able to get them away tonight."

"How do...?" Westcott began, rubbing his chin and looking from one man to the other.

Blessed hell but even Douglas had not been able to protect Merry and his wife. He was obviously shot, blood beginning to crust on the side of his head. "We'll get the constables and you said they?" Leslie asked, having expected only one man.

"Boucher was one of the men and the other was older, fat belly, sagging jowls," Douglas said cautiously. "Do you know the man?"

"Caron," Leslie all but whispered, realizing he'd made another mistake.

As if his prayers had been answered, the rain was beginning to stop and the clouds seemed to part so light from the moon hit the ground. They rode then, silence washing through his memories until they focused on Lacie.

She'd always intrigued him, even as a young girl. Her smiles gave him reason to grin. He felt pain wash through him, deep aching pain and an emptiness that was at once unusual yet not unexpected, not now, not that he'd finally come to realize he couldn't live without his wife.

He saw her pointing her gun at the men who nearly killed Flynt and heard her laughing with her sisters over something no one else understood and looking so young, her voice clear and precise. She could calculate numbers faster than anyone he knew. He smiled even as the pain ebbed and flowed deep inside him.

He would find her. He had to. There was no life for him if he didn't. He couldn't imagine facing the future without her.

Closing his eyes, he tried desperately to focus on the task at hand. He let the horse find its way, understood he had nothing to worry about as long as Douglas knew where he was going.

Without warning, Leslie saw Lacie in his imagination or inner conscious, he couldn't be sure. She was in a small room, lying on a ragged sofa. Her gown was wrinkled and torn. Her hair was straggling around her face. She was pale but he saw no fear, just deep all-encompassing pain. She was awake. He could practically imagine her thinking, plotting madly for a way to escape, and that gave him a reason to smile, at least for a second.

She had too much courage, but he wouldn't have her any other way. Then speaking to Douglas, "You and Westcott get Flynt then go stand guard at the door. Watch until I get back here with the law. Don't do anything unless it's an emergency of some sort. I know Lacie and she will try to escape rather than waiting for help." His heart pounded double time, his breath catching in his throat, thinking about that scenario.

"Now, how would you know such a thing? She will try to escape? That's too much foolishness. A woman should know her place. She should realize, she should wait for a man to come," Douglas said as he turned his horse to ride back to the city

Leslie watched him carefully, mumbling, "Done it before, put her life at risk thinking she could do things just as well as a man. I'm sure Merry will go along with whatever Lacie suggests. Should have put the fear of God into Lacie the first time she did something stupid instead of coddling her."

"She would still be in this situation. This was not their doing," Douglas pointed out dryly, "So would Merry. We just have to be there for them no matter what has happened or if they take matters into their hands and mess this all up. We will figure it out."

There was little conversation for the remaining miles. A profound silence encompassed them, darkening the mood even farther. Leslie ran one scenario over another one across his mind, understanding Lacie would never wait, would have known Douglas had been shot and would let that information twist her action into something untenable.

By the time they reached the city, the night was dark, gas lights the only illumination. What little moonlight they enjoyed earlier now vanished. After getting directions from Douglas to the building were the general and Nevil were keeping the women, Leslie pressed his horse to a faster pace, eager to put an end to this and see that justice would be carried out.

Leslie stopped at his townhouse, asking for a carriage to be sent to the address he gave the stable hand. Then made his way to the police station. Explaining the situation to the officer in charge, he was accompanied by two other men to the building.

Time seemed to tick by way too fast as they rode through the streets, buildings looming up around them. Clouds darkened the sky even more letting in no moonlight. He became the person in charge and with one purpose.

All Leslie wanted was to make sure his wife as well as his sister were left unharmed. So much could have happened in the time spent doing this the right way. He should have gone with his gut, and rode straight to the building. They would have surprised Caron and most likely killed him as well as Nevil. Then Lacie would be safe and in his arms right now. Merry would not have to worry about Nevil returning to threaten her life again.

A bit of moonlight splintered through the clouds. Leslie inhaled a deep breath. He saw Westcott and Flynt. The two constables were there to make sure everything was carried out according to the law.

"Where's Douglas?" he asked, concerned that he know every possibility. "He should be here with all of you."

"You said the lasses might try to escape. We learned from a man leaving that the girls were taken to the second floor. There's a window overlooking the alley and since you said they would try to save themselves, Douglas is standing beneath the window, waiting for that possible scenario. It's the only way to leave besides the front door."

"Good, now," Leslie turned to the constables, "you should go inside and find Denis Caron and Nevil Boucher. Try all the doors. Flynt and I will go upstairs. This should be easy. If the men are in the room with the ladies, I'll send for you. If not, we'll take them and leave. The carriage is waiting. I don't want to spend any more time than necessary standing outside this tenement doing nothing."

Douglas appeared around the corner of the building, smiling. "Merry dropped right into my arms."

Douglas' jacket was wrapped around her and she was leaning into him, as if trying to absorb his warmth. Leslie heard the sobs through the silence, knew he should calm himself before he spoke. It was not good.

"You jumped from the second floor, little fool," Leslie grit out before he could inquire about Lacie. "You should have your head examined."

"We didn't know when you would get here if ever." She spoke softly. "Lacie said we had to save ourselves and I agreed with her. There was nothing else I could do."

"Where's Lacie?" His voice was gruff, impatient. "She would have been the first one through the window. What aren't you telling me?"

"She's hurt so she couldn't jump." Merry's voice was soft, too quiet.

"What happened?" Leslie fought the urge to rush forward, needing to understand everything first.

"When the shot was fired, her horse reared and she fell off. She has bruised or broken ribs. We thought Douglas was dead." She gazed at him, her hand resting on his cheek.

Leslie saw the spark between them but brushed it off as his imagination. Douglas was much too old for his sister but not as old as Nevil.

"Nevil and Caron?" Leslie asked.

"Don't know. They left, said they'd be back in the morning. "There is another girl. They are using her, selling her to men for sex. She's in the room next to ours. Her name is Torra. She might not go with you willingly. From what I understand, she was starving and they pay her with food and clothing. She won't want to lose that, but maybe there is something else we can offer."

Leslie paused for a moment, thinking over his connections in town. There was a lady, Scarlett was her name. She ran a companion service. From what he could tell it was highly profitable. Her ladies escorted men to various events.

"I might have something for her. I know a lady, Miss Scarlett. She won't be a prisoner and she can earn her way, even choosing whether or not to have sex," Leslie said.

"Sir, can I take Merry to your townhouse? I'll have the carriage sent back immediately. It's not very far."

"No, wait here. Pray this won't take more than a few minutes. You can stay in the carriage with my sister."

Leslie turned to Flynt. "Shall we?" He pulled his pistol, determined to reach Lacie. For a second, he held his breath, understanding the danger for his wife. With Flynt and the constables behind him, they made their way to the second floor rooms. Merry had told him which room was theirs and which was Torra's.

He tried the knob but it was locked. Looking at Flynt, he waited for a moment before kicking the door in knowing the sound would alert Nevil and Denis. Inside he saw Lacie lying on the sofa, just as he imagined a few hours ago. She tried to sit but fell back, pain etched on her face. Instantly, he was beside her.

"Merry is all right?" she whispered. "Good." She closed her eyes, drawing in a shaky yet steady breath.

"What about you? Can you walk or should I carry you?"

His heart had nearly stopped, wishing he could take the agony into himself. He couldn't though and that fact sent him to his knees. He smoothed strands of hair from her face, touching her gently.

"I don't think I can walk." Her words were thin and thready. Leslie could barely hear them. "In any case, it will hurt no matter what you do."

With nothing more to say, he scooped her into his arms. Once inside the carriage, they waited for Flynt and news of Torra.

"When we get home, I'll bind the ribs and that will help a small amount. "In any case, whether or not anything is broken it will take time to heal. You will not be riding anytime soon. The baby?"

"I haven't lost the child." Then she saw the man with Merry. "Douglas, you're alive. I thought... thought they killed you. You must have followed the carriage. Thank you."

He nodded, holding Merry close, closer than what was appropriate, Leslie thought. Yet, he heard no protest from Merry. It seemed she needed his arms around her. Leslie wasn't going to say anything even while he didn't entirely approve.

"We have em, both of them. They won't be bothering you again. There's a penal ship heading for Botany Bay soon. Both will be on it, I'm sure. Have a good evening, Sir," one of the constables spoke up.

"Let me know when it sails. Just send a message to the townhouse," Leslie said as he gently stroked Lacie's back. He needed to be alone with her.

Flynt was there, Torra beside him, climbing into the carriage. "She's agreed to see Miss Scarlett. In any case, after Caron's arrest, she would be back on the streets and starving once more.

As the vehicle lumbered along, Leslie felt the quivers of pain rippling from Lacie. They seemed to be intense. A tiny whimper echoing inside Leslie's brain followed each bump. He had to wait, yet the ride to the house lasted eternally long. Blessed hell, but why did this seem to go on forever?

When they finally pulled to a stop, he let Torra and Flynt climb out in front of him then handing his precious wife to Flynt, he leapt from the carriage. He didn't wait to see what the others were doing. With Lacie once more in his arms, he strode into his house and directly to the bedroom. Servants appeared with bandages and bath water as well. Food and tea laced with willow bark was set on the bedside table.

He was alone with Lacie, blessedly and gratefully alone. She was safe and with him. He was never going to let her out of his sight again, he vowed, even knowing that would be next to impossible.

"Nevil and Denis are going to be tried in a few days and they'll be sent to the opposite side of the world on a prison ship. No one will ever hurt you again." He stroked her cheek, wishing he could put an end to the pain.

"Promise?" She looked up and graced him with a tiny smile. "At least it doesn't hurt to talk any more but whatever you do, don't make me laugh."

"At least not for another day or two," he told her.

~ * ~

"Is that bath for me?" she asked, wishing the task was already done. Lacie did want a bath, needed to wash the horrible hours out of her mind, but she didn't think that was possible. Judging the distance from where she was to where she wanted to go, seemed an unmanageable feat.

"Yes, it is, but drink this first. It's willow bark tea. It will help with the pain. I promise you'll feel better in no time." He held her while she drank and grimaced at the bitterness. When she stopped with half of the liquid gone, he said, "Drink it all."

"It is horrible, you know." She set the cup down, thinking she would wait a few seconds before tackling it yet again.

"You will feel better," he paused, touching her cheek with the back of his hand. "Probably not pain free but better. Now let's get you out of these clothes. I'll give them to one of the maids to burn. Don't ever want to see them again," Leslie said while he slowly unfastened the garments and eased them off her shoulders.

Gingerly, he touched her ribs, hating himself when she gasped yet at the same time trying to hold back the pain. She didn't want to worry him more. "I'm sorry. It hurts."

He smiled though. She was sitting on the edge of their bed stark naked without a single complaint. This was definitely a first for her. It seemed before she was always a bit shy. Perhaps she was just in too much pain to show emotion or shyness.

"The good news," he paused, his brows drawn together, "none are broken. When you finish with your bath, I will bind them and that will also help. You might be able to move, albeit slowly, without grimacing too much."

"How am I to get over there? Should I try to walk?" Once again, she was eyeing the distance between the two points.

He didn't answer but scooped her into his arms, carrying her once more. Then, "No, I'm going to pamper you until morning. By then you should start to do a few more things on your own."

She felt the hot water settle around her, and all she wanted right then was to stay here and sleep. His hands stroking her, with a sponge, surprised her, she wasn't sure why.

"Leslie?"

"Hush, just try to relax. I'll finish this then wash your hair." He continued and even if she'd wanted to protest, she couldn't. Before the accident and just because she was pregnant, he hovered, trying to do everything for her. Now, he would be unbearable.

Yet the sensations coursing through her were too heavenly, too delicious and when she didn't move, there was no pain. With her eyes closed, she imagined so many things and needed to ask Leslie about them. There must have been something else in the tea besides willow bark, because she felt as if she floated in an imaginary world.

When she opened her eyes, she was leaning against him and he was wrapping white bandages around her ribs. "I fell asleep? Didn't mean to but I... was there something else, did you drug me?"

"How is that?" he asked her, finishing and tying off the white linen strip. "Westcott might have had cook put something else in your tea. He does have a wealth of knowledge and has fixed me up any number of times."

"Not as much pain." She was telling the truth but the look in Leslie's eyes told her he didn't believe her. "Really," she reached upward to touch his face, pulling back quickly with the stab across her chest.

"Really?" One dark eyebrow rose in speculation. "Doesn't look that way to me, but I will try to believe you for the time being. Now then, we should dry your hair. I'll ring for some food as soon as your nightdress is on and your hair is dry."

He did everything for her and under normal circumstances, she would have complained but now... She realized she needed the help.

"You will understand that once I'm well you will cease this..." She almost laughed when he looked confused.

"Cease what?" he asked, one eyebrow slanted upward, a devilishly wicked smile on his face.

"Pampering, coddling, waiting on me. I won't have you continue in this vein for the rest of my pregnancy. Don't want you to get in the habit, thinking I need this much assistance." She understood from her sisters that at least the men in their lives acted exactly the same as Leslie was now for the duration of their pregnancy.

"Never." He slipped the opening of the gown over her head. "Can you put your arms into the sleeves?"

She did. "It seems as if I was just sick. I don't like this." She sounded petulant to herself as she watched him fasten the buttons.

"Of course you don't. No one likes to be confined to the bed, but I guarantee that within a day or two, you will be insisting that you are more than able to go downstairs and visit with your sisters when they come to check on you. I, of course, will tell you no and they should come to your room, but I'll wager you will win if you smile at me."

Westcott appeared unexpectedly with a tray of food and a bottle of wine, knocking then waiting for confirmation that it was safe to come into the room. "Just as you ordered sir. Is there anything else?"

"Not tonight. We just need time alone to talk and to sleep." Leslie almost laughed at the disapproving look his valet shot him. Blessed hell, but Westcott couldn't possibly believe he would force her this evening when her ribs hurt so much she couldn't move without pain. Leslie thought if anyone knew the workings of his mind, Westcott would.

"Very well," Westcott left, the door closing with a thud. Silence seemed to flood the room for a few seconds.

"What was that all about?" Lacie asked as he drew the comb through her hair. "Your man seemed angry with you."

"Westcott believes I would take you tonight, force you. By his expression, he's not even putting the gentler side to it, making love. Don't see how he could believe anything like that. He's known me forever, but he also understands a few other things about me. No, we won't make love again until the act won't hurt you. How is the baby? Have you had any cramping?"

"Luckily, no. Everything seems to be fine. My back got the brunt of the fall and perhaps it is a good thing that my ribs are hurt rather than the child. She rested her hands protectively on her belly then his hand covered hers.

"I'm pleased you both are well, but it's not..." he paused, seeming to think, "I don't think I can live without you and while I would be heartbroken if anything happened to our child..." He didn't have words to explain.

"We are both fine." She reached upward to touch the moisture slipping from his eyes.

Then he repeated as if he was trying to reassure himself. "I intend to make sure nothing else happens to you or this baby. Now, let's get you onto the bed and some food in your belly." He scooped her into his arms and brought her from the fireplace to the bed, her back resting against the headboard.

He poured her a glass of wine and dished up a plate of food, a little bit of everything on it. After that, he did the same for himself, settling on the opposite side of the bed.

"Now, is there anything you'd like to know?" He sipped the wine as he watched her waiting. "I'm sure your curiosity is getting the best of you."

"I've a million questions. Let's start with Merry."

She watched Merry and Douglas in the carriage ride back to the townhouse. If her guesses were right, Merry was smitten with the man and would not want to wait the years until she turned eighteen. Lacie was much older though when they were wed, and he would have to do some soul searching if Merry wanted to pursue the man, her bodyguard.

His brows drew together. "What do you want to know?"

By the look in your eyes you're thinking the same as I am. "Merry is half in love with the man and we both ken she is too young. Merry doesn't like to be told no or to wait for something she wants. What are you going to do?"

He was shaking his head and looking away from her, a clear indication that he didn't want to think about Merry and Douglas together in any way at least not tonight. "I don't know and I'm not at all sure I want to speak with either of them. Right now, all I'm concerned about is you. Well, hell. Merry and the bodyguard be damned."

"She is your sister and it's alright to worry about her."

She smiled, understanding why he didn't want the responsibility. He was a rake and understood what Douglas was thinking if he held the same emotions towards Merry.

"I'm not cut out to be a chaperone," he muttered.

"She is almost sixteen and he is about your age, perhaps a little younger?" she asked, wondering if Leslie would admit to being older than Douglas and the fact they wed when she was still seventeen.

"I don't ken how old the man is but he is too old for Merry," he said adamantly. "She will not lose her heart to that man."

"I'm afraid it might be a little too late for that." Lacie tried to make her point gently. "It is my guess that Merry fancies herself in love."

"Not if I keep her locked in her room," he muttered. "She's too young to know if she is in love or lust."

"Are you saying I had no idea if I was in love or lust?"

Anger began to build, but she tamped it down unwilling to allow him to know she loved him. She wasn't ready to tell the man now that he was insulting her as well as his sister. Male pride or arrogance, she wasn't sure.

Leslie ran his hands through his hair, clearly agitated. "One doesn't have anything to do with the other."

Lacie decided the best course of action would be to let what he just said slide and concentrate on Merry who needed someone on her side. "You let him hold her in his arms on the ride home and they were in the carriage I assume while you rescued me and Torra. Don't you think you might have sent the wrong message to Douglas?"

"All true. My mind was on you. Nowhere else." His voice was curt now and Lacie was sure he'd like her to stop pursuing this. "I'll deal with Merry and Douglas when you are healed, not one moment before. Nothing can happen in a few days. You and the child you are carrying are the most important in this entire scenario. Douglas will be dismissed since there is no more need for him."

She smiled, sipping her wine and staring at him over the rim of her glass. "You're sure about that."

"Of course, Merry is exhausted from the ordeal. She'll stay in bed most of tomorrow. You will begin to heal, and I'll stop hovering over you," he told her, touching her cheek with the back of his hand as if he had everything figured out. He was in charge after all.

"She was unharmed then when she dropped out of the second floor window?" Lacie asked, trying to put everything in order.

"Perfectly fine, seems Douglas caught her."

"Wearing almost nothing at all. He would have seen her, all of her, felt her, too, beneath that sheer gown," Lacie persisted, wishing she'd been able to protect Merry somehow. "You say he caught her."

"Wrapped his jacket around her so he most likely didn't see much of her," Leslie said. "He was ever the gentleman."

Lacie closed her eyes, attempting a long breath of air and was relieved when the pain didn't leave her gasping. "You believe that? You think Douglas didn't see her?"

Leslie sighed, once again running his hands through his hair leaving it endearingly standing on end. "I have to believe that he didn't see every part of her if I want to sleep tonight."

"Do you think he would go to her room? Just to check on her... if he cares about her at all?" Lacie asked, watching closely for a reaction. "Merry would let him in, you understand the fact here. Right?"

Lacie wasn't sure how she felt about Merry and Douglas. While she still remembered those earlier days and the way she was so lost in love over Leslie, she would have done anything for him, she wasn't sure that was the right scenario for Merry.

"I suppose I should go see what she... they are up to." Leslie stood but Lacie put a hand out to stop him. "For your own peace of mind, you would only embarrass your sister."

"I can't allow Douglas to take advantage of Merry. She's only fifteen and has no experience. If he kisses her and touches her and that's something she wants, she will..."

"Give him anything he wants?" Lacie remembered all too well how she behaved in exactly the same manner.

"Yes."

She smiled slightly, "What if it has already happened? Sit." Lacie patted the bed beside her. "I don't believe Douglas to be dishonorable. If Merry tells him the truth about her age, he would never take her innocence."

"Even if she is more than willing to hand it over to him? I

remember the day we were married. You would have let me make love to you and even before that if I'd pressed the point, I'm sure I could have seduced you."

"But you didn't because just like you, Douglas is honorable."

Trying to convince Leslie to let Merry forge her life the way she wanted it was not easy, especially when she planted the seeds of doubt.

"Excuse me, I won't go to her room if I find Douglas." He started to leave. "I would like to talk with him. We didn't have a chance to discuss just how he lost the two of you. Make sure the man kens Lacie's age as well."

"Other than the fact he was shot in the head and knocked off his horse. Merry and I thought he had died."

"That obviously didn't stop him, but I would still like to hear the details."

"Wait." Lacie stopped him again. "Tell me about Torra then you should go see to your sister. I need to sleep, can barely keep my eyes open but so much happened. I wasn't even a spectator." She stifled a yawn, suddenly feeling the events as well as the trauma of the last hour.

"There is a lady I've come to know and respect. Scarlett is her name. She has taken in abandoned and abused women, gives them a home and a chance to work. The more lucrative work they do is going with men who need a lady on their arm at certain events. There is no sex involved unless both parties are willing. Letti, as her friends call her, runs her business very well. I happen to know her history, but that conversation can wait."

"You mean she goes with men to events? What kind of events?" Lacie felt wide-awake suddenly.

"Anything the man wants to pay for. Some have taken her or the women she employs to the racetrack, or out to dinner. Some to a ball where they have to make an appearance but no, they will not be pursued by doting mothers with debutants to find husbands for."

"And you've used this woman, paid for her service?" Lacie asked, baffled that Leslie Stewart would do something like that yet feeling the rise of jealousy even while they spoke and supposedly was in his past.

"A number of times."

"She is not a mistress and you didn't take her to bed and you won't do it ever again."

"No to both and yes to the last." He smiled and kissed her on the cheek. "No worries, I'm going to see about Douglas and Merry. I'll be up in another couple of hours to check on you."

Lacie mulled over her husband's words, wondering about so many different things. She wondered what he would find when he was downstairs. The clock chimed nine times and she'd be willing to bet, both Merry and Douglas would be in the parlor talking and sipping the fine French brandy Leslie always kept there. She poured herself another glass of wine, watching the door and waiting for news.

She must have dozed, waking up when she felt the heat of Leslie's body and his arms around her. The pain was minimal and she thanked the tea for that and perhaps the half bottle of wine she consumed. She closed her eyes again, listening to the beat of his heart so close to her own. It seemed they beat as one.

Tiny kisses along her neck sent a familiar heat rushing to parts of her. "Leslie?"

"Hush... just relax and enjoy."

"Yes, how was Merry and did you find her still chaste and innocent?" she asked, smiling. She knew the answer simply because her husband seemed to be in a good mood.

"Yes." More kisses followed.

"They were in the parlor?" Her body shivered with the desire he created so quickly within her.

"Too bad you are hurt. I seem to be having a devil of a time stopping myself." Yet he drew away, her head now resting on his chest, her hand on his hard stomach.

"Everything was fine? Or was she stripped of that horrible sheer nightdress and he was having his bad boy way with her?" She needed answers from him and she was afraid he wasn't intending to give her a response.

"Merry was dressed in a simple day dress. She must have gone upstairs and changed then came down to talk to Douglas. They were sitting in different chairs, so I doubt if anything is going on between them."

"You didn't interrupt anything?" Lacie was almost disappointed in his answer as well as surprised.

"Nothing. I'm glad of that. Perhaps we both misjudged Merry's feelings toward him. I don't think either one is in love with the other. I'm glad to say that now I don't have to worry about her running off with him."

"I didn't misjudge anything," Lacie murmured. "I know what she told me before we were kidnapped."

~ * ~

Merry was grinning and feeling lighthearted the next day. She managed to talk Douglas into meeting her in a secluded place on Stewart land, and she talked the cook into packing a small picnic basket for the two of them. The sky was a beautiful wintertime blue and there were few clouds.

She hoped he would see fit to kiss her again.

Touching her finger to her lips she recalled vividly the kiss the night before while they waited for the others in the carriage. It had been unexpected but delicious. She'd never been touched or kissed like that before and suspected never would again unless it was Douglas doing the kissing. She simply had no use for any other man in her life.

In any case, she knew Douglas was going to be hers. She'd just die if he didn't kiss her again. He'd seen her, all of her, through the sheer gown, and undoubtedly felt most of her when he caught her. Just thinking about it made her heart speed and her breath catch. Unlike the unknown man she had her heart set on, she knew this man.

In the carriage, he didn't let her from his lap. When she looked at him, she couldn't take her gaze away. His deep blue eyes penetrated her soul and called out to her.

Lightly once then twice he brushed his lips across hers. Then he tugged on her bottom lip with his teeth. She'd never thought kissing was anything like that but in after thought, she realized he wanted her to open her mouth for him.

When she did, he traced her lips then her teeth with his tongue before exploring further. She didn't want the moment to end. Yet she gasped when his hand cupped her breast and he teased her nipple with his fingers, rolling the peak between them.

"Are you alright Merry?" he asked her when she let out the tiny noise he created by his touch, but he was grinning as if he knew the answer to her question.

In response, she moistened her lips, hoping he would kiss her again and he didn't disappoint. She prayed he wouldn't ask her how old she was. If he did, she would have to lie. Couldn't have him believing she was less than eighteen. Well, her birthday was in a few weeks so she decided she would tell him she was seventeen and would be eighteen then. A lie of two years but Lacie told her how Leslie kissed her way before her eighteenth birthday. She wouldn't let her brother behave like a hypocrite.

She was here, in her favorite spot and she didn't remember anything about the ride, being so immersed in her thoughts. The day was sunny and warm for the end of January. She had dressed in her best riding habit but wore no corset, just her chemise beneath, hoping he would touch her again, stroke her nipples. She would tell him how hot that made her feel and the strange ache in parts of her she'd never thought about before.

"Douglas." She pulled her horse to a stop. "You came. I'm so glad you did."

He was beside her, his hands reaching for her. When she slid into his arms, he held her close, her feet not touching the ground for several seconds. She didn't want the moment to end. She felt his hard length against her and hoped he appreciated the way she felt against him as much as she did.

"After last night I wouldn't have missed this for the world. We should talk," He told her, his voice gruff.

"Can we walk first," she asked, hopefully wanting the kiss before she had to tell him her age, "and maybe have some food? I'm starving."

She wasn't starving for food but for another kiss and maybe one after that.

Now that Nevil was gone from her life, she didn't need a bodyguard. It was so important she show him how much she needed him now, before she never saw him again.

He was showing a row of perfect white teeth. She wanted to laugh and grin back at him.

"Anything you want." He took the basket from the horse then brought it to the blanket he'd spread before she arrived. "You like this place? It's awfully secluded."

"It's my favorite, at least here in Scotland. There are other beautiful places in France." She found she was breathing hard, her heart pounding at just the gentle touch of her hand in his. Now he traced tiny circles on the underside of her wrist.

"I like it too. Reminds me of my home in the Highlands; rugged, secluded." He pulled her closer, draping an arm around her shoulder, his fingers nearly touching places where they shouldn't be but where she wanted them. She felt his breath whisper across her cheek when he spoke. "Should we go down by the creek? Someplace more private."

"More private than this?" Her voice very nearly squeaked

Then her breath once more catching in her throat all she could do was nod and lean into him absorbing his warmth and strength into her. She didn't want these moments here with him to ever end. This was the only man she wanted or would ever want. How to convince Douglas as well as her brother of that fact, she didn't know yet.

He stopped and turned her, lifting her chin. She moistened her lips in anticipation. "Are you going to kiss me again?"

"If you want me to," he told her as he slowly bent toward her.

"I do." She breathed into his mouth as it leisurely, enticingly closed over hers. Running her tongue along his teeth then into his mouth, touching his tongue with hers, tiny sounds of passion floated from her.

He groaned then pulled away before kissing her again, as if he wanted to absorb all of her into him. His hand closed over a breast. While she was lost in all the sensations he was creating, it seemed he'd unfastened her bodice. His hand was upon her breast, her naked flesh. It all seemed so much more intimate even than last night. Just as she had wanted, yearned for.

"Douglas," she said his name then his mouth closed over her nipple teasing and tasting through the fine lawn of her chemise. Her knees were wobbling. She could barely stand. "What are you doing?"

"Kissing you, just kissing, is that alright. I'll stop if you say the word."

"Kissing," she sighed softly. "I'm sure kissing is alright with Leslie. Mother used to say no harm would come from just kissing."

It seemed to Merry he paused then continued moving to the other nipple. "Come, let's go back to the blanket where we'll be more comfortable."

He swept her into his strong arms, carrying her. She was reminded of last night again and the way his touch created such delicious sensations. When she looked at him, his smile was wide. She hoped she pleased him.

On the blanket, he was lying on top of her. He whispered, "Tell me to stop, Merry."

"I don't want you to stop," she breathed softly.

He was above her, his forearms on the blanket and he was gazing into her eyes. "You should or perhaps I should be stronger." He groaned and rolled off her, pulling her bodice together and fastening what he'd undone.

She was disappointed, had hoped he would introduce her to another step in making love. "I like you to kiss me but I also want to understand what comes next." She sat up, running a fingertip along his jaw enjoying the feel of his day-old stubble.

"We should wait for what comes next. I have to leave Glasgow in a couple of days and go back to my home. I was going to ask your brother for..." he paused then looking away for a moment. "What did you bring for lunch?"

"What were you going to ask my brother for?" She didn't want to let that go, needed to learn everything, not liking the fact he was going home and most likely without her.

Cook packed the basket full of sandwiches and sweet tarts. There was a bottle of wine that she added to the basket.

"Is a ham sandwich fine for you?" She handed one to him without waiting for an answer then she uncorked the bottle of wine. It was a white Bordeaux from near her home in France. She'd hunted for a sweeter wine, more like an aperitif, the sauterne would have been perfect but she lost patience in her hunt, settling for the Bordeaux.

"I'd like to taste more of you..." He smiled as he bit into the food. "Thank you for this."

Taste more of me.

Unable to eat, her stomach rolling, "What did you want to ask my brother? If it was about me, I deserve to know." She sipped the wine, swallowing and hoping the liquid would calm her stomach as well as her nerves, which seemed to be pounding.

"Of course you deserve to know. I want you to come with me when I go home, but I understand he would never agree without a wedding even if I promised one afterwards." He stroked her cheek with the back of his hand. "I would like to make love to you right now, right here, but if a wedding is in our near future, we should wait."

"You're right of course, he wouldn't allow anything like that and when do you have to leave?"

Her hand was shaking so hard she had to set the glass down. At least he wanted her to go with him. She was glad about that and wished she could think of some way to make it happen.

"Tomorrow or the next day and you deserve a wedding, not some reading by the justice of the peace," he muttered.

"What if I don't care? That's pretty much what Leslie and Lacie had. It was a minister but Flynt had to force it and it was the second wedding." she asked emboldened by his words. "I'll go with you. It's my life after all."

"It's your brother's job to look after you until you turn of age. How old are you?" He was softly touching her with his lips and tongue and she was reminded of butterflies.

Butterfly kisses.

"I'll be eighteen in a couple of weeks."

Epilogue

"You made that look devilishly easy. Why no woman should complain about childbirth. I'm not seeing anything difficult in what you just did." Leslie said, a smirk on his handsome face as he sipped brandy.

Lacie punched him with her free hand. "You are a horrible, horrible man, Leslie Stewart. I heard you pacing outside the room and every time I screamed you were in here and Hope was pushing you out the door. If the look on your face said anything, you were terrified."

He ignored her words, gazing at her as she fed the baby, his heir. "Well, you did so well. I was proud of you. May I hold my son?" he asked, extending his hands for the tiny bundle as he seemed to have finished eating.

Actually, he found himself in awe of his wife and new son.

"Don't drop him."

She watched as he fumbled a bit with the child before settling alongside her on the bed stroking the child's soft cheek as he blew bubbles into the air.

"What should we name him? It must be something strong, yes, a good strong name. He will be the next Duke of Southcliff, you know. I will make sure he has all the proper training."

"You will not teach him to be a bad boy or a spy," she said, glaring at him. "You won't. Promise me."

"You want him to be like the men Flynt introduced to Bliss and Chelsea? I don't believe you for one second." He laughed, gently cuddling the newborn. With a bit of wonder in his voice, "We did this, we made this tiny miracle all by ourselves."

"We did," she agreed, smoothing the dark hair on the baby's head. "He looks just like you."

Leslie beamed at her words. Then, "I don't see how you can tell anything by the way he looks now. One can't even tell the color of his eyes yet."

"No, he has your eyes and that adorable way of frowning when something isn't' going as you planned it." She loved both males with all her heart. She'd never have trouble saying the words to her son but her husband... she sighed softly, closing her eyes for a second.

"What's wrong?"

She didn't want to explore right now whether or not he loved her. "We have to talk about Merry and what we are going to do to stop her moping."

"What about her?" He looked clearly confused then the child let out a huge wail.

"She left yesterday morning. Swore me to secrecy, but I didn't intend to keep the secret." She put a finger to his lips as if she knew he was about to protest the direction of her loyalties.

"Left for Bordeaux?" he queried.

"No, for the highlands to meet Douglas in Edinburgh. It seems she told him before he left she was a few weeks away from turning eighteen not sixteen. I did try to stop her, but in my defense, I did go into labor about that same time. All other thoughts vanished from my head. You have to go after her and bring her back before she makes a terrible mistake."

"I'm sure Merry and Douglas will sort things out. However, as soon as you are able to travel, we will pay them a visit and make sure everything has been done properly."

"She's only sixteen. Marriage is not the thing for her no matter what she thinks. Go after her or we may come to regret that decision. If it's true love, they both can wait until she is no longer a child."

"Very well, I will bring her back."

"Thank you."

"Lacie." He rose then and placed the baby in his cradle. "I should have said something a long time ago. I've known for such a long time."

Startled, she inhaled a deep breath, her insides fluttering nervously. "Should have told me what?"

Good God, but her mind raced with possible scenarios thinking of all his lovers and mistress who came before her and that he might not want her since he had his son and heir.

He placed her hand in his before bringing it to his lips to kiss her. "I love you, Lacie, and I've spent so much time loving you but never really believed in love before. I love you and will spend the rest of my life loving Lacie."

A breath of relief whooshed from her. "And I love you. I've known from that first kiss in the stables. I love the idea of loving Leslie.

He kissed her, long and deep. "When can we start making a new baby?"

In the coming years they did make more babies; two more boys then finally a girl. Along with her sisters and brother, they thrived and prospered. Leslie's lands in America prospered as Link helped establish the plantation as one of the best in the country.

Merry never married Douglas. He needed the money and an heiress not a child. Merry came to discover he was only using her just as Nevil had wanted to do. She swore never to fall in love again. Yet her thoughts traveled back to the man she saw in Paris as a little girl and again in Glasgow when she first arrived.

Coming Soon
by
Christine Young
at
Rogue Phoenix Press

Pleasing Arie

Chapter One

June 1824
Glasgow, Scotland

Victor, Arie's best friend and confidant, sat back in the plush chair with a glass of brandy in his hand, grinning, feeling like a besotted fool. "I took care of the little matter at hand. I believe you will be somewhat pleased. She is rare."

"So, the lady is ready to see me?" Arie had been too long without a woman. The little redhead he saw in the restaurant caught his attention, and Victor always made sure he got what he wanted. The moment he saw this woman all thoughts of Chelsea vanished from his head.

"I wouldn't go that far," Victor laughed, his mirth rolling off his tongue, his gaze and smirk focused on him. "Unless you want a battle on your hands. She is a spitfire. Her personality seems to fit the color of her hair. You'll have a devil of a time taming that one. She will talk to you but anything else..." Victor shrugged his broad shoulders, a wide smirk still on his face. "My advice, proceed with caution. Perhaps at this point, bribery should be contemplated. Perhaps you can win her over with the promise of jewels."

"Jewels? By all that's holy, I own the woman."

"She is Scottish to the core. Doubt if she has the same belief."

"My ladies are not able to teach her what will be expected of her? What you will expect when you go to see Alison. Still... there is potential. Hers is a beautiful woman's body, ripe to give pleasure a man will remember and come back for more." Arie rose, striding around the room, his gaze traveling upward to the rooms above. "They are not doing their job?"

"As I said, she is a redhead and Scotswoman, born and bred, stubborn to her very core." Victor followed the direction of Arie's gaze. "This will take time and untold patience, but I'm confident in the end she will see you as you wish her to see you."

"I should talk to her," Arie headed toward the staircase. A loud thud reverberated throughout, rocking the walls of the house then a scream that rent his pore eardrums. "What the bloody hell was that?" He started forward, held back by Victor.

"Hold it right where you are. I'll see what just happened. I'm assuming, nothing good." Victor didn't wait to see if he followed his directions but raced to the top floor.

All Arie saw was the back of Victor as he sped upstairs. With a huge breath of air, Arie sat down, sipping his drink and waiting for news. He really didn't have the patience for this but what did he expect? She was nothing like the women he was used to dealing with. In her home men might have dominated, her but she probably was able to come and go as she pleased. She'd been his prisoner now for days, held captive in the rooms on his third floor.

He'd already endured a lecture from Chelsea MacEwen, his friend, about buying women. Old habits were hard to break and just because he was a foreigner in Scotland, didn't mean he could change his true colors with a snap of his fingers or a lecture from his favorite lady. He would have wed Chelsea if she'd been willing to become his fourth wife. She was not. Arie didn't think she was even willing to be his first wife if that had been possible.

Restless, Arie didn't want to remain inside the stuffy confines of the house. He stepped outside, leaning against the porch railings, staring at the stars and the moon. Chelsea told him about the stars and what her husband Cam taught her. He'd been impressed. Cam had more facets about him than Arie realized at first. He wasn't even a sailor and he knew more about the stars than most sea captains. Arie had been surprised to discover Lord MacEwen was an expert in his field, astronomy, giving many guest lectures at the university.

A few minutes later Victor stood beside him, leaning on the railing, gazing at the brilliant night sky. Silence echoed around him for several minutes, dark brooding silence even drowning out the animal sounds. When he turned, Victor had a broad grin on his face, which belied the mood he found himself in.

"I take it everyone upstairs is still alive." Arie heard his deep breaths as well as the beat of his heart.

"Perhaps you should talk to Alison now. You've more patience than I have," Victor said laughing as if he knew something about the lady's present mood. "You should hear her words for yourself. A second hand rendition is never good. No, it's just never a good thing to hear about something from another man's point of view."

"Not sure I've the courage to confront the Scotswoman. She's a delicate wisp of a thing, and I'm down here cowering in my boots." Arie let out a long breath of air before finishing his drink. "I want her too much and doubt if I can be objective where she is concerned."

"She doesn't like the lock on the door or the clothing you've granted her. Doesn't seem to realize she has it a hell of a lot better here than in the whorehouse you rescued her from. Don't know how you're going to go about enlightening her though. She doesn't see things the same way you do."

"Doesn't appreciate the finer points of slavery," Arie's laugh didn't reach to his soul. He'd promised Chelsea he'd treat her right. Well, it had been several days since he bought Ali, and she was still far from compliant. He gave her more than any other women he owned, and he thought she would understand that fact but she didn't.

"She has no idea what waited for her and even if she does, what she doesn't understand is the difference between you and serving several different men every night. To her it's the same and repellent to her. She thinks she should have some say in her future."

"Perhaps I should leave her alone for a few more nights." Arie turned his attention to the light shining out the third floor window. He put her on the third floor because he knew if Chelsea was in that room, she would find a way to escape. He prayed Ali wasn't like that, reckless to a dangerous point and willing to risk anything as well as her life to escape him.

"Not all women are the same as the MacTavish girls," Victor reminded him pointedly, following Arie's gaze. "She might be feisty, but I doubt if she'll try to shimmy down that wall to the ground. It's a sheer drop and few would survive unscathed."

"She'd most likely kill herself if she tried. I don't think Chelsea would have tried this one either."

"No, there aren't enough sheets in Alison's room for her to tie them together so they would reach to the ground. I made sure of that," Victor grinned and Arie was sure he was thinking of something amusing about this situation. "Well, if you want to talk with her you should probably go now. If I were you, I wouldn't wait."

"Why? What difference would an hour make, or another few days?" Arie watched her, unsure of himself for the first time in his adult life. She was standing in front of the window, staring outside. Candlelight from her room caressed her hair, displaying the multitude of brilliant colors. He had an urgent need to run his fingers through the wild vivid strands, wanting her more now than the first time he saw her.

Victor lifted his shoulders nonchalantly, his smile broad. "She might be more angry in another hour. Who knows what she could be like in the morning, a redheaded Scotswoman? Right now she is somewhat biddable. I believe she's had several glasses of wine although she didn't touch her food. Might work in your favor, might not."

Arie ran his hands through his hair, frustrated by the situation, understanding all the rules he lived by for twenty-five years would not be applicable now. Ali lived by a different set. "Don't know what I'd say to her. Just want her in my bed, willing to give herself to me."

"Tell her why you bought her. Make her position in your life clear so there will be no second-guessing. She will come around to your way of thinking, eventually. She needs to comprehend how much better her life will be with you than in a whorehouse or on the streets. After all you have her best interest at heart." Victor strode into the house, pouring another glass of whiskey, chuckling softly, still cleared amused.

"Doubt if she'd like my reasons anymore than she enjoys being locked into that room, even though I've given her the entire floor." Arie figured he'd never be able to get close enough to the girl to seduce her to his way of thinking. "Maybe you have a point, but I expect you to be outside the door to rescue me if anything turns violent."

"You could bring her a gift," Victor repeated his earlier suggestion, holding up his hands to make his point. "Don't ask me what. No, wait a minute. You could bring her real clothing. Something you can't see through. I believe she would appreciate that."

"Doubt if baubles or clothing would ease her temper. She doesn't seem to be a lady who wants monetary things." Arie was stroking his chin, wondering what he could bring that might soothe her displeasure with him, completely ignoring the suggestion of clothing.

"She might like some clothes." Victor nearly laughed, repeating himself and it didn't go unnoticed by Arie.

"Then she might be more inclined to find a way down the side of the house. I don't intend to offer her the chance to kill herself." Arie was wondering about a dress for her. She might not be appreciating the harem clothes he'd given her. They were, after all, meant for a man to appreciate, not the woman. As for appreciating her, he hadn't even seen her wearing the soft lavender harem pants and bolero top.

"You don't want to chance her escape. She'd die on the streets," Victor said. "We both understand that fact. If you point that out to her, I'm sure she'll comprehend what you are trying to tell her. You are a true savior to that girl. She has no one else."

"But how will I know? I can't just give her a dress and unlock the door." He was thinking of the MacTavish girls. They would bolt the second they got the opportunity, see through clothing or none at all. Allison would die on the streets, either that or find herself abused by men. He meant to treat her special.

"Then you have to go to her and explain why she is here as well as her options," Victor said.

"She has none," Arie said, glancing upward once more.

"Exactly."

"I rescued her." Blood pounded in his head, the ache growing which each thud.

"That you did," Victor said agreeably.

"She should appreciate me."

"All true."

The silence between the two men was long and drawn out. Arie reconciled to meeting with Alison. She would come to recognize and accept her fate then he would treat her with the care and respect she would deserve. He thought on everything Chelsea told him days ago. It was nothing he wanted to hear, but he did listen and her words changed the way he meant to deal with Ali.

He gave her time and space to adjust to her new circumstances. Shouldn't she be adjusted by now?

He was a coward, he surmised thoughtfully, afraid of a tiny redheaded girl who stole his breath the first time he saw her. Victor had done well by him. He followed her and procured her for him before she was forced to entertain her first client in the whorehouse. Ali's circumstance decreed she would fall into his arms. From his vast experiences and when given the chance, all women, except Chelsea, fell into his arms. But...

But she fought Victor and railed against him, holding herself aloof as if she was royalty. Still he stood at the bottom of the staircase, sweat dripping from his brow and down his back. He'd never felt this way before and if he could, he'd give Ali everything she asked for.

Except her freedom.

He could never do that.

Victor stood beside him. "Perhaps you should give Ali her freedom then she'll fall into your arms. That's what you want, isn't it? Let her know she can come and go as she pleases."

"She would run and she has nowhere to flee; no money, no clothes, no nothing. She'd die on the streets or be violated," Arie said, wiping his brow with his sleeve, his hands shaking.

"Alison is not stupid. She has figured out that someone, most likely her stepfather sold her to the whorehouse and that you bought her. She will also understand she cannot make it in the outside world without help, most likely from a man. Perhaps you will have some bargaining chips with her if you present these facts to her."

"You think so?"

"No, but it's worth a try. Right now Alison is not thinking clearly. She does want to run from you and from all the bad things that have happened to her this last week. She might not have led a sheltered life, but I do believe she is an innocent in many ways. If you want her, you need to treat her as a virgin as well as give her your respect. She deserves nothing less."

"A virgin?" Arie didn't understand the words coming from his friend. This was a surprise to him, and he wasn't sure he wanted to deal with another innocent. "No wonder she is protesting so vehemently. Still I cannot believe she has never known a man intimately."

"I think so but I've been wrong about other things. When you first saw her, I was sure she would be quite willing."

"So where did we go wrong?"

"We didn't know the circumstances of the sale. I do now. It seems Fletcher Donovan and his nephew sold her and the mother was in agreement. But those two turned on Alison's mother. Sold her home and left her penniless. As we speak she is destitute and on the streets."

"She probably got what she deserved. They all need to be punished. It was Donovan and Leod who captured Chelsea and sold her to the same whorehouse. We should find the mother and see how she is faring. On second thought, I'm sure the Madam can find a suitable position for her at the brothel."

"The Madam too?" Victor asked. "Not sure she had any idea what was happening."

"She was greedy and wanted the money. Was contrite when I confronted her but this information about Ali is new to me."

"All the more reason to make sure Leod and Fletcher disappear forever. Leod apparently did not learn the first lesson I gave him."

"All will be taken care of," Victor said. "Just give the order."

"I want them taken and sold to a man who prefers men." Arie said, a smirk on his face. "I do believe that to be a fitting punishment for the two of them who are willing to abuse women for their own gain." He nearly stopped himself on those words because he understood that unknowingly he abused his women. He had three wives and all yet one barely tolerated him. The third wife said she loved him but...

Maybe that was a lie too.

"I will take care of it in the morning. I'm going upstairs with Tessa for a few hours, but I do think you should at least introduce yourself to your new concubine and decide for yourself on the next course of action."

Arie inhaled a long deep breath of air, downing his drink in a gulp before heading up the stairs. By the time he reached the top, he was breathing hard and sweating more profusely than at the bottom of the steps. The climb wasn't the cause but the fear of the confrontation. He had a lot to prove to himself, and he didn't know if he could change that much.

He nodded to the man stationed in front of the door, "Don't come in no matter what you think you hear. Not unless I tell you."

"Are you sure?"

"Positive."

Arie stared at the doorknob for a few seconds then slowly opened the door. Alison was still standing at the window, dressed in the see through lavender harem pants and bolero jacket he gave her a few days past. Without a second thought, he grinned, appreciating the view. From the back she was just as beautiful as he imagined, her vibrant red hair spilling to below her waist.

"Alison?"

"Go away."

"Afraid I can't do that." He stepped inside the room, closing the door behind him. The outside lock turned as he walked toward her. "We need to talk, to understand each other. I need you to understand why you are here rather than the brothel."

"Who are you?" Her voice quivered when she spoke, but her shoulders were stiff. Still she didn't turn around. He didn't need to see her face. Her visage was etched in his memory.

Arie understood this would not be easy between them, and he wasn't sure if she was terrified or angry, perhaps both. He hoped it was anger causing her body to shake. Anger he could deal with much easier than fear. He prayed she didn't cry and there would be no tears. Despite the lecture from Chelsea, Alison wasn't going anywhere. She was his.

In any case, Ali had nowhere to go. Donovan sold her house after selling her to the whorehouse. She had nothing save what he would give her. Without him she had no money, no home.

"My name is Arie." He stood beside her, looking out the window, his body barely touching her shoulder. A crescent moon stood out in a cloudless sky while brilliant stars emerged as the city lights dimmed even more with the hour.

"Then, Arie, what am I doing here?" she asked, her voice tense, anger simmering beneath each tight word. "You have no right to keep me prisoner."

"Do you want me to be brutally frank?" He smiled, wondering exactly how she would react when he gave her the truth of her existence now.

"Brutal?" she queried, her eyes wide with fury as she turned to look at him, her hands fisted at her sides. "Everything that has happened to me in the last couple of days has been brutal. I'm a free woman. You've no right to hold me here against my will."

"You didn't answer my question. I find I cannot continue on without an honest answer from you." He smiled, realizing this woman was not afraid of him; defiant yes, angry yes, but not afraid.

She turned away from him, her hands on the windowsill seeming to support all her weight. He was afraid when she learned the truth she would no longer be able to stand on her own.

"Why would you be anything less than honest?" Her voice quivered while her shoulders trembled. If he didn't miss his guess she was livid, willing to argue every point.

"Perhaps you should sit down first." He turned to the pillows and bedding gracing the floor behind them. "Have something to eat, a sip or two of the fine wine I've procured for us. You should relax."

"I'm not hungry or thirsty. I don't want to relax." She moved to look at the pillows then him. Her hands fisted at his sides, eyes still blazing. "I'll stand, thank you."

He shrugged wishing she would at least eat something even while he was enjoying the beautiful play of emotions. He would enjoy making love to her, the feel of her passion beneath him, "Suit yourself." Striding to the pillows set out for them, he held his cup out and a servant poured wine.

Relaxing and making himself comfortable, he sipped the liquid and watched her as she swayed slightly. She must be exhausted. He wanted nothing more than to make her life more comfortable, yet she was refusing at every turn.

"You really should sit down before you fall down," he said, patting the place beside him. Wishing he could bring all his plans with this lady to fruition this evening.

Slowly she walked toward him. For a few seconds she stood then she sat down as far away from him as possible. "I want to know the truth. What is it you want from me?"

"Ah, finally." He poured her wine and motioned for the servants to leave to an adjoining room. "You should sip it slowly."

She held the wine in shaking hands, her green eyes huge. She coughed slightly with the first sip. "I've never had wine or any spirits."

"A delicacy you might learn to enjoy. I can give you anything you want." He held his breath waiting for a response. "But you will have to give me what I ask for."

"What I want is to leave this place and you."

For a moment his heart sank then he slowly smiled. She would come to his viewpoint when he explained. "Where would you go? How would you eat? You have no clothing."

Her body seemed to wilt at his words before she stiffened with seeming determination. "I'll find a job. I'm not helpless."

"At the whorehouse?" he asked smoothly, hoping to make his point.

"No, I'm not a whore." She drank the entire glass of wine. He filled it again, hoping she would begin to feel more at ease.

"Do you have any skills?" He hoped she would understand she had few alternatives except whoring. "If you go out on the streets, you will only end up in a whorehouse or worse. I suppose if you were lucky you could find employment as a nanny or a wet nurse if you gave birth to a child of you own."

"There are worse things than a brothel?" She inhaled a long shaky breath seeming to think over what he said then she asked again. "What do you want from me?"

He no longer knew what to tell her. If she thought this was worse than a brothel, she was sadly mistaken. It would be hard to convince her she was wrong. "You could be out on the streets with no roof over your head, no food and no clothing." Frustration filled his soul. He needed to shake some sense into her. "I offer comforts I'm sure you never received at home. Inevitably, I would like you to warm my bed." He purposely avoided telling her he owned her. She was his concubine. There were no alternatives for her.

It seemed she did not listen to him, jumping to conclusions on her own. "I'm your prisoner though. You must want something in return, all men do." Her fists were clenched at her sides. If there had ever been a threat of tears, it vanished.

"If we please each other you could become my wife." There, it was an offer he had not meant to introduce to her at least not now.

"Is that what you want me for? Another wife?" Frown lines creased her brow. "I won't be a fourth wife."

"How did you know?" Gossip had never been something he could abide, and it seemed his servants were doing just that. Gossiping.

"There was talk, silly chatter from the women who were trying to teach me things you would want me to know. There was nothing intentional or malicious about the things they talked about. It was just women talking about men."

It seemed to Arie she sensed his anger. "So you say." They were all women. Of course she would defend them. "Well," he paused, thinking it was time for a change of subject, "do you care to show me what these fine women taught you?"

She blushed sweetly and he almost laughed. Dancing in the way of his people was not easy. He also hoped they taught her about what he expected and that she would be in his bed.

"I've two left feet and my hips don't move the same way theirs do." Her voice was lighter and it seemed she was laughing at herself.

For a second it seemed to him she forgot her anger as well as her desire to escape him.

His chuckle was soft and not meant to laugh at her. This was the first break in their serious conversation. "You should show me what you learned." He poured them both more wine, hoping she would loosen up some more, at least enough to show off her fledgling skills.

"I don't think so." She sipped the wine, leaning back and pulling a pillow across her. "You would only laugh or be appalled."

"Soon then," he prompted, disappointed she would not perform for him but encouraged that soon she would be more at ease in his presence. Perhaps this talk with her was a good thing. Victor had been right.

"What will you do for me if I dance. Not really sure one can call what I do dancing but..."

"What do you want?" He picked up a strand of her hair and held it in his hands. "So soft, silken, fire in my hands. Is every part of you this soft?" he murmured, staring at her lips, wanting desperately to kiss her.

"Soft...?" She swallowed hard. "I don't know what you mean."

"Your hair is like fire and it burns my soul. Did the women teach you how to kiss me?"

She pulled back, moving her head in denial as she did so. "What will you give me if I dance for you?"

"I repeat, what do you want?"

"To go for a ride on my mare."

"Your mare," Arie rubbed his chin, thinking. "Your entire household was purchased. Everything. Doubt if the mare is still there."

"You have the means. I'm sure you could offer whoever bought her enough money to buy my mare. Please find the dear girl and buy her back."

"Dance for me and I'll do it first thing tomorrow."

~ * ~

Alison had not expected the swift compliance to her wishes. Strangely she wasn't terrified of Arie, just furious with his arrogance and calm assumption she was his. One could say she was more fascinated by him than she could have ever imagined. She'd never met anyone like him.

Frustration and confusion had filled her since she first woke up in the brothel and was dressed in a flimsy see through gown. It seemed to her she jumped from one fire into another when Arie bought her at the auction. She ended up in this third story room two days ago. Now she had some hard decisions to make.

Ali didn't want to be attracted to the sultan. No, she wanted to despise the man who sought to make her a prisoner, a concubine. She needed to keep her anger simmering until he gave her what she really wanted. Her freedom. How was this so different from being a whore? Ah, his smile though sent a jolt straight through to her heart seeming to melt it. Watching him she had a difficult time remaining angry.

Now that she'd seen him, talked to him she could never hate him. His deep brown eyes shimmered with humor and something she wanted him to tell her. She just didn't know what it was he hid behind those fascinating dark brown eyes of his. They seemed to draw her to him tug at her heart inexorably. She had never met anyone comparable. His muscled chest was also something she'd never seen before. The sight left her with a nearly uncontrollable urge to touch him, run her fingers along his belly to feel the muscle beneath her fingers.

Mesmerized by him, she had this uncanny need to please this man, wanted to reach out and discover who the man really was.

Dancing for him would not please him. "If you promise not to laugh at me." The thought of failing as miserably as she knew she would left her shaking not with fear but with feelings of humiliation even while she wanted to laugh at herself.

"I would never laugh at you." Arie was grinning though his smile wide, appealing.

She knew he would laugh. It would not be possible for him to keep the amusement behind his teeth. "Then you are a saint." She rose then and inhaled a sharp breath, flashing his a smile. "Do I get music?"

Arie clapped his hands and two of his servants appeared. "Music for Ali."

With that said the music played and Ali began to move her hips and hands as she believed she'd been taught. But she was awkward and in no time winded from the attempt at belly dancing. The tempo picked up and she knew a shimmy was next, but not one part of her body seemed to work. Humor seemed to fill her then as she saw the look of utter horror on Arie's face. No, he wasn't laughing at her, he was horrified by what he witnessed.

"You're not pleased." She stopped, dragging in deep long breaths of well needed air. "I would seek to please you."

Giggles suddenly took over her body. She knew how terrible she was and the look on Arie's face was nothing she'd seen before. All her fears about the man vanished, at least for the moment. She fell on the pillows next to him, unable to stop the laughter.

"I want you to know I'm not laughing, but under the circumstances I'm having a devilishly hard time fulfilling my promise." He choked on the sip of wine, the liquid sputtering across his chest as a deep humorous rumble shook him.

She wanted to touch him, clean the liquid, reaching out she almost stroked him before she drew back her hand. His grin now was broad. His even white teeth glistened in the candlelight.

He nodded for the other women to leave and filled her glass again. "You know what you just did?"

"Earn my mare?" She accepted the glass but set it on a nearby table, feeling as if she shouldn't drink anymore, her mind a bit hazy.

"More than that. I'll also bring you something else to wear when we go riding. I enjoy your smile as well as your laughter. I want to spend more time with you. Don't let this sudden compliance to your wishes make you forget, I also want you in my bed." With the back of his hand, he touched her cheek, trailing a finger along her chin before following with a stroke down her neck.

"Thank you," she looked down, hiding her expression from him, unwilling to show him her gratitude when she wanted to stay angry. What he didn't know wouldn't hurt her. "I don't know what to say."

"Thank you was quite enough," he told her, rising from the pillows. "You look tired. You should sleep. I've the feeling you've managed very little sleep since you arrived here."

She sat up, staring at him, at the broad expanse of his chest, wondering what he would look like without clothes. What did a man look like wearing no clothing? "What if I don't want you to leave yet? I've been lonely."

"You want me to stay?" He sounded surprised yet his smile told her he was pleased.

Ali moistened her lips admitting she felt an instant connection to him, a connection she wanted to deny. "If you don't mind. You could tell me something about yourself."

"We do need to speak about why you are here and your options.

It seems you might be settling in now. I would like you to be happy and if not happy at least content."

"I still want my freedom," she bristled. "You will never own me."

"So much for progress," he mumbled.

"I didn't mean to give you the impression I wanted your attention." She suddenly didn't feel the least bit magnanimous. Her earlier anger simmering deep inside she realized the emotion would never be assuaged by a gift from a man who could afford anything.

"I understand. You only want me to buy your mare for you, but you don't need or want anything else to wear." He stroked his chin, his grin disappearing.

It seemed to Ali she had lost what little ground she made by dancing for him. He would not come around to her way of thinking. She stood then, accepting another glass of wine despite the fact she didn't want to drink it. At the window she gazed at the moon. It appeared the same as when she looked at it from her window at home, no longer her home.

From behind her he spoke. "You've gone through a great deal of trauma in the last few days butt Ali," he paused, "you are mine and the sooner you accept that fact the happier you'll be."

She whirled on him. "Never!" With a great deal of purpose she strode to him, tossing the liquid onto him and dousing his shirt with the liquid. Her breath caught in the back of her throat as she realized what she'd just done to the man who held her life in his hands.

For a few seconds he appeared shocked then a slow smooth grin spread across his too handsome face. A moment later his shirt was on the floor and he was bare chested, standing his hands on the fasteners of his soaked britches. Ali gasped at the pure male beauty she saw. Then her eyes widened as he was suddenly very nearly naked, his britches on the floor beside his shirt.

He clapped his hands and a woman appeared from a side room. "Would you please bring another pair of pants?"

"A shirt too?" she queried.

"Don't believe I want one. I find it's incredibly warm in this room tonight, perhaps hot." It seemed to Ali he searched her face for some sign of contrition. She didn't feel anything but awe as she stared at him unable to remove her gaze.

She pulled her lips together, retreating to the window and the incredible manly view. The long breath she inhaled was shaky, her knees trembling as she felt his presence so very close to her. Although he didn't touch her, she felt the heat emanate from his large, muscular body.

"What do you want?" she asked, her voice shaking, afraid of retaliation. If she'd done something like that to her so-called father, Fletcher Donovan, she would have been thrashed. He would have enjoyed taking a whip to her back.

"Only your sweet compliance but I'm resigned to the fact I will have to work harder to achieve that which I seek."

Still he didn't touch her, just stood beside her. "It was an impulse. I know I shouldn't have tossed the wine."

"Of course," he left her side. When she turned around he was sitting on a freshly made pallet with new coverings and pillows. "We talked about brutal honesty. Come sit." He was patting a spot beside him. "You should know what I need from you, yet I'm afraid you're not ready to hear the words or accept your fate."

She was shaking her head no, even while she strode toward him, sweat sliding between her breasts. Ali didn't want to sit. Standing was preferable when he held her future in his hands. Standing was preferable when she wanted to reach out and touch his chest, find out if it was as hard and unyielding as it appeared.

Then she did sit down, scooting as far from his as the pillows would allow. "Why am I your prisoner? Why did you say I was yours?"

He settled back, his arms spread wide on top of the pillows, his legs stretching out in front of him. "Because I bought you."

"It's not as simple as you try to make it. People cannot buy people." She didn't understand any of this even while she'd heard that Fletcher sold her to the brothel.

"People with power and money can do anything they please. It pleases me to own you and other things eventually. Whether you agree or not, you are mine. Now, no more discussion of this sort. Tell me more about yourself."

She needed to figure out what all he said meant to her. "If I say no, what then?"

"It doesn't matter what you say. I do care what you want but not where it concerns my ownership." His words were calm yet measured. "You will always be mine. Unless of course, I grow tired of you and this silliness and sell you to someone else."

"You can't do that!"

His smile told her otherwise. A shiver of fear slipped down her spine. At least here she was safe. It didn't seem he meant to abuse her.

For a few seconds she looked away from him, remembering her life from a few days past. It had been fraught with hard work and sometimes not knowing if there would be a next meal. Looking around the room, she was amazed at the opulence, the food and everything else that adorned the space she lived in and wondered what his quarters looked like.

"It is better than the whorehouse, I assume. I would have been able to walk out those doors though. As you say, as your possession I've not choices." She thought that might be true but wasn't sure.

"Not until you worked for the Madam long enough for her to make a profit. She would also keep your door locked. You would be forced to service several men each night."

"Do you have an answer for everything?" She found she was bitter, not at Arie for taking what he wanted but for her circumstances, for Fletcher who set all this in motion. He spoke the truth and she didn't want to admit it. "So I would have been kept behind a locked door."

"Yes." He sipped his wine and ate. "You should try the food. It's really quite good, much better than at the brothel. My cook is excellent. The spices he adds enhance the flavors."

"How would you know?" she shot back, angry once again at his arrogance and all knowing grin.

His chuckle sent her nerves on edge. "I've partaken of the food at said brothel several times. Now, if you don't mind, I'd like to learn something about you besides your love for your mare."

"She probably won't be there if you still plan on buying her for me. She is very old and can't be ridden." She was plucking at the sheer pants she wore. "I'll miss her even though she is a worthless nag. Obviously, I could not have ridden with you anyway."

He leaned forward then, his hand on top of hers, stilling it. His fingers wrapped around hers and she was startled by the gentleness. "I will do everything in my power to find her for you. I'm not an ogre. She will be kept in my stable and whenever I've the time, I'll ride with you. Not on your nag though. You must have a mare you can ride. I'll see to that too."

"Promise?" Her hopes lightened. Perhaps he spoke true. She could only hope even though she understood there would be a price to pay for his generosity.

"Yes, what would you like to know about me?"

"Anything you would want to share. What makes you so confidant you can buy a woman and no one cares?" She didn't want to sound belligerent but she couldn't help herself.

"Ah, people do care if it's the right woman. You have no man in your life. So, no one cares about your fate except me."

"I've no one to care about me," she repeated. She found her heart was breaking. Once not so long ago she thought her mother loved her.

"I'm confidant because I've always done what I pleased. I've lived my life in luxury with any woman who caught my fancy. You, my dear, catch my fancy." He placed his finger beneath her chin, "Don't ever believe that I don't care about you. I do more than you will ever know. I want only the best for you. If you are pleased then I'm a man well pleased."

"And I caught your fancy?" Once again she repeated his words, not really wanting to hear him agree yet beginning to realize she was better off than if she had not been a woman he wanted.

"The Madam told me you are not a virgin. Is that true?"

"Do you care?" She bristled again, remembering a time when she had been forced to kiss a man but she had not been violated. Fletcher had watched, grinning like a besotted fool and did nothing to stop the man who would not accept her no. Yet he finally did step in and pull the man from her.

"No, the truth will dictate how I proceed with you."

Ali inhaled a shaky breath, watching Arie intently. "A man who lived nearby." She stopped then, turning to the window to stare outside at the stars. The moon was no longer visible from her position.

"Go on," he urged.

"Fletcher thought I should wed this man so he brought him to me. I didn't even know his name. He kissed me and I shoved him away. I don't know if I'm a virgin or not." Once more she was plucking on her pants, pulling at the fabric revealing the dark red hair of her mound. She tried to stop her trembling fingers.

"Just a kiss," Arie's voice was gentle and soothing. "No, he didn't like the fact that I pushed him away. He hit me, punched me in the stomach. I never knew anything could hurt that bad."

His hand tightened around hers. "What did Fletcher do?"

"He ushered him from the house. I was surprised by that. He always hit mother when she did something he didn't like."

Arie's fists tightened, his eyes growing so dark they seemed to turn to ebony. "I have guesses about that but none of them are important. I'm sure you are still a virgin, Ali. Think hard and see if you can remember the man's name. I would like to speak with him. Is that the only kiss you've experienced?"

"Yes."

He brought her hand to his lips and placed a kiss on the back then he looked at her. "Was it that horrible?"

She blinked a few times before facing him. "I liked your kiss."

"That was hardly a kiss," he laughed.

She looked away, unable to meet his gaze. "Still I liked the way your lips felt on my hand."

"Perhaps before I leave tonight you would let me kiss you." He moved from the pillow to stride around the room.

His back was broad and his flesh well tanned such a contrast from her paleness. He was strong and proud. "I might like that." She was beginning to understand that her options were limited. Getting along with this man might serve her better than fighting and denying him the things he wanted. Perhaps she wanted them too.

"Good."

She was sure he was waiting for her to come to him but her feet wouldn't move. "If I kiss you, can I have something else to wear, that dress you spoke of maybe?"

"I promised you your mare tomorrow because you danced for me as well as clothing if we are to ride." He laughed then and she wondered what he was thinking.

"What I did was hardly a dance," she smiled at him, felt the mood suddenly lighten again. She was heartily pleased with that.

"Perhaps I'll give you two dresses then. Come here, one more if you kiss me." He motioned for her, beckoning to her.

Her body seemed to have a mind of its own and refused to move. Catching her bottom lip between her teeth, she inhaled a long deep steadying breath of air. She knew she would like that kiss, understood once she gave into a kiss, she would never be herself again. The only way to have control over this totally confidant man was to deny him.

"I believe I changed my mind," her words squeaked from her tight throat. "I don't think a kiss would work. I'm sure two dresses is too extravagant. One will suffice for now."

For a fleeting second his grin vanished but suddenly it was there on his face broader than ever before. "If that's what you wish."

He leaned on the windowsill, his back to her. She needed to know what he decided, how he truly was feeling about what she told him.

Ali stood beside him now, close to him, too close she decided when he turned suddenly his hands around her waist pulling her close. She knew she could break away if that was what she wanted. Instead, Ali closed her eyes for a moment before she let her lashes flutter open and gazed into his dark brown eyes, eyes that seemed to shimmer with raw passion.

Her heart raced so hard, she could not look away, could not refuse him as he slowly lowered his face so they were mere inches apart. "Do you want to kiss me? I would allow it if that is what you want?"

"Me kiss you?" she squeaked, her words barely audible.

"I would bring you some delicacy you might crave."

Her hands settled on his chest, moving, exploring, prowling as if she did this every day. Beneath her fingers his muscles flexed. She was acting like a ninny. Something needed to be done here before she lost herself to this man who demanded things of her she wasn't yet willing to give or even understand.

I can control him.

Controlling Arie would only happen when she kept her fascination with this man in check. Arie was everything she thought about in a man.

Everything Ali had ever imagined and knew was beyond her reach.

Beyond until now...

What would she have to do to gain his trust and respect? She would have to meet him part way and tempt him the other half.

Ali had no knowledge in the art of tempting a man. She didn't even know the rudiments of flirting. Perhaps others in his employ would be willing to give her some hints, teach her. If they understood her motives though they might relay the information to him and that would defeat her purpose. They seemed to tell him everything.

She inhaled a long ragged breath, gazing into his eyes. "I can't do that. Kiss you. I don't know how." The moment the last words were said she regretted them. He would find some way to turn them around to his advantage. She smushed her lips together, thinking, wondering just what would happen next.

The only thing she craved was discovering what his kiss felt like, if is lips were as soft and warm as they appeared. She wasn't about to let him know her thoughts and she had no reason to show him how inept at kissing she was, just as inept as dancing. He would be repulsed with her kisses and send her away, give her to another man. She knew she didn't want that.

Thinking she was way in over her head she pushed away from him, turning and walking towards the door.

"I'm tired now. It's been a long day." What a blatant lie. "Don't you think it's about time you left?" She stood beside it, hands clasped in front of her, watching his grin widen and she wondered just how that was possible but it was a fact.

"Not until I get my kiss." He sat down on the pallet where she would sleep, relaxed, observing her intently. Still watching her, he lazily stretched out, his long legs taking up the length of the bed.

She pushed hair from her face, exasperated by this arrogant and very stubborn streak. "You should learn to take no for an answer." She remained by the door, wishing she dared walk the distance and give him what he wanted.

"If I recall you didn't say no, just that you didn't know how."

"You should leave when asked."

"Why, when I don't have to?" He leaned back closing his eyes, his large hands behind his head. "This is comfortable. I made sure of it because one night, I hope in the not too distant future, I'll spend the evening here with you."

"A more distant than I'm sure you want to believe." She nodded her head toward the door. "I'm also sure you would like me to act more docile, but it's not in my nature."

"Neither docile or subservient would satisfy me. Now, I'll do what you ask as soon as I get that kiss."

Her eyes narrowed while she stared at him, "Then I suppose you'll have to stay the night." At the same time she was speaking the words she was looking around the room for a place where she could sleep.

"As you wish." He rose and for a moment she thought he meant to leave, but he unfastened his pants.

"You can't do that." Her voice strained with emotions and she wondered what devil got inside her to challenge him this way. He didn't care if she objected to him sleeping here with her. It was after all what he wanted all along.

Now he wore only his small clothes. Her throat tightened when she thought..."No, I'll kiss you then you can leave."

"Ah, but I think it might be too late for that. I find this bed quite comfortable."

"No, it's not." She rushed toward him, stumbled on the rug in her haste and together they fell on the bed, his arms wrapped tightly around her. The skimpy bolero jacket she wore rose, and she felt the naked flesh of his chest against her breasts. Her nipples tightened with the contact. A tiny sound erupted from the back of her throat.

"I like this position. You on top of me and I didn't even have to ask." He smoothed hair away from her face. "Are you going to kiss me?"

Her mouth touched his. Quickly she withdrew. "There."

"That was not a kiss." He laughed, his throaty chuckle sending shivers down her spine as she squirmed against him. His hands roamed the length of her back, up then down again, to finally stop on her bottom.

"I told you I didn't know how to kiss."

"Try again and make it last a wee bit longer. Perhaps you can give me a taste of your tongue. That's right. I'd like to savor you. You would taste of the sweet wine you just drank."

"My tongue?" Her body pressed against his trembled with raw passion. How the devil was she supposed to control him when she couldn't control herself?

"If you like."

"If I like?" she parroted.

I'm smarter than he is and stronger at least my will is stronger. I'm faster, my mind can be if I work at it.

"Press your lips against mine and I'll show you."

Ali pushed away from him, the tiny bit of distance making it easier for her to breathe. "Now you'll show me."

He grinned. "Any time."

"Alright then." She lowered herself so close to him she felt the whisper of his breath across her cheek. Then she touched her lips to his, closing her eyes and wondering how much a bit more time was. Gasping, her lashes flew open. His hand was behind her head, holding her close and his tongue swept across her lips. She was tempted to touch his with hers but held back, wishing she understood more. A tiny sound mewed in the back of her throat as her hips moved against his belly. His other hand swept up her back, touching, exploring naked flesh. When she gasped again, his tongue met hers then withdrew.

Then she found herself sitting next to him, her clothing askew. Quickly, she righted her pants and jacket Everything occurred so quickly and now it was like nothing transpired except she was hot, so very hot. Her body ached in places she never thought about before.

"Thank you," he told her before slipping on his pants and walking through the door shutting it behind him. "You can sleep alone tonight."

Breathing hard she raced to the door, tried to open it then collapsed onto the floor. Of course he locked it.

~ * ~

Victor relaxed in his room, Tessa, his favorite lady, handed him a drink before sitting down next to him. Wrapping an arm around her, he pulled her close. He figured he had about an hour before Arie gave up on his quest and knocked on his door.

Arie's mood would be questionable. So unlike himself in his

dealings with this new lady, Victor found it difficult to read his friend. He didn't understand how this one redheaded woman had Arie twisting and turning within himself, tying himself into knots. She was beautiful, yes. But...

He needed to bed the woman, show her he would treat her with the respect she deserved then get on with his life. Instead, he let his good friend Chelsea MacEwen tell him how to relate to this new woman, his concubine, a woman he owned. He was so off kilter it would be amusing if his temper wasn't frayed. A man could loose control in sensual matters. What he saw led him to belief Arie handed the reins over to the redhead.

"You seem preoccupied. Have I done something wrong?" Tessa asked, stroking Victor's chest and placing tiny kisses where her fingers had been. She raked her nails across his belly.

"Just worried." He picked up her hand, kissing the palm and running his tongue there before nibbling kisses the length of her arm.

"About Arie?" she queried. "I know it's none of my business but..."

"Hush." He placed a finger on her lips. "What you think or what I think will not change the way he goes forward with this lady. She is different somehow and he's not his usual self."

"I'm sorry." She was immediately contrite. "I'll go."

He reached out to her, "No, we've time yet."

"I don't know what you want."

"Kiss me and I'll show you."

She was more than eager to satisfy him. She trailed her tongue across his lower lip, prowling inside his mouth along his teeth and deeper.

More than an hour passed before the knock on his door woke him. Tessa left, quickly, wrapping a robe around her and walking by Arie with a nod.

"I see you've had a better night tonight than I have." Arie chuckled, which surprised him.

"You're in a good mood?" Victor pushed the covers back, rising and slipping on his pants. "Do you want to tell me anything?"

Arie was shaking his head while he poured a drink. "Would have liked to have stayed the night with her but," he held his hand up, "never expected that to happen in the first place. All in all the visit went surprisingly well."

"Maybe tomorrow?" Victor laughed, watching the man he'd called friend since they were just lads playing in Arie's father's harem.

"Not tomorrow. I'm going to make her wait for me and I'm going to take control, take charge of the direction this is going between the two of us. Right now she believes she has the upper hand and is dictating to me. Not any longer." Arie tossed his head back and laughed, leaving Victor bemused and wondering what happened in the third floor room this evening.

"What have you promised her?" Victor said, searching through the tray of food that was left over from earlier in the evening for something to eat. "Hopefully not the stars and moon."

"Her mare. Told her if she danced for me, I'd see if I could purchase it for her."

"Her mare? That's all?"

"Yes, the horse is old so I'm afraid the people who bought her home might have done away with it even though it's only been a few days since the property was sold."

"What do you want me to do?" Victor asked, knowing that Ali most likely won the first round between them.

"First thing in the morning you should go to the farm and talk to the owner. Pay him anything he wants. Then see if there is anywhere you can purchase another horse for her. One she will be able to ride. I'd like to take her outside the room, give her a small measure of independence. She needs to feel sunlight on her face and fresh air to scent."

"And a taste of freedom?"

"Just enough to let her appreciate what she has with me."

"You plan on buying her suitable clothing?" Victor asked laughing.

"I promised her a dress for a kiss."

Other Books by Christine Young
Available at Rogue Phoenix Press

My Sweet Broc
Bad Boys Book One

He's a bad bad boy...

Broc Wallace is a fun-loving rake who never thought any beautiful woman could melt his heart. He lives life in the present enjoying the camaraderie of his friends and the pleasures of his mistress. When Bliss races into his life, he is ill prepared to deal with her secrets or give up the tenor of his life. When the truth is revealed, he finds himself unable to forgive and forget the betrayal.

...but she's sweet for him

Bliss MacTavish knows she's playing with fire when she refuses to tell this bad boy her name. He tempts her with sweet whispers of seduction knowing her innocent nature will be unable to refuse all he yearns to give her. Deciding to follow her heart, she finds the repercussions more than she bargains for when she gives herself to this bad boy.

Crazy for Cam
Bad Boys Book Two

He's a bad bad boy...

Lord Cam MacEwen, Viscount of Rosehill, tries his best to be proper and court the lady of his dreams in the acceptable way. The feat proves impossible when the lady in question uses every means at her disposal to tempt him. He fights his jealousy for another man as well as the need to make her his own, finally giving in to her irresistible passion.

...but she's crazy for him.

Chelsea MacTavish wants the bad boy she fell in love with and kissed just before her eighteenth birthday. With feminine wiles and irresistible allure, the sensuous lady plans to best Cam at his game of hearts and make him forget his need to court her properly.

Falling for Flynt
Bad Boys Book Three

He's a bad, bad boy...

Fascinated by Hope's loss of memory yet haunted by her sultry beauty, Flynt is irresistibly drawn to the stoic miss—and into her troubles with the sultan who wants her for himself. When he discovers she is the sister of his best friend, his pride keeps him from pursuing her and making her his.

...but she's falling for him.

Raised in a harem but now penniless, alone and without her memory, Hope must discover a way to remember all that she has lost. She finds a way to continue with her life as a servant in Flynt's home. The first sight of Flynt steals Hope's breath as well as her heart. Can she overcome her fears and give herself to the man she fell in love with.

Dancing With Donal
Bad Boys Book Four

He's a bad bad boy...

Once a bad boy always a bad boy, Donal Chamberlin's carefree ways come crashing down around him when he meets the ravishingly beautiful Daryl MacTavish, the innocent little sister of one of his best friends. He is determined to win her heart as he sets his sights on marriage and an heir. His past gets in the way of his quest when a woman he once loved threatens Daryl's life.

... but she's dancing with him.

Daryl has seen the control her sister's husbands hold over them. She yearns for a life where she makes decisions for herself. No man will have power over her. But no man kisses her the way Donal does. No man can make her forget all her goals leaving her helpless to give up her dreams. Yet Donal is determined to dance through all the barriers she thrust in front of him, pursuing her until she says yes.

Foolish for Piper

The pickpocket...

Piper has spent her life surviving the streets of St. Giles Parish in London, a den of iniquity and crime. Masquerading as a boy she escapes the whorehouses the young girls are sent to as they come of age. The day she encounters Brett MacLachlan begins the same as every other one. When she picks his pocket, she has no idea her life is going to change irreversibly.

...and the mark

Handsome aristocrat Brett MacLachlan has come to London for his amusement only to find his world turned upside down by a thief and her dog. From the moment he spots her, Brett knows there is something intrinsically wrong. In his arms, Piper discovers passion and joy. Yet secrets of her past haunt her, and a scar will tell the true tale as well as her identity.

Taylor's Destiny

She traveled to another time and place to change destiny...

Enjoying a day of sailing, Taylor Maxwell never expected after a suffering a concussion she would wake up in another century. A resilient independent woman in the twenty-first century, the blond beauty is ill prepared for life in the 1800s. Her first sight of the naval captain who rescues her makes her heart stop, giving her hope for her future.

His life is transformed by a woman who appears from nowhere...

Born to a life of ease, Reid Stewart defies the dictates of those born to aristocracy and chooses a life of adventure in the navy and as a spy for the crown. When he discovers a nearly naked woman on the bow of small sailing ship, his heart warms. His love for Taylor and his need to protect her from a man who pursues her might cost him his life as well as hers.

Caitlin's Duke

She played a fiddle in an Irish pub....

Caitlin O'Shea Is the most beautiful woman Roc Leighton has ever seen. With her blue violet eyes and long black hair she captivates him. In turn he mesmerizes Caitlin. Caught in the power of his gaze as he watches her, she is wise enough to know he desires her but will never give his heart to her. Caitlin has vowed to never be any man's mistress.

And fell in love with an English Lord...

Roc knows the first time he watches her play the fiddle and dance around the pub, she will be his next mistress. Despite her protest, he will find a way to convince her that her place is with him. While Caitlin's determination to keep her vows, fate takes a cruel turn and she is forced to seek refuge with Roc.

Catching Meara
Book One in the McKenna Clan Series

Meara Thorton was a feisty, world-class computer hacker—cornered by the FBI and shockingly given the chance to be their newly acquired technical analyst. Brilliant and intuitive, yet aching with the loss of everyone she has cared about, her restless heart led her to discover a love she fought and a world she didn't know could possibly exist.

Sweet Sexy Sadie
Book Two in the McKenna Clan Series

From the first time Sadie's eyes met those of Brody McKenna in the hot Sierra Madre Mountains, theirs was a potent attraction—not gentle, slow, and easy, but hot, hard, and all-consuming. The daughter of a dysfunctional family, Sadie had dreams no man could wrench from her with hot sex and an all-consuming passion. She'd challenge this alpha male with all the strength she possessed. But her red hair, fiery temperament, and indomitable spirit obsessed Brody...and he knew he had to find a way to show her he was more than he appeared and convince her to make a life with him.

Sweet Misbehavin'
Book Three in the McKenna Clan Series

Cast adrift after fleeing the home of Jokul, the ice demon, Atantsi, a firestarter, grew to womanhood as she moved through time to keep the demon from finding her. Though stubborn and courageous, she was ill prepared to use powers she had not been taught. Her first sight of the intoxicating Carr McKenna left her breathless, and her second encounter gave her hope for a future she never thought she had.

A playboy, a second son and a shifter, a man who thought his life would be carefree, Carr McKenna was shocked to discover the woman he'd paid as an escort is a firestarter who is running for her life. He is the leader of all the McKennas around the world and that he has multiple powers. His passion for Margo and the need to defend her might cost him his life as well as hers.

Sweet Talkin' Sugar
Book Four in the McKenna Clan Series

Lyonesse McKenna, was dreaming or was she? From the instant Lyn saw Deacon McClain across a black jack table in a crowed Las Vegas casino the unmistakable attraction sent Lyn's senses flying into overdrive. Her family of shapeshifters believed in soul mates. She'd always been skeptical yet she couldn't help but question the way her heart sped when he looked at her.

When Deacon appeared in Las Vegas he knew his first job was to save Lyn from a Sea Demon, but the next order of business was to convince her he would someday mean more to her than she'd ever expected. But her stubborn nature and unbendable spirit consumed Deacon...and he had to chase away all the demons real and imagined in order to win her heart.

Sweet Surrender
Book Five in the McKenna Clan Series

Ripped from her family at the top of Infinity Cliff, Kimi McKenna finds herself thrust somewhere into the future. Dark elements threaten to destroy the earth unless Kimi can work together with the white witch to stop the destruction. Confused by her mate's role in the conspiracy, she refuses to acknowledge the connection. But amidst raging fire and attacks on the people she is coming to hold dear, she allows Maska O'keefe into her heart.

Maska O'keefe has loved the beautiful shapeshifter for years. Unable to save her life years ago, he vows to watch over her as he is given a second chance to convince her that even though he is a witch and not a shifter, they are indeed soul mates. Kimi's divided loyalties between her family and the cause she is now a part of will determine their relationship. Only the part she plays as the messiah can bring this to a conclusion in the final battle.

Dakota's Bride
The first book in the Lakota/Pinkerton Series

When Emma St. John received her brother's letter imploring her to escape her stepfather's vengeful scheme and to trust Dakota Barringer with her life, she was willing to chance it. But the handsome, brooding riverboat owner Emma found in Natchez a danger of another kind. For Emma soon found herself surrendering to an unrelenting desire.

Raised by the Sioux when his parents were killed, Dakota had been betrayed once before by a white woman. He wasn't about to trust another, especially one claiming that her stepfather, a powerful U.S. senator, had framed her as a murderess. But he couldn't let Emma's intoxicating effect on him. Now Dakota would risk his very life to protect the innocent beauty who had seduced him with her tender love.

My Angel
The second book in the Lakota/Pinkerton Series

A BEAUTY IN BUCKSKINS
When her father decided to send her to a finishing school back East, Angela Chamberlain refused to be confined to stuffy drawing rooms. Instead, the daring spitfire who could shoot like a man and ride like the

wind longed for a life of adventure and romance—and she knew exactly who could give it to her. Devil Blackmoor was a hired gun with a dangerous reputation. But Angela was willing to go to the ends of the earth to capture the handsome devil's heart.

A DEVIL IN DISGUISE

He'd come to America looking for excitement, but Devil Blackmoor got more than he bargained for when he encountered a beautiful rebel who answered his kisses with a wild innocence that touched his very soul. Yet standing between them were more obstacles than either ever dreamed. For Devil had strapped on a gun for the wrong man. And that made Angela his enemy. Now he'll have to choose between his duty and the woman he loves more than life.

The Locket
The third book in the Lakota/Pinkerton Series

The year is 1894. Seeking revenge for crimes against his family, Misha Petrovich follows a path that leads straight to Ariel Cameron's boarding house in Mist Harbor, Oregon. A family heirloom in Ariel's possession leads Misha to believe she is guilty. The locket has been handed down to the oldest girl in the Petrovich family for generations. Ariel is innocent of wrong doing, but her father is not. Misha is torn by his feelings for Ariel and his need for restitution against her father. Knowing that the relationship between them is fragile, Misha does everything in his power to protect Ariel's father. His efforts are to no avail when her father is shot. Ariel comes to realize Misha's steadfast courage and determination to protect her and her father despite what has happened to his family. Ariel's love and devotion heals Misha's heart.

The Talisman
The fourth book in the Lakota/Pinkerton Series

Running from a marriage that lasted one night, Dr. Moriah McKeown discovers the land she has settled on is coveted by determined and lawless men. Yet the proud young woman who once vowed never to abandon her home has second thoughts when her adopted children are threatened. Her only recourse is to enlist the aid of a dark, dangerous gun for hire.

Haunted by the past and a betrayal he will never forgive, Ian Civanovich uses his fast gun and his reckless courage to forget the faithlessness of a woman in his past. He will trust no female—nor will he rest until the threat hovering over Moriah McKeown is put to rest.

Forever His
The fifth book in the Lakota/Pinkerton Series

Struggling to come to terms with the part she played in Jacob St. John's death, Etta Barringer resigns from Pinkerton Agency and seeks peace and solace in a Rocky Mountain Cabin.
Jacob has vowed to discover the reason Etta has betrayed him, sold him out to his enemy and left him for dead.

Isolated in their cabin, they discover their love for each other and learn to trust. But the trust is shattered when Jacob learns she is married to his sworn enemy; the man who left him in the desert to die.

Allura's Secret
Twelve Dancing Princesses Book One

Allura McClellan is horrified by her father's decision to take out an ad in the Times awarding her to the man strong enough and smart enough to win her hand and uncover her secrets. She's an intelligent young woman who takes great delight in the freedom allotted to her by her father. She's well aware that marriage would effectively curtail the adventures she's shared with her sisters and cousins.

Hunter Gray is nothing like the other men who've arrived to vie for Allura's hand in marriage and everything that goes along with it. However, he is the first to refuse to concede defeat and pursue her despite her attempts to disguise her true appearance. It's her temperament that is of more concern to him than her looks. Hunter has worked all his life with the hope of someday owning his own land. Now that it looks like there's a very real possibility that everything he's ever wanted is within reach nothing is going to deter him – including Miss Allura's disagreeable disposition.

Amorica's Wager
Twelve Dancing Princesses Book Two

Amorica Hepburn was sent to London to find a husband. Finding a man was the last item on her agenda. With her two cousins, Amorica wagers she can dissuade her suitor before the others. Despite her efforts she discovers a chemistry that cannot be denied. Suddenly she is the arrogant man's wife, pledged to a marriage neither desire. But swept off to his ancestral home above the Dover cliffs and into his strong embrace, Amorica is soon possessed by a raging passion for the husband she had vowed to despise…

Damian Andrews couldn't afford to trust the emerald-eyed spitfire who happened upon his secret. Amorica's hatred of all men of his kind only inflames the war that rages between them. Still, he can not control the intense desire his stubborn bride inspires, or make her surrender to his will until he has conquered the headstrong beauty on the battlefield of love…

Ravyn's Marriage of Inconvenience
Twelve Dancing Princesses Book Three

A REGAL BEAUTY
When the duchess decides to wed her to a wastrel and a fop, Ravyn Grahm

takes matters into her own hands and declares her engagement to another man. Instead of fessing up and telling her great aunt what she has done, she goes through with the pretense. Ariec Lakeland is the bastard son of an earl and has a dangerous reputation. But Ravyn is willing to do most anything to keep the duchess from discovering the lie.

A DEVIL-MAY-CARE SMUGGLER

He'd bought land in America, looking to put down roots and end his life of adventure, but Ariec Lakeland got more than he bargained for when he encountered a beautiful heiress who made a promise she didn't want to keep. But the promise could not be undone and standing between them were more obstacles than either ever dreamed. Ariec had made plans to spend the rest of his life in America and that was at odds with Ravyn's plan of living in England and running her father's estate. Now, he'll have to choose between his dreams and the woman he loves more than life.

Christel's Sunrise
Twelve Dancing Princesses Book Four

He Made Her An Offer...

Life has thrown Christel McClellan some experiences that could have devastated a less determined woman. Beautiful, self-assured and fiercely independent, she is trying to forget the loss of her stillborn child. But is the child alive?

She Couldn't Deny...

Life is carefree for Ryder MacLaren who loves to see what is on the other side of the sunrise. Laird of Clan MacLaren, he is wealthy, handsome and happily unencumbered...until stunning Christel McClellan enters his life. When he hears her story, he believes the child she thought dead has been sold to a wealthy buyer.

Storm's Passion
Twelve Dancing Princesses Book Five

SHE MADE A PROPOSAL...

Life strikes Storm Graham a shattering blow when she learns her father has bartered her to a man she detests. Storm is beautiful, self–assured and fiercely independent, and refuses to be a pawn in her father's schemes, yet she can find no way out of this bargain made in hell. Going on the offensive she asks the wealthiest man on the eastern coast of England to marry her, never believing she might fall in love.

HE TRIED TO REFUSE...

For Hadden Johnston life has provided everything he ever wanted, including a sanctuary for homeless children. He is wealthy, handsome and happily unencumbered...until stunning Storm Graham marches into his life and proposes a marriage of convenience. Yet this type of marriage to a woman who inflames his senses is far from acceptable. If he's going to be tied down, he will move heaven and earth to have this woman warming his bed.

Gotta Have Fayth
Twelve Dancing Princesses Book Six

A regal beauty with raven hair and piercing blue eyes, Fayth Graham is unwilling to parade herself in front of the wealthy Lords of England during the season. Seeking a means to dissuade any man wishing to wed her, she seeks a way to ruin herself for marriage. When she unexpectedly meets a man with sparkling gray eyes and an infectious grin, she decides this is the man who will keep her from agreeing to obey.

He returned from six months at sea, looking for a few nights of pleasure with a willing lass, but Jarret Kinsley got more than he bargained for when he met a beautiful debutant who responded to his kisses with a wild innocence that touched his heart. Yet the obstacles looming between them might rip them apart. Both had vowed never to marry, so when consequences of their dalliances got in the way, Jarret would have to choose between the life he's always desired and the woman he loves more than life.

Ella's Pleasure
Twelve Dancing Princesses Book Seven

A WHISPER OF PLEASURE

Ella Hepburn was an auburn haired debutant from the harsh Scottish coastline—a wild innocent to be seduced and tamed. A spirited beauty, she captivated Drake Montgomerie's jaded heart—while succumbing to the smoldering desire she felt for her unyielding suitor.

A WHISPER OF DANGER

In Drake Montgomerie's glittering world of money and privilege, young Ella discovered passion and desire could overcome everything she'd been taught to resist—entangling Drake, the heir apparent, in a lethal coil of aristocratic family intrigue. But grave peril would only nurse the sparks of a love that knew no limits and a magnificent ecstasy that would not be denied.

Eveleen's Seduction
Twelve Dancing Princesses Book Eight

A WHISPER OF SEDUCTION

A brutal attack on Eveleen Hepburn's cherished island off the Scottish coastline leaves her shattered and bewildered. Learning a man she once trusted can kill as easily as he can breathe even though the deed saves her life, creates questions that need answers. An innocent beauty, she enchants Logan Maxwell's cynical heart—giving in to the raging passion she feels for her mysterious suitor.

A WHISPER OF INTRIGUE

In Logan's Maxwell's world of espionage and privilege, young Eveleen discovers truths about herself she never expected, and a need for passion and love can overcome all her fears if she learns to accept certain truths. She finds herself entangled in a lethal battle for land that was once owned by French nobility, taken from them during the revolution and sold to Maxwell. But grave peril would unleash the flames of love that simmers, creating a magical union that cannot be refuted.

Tavia's Deception
Twelve Dancing Princesses Book Nine

WHISPERS OF DECEPTION

When her father decides to send her to London for her season, Tavia Hepburn resolves to see the world instead. The raven haired beauty decides to disguise herself as a lad and find employment on a ship bound for Barcelona as a cabin boy. But she never bargains on finding passion and love to a red haired sea captain who rescues her from certain death.

WHISPERS OF MURDER

For James Macmurra, the world is black and white until he meets a young debutante, who turns his world upside down. He's unable to deny Tavia's intoxicating effect on him. In a match tense with obstacles, unwillingness to divulge secrets, and unforeseen peril, irresistible desire and passion grows into undeniable love. James would risk his life to shelter and protect the innocent debutante who seduces him with her sweet love.

Larena's Fascination
Twelve Dancing Princesses Book Ten

WHISPERS OF FASCINATION

Fiery, free spirited Larena Graham never wanted to marry a duke. She is thrilled to be in love with the fourth son of an aristocrat, Gavin Broon. But when it seems Gavin ignores her, she set her sights on politics and bettering human life. Unsuspecting intrigue and a plot against her, she continues her dangerous plans despite Gavin's wishes.

WHISPERS OF TRUST

Gavin has every intention of properly courting the beautiful Larena until he must leave the city in order to put his affairs in order. Returning to London, he finds the woman he means to make his own is embroiled in political protests that could lead to a prison ship. Larena must learn to trust the handsome Scotsman whose most pressing mission is to protect her and keep her from harm.

Tira's Education
Twelve Dancing Princesses Book Eleven

WHISPERS OF EDUCATION

Learning how to build ships is Tira Hepburn's only dream until she meets Jamie Lundin and her world is turned upside down. With her raven black hair and vivid green eyes, she tempts Jamie and pushes him to defy his vows. She never bargains on finding an irrevocable love and a passion to a man who cannot fulfill her dreams despite his burning desire for her.

WHISPERS OF A BARGAIN

Arrogant and self-assured Jamie is brought up short when Tira captures his heart. All his carefully made plans are put to the test when he decides to teach her the art of ship building if she will spend a week with him alone on his ship. He is unable to deny Tira's intoxicating effect on him. When Tira leaves him behind unwilling to live with him without the benefit of marriage, he races after her. Jamie will risk everything to shelter and protect the innocent debutante who seduces him with her sweet love.

Aidan's Love
Twelve Dancing Princesses Book Twelve
Whispers of Love

Aidan McLellan has loved since she first set eyes on him as a young girl. Spontaneous, wild and eager to grow up, Aidan haunts his waking thoughts day and night, insinuating herself into his life. With her fiery red hair and sparkling sapphire eyes, she seizes Blade's heart even while he tries to resist the innocent child until she becomes a woman.

Whispers of Courage

Blade has waited what seems a lifetime to claim the woman who captures his heart as a little girl. Claiming his inheritance before his younger brother takes what is rightfully his, Blade must convince Aidan of his sincerity after years of avoidance and wed her before his father dies so he can return home, securing his rightful place. Everything is put to the test when his life as well as Aidan's is threatened by the man who once called him brother.

Twelve Days to Love

When Archer Steele shows up at Calanthe Durand's failing plantation with an alligator over his shoulder, Cali thinks she's never seen a more handsome man. During the war she had to defend herself and her servants from both union and confederate soldiers. Independent and self-sufficient, she vows to never marry.

But Archer Steele has different ideas. The first time Archer sees Cali in town, he feels an instant attraction. He decides he will do everything and anything to convince the beautiful Miss Durand he is worthy of her love. During the weeks leading up to Christmas, he gives her twelve gifts in hopes she will fall in love with him. Yet they are faced with challenges they must overcome before Cali can commit to a marriage.

Door to Heaven

Jessica Lawrence is the stepdaughter of a woman born in the twentieth century transported back in time to the year 1868. An acclaimed suffragette, she raises Jessica to believe in the equality of women. Jess Law believes everything she was taught, and when the time is right she becomes a private investigator. Courageous and impetuous, Jess finds danger in her quest to save all women from white slavery. Her passionate mission results in a wedding to Roc Newman, a man she knows can steal her heart...

Roc can't trust the sapphire-eyed spitfire who invades his home in search of secret papers and knocks him flat with her karate moves. Jessica's refusal to obey his wishes serves to inflame the war between them. Still, he cannot control the intense desire his reluctant bride inspires, or make her surrender her independence, until he has conquered the headstrong beauty on the battlefield of love...

Rebel Heart

HER REBEL SPIRIT DEFIED HIS OUTSIDERS SOUL...She was velvet and silk, eyes the color of a summer storm and amber hair. Victoria DeMontville, because of a promise and a codicil to her father's will, was forced to marry one man to protect her from another. She hated Cameron Savage with a fierce passion. But to hold on to her genetic research and find a cure for the deadly Signe virus, she must pretend to love the enemy at her door, come with weapons of fire to melt her icy heart...

HIS OUTSIDERS TOUCH IGNITED RAGING PASSIONS...⸢⸤SEP⸥⸣He wore a mask, disguised as the Phantom, a true legend come to life. Even as war and debate over new genetic research engulfed them all, he would find his greatest adversary in the beauty who'd branded him an outsider and barbarian, the woman he was born to possess, his soul mate.

Safari Moon

Solo St. John, a wildlife photographer, is preparing for a trip to Alaska. Suddenly, Solo finds women of all sorts invading his privacy, his home and his office, all cooing nonsense words and blatantly throwing themselves at him. Solo doesn't know why, and he has no idea how to rid himself of the persistent women. He finally decides to beg a favor of his best buddy Nyssa Harrington.

In love with Solo for the past ten years and knowing he doesn't return her feelings Nyssa doesn't want to talk to Solo. She knows if she accepts his phone call, she will not be able to resist the temptation to hope again.

Straight to Heaven

Running from demons, Alexandra McMurdie stumbles into Forbidden Ground where up is down and elements of nature are contested. Though a strong independent woman in the twenty-first century' she is unprepared for life in the 1800s. Her first site of the formidable James Lawrence makes her heart skip a beat, giving her cause to reconsider her desperate need to find a way home.

Born with a silver spoon, James' life was torn apart during the War Between the States. Moving west he vows to put the life he once knew in the past. When he discovers a half-frozen woman near Gold Hill, his heart begins to thaw. His love for Alexandra and his need to keep her from a man who has pursued her through time might cost him his life as well as hers.

A Valentine's Anthology

The Lending Library-a fantasy by Christie L. Kraemer

Faeries try to fit into the human world when the forest where they make their home is destroyed by a mysterious enemy.

Chasing Rainbows-a contemporary romance by Genene Valleau

An eccentric aunt, an inventive uncle, a mother who wears poodle skirts, and a brother who wears pearls provide a hilarious backdrop for the courtship of a young woman who yearns for a "normal" family.

The Gift-an historical romance by Christine Young

A man and a woman on opposite sides of the Civil War get a second chance at love after one final battle returns soldiers to their war-torn homes to rebuild their lives.

A St. Patrick's Day Tale

Christine Young, C. L. Kraemer, Genene Valleau

Tumble through time…

…to Ireland in 1817, when tensions are high between Protestants and Catholics and fae people guide the fate of villagers. A lovely Catholic lass stumbles upon the weakly ritual fisticuffing between Irish lads. She falls into the lap of a handsome young Protestant. Family ties, grudges, and two conniving faeries threaten their budding love. But the faeries outsmart themselves when they hijack a time machine that has mysteriously appeared in their forest and are whisked to…

…Eugene, Oregon in the 20th century, amid a property feud between the local faeries and night elves. The conniving faeries from Olde Ireland try to stir up more mischief. However, a warrior gnome convinces the magic folk to control their own destiny, and forces the intruding faeries to take refuge in the time machine again, spinning their way toward…

…A modern day castle in western Oregon. An eccentric inventor is determined to reclaim his wayward time machine and save his beloved wife from her latest misadventure. If only they can travel safely past the black hole…

a May Day Anthology

Christine Young, C. L. Kraemer, Rosemary Indra, Genene Valleau

Highland Miracle — Christine Young

HURTLED THROUGH TIME, Sean Michael Sterling, landed in the midst of a May Day celebration he didn't understand, assuming the role of Laird Sterling.
ILLIGITAMATE CHILD OF NOBILITY, Reagan Douglas searches for a way out of her half brother's house.

Defying the Odds — C.L. Kraemer

The night elves on the hill aren't happy without their magic. They concoct a plan to punish those who were involved in the act that rendered them almost human. Meanwhile, Uther, the rogue night elf, has returned to woo the Librarian to be his eternal mate.

Love in Bloom — Rosemary Indra

When childhood friends reunite it takes two fairies and a matchmaking daughter to help them admit their true love for each other.

No More Poodle Skirts — Genie Gabriel

After drifting for years in the innocent age of the 1950s, a woman struggles to join today's world by finding a career and a new love, with some help from her zany family.

Once Upon a Christmas Moon

Christine Young, C. L. Kraemer, Genene Valleau

TWELVE DAYS TO LOVE

When Archer Steele shows up at Calanthe Durand's failing plantation with an alligator over his shoulder, Cali thinks she's never seen a more handsome man. During the war she had to defend herself and her servants from both union and confederate soldiers. Independent and self-sufficient, she vows to never marry. But Archer Steele has different ideas. The first time Archer sees Cali in town, he feels an instant attraction. He decides he will do everything and anything to convince the beautiful Miss Durand he is worthy of her love. During the weeks leading up to Christmas, he gives her twelve gifts in hopes she will fall in love with him.

BOOTS AND BLADES

An ancient evil from the old country has arrived in the high desert of Oregon. Gnome children are vanishing then re-appearing, showing various stages of traumatization. Tiamoon, warrior gnome, will put her skills to use alongside Killian, a handsome warrior, also in need of a cause.

CHRISTMAS PAWSIBILITIES

With their world destroyed and their space ship malfunctioning, the dogizens of Planet Canid have little choice but to crash land on Earth. They face tortuous experiments at the hands of the Geeks in Green...or they can trust an eccentric inventor and his zany family to deliver the Canine Queen's puppies and help them celebrate new lives.

*VISIT OUR WEBSITE
FOR THE FULL INVENTORY
OF QUALITY BOOKS:*
http://www.roguephoenixpress.com

Rogue Phoenix Press

Representing Excellence in Publishing

*Quality trade paperbacks and downloads
in multiple formats,
in genres ranging from historical to contemporary romance,
mystery and science fiction.
Visit the website then bookmark it.
We add new titles each month!*

www.ingramcontent.com/pod-product-compliance
Lightning Source LLC
Chambersburg PA
CBHW070650180626
46817CB00006B/2306